In countless ways, life resembl[...] family, education, environment, fri[...] mination, timing, and luck. It is up [...] with his or her own personal puzzle pieces, and that is when choice becomes a factor.

– Richard Malone

Reflection of Memories is a poignant tale of love and loss that kept me reading late into the night. Tesa Jones has created a beautiful and vivid story, and I was glad to lose myself in the characters.

– Libby Kirsch, Emmy Award winning journalist,
and author of the Stella Reynolds Mystery Series

Reflection of Memories is a story of love, loss and finding oneself. Jones is a masterful storyteller who takes you on a journey of self-discovery through the eyes of her characters. Readers of *Cobwebs of Time* will be thrilled to meet Brad and Rick again and understand their roots. You won't be able to put this book down!

– Kim Ranney

This impassioned love story has complex characters who become more and more endearing with each turn of the page.

– Terry Kingery

Reflection of Memories brought back precious times and historical events during my childhood experiences. I felt as if I could close my eyes, and I was actually in the story reliving my own life.

– James H. Lynch

The attention to historical detail is impressive and adds such an authentic note to this heartfelt love story.

– Brittany Dixon

With *Reflection of Memories*, Tesa Jones delivers a prequel as wonderful as her previous novel *Cobwebs of Time*. It's about love, family, history and human communication – a real page-turner. I absolutely love these books and feel a deep connection to the well-defined characters.

– Brian Ranney

REFLECTION OF MEMORIES

TESA JONES

ARCHWAY
PUBLISHING

Archway Publishing books may be ordered through booksellers or by contacting:

Archway Publishing
1663 Liberty Drive
Bloomington, IN 47403
www.archwaypublishing.com
1 (888) 242-5904

ISBN: 978-1-4808-4749-1 (sc)
ISBN: 978-1-4808-4750-7 (hc)
ISBN: 978-1-4808-4751-4 (e)

Library of Congress Control Number: 2017909881

Print information available on the last page.

Archway Publishing rev. date: 07/17/2017

Acknowledgements

I wish to thank Debi Sorber and Terry Kingery for plowing through the first draft of my manuscript; your insightful feedback helped polish my story. I am indebted to artist Ms. Kelly Myatt St. Clair, who agreed to read <u>Reflection of Memories</u>, embrace the narrative, and create the perfect drawing to depict my beloved characters as children. Jim Lynch, who is one of the few remaining living members of my parents' generation, thank you for allowing me to interview you about details during those early years of this family saga. Your perspective helped me empathize and understand how it felt to live during that era. Janet Scafetta, Mike Abney, Jim & Michelle Truett, Barbara Preston, Sue Quartiero, Deb Allenspach, Brittany Dixon, Terry Caruthers, Pat Dremel and Rosie Mitchell – even though you may not realize it – your words of encouragement gave me the confidence to climb over the initial hurdles and travel the long, often arduous path to completion.

Jan Brittain, Mark and Libra Pitts, Monica Humpal, Denise Addington, Katy Law, and Shirley Huffman – you are inspirational beacons in my life. Thank **you** and my entire church family for lifting me up! Your bountiful faith and loving spirits guide me during smooth, as well as, rocky roads.

Ellen Kinsella of Eye-B-4-E Editorial Service – thank you for your keen "eye", professional service and patience. You were instrumental in completing the first phase of this creative journey. Libby Kirsch – thank you for taking the time out of your busy life to give me advice. I truly appreciate Randy Clayton of Archway Publishing for his calm demeanor; he made me feel welcomed and relaxed from the very first day. I also want to thank Kayla Stobaugh, who kept me organized, and Lauren Holmes, who brightened some of the more difficult days.

To my entire Ranney/Jones family – especially Brian and Kim, who volunteered to read the rough drafts of <u>Reflection of Memories</u>; you provided wonderful suggestions and gave me the courage to move forward.

Roger Jones, Shelby Sims, and Rick Jones – "*thank you*" for loving me and always believing in me. You are my heroes. And finally – Haley, Lexi, Natalie, Rusty and Luke – you inspire *me* to be a better person. I hope one day – when you are older – you will read this story – learn from it – reach for *your* goals, find *your* lifetime partner and fill *your* hearts with the happiness that only true love and good choices can bring.

Part I

The Early Years

Getting to Know You

1

Richard

I was born on April Fools' Day, 1931 – and so was the love of my life. Herbert Hoover was president. It was the year the Empire State Building was completed, construction started on the Boulder Dam, and the last of Henry Ford's Model A was produced. Prohibition was still the law of the land. The tailspin of the stock market crash was old news; however, the ramifications of it were reaping havoc on the economy. While I was learning how to walk, Franklin Roosevelt was inaugurated and nearly a quarter of the population was unemployed. Many of them were standing in bread lines. Mother Nature contributed to the nation's downward spiral by creating several years of severe drought; adding insult to injury, violent winds stripped the farmers' land of topsoil, generating dust storms that traveled hundreds of miles and rained a black cloud of dirt on cities as far east as our nation's capital. Families lost their farms and food prices hit record highs. My parents – James and Victoria Malone – were poor, but we were not the only people in America living in poverty. Our country was besieged by a devastating depression, and it felt as if the suffering would go on forever.

Wait! I am getting a little ahead of myself.

When a person reflects upon his life, should he not first ponder the era directly *before* he comes into the world? Does that time not have an enormous impact on him? In countless ways, life resembles a puzzle. There are many pieces: faith, family, education, environment, friendships, opportunities, hard work, determination, timing, and luck. It is up to each individual to decide what to do with his or her own personal puzzle pieces, and that is when choice becomes a factor.

I believe my father, James Malone, was happy at one time in his life. However, during his life's journey he had more than his share of misery – enough sorrow to break a person's heart in two.

James Malone was born in 1899 to parents who'd lived in America all of their lives. He had a rather mundane childhood and completed five years of education before quitting school at age twelve to work as a picker in the coal mines of western Pennsylvania. Two years later, dozens of men died in a mine explosion – one of them was his father. James was scheduled to work that shift, but had stayed home because he had a fever. His father – my grandfather – had taken the shift in his place. James carried the guilt of his father's death like an albatross; it weighed heavily upon his heart.

Several years later, on April 6, 1917, President Woodrow Wilson said, "The world must be made safe for democracy," and Congress united with the Allies in Europe by declaring war on Germany. The next day, James Malone, who was eighteen years old, enlisted in the Army. He was the first person in our town to volunteer. At the time, he was still naïve enough to believe that war – in some way – was the road to becoming a hero.

Private James Malone saw minimal combat during the first year he was in the Army. However, in the summer of 1918, while he was with the Allies at a town called Chateau-Thierry, holding their position and protecting Paris, he found himself in a major battle. I must have heard the story a hundred times. My father spoke of the noise, the smells, the blood, and the chaos. When he described the German artillery, he always seemed in awe of their weapons. The persistent cannons pounded the town. In addition to the constant barrage of bullets, gigantic chunks of concrete rained in devastating destruction.

Out of sheer tenacity, the Allied troops held the Germans at Chateau-Thierry and stopped their advancement to Paris. Although the encounter was a military success, it was the end of the war for Private James Malone. During the battle, one of the artillery shells hit the building next to where James was positioned. The impact created an avalanche of bricks, boards and rubble that cascaded around him. In spite of the rapid German machine gun fire during the attack, he was never wounded by bullets; instead, the exploding debris buried most of his body and crushed his left arm. At first, he was in shock and could feel nothing. When his buddies and the medic came to dig him out, they had to amputate two inches above the left elbow in order to pull him from the wreckage. At that point, he passed out from the pain.

Two-and-a-half months later, Private James Malone was home. He automatically knew he would not be able to get his old job back in the mines so he searched elsewhere for wages. Although the tide had turned and it appeared as if there would eventually be a victory for the Allies, the war still raged in Europe; consequently, there were very few young men in town. Most of them had either volunteered or been drafted. As a result, James was able to get a job at Randall Miller's store, which was a little over a mile from home.

On November 11, 1918, Germany agreed to the terms for peace. The Great War was over, and our soldiers returned to American soil. Although the military battles had ended and nations, including the Big Four, were at the Paris Peace Conference, there was a new horrific global enemy looming on the horizon. During the last months of 1918 and the first half of 1919, there was an epidemic of influenza. It wiped out twenty million people around the world – 500,000 of them were Americans. One of them was James' mother. At age twenty, James was alone.

After the Great War, James worked fifty hours a week at Randall Miller's store. Nearly a decade earlier, the owner had transformed the backroom of the store into a nickelodeon; hence, my father had more than one job to perform. In addition to working behind the counter and helping the customers, he also took people's nickels when they came to see the motion pictures. Because the town was nestled in the back hills of Pennsylvania, more often than not, the movies had been around for a while. Charlie Chaplin's *The Tramp*, Mary Pickford's *The Poor Little Rich Girl*, and the controversial epic *Birth of a Nation* were as much as five years old before they were played at Miller's Nickelodeon. But it mattered not what was on the screen, the people came again and again. With his one hand, James proudly collected the coins.

In the summer of 1922, while James was working behind the counter, a young girl named Victoria Bradley came into Miller's store. Victoria, who would eventually become my mother, was of English and French descent. She had lived in the area since 1912 when she, her English father and French mother had come to America via Ellis Island in New York City. I suppose, because she was a mere seven-year-old child at the time, James didn't notice her when she first arrived in town. I'm equally certain that he didn't notice her for the next decade because she was a freckled-faced, pigtailed, slip of a girl who didn't attract attention at all. But at age seventeen, Victoria Bradley had turned into a lovely young woman; consequently, when she entered the store on that warm June afternoon in 1922, my father was completely overwhelmed by his instantaneous emotions. In fact, he nearly fell off of the ladder trying to assist her requests.

Victoria Bradley was a quiet, demure girl. She didn't talk much, but she loved to listen, and James rambled on and on to keep her in the store. Little did he know, Victoria was constantly making excuses to go to Miller's store simply because she wanted to be with *him*. James always seemed insecure about the fact that he didn't have a left arm, but Victoria never seemed to notice. She was always fixated on his face and his words, not his body.

It wasn't until James discerned Victoria only came to Miller's Nickelodeon when he was on duty that he began to realize she might return his affections. One evening, after all of the nickels were taken, James quietly sat next to Victoria and watched Douglas Fairbanks, Sr. in *The Mark of Zorro*. Halfway through the show, he placed his hand on top of hers. To his utter delight, Victoria twisted her hand until she could wrap her fingers around his, and she leaned in her seat so their shoulders touched. Neither spoke; instead, they sat spellbound by the magic on the screen.

Three months later, James Malone and Victoria Bradley were married. With his new bride's arms locked around his neck, James scooped Victoria up with his right arm and carried her over the threshold of his house on the south side of town. If Victoria was shocked by the location or the small size of her new log cabin home, she never spoke of it; instead, she enthusiastically went about the business of being a wife and homemaker. The downstairs was one large room with the living area on one side and the bedroom on the other. There were no doors for privacy. Instead, the stairs, which led up to the loft, divided the two living spaces. In the center of the room, there was a table and benches where meals were eaten. In one corner, there was a large wood-burning stove used for cooking; it also was the source of heat during the winter months. There was no electricity. Instead, candles with glass globes were strategically placed around the room. Next to the stove, there were two portable porcelain basins for washing dishes. Water had to be brought in from the well outside because there was no indoor plumbing – nor was there an indoor bathroom. The outhouse was forty feet from the back door.

When Victoria saw her marital bed for the first time, she was pleased. As it turned out, the quilt she had made and tucked away in her hope chest was perfect. The beautiful pink, blue and yellow colors instantly livened up the room. It was the only quilt I could ever remember seeing on my parents' bed. She always spoke shyly and reverently of that part of the house.

The loft had very little furniture – a couple of worn-out mattresses and a few wooden boxes in which to keep clothing. As Victoria glanced around the room, James said, "Let's fill this loft with the laughter of children." Even though the statement made his new bride blush, it quickly became Victoria's dream too. On October 18, 1923, my brother was born. They named him Calvin after Calvin Coolidge, the 30th president of the United States. My brother was strong, healthy and growing like a weed – much like our country's stock market, which was booming in a spectacular manner.

Although much of America was thriving in the post-war era, Victoria was having difficulty "filling the loft with the laughter of children." She had two miscarriages during 1924 and 1925. Even more tragic was her pregnancy in 1927. She contracted the German Measles during the first trimester; as a result, the baby girl was born with serious birth defects and died within hours of delivery. Victoria went into a deep depression. She blamed herself.

James, with the help of some neighbors, tried to cheer her spirits by improving things around the house. There was still no indoor bathroom, but he did lay pipe so they could have running water in the new porcelain sink he purchased, and he did buy an ice box so my mother could keep the food cold and fresh for the duration the block remained frozen. Even though they had very few modern appliances to make it worthwhile, James did connect with the county electricity. With his bonus money, which he usually put in the bank, he made an extravagant purchase: *a radio*. He bought the new contraption in hopes his wife would find it entertaining. Eventually, Victoria did begin to listen to the news, a couple of programs, some music and sporting events. Often, people heard her singing to songs like *Let a Smile Be Your Umbrella, Makin' Whoopee* and her personal favorite, *My Heart Stood Still*. Much to James' delight, she also developed a love for baseball and cheered for Babe Ruth and the New York Yankees.

Across town, during the mid-1920s, things were changing on a daily basis. There were recently paved roads and a new brick school with a classroom for every grade to replace the old, wooden schoolhouse that could no longer hold all of the children. The building also had a library and a gymnasium. There were more than a dozen new homes sprouting up and a car in nearly every garage in that part of town. Original houses were renovated to include electricity and indoor plumbing. Many people on the other side of town were borrowing money or using the installment plan to buy modern appliances like electric refrigerators and furnaces. In fact, these modern conveniences were not the sole reason people borrowed money. Because the stock market was growing at such a rapid pace, many of the people north of town were engaging in speculation and buying on margin in order to take advantage of the escalating value; in other words, they were borrowing money to buy stocks. James and Victoria didn't trust the stock market. Instead, they put every dollar they could save into the bank.

Victoria announced she was pregnant in early 1929; once again, she began to believe in her dream of "filling the loft with the laughter of children." She was extremely wary and took extra precautions to assure a healthy baby. James was overly protective and insisted he do all of the heavy work around the house. Calvin – at age five – had his share of chores to help his mother.

While the child grew in the womb, the town continued to thrive. Shortly after Herbert Hoover's Inauguration in March of 1929, Randall Miller, James' boss, sold all of his stocks. With the profits, he built a new general store that carried twice as many products, a gas station to accommodate the ever-increasing number of cars in the town, and the most beautiful movie theater anyone had ever seen. The grand opening was held on the Fourth of July. At noon, Mr. Miller ceremoniously tore down the old nickelodeon and opened the doors to Miller's General Store on West Street, Miller's Gas Station on Maple Street, and Miller's Grand Palace on Main Street.

It was perhaps the most excitement the people of the town had ever seen. There was a parade, of course – after all it was the Fourth of July. A band played. There was a lot of flag waving and cheering as the Veterans of the Civil War, the Spanish American War and the Great War all marched in their uniforms. Private James Malone participated. His left sleeve was pinned meticulously so it did not dangle by his side. He looked regal and proud. When James marched by his wife and child, who were standing on the curb cheering with the rest of the townspeople, he nodded his head slightly and winked. Calvin waved his flag enthusiastically, and Victoria blew him an imaginary kiss.

Afterward, there were speeches, more cheering, a pie eating contest, a three-legged sack race and a picnic. To the delight of every person in town, Mr. Miller announced the first movie to be played in his theater: Al Jolson in *The Jazz Singer*. Although *talkies* had been out for over a year, no one at the picnic had seen one. The crowd cheered wildly. When the clapping stopped, Randall Miller proudly stated the next scheduled movie would be an animated show entitled *Steamboat*, and the new cartoon star was Walt Disney's Mickey Mouse. There was another enormous round of applause.

The euphoric and prosperous feelings of the day began to envelop James Malone, and he considered selling his cabin and moving to the north side of town where the houses were new and filled with modern conveniences. He was told a person needed a few hundred dollars to make the initial payment on a house, and the bank would loan him the rest. James calculated his financial situation and decided if he diligently saved until the end of the year, he would have enough money to make the down payment and still have a small "nest egg" for his family. When James told Victoria about his plan, she gladly supported him. Together, they began to dream of moving into a new home.

But like the nation's economy, James and Victoria's dreams were built on a house of cards. My sister Elizabeth was born on *Black Tuesday* – October 29, 1929 – during the stock market crash. Before the month was over, there were catastrophic losses of over $25 billion. James and Victoria counted their blessings because they had a healthy baby girl and because they had put their money in the bank instead of the stock market. Unfortunately, counting their blessings was not nearly good enough.

Two weeks before Christmas, Calvin and Elizabeth came down

with Whooping Cough. At first, my parents thought it was the common cold, but then their fevers spiked and their breathing became labored. It wasn't long before the room was filled with the high-pitched whooping noise the children made as they tried desperately to catch their breath. The house was immediately quarantined, and the doctor no longer came to see them. James and Victoria worked around the clock to save their children. When Victoria was not tending to them, she was down on her knees praying to God. Neither James nor his wife slept for more than an hour at a time.

During the second stage of the disease, the children began to spit up huge globs of mucus. Victoria tried valiantly to scoop it out of their throats and keep the airway clear of the suffocating phlegm. When Calvin and Elizabeth had a coughing fit at the same time, the sound bounced off of the walls like a rubber ball, echoing and magnifying the ghastly racket. Elizabeth convulsed on several occasions, which struck fear in James' and Victoria's hearts. Christmas came and went without anyone in the house realizing the holiday had passed. Four days later, Elizabeth went into another convulsion. Seconds after it was over, the infant rested peacefully in Victoria's arms. She intuitively knew baby Elizabeth was dead. Victoria was on the verge of a crying jag when Calvin began another coughing spell. The mucus was streaming down his chin. Victoria's maternal instincts took over, and she moved like a robot, doing what was necessary to keep her remaining child alive.

The following day, while James made arrangements to bury Elizabeth, he discovered the bank – which held his life's savings – had closed its doors. Except for the cash in the glass jar on the shelf near the sink, all of their money was gone. James didn't have the heart to tell his wife. She was already dealing with enough tragedy. He wanted to protect her from any additional pain, so he made a pact to keep the secret until he felt his wife was strong enough to handle the news.

Because Calvin could not be left alone, Victoria was unable to attend her baby's meager funeral. Elizabeth was buried with only her father and the pastor standing over the grave. It was an added stab in Victoria's heart.

For an additional three weeks, Victoria nursed Calvin. He tittered on the edge several times, and it looked as if he might not see the spring.

Although James went back to work in January, Victoria refused to leave the house. It was March before Calvin was strong enough to venture outside for more than a few minutes at a time. When the crocuses began to bloom, Victoria took her son on walks around the town. Although, my mother had heard over the radio about the financial situation with the stock market and how banks were constantly closing all across America, she had no idea *her* bank had shut its doors months earlier. When she saw the boarded windows of the vacated bank on Main Street, the evidence of her financial loss became a reality. Victoria sat on the curb and sobbed. Calvin patted his mother on the shoulder and said, "Don't worry, Mommy, everything will be okay." Victoria surrounded her son with both arms and gave way to her tears.

2

A year later, on April Fools' Day 1931, I was born. My parents considered naming me after the president of the United States, but no one in our town liked Herbert Hoover anymore. His political slogan of "A Chicken in Every Pot and a Car in Every Garage" had backfired on him. Most people could not afford a car, and many were unable to buy food. In America, nearly twelve million people were out of work. They pointed at President Hoover and placed the blame for their monetary misery on him. Needless to say, my parents vetoed the idea of calling me Herbert; instead, they named me Richard. My mother told me numerous times that Richard was a strong name – a confident name – a name for kings.

I did not know I was born in a home of poverty, nor did I realize the nation was in a depression. I only knew my mother smelled sweet, her voice was like that of an angel, and when I was snuggled in her arms, I felt safe and warm.

At the time of my birth, my mother was nearly twenty-six years old, my father was thirty-two, and my brother Calvin was seven and a half. Our family continued to live in that small cabin on the south side of town. We still did not have a car, a telephone, a refrigerator, a furnace or an indoor bathroom, but the tiny house was mortgage-free, and my father still had a job at the Grand Palace. For the longest time, I couldn't figure out why my father spent his afternoons and evenings in such a majestic place while we lived in a small cabin. It was several years before

I realized my father didn't own the movie theater; instead, he was simply the man who took the tickets.

In the spring of 1932, many of our town's veterans traveled to Washington, D.C. to support a bill in Congress, which would authorize the government to pay a bonus of $500 to the veterans of the Great War. The peaceful protesters were called the Bonus Army. Those veterans, who were lucky enough to have a job in the mines or any of the other businesses in town, did not go to the nation's capital. My father, who feared losing his job at the Grand Palace if he left, was not a participant either. The unfortunate men who had not worked in more than two years and were desperately trying to find a way to feed their families, made the journey. They pitched their tents on the Mall in front of the Capitol and waited for the Senate to vote on the bill.

It was an election year. Due to the devastating economy, President Hoover was unpopular with the people. If he had been able to get the bill passed on June 17, perhaps the president would have won support from some of the voters, but it was not meant to be – the bill did not pass. In July, many in the Bonus Army refused to leave and continued to protest the outcome of the bill. As a result, soldiers under the command of General Douglas MacArthur and his aide Major Dwight D. Eisenhower arrived on the scene to forcibly remove the protesters.

Newspapers and radio gave detailed accounts of what happened, but the personal stories told by the townspeople upon their return made everyone's hair stand on end. Apparently, bayonets were used to nudge the veterans off of the Mall. The soldiers, who were wearing gas masks, set off tear-gas bombs. As soon as the people moved out of their makeshift, temporary homes in front of the Capitol, the soldiers set fire to the shantytown. A couple of people were shot, dozens were injured and an eleven-month-old baby died. Americans were shocked and appalled.

Franklin D. Roosevelt, the democratic candidate for president, took advantage of Hoover's political suicide. Roosevelt promised a "New Deal" for Americans. In his platform, he stated he would turn unemployment around, give aid to the farmers, balance the budget, and end Prohibition. In November – on Election Day – Franklin Roosevelt beat Herbert Hoover by a landslide. His electoral vote margin was 472 to

59, and he won 42 of the 48 states. My parents, as did most Americans, began to hope again.

<h2 style="text-align:center">3</h2>

I do not have many memories prior to being five years old, only the wonderful smell of my mother and the sweet way she sang to me while I was sitting in her lap. It wasn't until my fifth birthday my memories became clearer. During that summer, our family sat around the radio and listened as Jesse Owens won four gold medals at the 1936 Summer Olympics in Berlin, Germany. My father talked about an evil man named Adolf Hitler, who believed Germans were superior to everyone else and certainly more superior to colored folks or Jews. Jesse Owens and his Negro teammates won ten medals during the competition. Ironically, even though Germany won the most medals during the Games, the entire German men's track and field team earned fewer medals than the small number of American colored track and field athletes.

When the radio announcer reported the statistic, my father stood up, clapped his hands and said, "That ought to put that damn Nazi in his place and show him he's not so superior after all."

My mother instantly looked up from her knitting and said, "James, please do not say swear words in front of the children." My mother's voice was rather stern. She rarely spoke in that fashion.

I wasn't sure what the term "swear words" meant, but I was certain it was not a good thing. I was also not sure if the "swear word" was "Nazi" or "damn" – or maybe both together – I only knew I had never heard the words before that day.

"I'm sorry, Victoria," my father apologized. "I wish I could ignore what is going on over there, but I cannot. Hitler is such an evil man. We should all be terrified of him. His Third Reich is getting stronger and stronger every day. He took back the Rhineland and not a single shot was fired. What's the matter with Chamberlain? Can't he see what Hitler is doing?" My father's voice became even more passionate. "For God's sake, Hitler's in violation of most of the terms of the Treaty of Versailles, and no one's doing anything about it!" Whenever my father spoke of Hitler, he always rubbed the stump of his left arm and talked about what it was like to fight the Germans in the Great War. He often became pensive, and his brow wrinkled as he drifted off in his own private thoughts. My mother would change the mood in the room by changing the radio station so we could all listen to *Amos and Andy.* Whenever that program was on the air, our home would instantly fill with laughter. My mother would knit, and my father would stoke the stove, both chuckling the entire time. The cheerful atmosphere was contagious; Calvin and I often laughed so hard our sides ached.

4

The following year, in 1937, my mother worked at the big house on the hill. After school, Calvin walked to the newsstand and occasionally had the opportunity to sell *Extras*, but I had no place to go; therefore, I had to tag along with my mother while she cleaned the rooms in the gigantic mansion. I had never seen anything so big. In fact, it was bigger than the Grand Palace on Main Street. The house had marble floors and paintings on the wall, which were bigger than I was. My mother showed me the indoor bathroom and said if I was careful, I could use it when I found the need. I looked inside and was shocked by what I saw. There was a pull chain toilet and a bathtub big enough for a person to sit in it. I'd never seen one of those modern contraptions. I bathed with a cloth, some soap and a porcelain basin. When I was done, I threw the dirty water outside.

Much to my amazement, I realized my whole house could fit in the staircase that led up to the second floor. My mother told me I was never allowed to go up there; then, she led me into a room filled with books. She gently sat me in a big cushy chair and pleaded with me not to move. The radio in the corner was on – its dial was set to a show I knew my mother often listened to when she was doing her chores at home: *The Guiding Light.*

"Richard," my mother quietly spoke. "Please don't touch anything in the room. I promise I won't take long. If you are really good, perhaps you can listen to *The Green Hornet* tonight after dinner." She kissed me sweetly on the cheek and patted my hair. "You're a good boy, Richard. Mommy loves you very much."

As promised, I sat quietly in the chair. I was afraid if I ventured out on my own, I would surely get lost. At first, I was bored and lonely, but then something interesting happened. I met Caroline Sue. Normally, I didn't look at girls too much – they were silly creatures who wanted to talk about dolls and pretend to play house, but Caroline Sue seemed different. She didn't look like any of the girls who lived on my street. Her long, curly hair was clean and shiny. It was the color of the sky at midnight when there was no moon. There was a light blue ribbon holding the ringlets away from her face, but when she moved – even a little bit – the curls seemed to dance on her shoulders. Her eyes were dark brown –really dark brown – so dark, I couldn't even see the little black circles in the middle of her eyes. Her cheeks were flushed as if she had been running, and she had a splash of tiny freckles on her nose. This little girl had an aura about her. I instantly knew she was not the daughter of one of the women who cleaned the house. Quite the contrary, she looked as if she *belonged* here.

When Caroline Sue came in the room, she immediately shut the door behind her. After crossing her arms and staring at me for a full minute in silence, she cocked an eyebrow and said, "Who are you?"

"My name's Richard. What's your name?"

"Caroline Sue." She said in a bit of a snooty fashion, as if I should have known without asking.

As I tried to repeat it, I struggled with the pronunciation. "Carley Sue?"

"No, silly! Caroline." She slowly said it again. "Caroline."

Again, I tried. "Carley?"

"You don't talk very well, do you?" She said as she confidently approached me.

Until that moment, I had never realized I didn't talk well. No one in my family had ever said anything about the way I talked. Her statement made me feel insecure and even more out of place than I had when I initially entered the room. I sat in silence waiting for her next comment.

Caroline was a little girl. In order for her to sit in the outsized chair, she had to first use her arms to pull herself up enough to position her body in it. After she succeeded in getting in the chair, she scooted herself back until she could lean against the upholstery. Once again, she crossed her arms and stared at me. After doing so, she spoke, "I tell you what," Caroline stated. "You can call me Carley, if I can call you Ricky."

"But my name is Richard." I replied, a little baffled by her offer.

"Yes, I know. But Richard is such a big person name. And you're not a big person yet. Besides, wouldn't it be fun to have different names only we use for each other?"

"I guess it would be okay." I tentatively responded. We eyed each other for a while in silence, and then I asked, "Why are you wearing those funny pants? Girls are supposed to wear dresses."

"They're riding pants, silly! Don't you know anything?"

"Riding pants?" I responded. Then I asked, "Do you have a horse?"

"No, I don't have a horse. I have a pony. It's in the stable behind the house." She paused. "Do you know how to ride?"

Again, I felt instantly insecure. How could this tiny, little girl possibly know how to do something that I couldn't? Shyly, I responded, "No. I don't know anything about horses or ponies, except for what I see at the motion picture shows."

"I wish somebody else knew how to ride. It's so boring to do it all by myself." Caroline's shoulders slouched in disappointment, and she puffed out her lower lip in a pouting fashion.

There was at least a full minute of awkward silence before I asked the all-important question – the obvious one – the question kids ask when they are jockeying for status in a relationship. "How old are you?"

Caroline didn't even hesitate. "Six." She answered. "Actually, I'm six and a half. I'll be seven on April 1st."

I instantly sat up in my chair. "April 1st is *your* birthday? That's impossible. April 1st is *my* birthday!"

"You silly goose!" Caroline laughed. "More than one person can be born in a day!" Again she chuckled as if she had discovered the most delightful secret. "Isn't it wonderful we have the same birthday! I've never known anyone who was born on *my* birthday!"

"Has anyone ever made fun of you on your birthday?" I asked shyly.

"No. Why would anyone make fun of a person on her birthday?" Caroline seemed genuinely interested when she asked, "Has anyone ever made fun of *you* on *your* birthday?"

"Yes." I responded. "On my last birthday." I glanced up to see if she were listening. "People played a joke on me and screamed *April Fools* afterward."

"What kind of joke?"

"This big kid who lives down the street from me said they had seen my mother and father buy a bicycle for me as a present for my birthday, and he asked me if I liked my new bike." I paused for a moment because I couldn't – for the life of me – figure out why I was confessing this to a pint-sized little girl. When she leaned toward me and smiled as if she were truly interested in what I had to say, I got the courage to continue. "When I told him I didn't have a new bike, he told me I should go straight home and it would be there in the house wrapped in a great big red ribbon. So I raced home, but there was no bike. I asked my mom where the bike was, and she looked puzzled and said 'what bike?' I went back down the street and told the boy there was no bike. He and his friends screamed *April Fools*! And they laughed and laughed and laughed." Tears sprang uncontrollably to my eyes. I looked down at my hands because I didn't want Caroline to see I was crying.

"That's awful!" Caroline interjected. "Those boys were mean to you."

"I don't think they knew how much I wanted a bicycle. Okay – so maybe I'm too small to ride a bike yet, but some day I'm going to learn. And some day, I'm going to have a bike. I'm going to make lots and lots of money, and I'm going to buy the best bike in the whole wide world."

"Why did those boys say *April Fools* to you?" Caroline asked. "Do you know what it means?"

"Yes." I spoke softly. "That night, I went home and told my mother what had happened. My mom looked sad. She even got her handkerchief out and blew her nose. I think she was crying. I don't like it when my mother cries. It makes me feel bad." I looked around the room for a few seconds before I continued. "My mother sat in her special chair by the door, and I crawled onto her lap. She wrapped her arms around me and hummed my favorite tune – the one she made up special for me." I looked Caroline straight in the eyes as I continued to tell her about my sixth birthday. "Then my mother told me about April Fools' Day. She said in some countries it's a day for jokes, and the person who gets to be the butt of the joke is an *April Fool*. My mother told me no one is sure how it started, but some people think it began way back – a long time ago – before Mommy was born – even before Mommy's Mommy was born – even before Mommy's Mommy's Mommy was born – a *really* long time ago! Back then, the first day of the year was on April 1st, and

17

people gave gifts to each other on the first day of each year. When the calendar was rearranged and January 1st became the first day of the year, people continued to give gifts on April 1st, but instead of the gifts being special, they were more like a joke. My mother said some people think it began in France – that's where my mother was born." I paused. "And I said that I don't think I like France very much – not if they make up stupid, mean things like *April Fools.*"

"You're right, Ricky." Caroline sympathized. "I hope no one ever makes me an *April Fool.* I don't want to be an *April Fool.* I think it might hurt too much."

I sat in silence for a long time before speaking again, "You know something, Carley?" I tried to pronounce her name correctly, but it still came out sounding wrong.

"What?"

"You kind of look like you might be bratty, but you're nice."

"Thank you. I think you're nice too." With a smile on her face, she asked, "Do you want to be friends?"

"I've never been friends with a girl before." I paused. "But I guess it would be okay."

"Wonderful!" Caroline clapped her hands enthusiastically. "Since we are friends, would you like to go to the Grand Palace with me for the Saturday matinee? *The Little Colonel* is playing. I love Shirley Temple. Don't you?"

"Yeah. She's funny, and she sings real good." I responded.

Caroline sat up in her chair – proud like a peacock. "Father tells me I am precocious like Shirley Temple."

"What does precocious mean?" I asked.

"I don't know, and I'm not sure if it's a good thing or not, but when my father says it he smiles at me." Caroline paused a moment. "Well, do you want to go to see *The Little Colonel* with me?

"Okay. I'll meet you there."

5

The following Saturday afternoon I stood next to my father, who was taking tickets at the lobby door of the Grand Palace, and waited for Caroline Sue. I was beginning to think she was not coming, when a brand new, shining, black 1937 Packard stopped at the entrance to the theater. A chauffer got out and opened the passenger door. Caroline Sue stepped out on to the curb.

When she saw me through the crowd, she waved enthusiastically. "Hi, Ricky," she shouted. "Sorry I'm late."

"It's okay, Carley. The movie hasn't started yet. They are still playing the newsreels." I answered.

To my complete surprise, Caroline didn't purchase a ticket. Instead, she marched right passed my father, as if he weren't even there. My dad didn't stop her; in fact, he nodded in her direction, smiled and said, "Good afternoon, Miss Caroline Sue."

"Good afternoon to you, too, Mr. Malone." Caroline replied with a smile.

I was about to ask her how she was able to get past my father without buying a ticket when the music for the feature film resonated in the lobby. Caroline grabbed my hand and jerked me in the direction of the balcony. "Hurry! I don't want to miss a second," she said. I obediently followed.

When *The Little Colonel* was over, Caroline and I stood outside in the oppressive August heat while she waited for the Packard to pick her up. My curiosity got the best of me, and I finally confronted Caroline. "When you got here this afternoon, you didn't buy a ticket."

"Why should I?" she asked.

"Because everyone has to buy a ticket." I stated frankly.

"Silly goose!" Caroline chuckled. "I don't have to buy a ticket. My father *owns* the Grand Palace."

"No, he doesn't!" I stubbornly responded. "*My* father owns the theater!" Why was Caroline lying? After all, everyone knew it was *my* father who owned the theater. "Can't you see?" I pointed to my father. "It's *my* father who dresses up in the fancy red suit with all of the gold embroidery on it and greets everyone at the door. And *he's* the person who takes the tickets when the people go inside."

"Mr. Malone is *your* father?" Caroline seemed completely surprised by the news. "I didn't know that. He's really nice, but he doesn't own the Grand Palace." Caroline grabbed my hand and led me out into the street. She pointed to the gigantic sign over the theater. "What does that say?" she asked. When I didn't respond, she continued. "It says *Miller's Grand Palace.*" Caroline stated firmly. "Miller! That's *my* name. Caroline Sue Miller."

I stood in silence for several seconds. Never in my short life, had I felt so humiliated. I didn't look at the sign; in fact, I didn't even look at Caroline. Finally, I responded, "I don't know what the sign says. I don't know how to read." I wasn't sure what embarrassed me more: the fact I couldn't read the sign and she could, or the fact I felt like such a fool for believing my father owned the theater.

"You don't know how to read?" Caroline seemed truly mystified. I thought everyone knew how to read at least a little bit."

"I don't go to first grade until next month. And neither do you! How come *you* already know how to read?"

"Miss Mavis teaches me. She comes every day at 10:00 – except Saturdays and Sundays," Caroline said as she led us both back to the safety of the sidewalk. "She taught me my ABCs a year ago. I can even write all of the upper- and lower-case letters. And I can write sentences too!" Caroline added proudly. "Father told me I'm very, very smart and – one day – I'm going to go to college. And he told me, even though I am a girl, I can be anything I want to be. Anything at all!"

Caroline must have sensed my solemn mood. She gently put her hand in mine and squeezed it. Instead of her gesture making me feel more insecure; to my amazement, I began to relax.

"Doesn't your mother read to you and teach you the ABCs?" Caroline asked.

I pondered the question for quite a while before I responded, "I don't think my mother knows how to read." I replied. "I've never seen her do it." Then I added, "Does your mother ever read to you?"

"I don't have a mother." Caroline answered in a rather matter-of-fact tone. "My mother died the day I was born."

"Oh!" This time, I was the one who reached for Caroline's hand and gently squeezed it. I thought about what it would be like for me if I didn't have my mother. The idea made me terribly sad. "I'm sorry. It must be hard not to have a mother. I hope nothing ever happens to my mother."

As I was finishing my sentence, the Packard stopped in front of us. The chauffer opened the door and Caroline climbed into the car.

Seconds later, an elderly lady also got into the car. "Who's that?" I asked as I pointed to the woman.

"Oh, her?" she replied. "She's one of my father's workers. She follows me everywhere." Caroline sneered at the woman. "It's so annoying."

"I didn't see her when you came to the theater."

"You might not have seen her, but she was there!" Caroline responded with an exasperated tone. Then she smiled. "Are you going to come with your mother to the house next week?"

"Probably," I responded.

"Wonderful!" Caroline stated. "I had a good time today, Ricky."

"Bye, Carley." The chauffer shut the door before I could say anything else. I realized I, too, had a good time. Even though I'd never had a friend who was a girl, I liked Caroline. She was a little bratty, but she was fun.

<h1 style="text-align:center">6</h1>

Generally on Saturdays, my father was home long enough to eat dinner. The rest of the time, he spent at the Grand Palace because movies played several times during the weekend. He, more often than not, ate quickly and didn't talk during the meal, but this particular Saturday night, he interrupted my brother Calvin's discussion about his rapidly approaching 14th birthday.

"Richard," my father interjected. "When you told me you were going to meet a friend at the Grand Palace, I didn't know your friend was going to be Caroline Sue Miller." He glanced across the table at my mother. The expression on his face was stern. "How did this happen, Victoria?"

"I was unaware they even knew each other." My mother spoke hesitantly. She turned her attention to me and inquired, "Did you meet Miss Caroline when we were at the big house last week, Richard?"

"Yes, Ma'am," I replied. "Carley came into the room while I was waiting for you." I was still unable to pronounce Caroline's name properly but no one seemed to notice or care.

"Victoria," my father addressed my mother in a cautionary tone. "I don't think this is a good idea."

"They are little children, James," my mother replied softly. "What harm can there be?"

"We live on the south side of town. She lives on the north side." My father raised his voice slightly. "Don't you see a potential problem here?"

I could not understand why my parents were concerned. After all, I had tons of friends; plus, Calvin and I had always been allowed to run freely through town and the surrounding area as long as we got our chores done on time and we were at the table – hands and faces washed – when dinner was served. *What could possibly be the problem?*

"I don't like it, Victoria." My father swallowed his last bite and pushed himself away from the table. "Richard," he directed his attention to me. "I hope you realize if you come to the theater with Caroline Sue Miller, I can't let you in without a ticket. Do you understand?" My father did not wait for an answer. He stood up and walked to the door. "I have to leave or I'll be late for the next showing. We'll talk about this when I get home."

My father left. The moment the door shut behind him, Calvin returned the conversation to highlights of his 14th birthday, and my mother sat quietly in her seat. She wasn't listening to a word my brother said.

7

That night, while Calvin and I lay on our mattresses in the loft, I asked him the question that had been bothering me all day. "Did you know Dad doesn't own the Grand Palace?"

"What?" Calvin let out a small chuckle.

"You heard me." I responded, but I repeated myself anyway. "Did you know Dad doesn't own the theater?"

"Of course, I know that," my brother responded.

"I feel so stupid." I whispered the words. "I figured that because we never had to pay the quarter for a ticket then Dad must own the place. And Dad is always there – every day – and he wears that nifty suit with the gold buttons and the braids on his shoulders. No one else wears that suit –only Dad."

"Do you want to know a secret, Richard?" Calvin asked in a mischievous manner. He didn't wait for a reply; instead, he continued, "When I was your age –about the time my two front teeth fell out – like yours – I thought Dad owned the Grand Palace too."

"Really?"

"Yeah," my brother continued. "And for the same reasons. In fact, I couldn't figure out why Dad owned this gigantic theater and we lived in such a little house. It might sound silly, but sometimes, I even wished we lived at the Grand Palace instead of here."

I instantly sat up. "Yeah!" I interrupted. "That's exactly what I thought."

"We're not rich." Calvin changed the subject and spoke softly. "You know that – don't you, Richard?"

"You mean, we're not rich like the people with the big house on the hill. Carley's house?" I responded.

"We're *definitely* not rich like the Millers." Calvin paused. "In fact, we are lucky Dad even has a job. Dad's lucky Mr. Miller hired him when he came back from the Great War with only one arm. And – before you were born – when most of the men in town lost their jobs and their money, Mr. Miller let Dad keep his job at the Grand Palace. Most of my friends' fathers don't have jobs, and they have both arms. Kids my age are riding the rails looking for work and taking any job they can get, because there isn't enough food at their homes. After I turn fourteen, I'm going to stop selling the *Extras* and get another job. Mr. Miller said he would let me stock the shelves at the General Store for a couple of hours every day after school. If I work really hard, I'll make three, maybe four bucks a week."

"You're going to stop selling the *Extras*?" I asked. For as long as I could remember, my brother had spent his afternoons at the newsstand on the corner of Main and Maple. When the news warranted an *Extra* addition, he waved the papers in the air and scream, "Extra! Extra! Read all about it."

"Yes." Calvin said. "I get twenty-five cents to sell the *Extras*, but they only print them when something big happens. I want a job that will give me a consistent income."

"How old do you have to be to sell the *Extras*?"

"I was seven when I sold my first one." Calvin paused. "Are you interested in doing it?"

"Is it hard to do?" I inquired in a timid voice.

"No. Not really. You kind of have to get people excited about what's in the paper so they will buy it, but that's not hard to do." Calvin paused.

"For example, last May when the Hindenburg blew up, I screamed 'Extra! Extra! Thirty-six people die in an explosion in the sky! Read all about it!'" My brother threw his hands up in the air in a wild, excited gesture. "My papers were gone in twenty minutes." He paused to collect his thoughts. "And the day Jean Harlow died – that was another busy day. All I had to say was 'Blond Bombshell' and the men came running. Of course, the biggest seller is always a story about Hitler or Germany – those papers sell like hotcakes. People start reading the paper the second they buy it. They shake their heads and mutter in disgust."

"Do you think I could get the job at the newsstand when you start working at the General Store?" I asked. "Dad made it sound like I won't be able to get into the Grand Palace anymore without buying a ticket."

"You know, Richard," my brother spoke softly. "Dad could probably lose his job if Mr. Miller ever found out that he let all of us get in the motion picture show for free any time we wanted."

I felt the guilt wash over me. It was a unpleasant feeling. "I didn't know he could get into trouble."

"I tell you what," Calvin said confidently. "I'll talk to the man at the newsstand tomorrow and ask him if you can step into my shoes when I leave. Okay?"

"Okay!" It would be nice to make some money of my own.

8

My mother stopped taking me to the house on the hill, so I didn't get to see Caroline again until the first day of school. We were in the same classroom, but it didn't take me long to figure out that she was in the *smart* reading group, and I was not. She didn't seem bothered by it. To my surprise, she offered to give up her recess time so she could help me learn my ABCs. In a strange way, I felt the need to make her proud of me; consequently, I concentrated and worked extra at home. Every time I'd learn something new, Caroline would squeal with delight and say, "You're so smart, Ricky!" I, of course, would beam with pride and work twice as hard so I could make her smile again. I asked her once why she stayed with me instead of playing with the other kids during recess and she always said, "Because you're my friend, you silly goose!"

In mid-October, Calvin turned fourteen. As he predicted, my

brother worked at Miller's General Store, and I inherited his job at the newsstand. Calvin was right. It wasn't difficult at all. In fact, I rather enjoyed it. On the days there was an *Extra* to sell, I walked the block, yelling my slogan, and sold the papers quickly, which meant I could spend the remainder of the afternoon playing with my buddies. On the slower days, I looked at the words in the newspaper and tried to find any of those words I'd learned in school. Every once in a while, Caroline would sneak out of the house and come to the corner. She helped me sell the papers. Those days were especially enjoyable because Caroline always came up with the best *Extra* slogans. Nine times out of ten, she could make them rhyme. When we were done, she helped me with my homework. On warm days, we played marbles on the sidewalk, or walked down to the river and skipped stones, or sat on the water's edge and talked about tadpoles and frogs and fish, or looked at the sky and made up imaginary stories about the shapes the clouds created. Often we discussed the latest episode of *The Lone Ranger* or *The Green Hornet* or *The Mark of Zorro*, which had been on the radio the previous night. I had a lot of friends, but Caroline was my favorite. It was kind of weird. Who ever heard of boys having girls for friends, but Caroline didn't act like a girl, and she liked to talk about and do the things I enjoyed.

During the winter months, I rarely saw Caroline outside of school and church. At school, we were able to spend a little time together when we weren't doing our lessons, but on Sundays, even though I saw her at church, I didn't get to talk to her. She sat in the first pew with her father, and I sat in the back of the church with my parents and Calvin. I tried to get my parents to move closer to the front of the church, but my father insisted we must always sit in the back. After Sunday sermon, Caroline's father moved her so rapidly to the Packard, she and I were lucky if we even got the chance to say "hello" to each other.

Throughout January, February and March, it snowed a lot, which didn't allow us any extra time for outside activities or any time for Caroline to help me with my reading. At night, after all of my chores were done, I pulled my schoolbooks out and asked my mother for help. Although my mother tried, she wasn't good at it, and I could tell she was embarrassed she couldn't help me. I patted her on the shoulder and said, "Maybe, Mom, I can practice reading to you. The teacher says the more I do it, the better I will get."

My mother embraced me warmly and kissed my cheek. There were tears glistening in her eyes. Her voice was soothing and sympathetic when she spoke. "Remember, my beautiful son, we named you Richard because it is strong name – a proud name – a name for kings. You are very smart and very brave. You can grow up to be anything you want to be. Don't let anyone tell you otherwise and don't let anything stop you from reaching for your dreams." A solitary tear traveled down her cheek.

"It's okay, Mommy. Please don't cry. Like you said, I'm going to grow up some day, and I promise I'm going to make lots of money and live in a grand house. It will have a pull chain toilet and a furnace and a telephone and a real refrigerator, and I'll have a car. You and Father can live with me. And you won't have to clean other people's houses anymore." I touched my mother's cheek and wiped away the tears, but they kept coming. "Please don't cry, Mommy. It will be okay. I'm going to learn how to read and then everything will be okay."

9

On April 1, 1938, the teacher brought in a fancy cake to celebrate Caroline's seventh birthday. Part of me was confused and maybe even a little jealous when I realized Caroline's birthday was the only birthday celebrated during the entire year. The teacher didn't bring in a cake for any of the other students, nor did the class sing "Happy Birthday" to any child when it was his or her special day.

But another part of me was happy and excited because when Caroline walked to the front of the class and turned around, she searched the room with her eyes until she found me standing in the corner by the coat closet. Caroline instantly smiled and waved in my direction. "Ricky! Come here. It's your birthday too!" She waited patiently until I joined her by the birthday cake. "Will you help me blow out the candles?"

"Okay," I replied.

Together, we bent toward the flames, counted to three and blew out all of the candles. As the smoke surrounded us, it looked as if Caroline were going to kiss me on the cheek, but I quickly stood up because I didn't want her to do that in front of all the other kids. That would be too embarrassing, and someone would surely make a joke out of it; after all, it *was* April Fools' Day.

After school, I walked to the corner of Main and Maple to sell the *Extras*. When Caroline caught up with me, she handed me a present. "Happy Birthday, Ricky!" She stated enthusiastically.

"I'm sorry," I replied. "I didn't get you anything."

Much to my surprise, Caroline seemed perfectly content with the fact she was giving a gift, but not receiving one. "That's okay," she cheerfully replied. "Open it! I hope you like what I got you."

When I stripped off the paper, I discovered a wooden box with hinges and a handle. I opened the latch and looked inside of it. The box was divided into cubicles. In each cubicle was an assortment of fishing equipment: hooks, weights and string. "Wow!" I expressed my surprise. "This is fantastic!"

"And look!" Caroline pointed to several of the cubicles. "There's extra string – so when I'm with you, I can drop a line and fish too!"

"Thanks, Caroline." I spoke with honest joy. It was the first time I'd ever pronounced her name correctly and that accomplishment added to my pleasure, but when I looked at her, she seemed disappointed. "What's wrong?"

"You called me Caroline."

"Yeah! I know! I finally said it right!" I stated proudly.

"I like it when you call me Carley."

"Okay. Then I'll keep calling you Carley." *Girls!* I thought to myself. Sometimes they were so weird. I closed the box and walked towards the newsstand. Caroline followed.

"Can I ask you a question?"

"Sure," I replied.

"In school today, when you blew out the candles, did you make a wish?"

"Yes. Did you?" I asked.

"Yes," Caroline answered. "I'll tell my wish if you tell yours."

"I wished that one day I will be able to read as good as you." I almost whispered the words.

"I wished we would forever and always be friends."

10

In 1938, I sold a lot of *Extras*. It seemed like something important was happening almost every single day. For example, at age twenty-four, America's Heavyweight Champion Joe Louis beat Germany's Max Schmeling in a rematch. It would not have been such amazing news except for two details. First, it was well publicized and dubbed a test for superiority between the two nations. And second, Louis beat the German in 2:04 of the First Round. Needless to say, I sold all the *Extras* on that day.

During 1938, Hollywood was reaching a peak. There was a flood of movies released, which meant the Grand Palace was extremely busy, and my father was manning the door. In spite of the fact the country was still – after nearly a decade – in a depression, and money was tight for most of the town's residents, people managed to hoard their pennies until they had enough for a ticket to see Jimmy Stewart, Katharine Hepburn, Cary Grant, James Cagney, Bette Davis and dozens of other dazzling stars. It was the townspeople's way of putting their troubles aside for a little while and losing themselves in the magic of the silver screen. The people who bought the *Extras* couldn't get enough news about Hollywood's treasures.

Also during this time, President Roosevelt signed a bill called The Fair Labor Standards Act, which implemented a minimum wage of twenty-five cents per hour; as a result, my father made additional money for all of the hours he spent at the Grand Palace, and my brother also had an increase for the time he spent stocking shelves at Miller's General Store. Calvin asked for extra hours, and the manager gave them to him. My brother had dreams of buying a car when he turned fifteen – maybe it would be an old car – but a car nonetheless.

In addition, Thorton Wilder wrote a play called "Our Town" that won a Pulitzer Prize, which seemed like a big deal to all of the grownups. The drama class at our high school reenacted a couple scenes. My brother earned a small part in the play, so my family went to watch Calvin perform. At the curtain call, my parents cheered wildly. The local paper praised the school play and even mentioned Calvin's name in the article. My mother proudly clipped it out and put it in her beloved scrapbook.

In addition, whenever there was an *Extra* to sell during the summer, there was an abundance of information about the epidemic of polio across the country, but for some reason there were not many cases in our neighborhood. My mother said it was because she prayed a hundred times a day.

Even though there were numerous topics, which tempted patrons to purchase an *Extra*, the news that often monopolized the pages was information about Germany and Adolf Hitler. During that year, Hitler and his Nazis invaded Austria and Czechoslovakia. He took over both countries without a single shot being fired. Neville Chamberlain, the British prime minister, seemed to think allowing Germany to annex those countries was the only way to keep the peace, but my father adamantly disagreed with him. Often, my father screeched his rage while we sat around the dinner table. "Someone please explain to me why we even fought in the Great War. Those damn Nazis are like a disease that keeps spreading. We have to stop them, strangle them, and kill them! Why doesn't Great Britain or France do something? Don't they know Hitler is eventually going to come after *them*?"

"James! Please! You're scaring the children," my mother tried to keep her voice calm, but everyone at the table knew she was also agitated.

"They *should* be scared, Victoria." He pointed a finger at Calvin and then at me. "And *you* should be scared too." He turned his attention to his wife. "You have *sons*! Do you want them to go to war and come back with one arm blown off – or worse yet – be buried in an unmarked grave in a country you will never see?"

That night, I woke up from a deep slumber to find my mother sitting between my mattress and Calvin's. She was staring at me and wringing her beautifully embroidered handkerchief. There were no tears in her eyes, but she looked sad. "It is okay, Mommy." I whispered so I wouldn't awaken my brother. "If I have to go to war, I can kill the damn Nazis. I'm not afraid."

"Oh, my sweet Richard," my mother spoke softly. "You are my brave little boy."

"I'm not so very little anymore, Mommy." I stated.

"You're right," she replied. "You're growing up quickly, but you will always be *my* little boy – no matter how big you become – you will always be *my* little boy." She gentled kissed me on the cheek. "Go back to sleep, little man. Tomorrow is a school day."

11

Three important events occurred in my life during 1939. The first happened on September 1ˢᵗ, when Hilter invaded Poland. Two days later, Great Britain and France declared war on Germany, and my father's biggest nightmare began to take shape. Every night at dinner, he spoke of nothing but the conflict in Europe. The anxiety amongst the townspeople was equally as strong. Every day, I sold out of *Extras* within thirty minutes; as a result, twice as many were printed, and my wages were doubled.

The second major occurrence happened in October when I finally reaped the reward from all of my hard work in school. I was moved up to the highest reading group in my third-grade class. Caroline saved the seat next to her, and a tradition began – from that day on we always sat beside each other during reading circle. I was so proud of myself, and I couldn't wait to go home to tell my mother. She immediately threw her arms around me and said, "I knew you could do it. I'm so proud of you, Richard." She baked a cake to celebrate the occasion. In our family, this was an exceptional treat because cakes were only baked on birthdays. That night, at dinner, we didn't talk about Hitler or the Nazis or Germany. Instead, we talked about books and school.

The third major incident occurred at the Grand Palace while Caroline and I were watching *Gone With The Wind*. It was a Saturday, and I – like everyone else in town – couldn't wait to see the movie that had caused such a commotion all across the country. Most movies cost a quarter, but in order to get into *this* movie, I needed fifty cents. With my raise for selling the *Extras*, it took me one day. Caroline and I met in the lobby, went up to the balcony where we usually sat, and waited for the main event to start. The theater was packed – not a vacant seat in the house. I could feel the excitement in the air. When the lights dimmed, the red velvet curtains opened, and the overture began to play. Caroline reached for my hand. She didn't say a word; in fact, no one in the audience spoke throughout the first half of the movie. They were all spellbound and focused on the gigantic screen. Caroline squeezed my hand even tighter during the scene when Rhett Butler helped Scarlett, Melanie, Prissy and the baby escape from Atlanta. With her free hand, Caroline covered her eyes while the explosions occurred on the railroad tracks, and she winced when it appeared as if they were not going to get out in time. At the bridge, when Rhett kissed Scarlett before he left to join the Confederate Army, I looked at Caroline. She was totally and completely absorbed in the story.

At Intermission, we raced to the lobby in order to be first in line for popcorn, but there were dozens of people in front of us. Caroline was nervous because she didn't think we would make it back to our seats before the curtains opened again. Luckily, we did. As soon as the lights dimmed and the velvet curtains opened, Caroline reached for my hand. Every once in a while, she let go in order to get a handful of popcorn; however, throughout the majority of the movie, she squeezed my fingers tightly.

At the end, when Rhett Butler said, "Frankly, my dear, I don't give a damn!" I could hear several of the women in the theater gasp in shock. No such words had ever been spoken in a movie. Even though the ladies were all a buzz, Caroline was silent and riveted to her seat. Seconds later, as the audience was giving a resounding applause, I glanced at Caroline and she looked at me. She didn't say a word, and it happened without any warning at all.

Caroline Sue Miller kissed me. It was quick – over in an instant. I was so stunned, I couldn't speak. Moments later, the lights came on. Caroline stood up. So did I. We waited patiently and quietly as the people trickled out of the theater. Not once did she ever speak of that kiss, and neither did I.

Girls! Sometimes, they acted so weird!

12

By April Fools' Day 1941 – when I turned double digits – life in my town had changed considerably. A decade earlier, most of the men were unemployed, the mines were basically idle, there was an economic depression choking the country, and an aura of despondency encompassed the people of the town. President Roosevelt's New Deal had given Americans hope and the promise of turning our economy around, but – in actuality – his ideas never worked as well as planned. It wasn't until Hitler's war in Europe that factories were reopened and men were able to find gainful employment. Roosevelt's *Cash and Carry* policy benefited Britain, handicapped Germany and pacified those American isolationists who did not want to get involved in Europe's war. The increasing need for military supplies generated manufacturing jobs and greatly improved our nation's economy. Our mines were at full capacity again. There were jobs available for men who wanted to work. My father was still employed at the Grand Palace, but instead of simply taking tickets, he was now the night manager. We still lived on the south side of town, but with his increased wages, he had improved our home. As in the past, Calvin and I slept in the loft, but my parents had built an addition on to the house so they could have a private bedroom with a door, instead of a curtain. There was still no bathroom; we still used chamber pots and the outhouse. Several times a week, my father said, "If things keep getting better, perhaps we can sell this place and move to the north side of town."

Calvin, at age seventeen, had two jobs. He stocked supplies at Miller's General Store in the evenings, and he delivered milk before school three days a week. Last year, he had reached his dream of buying a car: an old Chrysler Imperial. It was rather beat up and had rust damage in several areas, but it ran like a top. Calvin was fiercely proud of his automobile.

My mom was still working for Mr. Miller, cleaning the big house on the hill, and I could tell, by conversations I overheard, my father was not happy with the situation. My parents were expecting a baby. Apparently, the child was due in November, and my mother's pregnancy was not going smoothly. Although Mother was thrilled there would soon be a baby in the family again, my father feared her health was in danger. When he insisted she quit, my mother replied, "But, James, we need the money." And my father sternly debated, "You know what the doctor said, Victoria!" Then with a softer voice, he added, "I need *you* more than we need a new house." No matter how many times my father insisted, my mother refused to quit. I often heard my father say, "Victoria, you are the kindest, gentlest, most wonderful person in the world, but you can be so stubborn sometimes!" Then he left the room in a huff.

I was also working on a regular basis. In the morning, I delivered the daily paper to the residences of the north side of town, in the afternoon I sold the *Extras*. I, like my brother, had also realized a dream. I had a bike. It wasn't brand new, but it was perfect for me. After my parents bought it from Mr. Miller, Caroline told me she had purposely asked for a bike for Christmas knowing she didn't want one. When it sat in the garage for three months in a row, Caroline's father threatened to sell it and she – giggling under her breath – allowed him to sell it to my mother. Caroline never confessed her manipulation to her father, but she proudly told me about it one sunny spring afternoon while we were fishing at the river.

"Last fall, I saw you looking at the bike in the store window," Caroline said. "You told me a zillion times your parents could never afford to buy you a new bike, and you were saving all of your money so *you* could buy one, but you said it would take another year and a half until you had enough to buy *that* bike. So I thought if I could get my father to buy it for *me* and I never rode it – he would eventually sell it for a lot less than the original price, but the bike would still be brand new."

"You did this for me?" I was flabbergasted.

"Of course," she replied nonchalantly.

"Why?"

"Because we're friends, you silly goose!" Upon making that statement, Caroline put another worm on her hook and dropped the line in the water.

I wasn't quite sure how to respond, so I simply said, "Thanks, Carley."

She smiled widely at me and then turned her attention to the fish nibbling at her bait.

13

During the summer, two subjects monopolized the newspapers: the war in Europe and baseball. German Luftwaffe seriously damaged London during the Blitz, and the Nazis marched through Greece and Yugoslavia. In addition, Hitler reneged on his non-aggression pact with Stalin and invaded the Soviet Union. When Americans talked about whether or not the United States should join the Allies, our country was divided. No matter where I went in town, I could hear a heated argument. Germany, Italy and Japan had previously signed a mutual defense treaty known as the Tripartite Pact, which guaranteed each of those nations the support of the other should they be invaded by an enemy. Due to this alliance, some Americans feared a military nightmare – a war across two oceans – and they wanted no part of it. "This is not our war," they shouted. "We should not get involved!" Although most people were in favor of Roosevelt's economy boosting cash-and-carry provision, which allowed countries to buy our American products as long as they paid for them in cash and carried them back to *their* countries on *their* ships, many people didn't think it was enough support for the Allies. Isolationists screamed, "We will not fight on foreign soil!" While others screamed, "No country will ever be safe as long as that madman Hilter is in power. We must join the fight!" President Roosevelt repeatedly stated, "This country is not going to war." Then he added, "except in case of attack."

Throughout the summer of 1941, the debate raged on.

Baseball was a wonderful diversion from the talk of war, and fans were glued to their radios or flocked to the stadiums all across the country for an afternoon of entertainment. By the end of August, my mother's belly had grown quite large. She was expecting twins, and the doctor seemed increasingly more concerned for her health. Finally, she conceded to my father's request and stayed home, spending most of her time lying in bed and listening to the radio. Like the rest of the country, baseball was her favorite pastime. It was an incredible season, but two players stood out as the brightest and the best: Ted Williams and Joe DiMaggio. When Boston Red Sox player Ted Williams batted .406 for the season, some fans arguably called him the greatest hitter in baseball history, but my mother vehemently disagreed. She was an adamant New York Yankees fan, and she loved "Joltin' Joe" DiMaggio. She could rattle off stats faster than anyone I knew. My mother argued even though "the Yankee Clipper" didn't have as high of a batting average of Ted Williams, he was consistent with his major league record of fifty-six straight games with a hit, and he was the American League's MVP choice for 1939 *and* was a strong candidate to win it again at the end of the 1941 season.

Even though my mother was constantly talking about baseball or humming one of the latest tunes or smiling at me when I brought home good grades, I knew she was putting on a brave façade. She rarely got out of bed. More often than not, Dad or Calvin made dinner, and we all cleaned the house so she didn't have to do it. My father didn't even try to pretend everything was okay. He hovered over my mother constantly. Even at my young age, I knew there was something wrong.

I spent most of my free time sitting on my mother's bed. When we weren't listening to the radio or talking about the events of the day, I read to her from books I had gotten at the library. My mother was amazed at how well I read, and she told me at least once a day that she was proud. She also said, on more than one occasion, "Always hold your head high, Richard. No matter what happens in your life, always do the best you can do. Make good choices and take responsibility for your actions. Be proud of who you are, and never give up on your dreams." She patted my hand gently. "And remember what Babe Ruth says . . . It's hard to beat a person who never gives up." When she spoke she was smiling, but I could tell there were tears welling up in her eyes, and for some reason, she looked sad.

Although the twins weren't due until November, my mother went into premature labor a month early. Calvin and I had both been born – with the help of a midwife – in our home, but at the first sign of labor pains with the twins, my father asked Calvin to drive us to the clinic. I sat in the front seat of the Chrysler Imperial, and my parents sat in the back. Dad looked scared, and Mom looked ashen. No one said a word.

When we arrived at the clinic, Calvin dropped my parents off at the main entrance, and we went to find a parking space. I turned around in my seat so I could watch my mother walk toward the door. She was leaning heavily on my father, and he had his good arm wrapped protectively around her. They were moving slowly. I wanted to get out of the car and race toward them. Something inside of me screamed to run after her. My entire body trembled. I steadied my hand on the window and rushed to roll it down so I could yell "I love you" to my mother, but I didn't get the window down fast enough. She was already inside. I saw her for a fraction of a second before the door shut behind her.

It was the last time I saw my mother alive.

Calvin and I stayed in the waiting room for hours. My brother asked the nurse at least a dozen times what was happening, but she couldn't or wouldn't tell us. I had a sick feeling in my stomach, and it wouldn't go away. Finally, long after dark, my father came into the room. He wasn't crying, but I could tell he had been. His eyes were red and puffy. I didn't understand everything he said, but what I did hear was horrifying. One of the twins was still born. Apparently, it had been dead inside my mother's stomach for a few days. The other baby – also a girl – died shortly after she was born. Neither baby weighed more than three pounds.

"And Mommy? How is she?" My voice was quivering. Somehow, I knew – way down deep inside – I already knew.

My father looked first at Calvin and then at me. His mouth moved, but he didn't speak. He swallowed and tried again. "I have some bad news." He put his right arm around Calvin and the stump of his left arm around me.

"Your mother . . ." my father said.

"No!" I interrupted. "Don't say it!" I practically yelled the words. "I don't want to hear it." I pulled away from my father and backed up until I ran out of room and was imprisoned in the corner. "Don't say it! Don't say it! I don't want to hear it!" I covered my ears and shut my eyes. "No! No! Don't say it!" With my back against the wall and my eyes closed tightly, I cried, "If you say it, it will be real. Don't say it. Please, Dad, don't say it."

14

I had been to church every Sunday of my life, and all of those things I had learned while I was there affirmed – when a person dies – the body dies— but the spirit goes to heaven and lives on for eternity. While I was sitting in the front pew between my father and my brother, listening to the minister talk about my mother, none of those teachings I had learned in church mattered anymore. In my heart, I knew I was never going to see my mother again, and I didn't even get to say good-bye.

I didn't cry. I'd cried for three days prior to the funeral, and I wasn't going to cry in church where everyone could see me. My father didn't cry, and Calvin didn't cry either. If they could be brave, then I could be brave too. At some point during the service, a woman sang "Amazing Grace." I had always liked the song, but I knew – for the rest of my life – I would never be able to listen to that song again without thinking about my mother. Suddenly, I hated the tune.

When we got to the cemetery, Calvin was one of the pallbearers, but they told me I couldn't do it. They said I was too small, so I walked with my father directly behind the casket. I had no idea how many people were at the interment because I blocked it out and spent my time focusing on the sleeves of my jacket. They were too short – about two inches too short – and the cuffs of my white shirt showed more than they should. I kept remembering what my mother had said the previous summer. "My goodness, Richard," she had chuckled. "You have grown so much. We are going to have to get you another jacket. This one is way too small." Then she had smiled and stared at me for a while before adding, "My sweet Richard. You are quite the little man."

When the minister was finished speaking, he invited others to talk. A couple of people said a few words, but no one was saying the *right* words. I knew I had to find the courage to stand in front of all of those people and speak. Finally, when there was a break in the comments, I walked to the head of the coffin and looked out into the crowd. No one moved. No one spoke. I took a deep breath before I said, "My mother was a very nice person." I tried so hard not to cry. I kept my voice firm, and it didn't quiver – not once. And although I didn't think I was crying, in actuality, silent tears were streaming down my face. "She loved everyone and everything, but she especially loved my father, my brother, baseball and me." I tried to say more, but I knew I couldn't do it. My knees were starting to shake, and I was terrified I would open my mouth and no words would come out.

I stood there for what seemed like hours before the minister said a final blessing and dismissed the crowd. Everyone left – even my father and Calvin walked away – but I remained transfixed in that spot at the head of the coffin.

The sun went behind a cloud. The temperature quickly dropped, and it felt chilly. "Why did this happen, Mommy?" I muttered. "Why did God do this?" I touched the coffin and rubbed my fingers over the wood – back and forth – back and forth. The casket was smooth and cold. Tears welled up in my eyes and caused the flowers on top of the coffin to blur into a multi-colored collage. "I didn't even get to say good-bye. I didn't get to tell you that I love you one more time." I sniveled repeatedly and ran my finger under my nose to wipe away the moisture.

"That's not fair! Can you hear me, God? That's not fair at all." I choked on my tears.

"Richard."

I heard my name – soft and sweet. The word seemed to hang in the air. I couldn't see anything because the tears were blocking my vision.

"Richard."

There it was again – soft and sweet. Simultaneously, as I heard my name, a gentle breeze enveloped me like a warm, cozy quilt. In spite of the fact the sun was still behind clouds, I could feel a pocket of warmth surrounding me. It was comforting.

"Mommy?" I whispered. "Is that you?" I swore it was her voice. I could not see her through my tears, but I instinctively knew it was my mother.

"I'm okay, Richard. God is taking good care of me." Each syllable was as clear as a church bell.

"I miss you, Mommy," I spoke quietly. "Please come home."

"I can't, my little man," the words seemed to dance on the air, almost like music. "But always remember – I am with you. I can see you. I am watching. And I am proud."

"Mommy!" Without even touching my eyes, the tears dried up. I looked around, but no one was there. "Mommy?" A chilly breeze brushed across my face, and I was cold again. "Come back, Mommy. I want to say good-bye." I laid both of my hands on the coffin and listened carefully. Silence. I stood still for a long time and waited. Nothing happened.

"Richard." My father's voice broke the silence. "What are you doing, son?"

"I'm talking to Mommy." I replied honestly.

"Of course, you are." He gently patted my shoulder.

"No," I added. "I mean . . . I'm *really* talking to Mommy." I bravely continued. "And she's talking to me."

My father bent down so his face was level with mine. His tone was tender. "You don't actually believe that. Do you, Richard?" He looked me squarely in the eyes.

"You don't understand, Dad." I insisted. "I can *hear* her."

"Of course, you can, son." He put his hand on my chest before he continued, "You can hear her in your heart."

When I looked at my father, I saw huge tears in his eyes. His grief was etched in the lines of his face. I automatically knew it was futile to argue with him because – to do so – would cause him more pain.

"Richard," my father embraced me. "You need to come home now."

"Can I please stay here a little bit longer?" I pleaded. "I can walk – it's not far. I promise I will come home soon."

"Will you be alright?"

"Yes, Dad. I will be fine."

"Okay. But don't stay long." After my father hugged me again, he turned and walked away. His head was down, and his shoulders were slumped.

I stood in silence by my mother's coffin, willing her voice to return. Attentively, I listened, but all I seemed to be able to hear was the tune "Amazing Grace", and I knew I was subconsciously humming it in my own mind.

Without any warning at all, Caroline appeared by my side. Even though I didn't see her at the church or in the crowd during the interment, I knew she had been there.

"I'm sorry about what happened to your mother," Caroline said reverently.

I didn't respond to her comment for a long time. Slowly, I turned my head, looked into her eyes and said, "I've been talking to my mother." I paused, a bit wary of my next statement. "And she's been talking to me."

"You can hear her voice?" Caroline asked in a surprised manner.

"Yes."

There was no hesitation in Caroline's words when she asked, "What did she say?"

"She told me God was taking good care of her and that she was watching me – she would always be watching me – and she told me she was proud of me." I stated the words firmly because I wanted Caroline to believe me. "I *know* I heard her voice." I continued. "I *know* I did!" I lowered my voice before adding, "But when I told my father about it, he didn't believe me."

Caroline slipped her hand into mine and squeezed my fingers tenderly. "I believe you," she said without a hint of reservation.

I thought she was going to speak again, but she didn't. Caroline simply stood next to me – shoulder-to-shoulder – hand-in-hand – quietly.

15

To the best of my memory, *Extras* were never sold on Sundays. However, on December 7, 1941, there was an exception. Four hours after church, I was on the corner of Maple and Main screaming, "The Japs bombed Pearl Harbor! Read all about it." I sold over 350 *Extras* that day. My voice was horse, my knees were weak, and my heart was heavy. It was the first time I ever sold the *Extras* and felt fear in the pit of my stomach. Losing my mother had changed everything in our family – the promise of global war changed everything in America.

16

Twenty-seven hours after Pearl Harbor was bombed, President Franklin D. Roosevelt declared war on Japan. On December 11th, Germany and Italy came to Japan's aid and declared war on the United States. America was entangled in yet another world war.

My father would not let Calvin join the army until he graduated from high school in the spring of 1942. A week after commencement, we stood outside the county courthouse waiting for the military bus. Calvin and three dozen of his classmates stood in a line as a sergeant rattled off each of their names. When Calvin's name was called, he checked in, loaded his bags, and then came to say good-bye. Stoically, he hugged my father. Neither said a word. I think they were both afraid their voices would not be strong enough to handle a conversation, but their eyes spoke volumes. I could see all of my father's memories of war reflected in his expression; at the same time, I could see Calvin's anticipation, his patriotism, and his trepidation. For the first time in my life, I saw my brother as a man. He towered over me, and even though his face barely needed the use of a razor on more than a weekly basis, he had an aura about him that exuded maturity.

After sharing a firm handshake with my father, Calvin laid his arm on my shoulder and guided me away from the crowd. When we reached the maple tree by the courthouse steps, Calvin stopped – so did I. My brother managed a valiant smile before he spoke. "Richard, I have a couple of favors I need to ask of you."

Without taking my eyes off of his, I nodded.

"First," he smiled again. "I want you to take care of my baseball card collection. It's under the right corner of my mattress. There are two boxes. You know what they look like. The big one has the cards I'm willing to trade. I trust you. You know how to make a good deal. See if you can get a Gehrig card. Jerry Adams has one. It's in perfect condition. I've been trying to trade for it or win it off of him for a year, but Jerry's the luckiest son of a gun around." Calvin paused. "In the smaller box, you'll find my best cards. You know the ones: Babe Ruth, Ty Cobb, Joe DiMaggio, Ted Williams . . . the big dogs. There's also a Stan Musial card from his rookie year, and a half a dozen others. I think Musial might turn out to be a pretty good ball player, so keep that card in the small box." Calvin broke eye contact, glanced away into the distance before returning his eyes to mine and speaking again. His voice was solemn. "Take good care of my cards, Richard. Someday, when I have a family, I want to give those cards to my son."

Calvin slowly inhaled and held his breath for several seconds before releasing it in an equally slow manner. When he was done, my brother pulled a set of keys out of his pocket and ceremoniously placed them in my hand. "I'd give these to Dad, but he can't drive – not with only one arm." Calvin spoke firmly. "I expect you to take good care of my car, Richard. If you were a few inches taller, I'd teach you how to drive, and you could use it while I'm gone, but you're not ready yet – maybe in a couple of years. Promise me – you won't take the car on any joy rides. Look at me, Richard!" We made eye contact. "You can't press the pedals and see over the dashboard at the same time. When I come home, you'll be older and taller – I'll teach you how to drive – I promise. But – in return – you have to promise me – you will take care of the Chrysler. Wash it at least once a month. Start the engine every week. Let it run for a few minutes." He smiled assuredly. "I expect it to be here – intact – when I get back. I'm counting on you, Richard. Can you handle it?"

I didn't trust my voice, so I nodded affirmatively.

Calvin swallowed, glanced to the side for a moment and then made eye contact again. "If anything happens to me, Richard – the car and the cards are yours."

"I don't want them, Calvin." I choked on the words. "I want you to come home." I threw my arms around him and held my brother as strongly as I could.

"One more thing, Richard." Calvin continued to hug me. "Watch over Dad. Since Mom died, he has been drinking a lot. Too much. I'm worried about him."

Moments later, Calvin was on the bus, waving from the window. I gripped the keys tightly in my fist – one of the prongs broke the skin. Blood seeped through my clenched fingers.

2

Caroline

I fell in love with Ricky Malone the first time I saw him sitting in my father's library when I was six years old. Most people would say it was a silly schoolgirl crush – but in my heart, I instantly knew he was the boy for me. There was something magical about him. It wasn't the jocular fact we were both born on the same day. It wasn't because he was the cutest of all the boys in town, and he had an adorable smile that made my little-girl pulse race whenever he aimed it in my direction. Nor was it the fact he had eyes the color of the sky – and when he was happy they twinkled like sapphires in the sunshine. No! It was so much more. Ricky loved doing the same things I enjoyed. In addition, he was the only person I ever knew who didn't want to spend time with me simply because I had a lot of toys.

I didn't have any *real* friends. I learned at a young age that people were nice to me because my father was rich, but Ricky never treated me like that. He didn't seem to care that I lived in the biggest house in town, had a pony, and more toys than I could possibly play with in an entire lifetime. Ricky was happiest with a bag of marbles or a homemade fishing pole or a quarter for the Saturday matinee. When I was with him, I was happy too.

Being the only child of the wealthiest man in a hundred-mile radius gave me an instant reputation for being a spoiled brat. Perhaps I was a little bit spoiled; after all, I did get any tangible thing I wanted. However – truth be told – I was horribly lonely.

Some people say a person's destiny in life hinges on luck and timing. In my father's case, it's probably true. On many occasions, my father told me the story of how he made his fortune. Apparently, his father – my grandfather – had worked long and hard in the mines. My grandfather managed to save enough money to start a little general store in town. When my father was old enough, he worked alongside his father, and they put every dime of profit back into the store. About the time the

United States got into the Great War with Germany, my grandfather died; as a result, when Ricky Malone's father went off to war, my father stayed in town to run the general store. During the decade after the Great War, my father invested heavily in the stock market and did remarkably well. In spite of the fact the market was still soaring in the spring of 1929, my father sold every bit of his stock. With a dream of expansion, he tore down the original general store and built a new one. He also built a gas station, a movie theater and our beautiful house on the hill which overlooked the town. All of it was built with profits from the stocks. Miraculously, he had no debt. Several months later, the stock market crashed and the local bank failed. The mines were running at a minimum, and most of the people in town were out of work. It looked as if they would be unable to purchase gasoline from my father's station or goods in his store or go to a movie in his theater. Although my father had been lucky to sell at the most opportune time, he feared all of his businesses would fail because no one could afford to patronize them. He pondered the situation and realized he needed to create jobs for as many men as possible. No one worked full time. Instead, my father hired three times the number of employees he needed, but gave them one-third the number of work hours. This allowed more men the ability to earn *some* wages, and those families spent their money in his businesses. Therefore, money circulated, and my father stayed afloat.

During the last two years of Herbert Hoover's term as president, my father barely broke even, but he did manage to keep all of his businesses open and stay out of debt. Fortunately, everything began to slowly turn around when Roosevelt was inaugurated in 1933. Part of the president's New Deal was a program called the Civilian Conservation Corps (CCC), which directly affected our town. The CCC hired young men between the ages of eighteen to twenty-five to work on projects across the country. Most of the boys in our town who were of that age joined the program. They built roads and developed parks. Many of those employed by the CCC traveled to the Great Plains and planted millions of trees in hopes of preventing another Dust Bowl in the future. Because the young men were given uniforms, meals and lodging for free, a portion of their salary was withheld. They were allowed to keep five dollars of their monthly wages. The remaining twenty-five dollars was automatically sent to their families at the end of each month. This meant the townspeople had additional money to spend in my father's businesses.

By the time I was five years old, money began to flow again in our town, and my father began to dream of expanding his business. He hired fifteen to twenty people on a daily basis – paying them a nominal stipend – to build a new grocery store. My father was willing to pay cash. Thus, he was able to get the labor for a fraction of the cost, and the materials for a pittance. People had jobs, the town prospered, and my father increased his wealth. As soon as one project was over, he started another one. The invention of hand-held power tools made the construction of each project faster and easier. My father built a clinic and encouraged doctors and dentists to move to our town. He built a barbershop, a saloon and a pharmacy. He remodeled the bank and opened it for business, using his own money to back it. Whenever an unfortunate family was unable to pay their mortgage, my father purchased their house for a song and then rented it back to the family. Those families felt blessed they were not forced from their homes – while at the same time my father was turning a profit on their misfortune. He owned dozens of houses on both the north and the south side of town. As a result of his monopoly with businesses and homes, people began to give our town the nickname Millersville after my family. They did this as a direct result of the fact some thought of my father as a savior because he had resurrected a ghost town, while others thought of him as a dictator because he *owned* the town.

At the end of the 1930s, much of Europe was at war. All of the mines surrounding our town were reopened and working to capacity in order to meet the demand from abroad. Although there were still pockets of people in America who were affected by the Depression, the worst was over in our town. It was thriving, and my father was becoming wealthier by the day.

I was born during my father's monetary hardships – after he built the movie theater, the general store and the gas station, but before those businesses became financially sound and successful. When I reflected upon my youth, I often wondered what my life would have been like if there hadn't been a depression. Would my father have had more time to spend with me? And I wondered, too, if my mother had not died on the day I was born – would my father have loved me more? If we had been a normal family living during a normal era in history, would I still have been the same little child who roamed aimlessly around that gigantic house looking for something or someone who could make me feel as if the building I lived in was actually a home instead of a symbol of wealth.

Father was a stern, demanding man. He commanded respect, and he expected success. He worked hard and dedicated all of his energy to the next financial goal. He was never satisfied with what he had – he always wanted more. I can't remember exactly how old I was when I realized I was a part of his affluent façade. He dressed me in the most expensive clothes, hired the best tutors to educate me, and paraded me around in public as if I were a trophy. I often heard him say, "Caroline might not be a boy, but she's the smartest girl in three states." I was never sure what my father meant by his statement. Would he have boasted about me if I weren't smart? Would he have been prouder of me had I been born a boy?

I could have received my entire education from tutors, but being tutored at home was a lonely existence. I begged my father to let me go to public school. I had two reasons for this request. First, I wanted to be with other children my own age; secondly, I wanted to be with Ricky Malone. It took a great deal of pleading, but finally my father agreed. There was little doubt in my mind that my father succumbed to my pleas because he knew I would shine brightly in the school system, which would reflect positively on him.

2

The summer of 1943 was a milestone for me. At age twelve, I began to notice that my body was changing. My hips developed curves, my breasts swelled to the size of large oranges, hair began to grow on private areas of my body, and – for a couple of months – I was taller than Ricky. I often felt awkward, yet at the same time, it was a mystifying and exciting feeling. I heard girls huddled in groups, giggling about personal things, but they never let me in on their conversations. I always felt like the outsider. I longed for a mother, a sister, or a best friend like the other girls had, but I realized my only *real* friend was Ricky Malone.

Because my father was often traveling on business and I never made a connection with any of the girls in town, I spent most of my time alone.

Throughout the majority of the summer, I was reading a book, riding my pony, or teaching myself how to use the Singer sewing machine I'd gotten for my twelfth birthday. The rest of the time I spent with Ricky.

Ricky worked three jobs. In the morning – before the sun came up – Ricky delivered the daily paper to most of the residences on the north side of town. For three hours after breakfast, he worked in my father's general store stocking supplies. It was the same job his brother had done before the war. And in the evening, he was at the newsstand. Due to the ever-changing information regarding the battles on both fronts, there were often *Extras* to be sold, and Ricky wanted to be the one to sell them.

During the hottest part of the day, when the sun was high and the heat was the most intense, I could always find Ricky in one of two places: sitting beside his mother's grave or relaxing by the river. I spent as many afternoons with him as possible. Sometimes I sat quietly beside him at the cemetery. Ricky often read out loud from his brother's letters or articles in the newspaper, and we'd talk about the war. Other times, we played marbles or flipped baseball cards with some of the kids from his neighborhood. On those days when it was too hot to do anything physical, the logical solution was to strip down to our underwear and dive into the water. But, mostly, Ricky and I sat on the edge of the river, makeshift poles in our hands, and waited for a hungry fish to take the bait.

On one particularly steamy day in late August, Ricky and I sat by the water's edge with our feet dangling in the river and our poles in hand. He was talking about Calvin's latest letters – three came in one day. It wasn't unusual for the letters to arrive in groups; in fact, a letter could be weeks old before Ricky received it. Needless to say, soldiers were not allowed to write any specific details about military information – so Calvin's letters were on more of a personal level. In February, he had written about the extreme heat and the sand, which gave us our first major clue concerning his location. Between the newsreels shown before movies, the articles we read in the newspapers, and Calvin's letters, Ricky and I used deductive reasoning and figured his brother had spent his first year in the army fighting in northern Africa.

Although Calvin never mentioned it in his correspondence, we read in the newspaper about the battles at Kasserine Pass near Tunisia, which took place in February. The day after the military maneuver was reveled in the headlines, I brought a map to show Ricky, and it became obvious why the German general named Rommel was defending that area in Africa. Tunis was a short distance across the Mediterranean Sea to Sicily, and Sicily led to Italy, and Italy bordered Germany. As we read about the battles in the newspapers, we marked Calvin's location on the map.

Our troops, led by Lieutenant General Dwight D. Eisenhower, invaded Sicily in July. Mussolini fell from power two weeks later. By August 17th, the Germans evacuated Sicily, and the Allies controlled it. Although it appeared as if the Italian government would soon surrender, the German army still controlled Italy.

According to one of his letters, Calvin was cited for bravery and promoted to corporal. When Ricky talked about the battles and his brother, it gave him great pride to know Calvin was part of it. "It won't be long now before Italy surrenders!" Ricky said as he pointed to another article in the paper. "And we're going to run those Germans right out of there."

On this particular day in late August, I was listening halfheartedly to Ricky. I had something personal on my mind. Desperately, I wanted to talk to him about it, but I didn't know how.

"The sooner they annihilate those damn Nazis, the sooner Calvin can come home. I want him to see his car. I've taken such great care of the Chrysler. I've polished it so much it sparkles! On a sunny day, it hurts the eyes to look at it." Ricky pulled his line in order to recast it. "I'm almost tall enough to drive. By the time Calvin comes back, I *will* be tall enough – he's going to teach me," Ricky announced. It wasn't the first time he had made that statement. Ricky talked about his brother's car almost every time we were together. "I can't believe it's almost Labor Day. This summer went by so quickly." Ricky glanced in my direction. "Hey, Carley. You're awfully quiet today. Is anything wrong?"

"I think I'm going to burst if I don't tell someone." I didn't look at Ricky; instead, I stared out across the water.

"You look sort of sick." Ricky's voice was beginning to make the change. Sometimes it was deep and didn't sound like him at all – while other times it squeaked when he spoke. This was one of those occasions when his voice cracked. "You look pale. Do you have a fever?"

"If I tell you," I said. "You have to promise you won't tell anyone."

"What is it, Carley?" Ricky seemed genuinely worried.

I took a deep breath before I spoke. "I think I'm dying." My voice quivered slightly.

"What?" Ricky dropped his fishing pole and raced to my side. "What's the matter? What happened?"

"I'm scared," I whispered. "I don't know what to do, and I don't know who to talk to about it."

"You can tell me!" Ricky insisted. "Carley, you're scaring me. Tell me what's happened. Right now!"

"I'm bleeding." Tears welled up in my eyes.

"Where?" Ricky looked on my arms and legs, searching for traces of blood, but he couldn't find any. "I don't see anything."

"I'm bleeding in a strange place." As calmly as possible, I continued to speak. "I think my insides are falling out. And it hurts right here in my stomach." I cupped my abdomen and bent over slightly.

Ricky moved my hands and looked at my waistline. "I don't see anything. Where are you bleeding?" Ricky's voice seemed anxious.

"I'm bleeding here . . . between my legs. I noticed it yesterday, and I can't make it stop." Verbalizing my fears gave me some relief. Ricky was so smart. He would know what to do. I waited for a response.

"We have to go to the doctor's office. Now!" Ricky grabbed my hand and pulled me up. Together we walked the half a mile to Dr. Thompson's office, which was also his home. When we arrived, Ricky did all of the talking. He walked to the desk in the front parlor and said to the receptionist, "We have an emergency. My friend, Caroline Sue Miller, *has* to see the doctor right away!" He spoke with composure and an amazingly mature voice.

Needless to say, the mention of my name had people jumping to his command. Less than a minute later, I was sitting in a doctor's office. Ricky was at my side, nervously stroking my hand. "It will be alright, Carley. Doc Thompson will take care of you. I promise." Although his voice was calm, his eyes were wide with fear.

When Dr. Thompson entered the room, he first looked at me. "Hello, Caroline Sue," he said. After acknowledging my presence, he glanced at Ricky and frowned. "Aren't you Richard Malone?" Dr. Thompson asked. "James Malone's son?"

"Yes, sir." Ricky replied.

"And what exactly are you two doing here?" The doctor crossed his arms over his chest.

"She's sick, doc! She's really sick. You have to help her." Ricky said in a near panic.

"First of all," the doctor looked at Ricky. "I'm going to ask you to leave. Then I'm going to examine Miss Miller." When Ricky left the room, the doctor directed his attention to me. "So . . . tell me . . . what seems to be the problem, Caroline?"

I closed my eyes tightly before answering, "I think I'm dying."

"Can you tell me your symptoms?" Dr. Thompson politely asked. When I finished describing what had happened, he began to chuckle. "You're not dying, Caroline. In fact, you don't even need a doctor. You need a mother. Unfortunately, you don't have one of those, do you?" He seemed truly sympathetic as he patted my shoulder. "Perhaps this will help," he added and handed me a pamphlet with the word Menstruation on it. "Read this. It will answer all of your questions."

I looked first at the pamphlet and then at the doctor. "So! I'm okay?" I inquired.

"Yes. You will be fine. What you are experiencing is part of becoming a woman. If you have any more questions after you've read the pamphlet, you can come ask me." Dr. Thompson paused and then added, "I didn't know you knew Richard Malone." He didn't wait for an answer. "Isn't he from South Side?"

"Yes. He lives on the south side of town."

The doctor shook his head. "You shouldn't be hanging around with the likes of him, Caroline. I don't think your father would approve."

I was truly stunned by the doctor's comment. I couldn't imagine why it would matter where Ricky lived. My curiosity spiked. In the six years I had known Ricky, I had never been to his home. On numerous occasions, I had suggested meeting him at his house, but Ricky had always vetoed the idea; consequently, I'd never seen where he lived. In fact, I didn't even know his address.

"Caroline," Dr. Thompson said. "That Malone kid isn't taking advantage of you, is he?"

"What do you mean?"

"He isn't," the doctor paused. "How shall I say this?" He paused again. "Richard isn't touching you, or anything like that, is he?"

I felt uncomfortable. I couldn't imagine why the doctor was asking me that question. "Ricky and I are friends. We have been friends for years. Years!" I insisted. "We fish, go to the movies, play marbles. I use to help him with his homework and teach him how to read, but he's so good now . . . sometimes, he teaches me." I laughed.

"How old is he?" There was a frown on Dr. Thompson's face when he asked the question.

"Twelve. Like me," I answered.

"He's twelve?" Dr. Thompson rubbed his chin in silence. "He looks older." The doctor pointed his finger at me and firmly added, "You watch out for him. He's trouble with a capital T!"

<h1 style="text-align:center">3</h1>

While American troops were fighting the Japanese in the Pacific and the Allies were struggling for victory in Europe, Ricky and I started another school year. Our teachers incorporated the war into our curriculum so we would better understand what was happening. People never spoke of surrender. Instead, the chant was "Now we're in it, we have to win it!" Everyone was willing to pull his or her own weight. There were ration stamps for items we had once taken for granted; for example, meat, flour, sugar and coffee were no longer staples in a kitchen – they were luxury items. Fuel was needed for military equipment like tanks, jeeps and airplanes. Consequently, my father's gas station was allotted a certain amount of gasoline, and customers were given coupons for three gallons of gas per week. People walked or rode bicycles whenever possible, and rarely did you hear of anyone traveling a long distance in an automobile. The price of gasoline was nearly twenty cents a gallon! Astronomical!

Hollywood did its part to support the war effort. The country was flooded with movies that promoted American soldiers as heroes and depicted the enemy as evil. Newsreels, portraying patriotism and valor, were shown in all of the theaters. A documentary entitled "Why We Fight" by Frank Capra played in major theaters and helped to explain the causes of the war. During the course of the year, *Casablanca* was the most popular movie shown at the Grand Palace. Ricky and I saw it three times in one week. Next to *Gone With The Wind*, it was – without a doubt – my favorite movie. I adored Ingrid Bergman and Humphrey Bogart.

In addition, actors and actresses used their stardom to sell War Bonds. They traveled across the country raising money for the war effort. Tragically, Carol Lombard had died a year ago when her plane crashed during one such promotion. On that day, while Ricky sold the *Extras,* I cried. All I could think about was poor Clark Gable. He was so in love with her.

The war was changing our country. The people in towns all over America were beginning to feel the pinch. Because most of the young men were fighting in the war, women – who had never worked anywhere except their own homes – had to take over jobs that were once filled by men. Women worked in factories and shipyards handling tools most of them had never touched before the war; as a result, they acquired the nickname *Rosie the Riveter.* While their brothers, fathers, husbands and sons were engaged in combat, the women who lived on farms worked the land in order to produce food for the troops. Some women joined the military and held noncombatant jobs such as nurse, mechanic, clerk, cook or driver. Fifteen million women left their household duties in order to work for the cause. Many of them were finding a great deal of personal satisfaction in the workplace.

4

The following spring, after Ricky's and my thirteenth birthdays, I began to see a difference in the way my friend behaved around me. Whereas we had once been so comfortable together, Ricky began to stammer during our conversations, and often I caught him staring at me – especially in school. Our desks were next to each other in the front row. Several times a day – when I looked in his direction – I noticed – instead of watching the teacher, Ricky was gazing at me as if he were lost in thought. The moment I smiled at him, he looked away. His behavior was definitely odd.

Another strange incident occurred in May. While Ricky stood behind me in the cafeteria line, I felt a slight tug at my hair. The instant I twirled around, I discovered he was touching my ringlets.

"What are you doing?" I asked.

Ricky blushed as he turned a light shade of red. "Nothing!" he muttered, and he dropped his hand before looking away as if he were interested in the conversation three boys were having a short distance away.

"What's wrong?" I inquired.

"Nothing!" he repeated curtly. Ricky brought his attention back to me before stammering in a voice that was barely more than a whisper, "I guess I never realized how soft your hair is." He looked down at his feet and then glanced around the room, dismissing the conversation.

Two weeks later, on an unseasonably hot Saturday in late May, Ricky and I were swimming in the river with a dozen other kids – mostly boys. It was a grand day filled with laughter and water games. A thick rope hung from a massive oak branch, which enabled us to swing out over the river and splash loudly when we landed in the water. Repeatedly, we took our turns. Ricky was always able to travel the furthest and make the largest splash. Each time, after my turn with the rope, he extended his hand and helped me up the riverbank. On this particular day – as Ricky assisted me – I noticed he focused a great deal of attention on certain parts of my body. When I saw him looking at me, I blushed uncontrollably and felt a tingling sensation ripple over my spine and then settle in the pit of my stomach. It made me nervous, excited and surprisingly speechless.

Later in the day, Ricky and several of the older boys were sitting in a circle shooting marbles. Most of them were drinking Coca Colas, but a few of the older boys were drinking beer. I overheard fragments of their dialogue. It was obvious they were talking about girls in general, but the moment I overheard my name, I strategically positioned myself behind a tree and strained to hear the rest of their discussion. None of the boys seemed to notice I was within earshot of their conversation.

One of the older fellows said, "Caroline Sue has great gams. Those legs are starting to look a little like Betty Grable's."

"You're right! They're amazing!" Another boy added as he took a swig of beer. "In a couple of years, I wouldn't mind running my fingers up those thighs." His comment inspired an assortment of whistles and cheers from the group.

"Caroline's going to be a hot little number when she grows up," Jerry

Adams responded with a chuckle as he flicked his marble into the center pile. Even though Jerry was not quite fourteen, and was in the same class at school as Ricky and me, he was already drinking beer and talking as if he were much older than his age.

"She has great knockers too. A perfect handful!" One boy moved his opened palms in a circular pattern as if he were touching imaginary breasts.

"Cut it out, guys!" Ricky interjected. "Carley's thirteen years old. You shouldn't be talking about her like that."

"Caroline Sue Miller may be thirteen, but she moves like she's twenty. What a hot tomato!"

"I'm not kidding! Cut it out!" Ricky's voice could be heard clearly above the rest.

"What's your problem, Richard?" Jerry Adams, who had the lead marble, scooped up his catch before adding, "You and Caroline Sue got somethin' going?" He laughed. "Don't you think she's a little too high class for you?"

"She's just a kid." Ricky replied. He stared directly into the Jerry's eyes. "I don't want you talking about her like that." Ricky didn't even flinch. He may have been a few years younger than most of the boys in the group, but he was more than able to hold his own. During the last several months, he had grown significantly and was equal in height – regardless of age – to most of the boys in the circle. His job at the general store required him to unload, move and stock the majority of the inventory; therefore, he had developed large shoulder muscles and had bulked up his body.

"Jeepers!" One boy replied. "Looks like Richard is staking a claim."

"Don't be ridiculous!" Ricky stated firmly. He snatched the shooter out of the circle and positioned himself to make a play. "Shut up! All of you! Let's finish the game." Ricky stared directly at Jerry Adams. "Throw your Lou Gehrig card in the pile," he demanded. Everyone's attention shifted to the competition and became focused on the challenge.

"I'm not throwing my Gehrig card in the pile unless you toss in your Ty Cobb *and* your Fred Clark." Jerry sat upright and defied Ricky to take the bait. Ricky didn't move. "What's the matter?" Jerry jeered, "Don't think you're good enough?"

Ricky sat stalk still for what seemed like an eternity. All of the boys, even the ones who were drinking beer, didn't move a muscle. It was almost as if I were looking at a picture instead of a real-life scene. It appeared as if everyone was holding his breath. Ricky brushed his index finger in tiny rapid movements across his cheekbone as he concentrated and continued to stare at Jerry Adams. For the last couple of years, a fierce rivalry had developed between the two. It wasn't about who could win at marbles or who could catch the most fish in a day or who could go further on the rope swing. There was something more to their competitive spirit; in fact, there seemed to be a dangerous undercurrent between them.

Without a word, Ricky confidently pulled out two baseball cards and placed them on the pile. In return, Jerry threw in his Lou Gehrig card. The crowd gasped. Imaginary needles were darting between the competitors' eyes. It was the largest pot of the day – maybe the biggest pot of the year. Numerous coins, several paper bills, a package of Lucky Strikes, three Coca Colas, and fifteen baseball cards were in the pile, several of which were big name players.

Ricky flicked the marble and acquired the lead. Those boys, who had already lost their advantage and become spectators, positioned themselves behind the individual they supported. The crowd was divided: half for Jerry and half for Ricky. The tempo changed. It was no longer a quiet tension surrounding the game; instead, the boys were cheering boisterously for their favorite.

From my concealed vantage point, I continued to watch as they became increasingly more engrossed in their competition. To my amazement, I had a variety of emotions swimming around inside of me. I was curious, embarrassed, and unexpectedly pleased about the conversation I had overheard. It was rather exhilarating to know the boys were talking and thinking about me in such a grown-up way. Ironically, it made me feel pretty. As I thought about it, a pink blush washed over my face. But I wondered why Ricky didn't feel like the other boys. Instead, all he wanted to do was bet on the marbles. Didn't he think I had nice legs? Did he even notice I was growing up?

As I daydreamed, I lost track of the game until there was a robust roar from the crowd. I turned my attention back to the boys and saw

Jerry pulling the pile toward him. His friends were cheering loudly and slapping him playfully on the back as they congratulated him on his victory. Ricky, on the other hand, stood motionless as he watched Jerry stack the baseball cards in a neat pile and stuff them in his shirt pocket.

That evening, when we all scattered to go home for dinner, I made a detour in order to follow Ricky. We hadn't had the opportunity to talk during the latter part of the day. He seemed oddly sad and quiet, which led me to believe he might go to his mother's grave as he often did when he felt despondent. To my surprise, he did not. Instead, he headed south of town.

In all of the years I had known Ricky, I'd never been to his house. I suppose my curiosity had finally gotten the best of me, and I wanted to see where he lived. To my amazement – as I traveled a hundred feet behind him – the houses that lined the road began to change from two-story dwellings to small, dilapidated cabins which appeared to be more than a century old. Some of the windows were broken and held together by paper and tape. The shingles on a few of the roofs were gone, which meant they probably leaked in a storm. Some of the yards had fences, but most of those were falling down. Gates were hanging on one hinge. Posts stood askew. Almost every house had a small veranda with a rusty porch swing or a couple of metal chairs. There wasn't a house on the entire street that didn't need to be painted. Everywhere I looked, I could see lines of laundry flapping in the breeze. Occasionally, when a puff of air shifted slightly, I caught an aroma of manure. I thought it might be a dog's droppings, but when I glanced behind one of the dwellings, I could see there was an outhouse.

Ricky took a left on Southern Avenue. It wasn't even a paved street; instead, it was bluestone with scattered mud puddles from the last rain-storm. When I approached the corner to make the turn, I thought I had lost him. Ricky was no longer on the street. Luckily, out of the corner of my eye, I saw his red shirt and blue overalls seconds before he disap-peared inside of the third house on the right. I walked, as if in a trance, the remainder of the steps to his front yard.

Standing in silence, I absorbed the image of Ricky's home. It was small – a simple log cabin with a tiny brick addition on the side. I always knew Ricky's family didn't have much money, but I had no idea he was so poor. In spite of the shock, I knew I was in the correct place. Calvin's Chrysler Imperial was parked in the yard to the right of the house, and Ricky's bike was leaning against the porch railing.

"Oh, goodness!" I muttered to myself. "No wonder Ricky never wants me to come to his house." I turned to leave.

A half of a second later, the screened door opened. The squeaky hinges echoed in the air. James Malone stepped on to the porch. The sleeve of his left arm dangled loosely by his side – in his right hand – he held a bottle of beer. I searched for a place to hide, but there was no object nearby large enough to conceal me. Even before the door shut, Ricky's father saw me. At first, he didn't speak. Mr. Malone simply nodded in my direction and then drained his bottle. The majority of the times I had seen James Malone, he was at the Grand Palace. He always looked immaculate in his red suit with gold embroidery: clean-shaven and well groomed. Sadly – standing on that porch – he was anything but dapper. His clothes appeared rumpled. His hair was in total disarray, and he looked disoriented.

James Malone stared at me for a full ten seconds before he yelled, "Richard!" He paused. "You have company." His words were slurred.

My pulse raced erratically, and my feet felt as if they were mired in quicksand. I wanted to vanish – sink into the earth and disappear – but I couldn't move.

Carrying a wicker laundry basket, Ricky stepped on to the porch. "What did you say, Dad?" Before his father could respond, Ricky saw me. All of his actions seemed to be in slow motion. He propped the basket against the side of the house and took the steps in my direction. His face was masked with fury – anger was etched in his scowl.

Ricky broke the silence first. "What are you doing here, Caroline?" He demanded.

"I . . . I . . ." I tried to speak, but no words formed.

"If I wanted you to come to my house, I would have invited you!" He was furious.

"I . . . I . . ." Again I tried to speak.

"Get out of here! Go back to your fancy castle!" Ricky pointed north. He had a twisted snarl on his face. "Why did you come? You don't belong here!"

Tears streamed down my face. I pivoted and began the long trek home. My heart pounded wildly in my chest. I feared it would burst out of my ribcage. Desperately, I wanted to express a multitude of emotions, but I was completely unable to speak. I took four, maybe five steps, before Ricky was at my side. He grabbed my arm and held it firmly.

"It will be dark soon." His words were surly. "You can't walk alone." Ricky let go of my arm almost has harshly as he had grabbed it. Without saying a word, he walked with me – all of the way to my house – in silence.

5

Neither Ricky nor I spoke for several weeks. Not in church. Not in school. Every time we saw each other, he avoided me. I tried a couple of times to write a note, but I couldn't put my feelings on paper. At night, I tossed and turned because I was unable to sleep. At meals – instead of eating I pushed my food around on the plate – I had no appetite. I missed him, and it felt as if my heart was breaking.

On Tuesday afternoon June 6th, I rushed to the corner of Main and Maple because I was one hundred-percent certain I would find Ricky at the newsstand selling *Extras*, and I was right. He was yelling, "Extra! Extra! The Allies invade Normandy! Read all about it." Dozens of people surrounded Ricky as they clamored for a paper. The news was vague because the invasion was still in progress. France was six hours ahead of our time zone, and *Operation Overload,* which was the code name for the invasion, began that morning. Two thousand seven hundred ships carrying landing craft and 176,000 soldiers crossed the English Channel the previous night. In order to take control of the bridges and the railroad tracks, hundreds of paratroopers were dropped behind enemy lines. The French shore was hit on five beaches by troops from Canada, Britain and the United States. The word was already out – massive casualties, but the invasion appeared to be successful. Reporters were dubbing it "the longest day" and the largest sea borne invasion in history.

I stood on the corner and watched Ricky until all of the *Extras* were sold. His voice was hoarse – he could barely speak. Ricky looked exhausted. With apprehension, I approached him. When he saw me, it appeared as if he might turn away, but he hesitated. I didn't say a word; instead, I encircled him with my arms and laid my head on his shoulder.

"This is so scary." I muttered softly.

"Yes. But it's a good thing, Carley. It will be an important victory." Ricky spoke as he, too, put his arms around me. "We are going to win this war. I can feel it."

"According to the article, Eisenhower is the commander. Isn't he the general who commanded your brother's division in Italy?"

"Yes." Ricky responded. "Calvin wrote last winter that his division had been transferred out of Italy. He couldn't say where, but it's possible he *could* have been transferred to England. He said he was in a place where there was no fighting. He was not allowed to divulge his location, but he did say he felt safe – like he was on a holiday. He told me that he met a girl. Said she spoke English. They even went on a couple of dates." Ricky paused. Tears welled up in his eyes. "I don't know for sure, but his division could have been part of this invasion."

"Oh, my God!" I felt his anxiety and held Ricky as tightly as I could. "Do you think Calvin is alright?"

"I have no way of knowing." Ricky responded. "The telegrams will start coming in the next few days, and the casualty lists will be printed as soon as possible." He held his breath. "It will take a while before all of the deaths are reported."

"I'll pray for Calvin." I spoke softly.

"Calvin's a good soldier. He'll be okay." Ricky whispered. "He *has* to be okay. I don't think my father can take any more sorrow."

As we stood on the corner of Maple and Main, Ricky and I spoke of the newspaper article. We talked about Eisenhower, Hitler, the invasion, the Germans, the British, the French and Calvin. We didn't, however, talk about what had happened on that hot Saturday afternoon in May. I never mentioned his house. He never spoke of his anger. The subject was purposely dropped from our conversation, and our relationship reverted back to the solid friendship we shared.

6

With each day that passed, more casualties were reported and the printed list grew larger. There were heavy losses from our town. Mourning wreaths hung on dozens of doors throughout the neighborhood. Sisters, mothers and wives cried openly. Ricky and his father waited for news regarding Calvin. Finally, two weeks after the invasion, a letter arrived. Calvin was alive. Yes! He was one of the soldiers to cross the English Channel. Yes! He had been at Omaha Beach. Thousands of casualties. Dozens of his buddies were massacred as they penetrated the coastline. He wrote the sand was riddled with bodies and blood. And he feared the images would never fade from his memory.

Fortunately, Calvin had been unscathed during the battle and was currently marching toward Paris. According to him, the Frenchmen waved American flags and cheered when the U.S. troops traveled through a town, and the French women spontaneously kissed random soldiers while screaming, "Liberty! Liberty!" When Ricky shared his brother's letter with me, I could feel the euphoria in his correspondence. Surely the war would not last much longer.

One more school year was behind us and another summer was rapidly racing by. It was hot – unusually hot, but – once again – we squandered hours cooling our bodies in the river. Ricky spent the majority of his day working. He continued to deliver newspapers in the morning. When the news warranted a special edition, he sold *Extras* in the afternoon. He, also, worked as many as five hours a day at the general store unloading supplies and stocking the shelves. His savings account was growing.

When Ricky was working, I read or sewed.

For relaxation, Ricky spent at least three hours a week tinkering on his brother's Chrysler Imperial. He ran the engine multiple times and polished it monthly. In the two years since Calvin had joined the army, Ricky had grown a considerable amount – more than enough to touch the pedals and see over the dashboard. Occasionally, he drove the car around the block, but he would not tempt fate by taking it out of the neighborhood. And he never let anyone – including me – ride in the car with him.

During the summer of 1944, our relationship changed. I would like to think – as I reflect upon the past – I saw the transition coming, but I didn't. It was one of those monumental adolescent moments that simply happened without any forewarning at all.

Earlier in the day, Ricky and I had seen an encore showing of *Casablanca* at the Grand Palace. Instead of going to the river afterward like the rest of the kids, we took a long, leisurely walk that ended at the cemetery. As we sat by his mother's grave, Ricky talked a great deal about his family. His words were somber and philosophical. He spoke about his fear regarding the war and the possibility Calvin might not return. He talked about the fact his father often drank too much and seemed aimless since his mother's death. And he broached his own emotions about his mom. In all of the years I had known Ricky, he had never been so candid.

"I come here six, maybe seven times a month. It doesn't matter how hot or cold it is – doesn't matter if it's sunny or raining. Doesn't even matter if there is snow on the ground. I come here." Ricky paused and looked around at the neighboring gravestones. "I close my eyes. I wait. I listen." He sighed. "On the day my mother was buried, she spoke to me. I heard her! I'm *sure* I did! I want to hear her voice again." Ricky shook his head sadly. "But I never do." He picked haphazardly at pebbles wedged in the dirt and piled them on top of each other. "Sometimes, I think maybe I didn't actually hear her voice at all. Maybe it *was* in my imagination. But it seemed so *real*!"

"I think you heard her, Ricky. I really do." I paused. "I think God let her speak to you one more time with a human voice so you could know she was at peace." I placed my hand gently on top of his. We made eye contact. "But I don't think she's ever going to talk to you again – not that way. I think – maybe – from now on – you are going to have to listen to her from inside of your heart." I tenderly squeezed his hand. "It doesn't mean you can't still come here – sit by her grave – in order to feel close to her. And you can still talk – out loud if you need to – when you want to share something with her, because I think *she* can hear *you*. I *really* believe that! And I think she's watching over you – exactly like she said! But instead of being your mother – now she's your guardian angel."

Ricky smiled. "How did you get so smart, Carley?" He didn't wait for a response. "At least, I had a mother for ten years." He looked at me with a rueful expression. "You never even knew your mother. It must be hard not to ever have a mother at all." Ricky picked up a handful of small stones and began to throw them sidearm at the base of an oak tree that stood several feet away.

"It is." I responded. "Perhaps it doesn't hurt in the same way as it does for you. I didn't know my mother, so I didn't love her. But I wish I had." I watched a pair of birds fly quietly over our heads before continuing. "I feel guilty sometimes because I feel I'm responsible for her death. It was my fault she died. Childbirth was too much for her." I took a long, deep breath. "I think things would be different if I had a mother. Maybe I wouldn't be so lonely." I smirked slightly before continuing. "I guess my father loves me, but I don't think he likes me all that much. We live in that great big house, and I still feel like I'm always in the way."

"I remember your house." Ricky mechanically picked at the dirt underneath his nails. He focused on his action as if it were of vital importance. "I saw it once, but I remember it!" He was silent for a long time, and he didn't look at me when he spoke. "I wish you hadn't come to my house last spring. I never wanted you to see it." Ricky sighed. "When my mother lived there, it wasn't so bad. She made it seem like a palace, and she made me feel like a prince. But since she died – Dad basically sits in the corner and drinks until he goes to sleep. And all I can see is poverty. That house is horrible and ugly and dirty. It makes me feel worthless. I don't want to be like that – I don't want to be like *him*. I hate that house – and I hate this town." Ricky said. "Someday, I'm going to get out of here. And I'm never going to look back."

"Is that why you work so hard?" I asked.

"I save every penny." He threw the remainder of the stones all at once. When they hit the tree, the pebbles scattered in a dozen different directions. "I won't be a prisoner here. I won't! I'm getting out! I swear to God!"

"What do you want to do when you grow up?" I asked.

"I don't know," Ricky responded. "I only know – whatever I do with my life – I don't want to do it *here*."

"I know what I want to be!" I announced proudly. "I want to sew – design dresses. In fact, I want to make wardrobes for the movie stars."

"That's a pretty big dream." Ricky said as he stood up.

"Yes!" I stated confidently as I, too, stood up and brushed blades of grass from my clothes. "But if you don't dream big, then what's the point in dreaming at all?" I continued by adding, "On the radio, I heard Eleanor Roosevelt say, 'The future belongs to those who believe in the beauty of their dreams.' And I believe in my dream. Someday, I'm going to make it come true."

I caught a glimpse of Ricky out of the corner of my eye. He was staring at me again – like he did during those times in school. He looked mesmerized. During the past year, I rarely knew what he was thinking, and I was frequently perplexed when it came to our friendship. But – at that specific moment – I could read his thoughts – see his intentions reflected in his eyes. He was going to kiss me. My heart began to pound wildly in my chest, and I felt as if I couldn't breathe. I looked at him. We were inches apart. His eyes were a brilliant, clear blue – sparkling – like the sun reflecting off of the water. He leaned toward me – then hesitated. I took a tiny step in his direction. I didn't know what I was supposed to do. I only knew I desperately wanted him to kiss me – I had dreamed of it for as long as I could remember. As I stood there awaiting his move, my mind's eye flashed to the final scene at the airport during *Casablanca*. Ingrid Bergman – with tears in her eyes – tilted her head and Humphrey Bogart kissed her. Should I tilt my head? Should I close my eyes? Ricky's mouth was so close to mine, I could feel his warm breath on my lips. I didn't think. I simply reacted. Automatically, I tilted my head to the right – he bent his to the left. Our noses missed touching by a hair. He closed his eyes. I didn't. When our lips touched, I could feel the tiny hairs on his face as they ever so softly came in contact with my skin. Something magical happened inside of me. A tingling sensation flashed all over my body, and my knees became weak. I felt as if I had come to the end of a long journey – and I was home. Safe. Secure. Loved.

In the aftermath, we stood quietly drinking in the surrounding silence. Branches swayed in the breeze and leaves rustled creating a whisper of a medley. We were so still three deer walked within fifteen feet of us. Completely unaware of our presence, they stopped to graze for a few moments before wandering to the other side of the cemetery.

"Carley." Ricky said as his eyes continued to follow the deer's path. "Yes?"

"You're my best friend." He spoke the words softly – still motion-less – still looking straight ahead.

"You're my best friend too." I replied

Neither of us said another word.

7

"You will *not* see that Malone boy anymore!" My father's voice bellowed through the house. He was pacing behind his desk.

"But . . . " I stammered. Never in my life had I talked back to my father – I was quaking in my shoes. "He's my best friend."

"That's not the way I heard it. Bill Adams said he saw the two of you kissing at the cemetery last week. I will *not* have the town gossiping about *my* daughter!" He squashed his cigar in the crystal ashtray. "I forbid you to see him again."

"Ricky and I haven't done anything wrong!" I insisted. Tears formed in my eyes. I was terrified I'd cry in front of him. I didn't want him to see my weakness.

"Has he touched you?" my father demanded.

"No! Ricky would never do anything. He's a gentleman."

"You are such a naïve little girl. Don't you understand anything?"

"Ricky's not like that. We're friends! We've always been friends."

"I should have put a stop to this a long time ago." My father pointed a finger in my direction in order to keep me from interrupting. "Listen to me, young lady. You will *not* see Richard Malone any more. He's common trash. That Malone boy is going nowhere! And you are *not* traveling down that path with him."

"Why do you hate him?" I asked.

"I don't hate Richard. He isn't worth my time or my energy." My father paused. "When the Great War was over, James Malone came home a cripple. No one would hire a one-armed man. But I did. I gave him a job. I gave him a chance. He worked at my store, then took tickets at the Grand Palace and eventually became a manager. What did he do with it? Nothing! He still lives in the same dump he lived in when he was born. James could have gotten out. He could have made something of himself. But instead, he drank away his money and his self-respect. Now he's the janitor at the theater – and that's on the days he decides to show up for work."

"He drinks because his wife died."

"That's no excuse." My father sneered. "My wife died too. You don't see me wallowing in it. Besides, James Malone was weak *before* his wife died. He's pathetic. He's stupid. And his son is exactly like him."

"No!" I cried.

"You stay away from him!" My father demanded.

"I'm thirteen years old. I should be allowed to pick my own friends."

"He's not your friend, little missy! He's ultimately after my money. He thinks if he's nice to you, then he can get to *my* bank account!"

"Ricky doesn't care about your money."

"Caroline!" My father took several deep breaths until his voice became calm. "You have a lot to learn about life! And I will not let you make a mistake on that worthless piece of trash."

"You don't understand!" I screamed defiantly.

"You mind your manners, Caroline!" His words were steadfast and had an ominous tone. "And you listen to what I'm saying! Heed my words! If I catch you with that boy again or if I hear you've been together – I'll ship you off to boarding school so fast – it will take a week for your head to stop spinning." He raised his voice a notch. "Do you hear me?"

"Yes, sir!" I was quaking in my shoes. I had never seen my father so angry.

8

I didn't see Ricky for the rest of the summer; in fact – for the next five months, I only saw Ricky in church and at school. I wanted to call him on the phone, but I knew he didn't have one. I thought about writing him a letter, but I wasn't sure of his address. So I compromised and slipped him notes in class. We were cautious. Ricky and I didn't trust anyone because we didn't know who might turn out to be a traitor – for that reason we were careful to keep our correspondence and conversations a secret.

The more difficult it was for us to be together, the more frantically I wanted to be with Ricky. I thought about him all of the time. I even fantasized about kissing him again. Sometimes, at night, before I went to sleep – I balled my pillow up in my arms and pretended it was Ricky. I closed my eyes and imagined the way it was when he kissed me. I could feel his warm lips. If I concentrated hard enough, I could even feel the tiny hairs on his face as they brushed against my skin. Whenever I thought about Ricky, I had the most wonderful sensations. It felt as if butterflies were fluttering around in my stomach. I could feel my pulse quicken, and there was a throbbing sensation between my legs. In an indescribable way, I ached to be with him, but I was too afraid of my father's wrath to chance a private meeting.

In our notes we passed back and forth in school, Ricky and I discussed the war, his brother's letters, some rather boring information we learned in class, a scheduled test, a grade on an exam, who was winning at marbles or hop-scotch, and what movies were playing at the Grand Palace. I wanted desperately to tell him how I felt, and I wanted to hear about his emotions, but we never wrote a word about our personal thoughts. It didn't matter. I treasured every piece of paper and concealed them in a wooden box I kept hidden in my closet.

I adhered to my father's strident demands until December. Three days after Christmas, I overheard two of the chambermaids talking while they were changing the bedding in my father's room. One of them mentioned James Malone's eldest boy had died in the Ardennes Forest in Belgium at – what she referred to as – the Battle of the Bulge. I instantly raced to my father's library to see if the morning paper was still on his desk. There was a sick feeling in the pit of my stomach. I was terrified I would purge my breakfast. Repeatedly, I swallowed to keep the bile down. After locating the newspaper, I thumbed through the pages until I found the list of casualties. My entire body was shaking as I read the names from the middle of the list: Nelson, Newcomb, Norton, MacDonald, Mallory, Malone – Oh God! Malone! There it was! The letters screamed off of the page. Corporal Calvin Malone. Oh, my God!

I didn't bother to change clothes. Instead, I grabbed my coat and raced out the front door. Instinctively, I knew exactly where to go. And I was right. Ricky was there – sitting by his mother's grave. He didn't see me at first. Silently, I approached him, sat by his side, and reached for his hand. Ricky slowly turned his head and looked at me. His cheeks were dry, but I could see tears imprisoned in his eyes. Not a word was spoken. We wrapped our arms around each other, and he released his grief. Choking sobs came from deep within him. I held him as tightly as I could.

9

Winter seemed to last forever. We had an abnormal amount of snow and below average temperatures. Sledding was no longer a treat, and the cold was getting on people's nerves. Everyone had cabin fever. I thought spring would never come. Finally, by mid-April, it was warm enough for Ricky and me to spend some time together outside.

After passing notes in class, we planned to meet by the river at a location we had always called our special fishing hole. He brought two poles and the wooden tackle box I had given him years ago for his birthday. At first, we didn't talk a great deal – but that didn't matter. It felt comfortable merely to be with him.

As a rule, we avoided any discussion regarding why we could not be seen together in public. I knew if we talked of it, I would have to tell Ricky about my father's prejudice opinion in relation to his family. And I didn't want to do that – not ever. It would hurt too much – hurt him – hurt me. In spite of the fact we avoided the topic, I think he automatically knew – I could see the realization reflected in his eyes. A poignant sadness seemed to be mirrored in his countenance, and I could feel his anguish.

I also saw something else in his eyes. As a direct result of my innocence, I was not quite sure how to describe his expression, but I sensed a longing – perhaps a desire – a yearning. Those intangible emotions created a magnetic attraction between us. I wanted to touch him – his hand – his arm – his face – but I continually held back. There was an undercurrent of urgency every time we saw each other, but neither of us spoke of it. I was mystified by my reasons for imprisoning my emotions and harboring gestures that had once been so easy to convey.

As April melded into May and the days passed with warm sunshine and soft, sweet breezes, Ricky and I spent every available moment in our secluded spot. Our secret was safe – my father still believed we had broken off our friendship last summer. The irony of it all was the fact that the secrecy enhanced our need to see each other. My emotions began to multiple on a daily basis. The more I *couldn't* see him, the more I *wanted* to see him. When we were together – time flew by so rapidly – hours felt like seconds. And when we were apart – every minute felt like an eternity.

10

On May 8ᵗʰ, I was lying on my bed reading the latest edition of *The Saturday Evening Post* when I first heard the news over the radio. The war in Europe was over. My heart soared. Instantly, I ran downstairs to spread the news, but it was obvious the servants were already aware of the victory. They were cheering, laughing, hugging – hoots of joy were rebounding off of the walls. The cook smiled at me and said, "Isn't it wonderful, Miss Caroline! Surely Japan will surrender, too, and the war will finally be over. It is a shame President Roosevelt died before he could see this victory." The moment she finished her sentence, the cook turned her attention to the other servants, and I felt out of place. Alone. I could see the joy on their faces and the unity of their friendship, but there seemed to be no space in their circle for me. I desperately wanted to be a part of the celebration – I wanted to share the triumphant moment with someone.

I knew in my heart – all the way to my soul – there was only one person with whom I wanted to be. I raced out of the house, down the driveway, and headed toward Main Street. Horns were blaring, people were screaming, and confetti was everywhere – it floated in the air like a soft spring rain. Couples were kissing passionately. People were arm-in-arm – dancing. Children were running randomly in all directions. I could hear music. Apparently, the high school band had left practice and was playing patriotic songs in Town Square. As I raced passed them, I could hear Sousa's "Stars & Stripes Forever." Goosebumps flashed over my body, and I was overcome with an urgency to reach my destination. Frantically, I pushed my way through the crowd – searching for him. A couple of people stepped aside – the crowd thinned – and magically – there he was.

Ricky held an *Extra* high into the air – the headline stated in big, bold, black print – *Victory in Europe*! He was yelling the words causing his voice to be hoarse and raspy. I stood a few yards away. It was two – maybe three – seconds before he saw me.

Ricky's entire face beamed when he acknowledged my presence.

Instantly, he dropped the newspapers and took the paces between us. With strong, decisive arms, he embraced me and twirled me around in circles – laughing the entire time.

"I'm so glad you're here!" Ricky rejoiced. Without a second's hesitation, he kissed me. It wasn't sweet or tender or even affectionate like the last time he had kissed me; instead, it was vigorous, electric, and audacious. Our mouths were locked together like two sheets of welded steel. Although his feet were planted firmly on the sidewalk, mine were floating off the ground, and he held me in a bear-like hug so tightly I felt as if I were melding into his body. I held on to him with equal passion, praying the moment would last forever.

When we finally pulled our lips apart, he lowered me back to the ground. I knew I was standing on my own – however, my knees were so weak – I feared I'd collapse so I gently leaned against him – savoring his strength. My heart pounded fervently in my chest – I thought it might fly uncontrollably – like a spinning top – right out of my body. Our mouths were no more than a whisper away. I felt his breath caressing my lips, and I longed for him to kiss me again. Our eyes held each other spellbound as if an intangible device kept them from glancing elsewhere. In unison, we leaned toward each other. Slowly – this time – Ricky kissed me again – softly – gently – but it created within me a mysterious sensation that unleashed an entire new meaning to my emotions.

We were jarred back to reality when a couple of kids brushed by us banging pots and pans. I became aware of our surroundings. The corner of Main and Maple was packed with people celebrating the news. Most of them were ignoring us, but a few were focused on the teenage couple pasted together in passion. Despite the fact Ricky didn't want to let go of me, I instinctively pulled away and took three steps back.

I felt my father's eyes upon me before I saw him. When I turned around, I noticed him standing by the lamppost on the other side of the street. My father's face was masked with rage. Upon realizing our predicament, I began to shake uncontrollably. Ricky grasped our dilemma, but instead of cowering, he defiantly put his arm around me in a protective manner and pulled me close.

"It will be okay, Carley," Ricky spoke in a firm voice. He sounded self-assured.

"No, it won't," I murmured. "It's not going to be okay. It's never going to be the same again." I knew it as surely as if I had already seen my future produced as a movie and shown on the silver screen.

"Caroline!" My father bellowed. "Come here!"

"Don't go." Ricky stated.

"What other choice do I have?" I responded. I looked at Ricky – pleading with my eyes for a solution, but I knew there was none.

Ricky clamped onto my hand and commanded my attention. "I'll meet you at the river – tomorrow – 4:00."

I gripped his hand one more time before letting go and taking the paces toward my father.

11

I was able to sneak quietly out of the house at 4:00 the following day. I wanted to leave earlier, but I had to wait for my father to depart in order to assure a safe passage out of the back door. I was careful to avoid all of the servants who had sworn an allegiance to my father. None of them felt any loyalty to me, so I didn't trust anyone with my tryst. I ran the entire way to the river, praying Ricky would still be waiting for me. Thankfully, he was. The moment he saw me, his expression transformed from apprehension to delight. He took the paces between us. Without hesitation, Ricky wrapped his arms around me. It was a warm, wonderful feeling to be in his embrace.

"Are you okay?" he inquired.

"My father's going to send me away." I choked on the words.

"He can't do that!" Ricky was adamant.

"Yes. He can. And he will," I responded in a defeated tone. "Father thought about sending me to Europe, but he said the cities over there are so destroyed by the war – it wouldn't be a good place for me, so he spent the entire morning calling boarding schools in the East." My voice began to quiver, and breathing became laborious. "I don't even know where he is sending me. He told me to pack my bags – I'm leaving tomorrow, and I'll find out about the school when I get there." I leaned against Ricky hoping to gain strength from his touch. "He's not even going to let me stay and finish this school year here. Father said he'd fix it with my teachers. Make sure my grades are complete, and I'll start off next year at the new school."

"We can run away." Ricky interjected as if it were the most brilliant idea in the world. "I have some money. We can run away – you and me! I have Calvin's car. We can do it."

"Would you really do that for me, Ricky?" I stared into his eyes, hoping for a miracle.

"Yes," he responded. "There is nothing in this town for me. I would leave in a second. Come with me, Carley. You don't even need to go back to your father's house. We can turn our backs and walk away."

"Ricky," I interrupted as the sensible side of me took control. "You haven't driven Calvin's car since he died, and you barely knew how to drive it then. Did you ever take it more than three blocks from your house?" I paused. "I doubt it. And how much money could you possibly have? Forty dollars? Fifty?"

"I have ninety seven dollars and sixty-five cents in the bank." Ricky stated proudly. "Maybe it's not enough money to buy a fancy house on a hill – but it's enough to get the heck out of this town."

"We're fourteen years old," I said. "We have to be practical."

"I don't want to be practical," Ricky declared emphatically. "Come with me. We can leave tonight."

I stared at Ricky. He seemed much older – wiser. How did he do that? When did he change from that adorable little boy who sat in the chair in my father's library to this confident, defiant person standing in front of me now? Why was it – I still felt fourteen? Frightened and insecure. And he looked grown up – assured – poised – in control. Why couldn't I have his fortitude – his resolve? How could it be – in one day he discovered himself – knew what he wanted – and had the courage to reach for it at any cost, and I still felt like a terrified teenager who was too afraid of her own shadow to take a stand on anything?

"I wish I had your courage." I muttered softly as I stared futilely across the river. I was such a coward – I couldn't even look him in the eyes.

"Don't go, Carley."

"I'll write you." I paused. "I promise. I'll write you every day."

3

Richard

On the Wednesday after Election Day 1948, two huge events occurred – one impacted the nation, and the other affected my life.

Throughout the 1948 election year, the Democratic Party was divided. Southern democrats formed the Dixiecrat Party and nominated Strom Thurmond of South Carolina. They campaigned against a strong civil rights program. Liberal democrats created the Progressive Party with former Vice President Wallace as their candidate. Harry Truman, who had inherited the presidency in April of 1945 when Franklin Roosevelt died, was the official candidate nominated at the Democratic Convention, but everyone expected him to lose to the republican ticket of Thomas Dewey for president and Earl Warren as his running mate. Newspapers were so certain of Dewey's landslide victory they prematurely printed the morning's paper with headlines reading "*Dewey Defeats Truman*" before the final results were counted; consequently, after football practice on Wednesday, I went directly to the corner of Maple and Main to sell *Extras* that retracted the morning headlines. The words across the top of the newspaper read – *Truman Wins Biggest Upset in Political History.*

I was assertively waving the *Extra* over my head when the second momentous event occurred. For some unknown reason, I stopped advertising the headline in mid-sentence. The hairs on the back of my neck began to prickle at my skin and a warm sensation flooded over my body. My senses were on full alert. I pivoted quickly to my left and discovered Caroline Sue Miller an arm's length away.

I had not seen Caroline in nearly three and a half years, nor had I received any of the letters she had so adamantly promised me. For the first three months after she left, I went to the mailbox every single day – hoping for a letter and a mailing address so I could write her in return. But there was nothing. To the best of my knowledge, she had not returned to our town since that day – an eternity ago – when her father had exiled her. I couldn't fathom one single reason why she would be here now – in the middle of the week – standing on the corner of Maple and Main like nothing bad had ever happened between us.

The moment I saw her, I felt as if I had been sucker punched in the gut. The wind was knocked out of me. I couldn't think. I surely couldn't talk. In fact, it was difficult to breathe. To say Caroline looked good would be a gross understatement. When Caroline Sue was ten years old, she was cute. When she was fourteen, Caroline was pretty. But as a senior in high school, Caroline Sue Miller was beyond beautiful. The first words that came to mind were stunningly gorgeous and incredibly beguiling. Her jet-black hair hung loosely, and the ringlets danced on her shoulders. Caroline's skin looked soft as silk and was the color of cream. The freckles she had as a child were gone and a slight blush was present on her cheeks. Caroline Sue Miller looked a lot like Elizabeth Taylor, except instead of having eyes the shade of violets, her eyes were pools of rich, dark chocolate. I was instantly captivated.

"Hello, stranger," Caroline spoke confidently. Her lips curved provocatively at the corners, and her smile teased me. When I didn't respond, she added, "I thought I might find you here." She pointed to the newspaper. "Amazing news, don't you think?"

Completely flabbergasted, I remained silent and continued to stare into her eyes as if I had lost my soul in her pupils.

"Don't you remember me, Richard?" For the first time, Caroline seemed slightly off balance.

"Of course," I finally found my voice. "I remember you." I felt as if I was trembling to the marrow of my bones, but – to my surprise – I sounded and acted in control. "You look wonderful, Caroline."

"Thank you," she replied as a wide and warm smile spread across her face. "And look at you! You're all grown up – taller – stronger."

"I play football."

"What position?"

"I'm a receiver on the offense, but sometimes I play linebacker on defense."

"I guess I'll have to come to the game Saturday and see for myself." Caroline spoke in a coy manner.

"You'll be here on Saturday?" I asked hesitantly.

"Yes," she answered. "I am going to finish the school year here."

"Really?" My curiosity overcame my nervousness. "I thought you were attending boarding school."

"I was." Caroline paused. "There was a fire on campus. The dormitory burned down and so did one of the classroom buildings. Apparently, there was a problem with the electrical wiring. Thank goodness no one was hurt. All of the students were sent home. So," she shrugged her shoulders nonchalantly. "Looks like I'll be finishing high school here."

"Oh." I could think of nothing else to say. Part of me was absolutely thrilled to see her again. Flashbacks of incredible childhood memories resonated in my mind – sweet memories – enjoyable memories – comfortable, safe memories. Yet there was another part of me that was frustrated, anxious, and even angry Caroline was back in town. I still remembered quite vividly the years we had spent together – and especially the *last* year – the year when our friendship had evolved into something more tender and heartfelt. I had been mysteriously attracted to Caroline. Sensing we had been more than friends, I had been drawn to her because she was beautiful – tempting – forbidden, and I felt an ache in my chest – a craving – a desire. I couldn't explain it. I only knew when she left, I felt empty inside, and I resented the fact – during the course of three and a half years – she had never bothered to contact me – not once!

More than a minute passed without words spoken. Several individuals purchased newspapers from my pile and gave me the necessary coins without comment. Our silence created an awkward and uncomfortable gulf between us. All I seemed able to do was stare at her in a dumbfounded manner.

Finally, Caroline spoke, "I better get going. Father is expecting me for dinner." She smiled, and it caused her eyes to sparkle involuntarily. "Perhaps I will see you in school tomorrow." She didn't wait for a reply; instead, she casually walked toward her home.

It was at least five minutes before my heart returned to its normal, steady beat.

2

The following day, I saw Caroline in school; in fact, she was in my

English class. Much to my chagrin, when Caroline entered the room, she was holding hands with Jerry Adams, the quarterback of our team, and enjoying the chatter of several male and female followers. A couple of students agreed to change desks so Caroline and Jerry could sit next to each other. To my horror, I discovered she had taken the desk directly in front of mine, but she did not acknowledge me. Caroline was obviously enthralled with Jerry's company and unaware of my presence.

I didn't hear a word the teacher said during the entire class. Instead, I was completely mesmerized by Caroline's ponytail. Whenever Caroline made even the slightest move, the ends of her hair brushed against the soft skin of her neck. It appeared as if she was moving in slow motion, and I was caught up in the action. Secretly, I wanted to undo the ribbon that imprisoned her hair and let all of the strands flow freely. To my amazement, I realized I wanted to touch her – run my fingers through those jet-black ringlets.

During my high school years, I'd been with a lot of girls. Some were nice girls who wanted to neck in the front seat of my car and steam up the windows of my Chrysler, but they weren't willing in do anything serious. And then there were a few girls who were more interested in body contact than going to the movies or a sock hop. Those girls enjoyed climbing into the backseat of my car. Within fifteen minutes, our clothes were peeled off and our physical needs were met. A date with one of those girls was always a fabulous evening. My sexual appetite was quenched.

I wasn't sure why, but for some unknown reason, I never wanted for a girl. They were always in abundance. Perhaps it was because I appeared older than I was – perhaps it was because I played football – perhaps it was because, as one girl said, I looked a little like Cary Grant. But – thankfully – for whatever reason, I had more than my share of willing young ladies, and I never felt even the slightest bit awkward around any of them.

Until now!

As I sat behind Caroline, I realized my pulse was racing, my palms were damp and my attention span was nil because I could only think about her.

What was happening to me?

3

As the weeks passed, I began to feel as if my life was spinning out of control. Although I had never been a contender for valedictorian, my grades had always been pretty decent, but in the last month they had begun to spiral downward. My father didn't care one way or the other about my report card – in fact, he never even looked at it – but I was frustrated with my lack of concentration in the classroom. I *wanted* to do well. I knew my future depended upon it.

Regarding my social life, I had stopped pursuing those *nice* girls; instead, I asked the *willing* girls who would entertain my needs. Although I was being sexually satisfied on a regular basis, I didn't feel fulfilled. I was constantly tense and anxious. Sleep often eluded me. In the past, I could always count on instant slumber the moment my head hit the pillow, but now I tossed and turned most of the night and rarely woke up refreshed.

During football practice, when I played my defensive position, all I wanted to do was sack the quarterback and drill Jerry Adams into the dirt. It galled me to no end to see him prance around school with his arm draped around Caroline, and I knew he was getting plenty of action on the side. In the locker room, he frequently bragged about one girl or another. He kept souvenirs of his conquests to show the other players. Usually, those mementos were panties. He had at least six stuffed in his locker, and he was always boasting Caroline's would soon be added to his collection.

Although I'd known Jerry Adams most of my life, I'd never liked him. He was arrogant, rude, and a spoiled rich kid. Even though he wasn't the most qualified for the position, Jerry was the quarterback on our team. He never earned the spot on the roster; instead, he got it because his father demanded his son be the captain *and* the quarterback. Jerry aspired to attend Harvard next year, and he boasted leadership qualities looked good on college applications. Like his father, Jerry got whatever he wanted and was never held accountable for his actions on or off of the playing field. In practice and especially during the games, the coach never accused him of doing anything wrong. An error with the football was always another player's fault. In the classroom or in town, his father could fix any mistake Jerry made. It didn't take a genius to figure out – the coach, along with the rest of the townspeople, played favorites when it came to Bill Adams' only child.

Shortly before the Second World War, Bill Adams had purchased several hundred acres of the land north of town. After the war, the population exploded, and the people needed homes. Between Randall Miller's businesses and Bill Adams' land, the two men had a monopoly on the area. What one didn't own, the other did. In addition to their wealth, the Adams and the Miller names intimidated most of the people, including my high school coach; consequently, Jerry Adams was allowed to do and say anything he wanted.

Rumor had it – Jerry's father and Caroline's father had discussed a marital agreement, which would combine the Adams and Randall families. The thought sickened me.

4

Throughout my senior year in high school, I rarely spoke to Caroline. Once in a while, I saw her glancing in my direction, but usually, she kept to her group of friends and I stayed with mine. As far as I was concerned, she was too popular for me. Not only was she Queen of the Harvest Ball and Jerry Adams' girlfriend, she was from the north side of town, and I had learned – many years ago – the people who lived in North Side were in a league of their own. I didn't belong.

Even though Caroline Sue Miller and I were no longer friends, it still galled me to hear Jerry Adams speak of her as if she were his latest conquest. In February, during gym class, he pulled a pair of silk panties out of his pocket and announced they were Caroline's. Half of the fellows in the locker room rushed over to gawk at his prize and listen as he told the story of his night of bliss after the Valentine's Day dance. I thought my head was going to explode. The idea of Caroline with Jerry Adams made me nauseous. When I left the room, I nearly put my fist through the door. Luckily, I didn't break any bones in my hand, but I did peel the skin right off of my knuckles. Damn! It hurt.

It didn't help matters when many of the seniors received college acceptance letters, and I had no concrete plans for my future. There was no way I could attend college. I had fairly decent grades, but I didn't have the money. It felt like salt in an open wound when I heard Jerry Adams was going to Penn State in the fall. Most of the boys from the north side of town were celebrating their acceptance to prestigious universities. Caroline, the first girl in the entire history of our high school to apply to college, was going to Radcliffe.

Her father had enough money to buy a department store full of clothes, but Caroline always wore outfits she made. Ninety percent of her entire wardrobe was created on her Singer sewing machine. She was an incredible seamstress. I often overheard her conversations as she told her snotty, rich friends that she was going to college to get her degree in business, but her dream was to design clothing for the movie stars.

People flocked around Jerry and Caroline, and the couple thrived from the attention. They were magnets for admiring peers. Classmates loved them – showered them with praise and affection – followed them around as if they were the king and queen of the town.

5

Aside from graduation, the Spring Ball was the biggest social gala of the high school year. Normally, I would blow the occasion off as trivial, but I knew it was a sure fire score with any girl I took to the event so I pondered my choice carefully. After much deliberation, I asked Dorothy Jamison. She wasn't the best looking girl in the senior class, but she did have eyes like Bette Davis and a body like Rita Hayworth; plus, she was willing to go the distance in the back seat of my Chrysler. Fortunately, she was thrilled with my invitation and accepted instantly. The dance was always held on the first Saturday in April. Ironically, the first Saturday in April was also my birthday, so I automatically knew what *present* I wanted from Dorothy. I smiled as I anticipated the evening.

I was quickly bored at the event. It wasn't the music because the band played a lot of Glenn Miller and Frank Sinatra tunes, which I liked. It wasn't the dancing because I knew all the latest steps, and I had a string of girls willing to jitterbug with me. Nor was it the beverage, because someone had spiked the punch with a flask of vodka. Comically, the chaperones didn't even notice, and most of the guests were tipsy. It wasn't Dorothy's fault either. She was her usual gregarious self, tempting and teasing me of events to come. Normally, I would have enjoyed myself immensely.

My disappointment in the event lay with one of the other guests –truth be told – it was *two* of the other guests: Jerry Adams and Caroline Sue Miller. The night before the Spring Ball, Randall Miller hosted an elaborate party at the country club. Several hundred people – some from as far away as Philadelphia and New York – were invited. In addition, all of the haughty rich kids from school were also included. Needless to say, I was not on the invitation list. I heard through the grapevine – during the festivities – Randall Miller announced the engagement of his daughter. The wedding of Caroline Sue Miller and Jerry Adams was scheduled for July and promised to be the event of the decade. Of course, there was a thunderous applause for the couple. I also heard Randall Miller and Bill Adams, the two wealthiest men in town, stood side-by-side next to the engaged couple – all with hands clasped together and held high over their heads. Everyone within a hundred-mile radius automatically knew a union between the Adams and Miller families would further strengthen their affluence and the town's reputation.

Caroline and I had not been friends for a long time, but that didn't seem to soften the blow to my ego. Nor did it help that most of the attention during the evening was on them. People were constantly crowded around Jerry and Caroline, gushing over her ring and clamoring for the details of the wedding. I felt as if I were tied up in knots. As a result of the news of Caroline's engagement, I was not in the mood to dance with my date. Instead, I was more inclined to ditch the party, drive to the quarry, and park on Lover's Lane – let Dorothy give me my birthday gift. Perhaps the action would release some of my pent up tension.

As I approached my date, a fellow ambushed her and asked her to dance. With a nod and a smile, I encouraged Dorothy to join him. What the heck, I was becoming less and less interested in a trip to the back seat of my car and more and more interested in going home and getting a head start on sleeping off the hangover I was going to have in the morning. Dorothy and I had polished off my personal flask before we came to the dance, and the added drinks from the punch bowl had enhanced the buzz. My head was starting to spin a little bit.

I leaned against the wall, tugged at my tie to loosen it and watched the festivities. In a few months, I'd be done with high school and out of this one-horse town. There was nothing here for me. I wasn't sure exactly what I was going to do – maybe head east: New York City. Maybe west: Chicago.

I never heard her approach. She didn't make a sound. I smelled her perfume before I even looked in her direction. Standing to my left – quiet and beautiful – stood Caroline Sue Miller. She was alone. When I looked at her, she remained silent – smiling.

I tried to be casual and composed, giving her a lukewarm nod. She didn't speak, nor did she walk away. In my awkwardness, I reached in my pocket and withdrew a pack of *Blackjack* gum. I put a piece in my mouth and then offered one to her. She accepted it.

I finally broke the silence. "Are you having a good time, Caroline?"

She didn't respond; instead, she continued to look at me. Her beautiful, dark brown eyes were wide, sparkling and harbored an inquisitive glint. After what seemed to be an eternity, Caroline broke the silence and spoke softly, "Happy 18th Birthday!"

"Same to you!" I bowed slightly to augment my greeting.

"How nice of the senior class to schedule the spring dance on our birthdays." She chuckled slightly, almost as if she were nervous.

"I doubt anyone in this room even knows it's my birthday, but from what I've seen tonight, there are plenty of people who remember that it's yours."

"When the refreshment committee brought the cake out, I looked all over the room hoping you would help me blow out the candles. I couldn't find you."

I remembered the moment. Caroline and Jerry had stood together, hand-in-hand, while the crowd sang to her. She *had* glanced around the room several times. In fact, it did appear as if she had been looking for someone. *Could it really have been me?* I didn't respond.

I could think of no clever words to keep Caroline in the conversation. When I finally did speak, my voice sounded monotone. "It's a red-letter day for me." I didn't even look at her.

"How so?" she inquired.

"I'm eighteen – I registered for the Selective Service today." I shrugged apathetically.

"Thank goodness the war is long over. Even if you are drafted, you'll be safe." Caroline tenderly touched my arm.

I summoned the courage to look at her face. To my surprise, there was concern in her expression. *Was she really worried about whether or not I might be drafted?*

Caroline gazed at me for several seconds before bluntly asking, "Any chance I can talk you into taking me for a drive?"

I nearly choked on my own saliva. Caroline Sue Miller hadn't so much as given me two minutes out of any day since she had come back to town – and here she was – suggesting we leave the party – together! I was confused and felt slightly unhinged.

"I always wanted to ride in the Chrysler. When we were kids, you'd never let me sit in it. I've seen you drive it to school every day, and I see you let other girls," she stuttered before continuing, "you let other people ride in it."

"Don't you think your fiancé might object if you left the dance without him?"

"Jerry's busy flirting with a couple of girls over by the punch bowl." Caroline paused. "He won't miss me."

Oh! I thought to myself. So *that* was it. She wanted to make her brand new fiancé jealous, and she wanted to use me in order to accomplish her goal. Well! I squared my shoulders indignantly. I wanted no part of her tactics. Without a word, I made a move to leave.

Caroline reached for my hand. "Richard, please." She squeezed my fingers gently. "Take me out of here." There was a pleading quality to her voice, and those vibrant brown eyes of hers seemed sad and suppliant.

I was powerless to resist. "Okay," I finally responded. "Where would you like to go?"

"Will you take to me to the river?" A tiny smile spread across her lips. She continued, "Where we used to fish."

I hesitated for a second.

"Please?" Her word sounded more like a timid question, than a request.

Together we walked out of the building and to the car. When I opened the door for her, she brushed against my body in order to get in the Chrysler, and I could smell the faint odor of *Blackjack* gum and bourbon on her breath. She had been drinking. I wondered if that was the reason for her brave and questionable advances toward me. My heart was pounding wildly in my chest. I had no idea why she had chosen today – of all days – to approach me. Was it some kind of *April Fool's* joke? Every year, on my birthday, I feared someone would play a trick on me and make me feel like an idiot-stick as those North-Side boys had done with the bike when I was a kid. I couldn't believe Caroline would be party to anything so devious. But, then again, Caroline and I hadn't been friends for several years. I was no longer certain what Caroline Sue Miller was capable of doing.

As I drove silently to the river, Caroline's reason for luring me away from the dance was uppermost in my mind, and I wanted to be one step ahead of her before any joke blew up in my face. I remained silent, pensive. Caroline didn't speak either, but I could feel her eyes on me. There was an excitement brewing inside of me, and a sexual tension was building. I was powerless to combat it. I hadn't been this close to Caroline in a long time – I'd forgotten the impact she had on me. I felt slightly dizzy – partially due to the whiskey I'd put in my Coke and partially because I was feeling quite intoxicated sitting in the car with her. In the years since I had discovered girls and their many attributes and talents, I had never felt uncomfortable or tongue-tied around any of them. Some were to be respected – some enjoyed – but none of them made me feel horribly nervous or apprehensive as I did at this moment.

Once we reached our destination, I drove off of the road and surged a little closer to the river. When it was no longer possible to drive the car further, I put the gearshift in park and turned off the lights. There was complete silence. No breeze. No rustling of branches. No birds singing. No woodland creatures chirping. Ironically, the silence was deafening. I felt as if I were going to explode if Caroline didn't speak. My antici-pation, my fear, my attraction to her swirled around inside of my head creating chaos and uncertainty. It was hard to breathe. Caroline Sue Miller and Jerry Adams publicly announced their engagement a little more than twenty-four hours ago.

Why was she here with me? What did she want?

"Caroline," I attempted to broach the subject.

"Please don't call me Caroline," she interrupted with a voice that was barely more than a whisper. "Call me Carley, like you did when we were kids."

The moon was bright, nearly full. Resembling a spotlight, the moonbeams shone in the car, and Caroline's face radiated from the glow. No matter how hard I searched, there was no readable expression in her eyes.

"I love this place." Caroline looked toward the river as if she could replay memories and visualize them in the distant. "Most of the happiest moments of my life were right here . . . on this river." She turned her head and looked directly at me. "And all of my good memories . . . all of my happy memories . . . *all* of them . . ." Her lower lip quivered slightly. "You're in all of those memories, Richard." She hung the statement in the air as if it were tangible. Her eyes challenged me to speak, but I was so breathless and my heart was beating so frantically, I couldn't utter a word. Quietly, Caroline inched toward me. She looked slightly frightened, but at the same time, she appeared determined.

She slid across the bench seat of my Chrysler like a panther moving stealthy toward her prey – even the satin on her dress didn't make a sound. Her eyes never left mine. They were captivating and incredibly beguiling – I thought I was going to lose myself in them. More than anything in the world, I wanted to wrap my arms around Caroline and pull her toward me, but I couldn't move. My heart continued to beat progressively faster and more irregularly. I feared it would catapult from my chest. For the last several months – since her return – I had secretly dreamed of Caroline coming toward me in the exact manner in which she was doing now. Sometimes those dreams seemed real; I could almost feel her in my arms. During the day, the fantasies were – to a certain extent – disturbing and painful – yes – painful – I pushed them from my mind. I did not let my imagination intrude my waking hours. It hurt too much when I saw Jerry and Caroline walking together in the halls of the school, and I did not want to subject myself to the agony. But, at night, when my subconscious emotions took command, Caroline invaded my dreams. When she came to me in that surreal manner, I was defenseless and unable to control my desires.

The practical side of me was certain this moment was not real – perhaps – I was dreaming – again. Caroline and me – in the Chrysler – alone – it was too good to be true. As I sat frozen in one position, Caroline continued to move closer – so close her perfume embraced me. The scent was as enticing as forbidden fruit, and I felt as if I was lost forever in the spell it created. She moved at an excruciatingly slow speed, and the slower she moved the more rapidly my heart pounded.

When her mouth was inches from mine, Caroline stopped. Her warm, sweet breath caressed my face. As I studied her expression, I saw an intense yearning in her eyes, which doubled my desire and made me feel as if I were on fire. The bright moonlight enabled me to see a pulse through the soft skin on the side of her neck. The vein was beating widely as if a drummer were pounding out the rhythm of a vigorous Sousa march.

Caroline's lips moved. At first, no words came out of her mouth. When she attempted to speak a second time, she was successful. "Remember," she whispered. "Remember when we were little kids . . ." she paused for a moment before continuing, "we sat in the balcony and watched *Gone With The Wind*. When the movie was over . . . I kissed you. Do you remember?"

"Yes." I choked on the word, but the syllable managed to come out of my mouth audibly.

"Could I . . ." Caroline paused. "Would you mind if I kissed you again?"

The instant her question was completed, something snapped inside of me. I no longer felt imprisoned by my uncertainties and emotions; consequently, my passion took command. Instead of Caroline moving toward me, I traveled with lightning speed in her direction. My arms encircled her, and I pulled her to me. I was hot and hungry, starving for her touch. A thought flashed through my mind – *was I being too strong, too violent, too passionate?* I brushed the concept away because I could feel an equal fervor exuding from her. Our mouths collided like bolts of lightning on a hot, steamy summer night. She opened her mouth to me, allowing me to taste her tongue and savor its sweetness. My fingers ripped at the bobby pins, which kept her hair captive in a twist behind her head, and I wanted desperately to free the strands so my hands could become entangled in her hair.

As I tore out the pins in Caroline's tresses, she ripped at my clothes. All the while, as we fiercely tasted each other's pleasures, our lips remained connected. Never in my life had I been so consumed – almost as if wildfires were raging out of control throughout my entire body. It was exciting and overwhelming at the same time. I wanted to be lost in this moment forever.

My lips began to travel. I kissed her neck and felt the drumbeat of her pulse on my tongue. As I sucked the tender skin into my mouth, I discovered the flavor was remarkably sweet. My actions seemed to generate a wild response from Caroline, and she continued to tear at my clothes until her fingers were free to touch my bare chest. She yanked on my tie and pushed the material of my jacket off my shoulders. Her actions imprisoned my arms and kept me from touching her. Frantically, I took the coat off and tossed it on the backseat. When I was free of the cumbersome garment, I encircled her again. Now that Caroline was in my arms, I didn't want to let her go – not even for an instant.

Over and over again, I mumbled her name, "Carley. Carley! Carley!" Each time I said it, she held me tighter with an embrace so powerful it excited me even more. Before I knew what was happening, my shirt was peeled off and her fingers were all over my skin. It felt as if thousands of tiny electric bolts raced through my veins. I couldn't think; in fact, I didn't want to think. I was consumed with the obsession to taste, touch, smell and devour every ounce of her.

The zipper on her dress was strategically placed on the side so the back was unencumbered and the transparent chiffon material was not disturbed. Caroline yanked at the zipper, trying to pull it down. "Help me, Richard. I can't make it work." She seemed in a panic, and there was a slight tremor to her words. She paused a moment and looked pleadingly into my eyes. When she spoke, the sexual undertones vibrated in her voice. "Please."

I began to tug at the metal zipper. Without much effort, it went down. Caroline was in my arms again expressing a heightened passion. She took my hands and placed them on her breasts. They were swollen with desire, and I could barely contain myself. I kissed and licked and teased her with my tongue. There was such a fever racing between us – we were engulfed by it.

As I tried to reposition myself in order to give us more room, my elbow hit the horn, and it blared through the quiet night air. I was jolted into awareness. To my surprise, I noticed Caroline was no longer wearing her light blue chiffon party dress. It was gone. *When* did that happen?

How did it happen? I looked at Caroline. She was lying on the seat, facing me, arms outstretched and welcoming. Her breasts, mountains in the moonlight, were glistening. I hesitated a moment, then Caroline began to jerk at my belt. It was as if she were a mad-woman, crazed, out of control. Her fervent passion was contagious. I no longer had any control over my thoughts or actions. I plunged toward her with one thought in mind. Frantically, we groped at each other, kissing, fondling, licking, sucking. My world was beyond perfect. This was heaven, and I was ecstatic.

When all of my clothes were shed, I adjusted my body until I was in a position to consummate our relationship. I made a short thrusting movement, but then I stopped. It was as if an alarm went off inside my head. Something wasn't quite right. The blood in my brain was pounding incessantly, which made it difficult to think. I was panting – so was Caroline. *Think!* Then – like a flash of lightning – I understood.

"Oh, my God!" I whispered the words. Caroline had never been with anyone before – not like this. I didn't need words for proof – I could feel the barrier – she was a virgin! Images of Jerry Adams holding silk panties and boasting about his conquests raced across my mind, and then I saw him grinning as he waved his newest pair of panties – claiming they belonged to Caroline Sue Miller. I remembered the envy and the jealousy which had raged through me. I had been crazy with the emotions. Now – this moment – I realized Jerry Adams had been lying. He had never been with Caroline; in fact, she had never been with any man.

I tried to capture some control over my breathing, but it was a lost cause. I felt as if I'd been running for hours without a break. Caroline was equally struggling. She, too, was breathless. There seemed to be an intangible bridge between our eyes. Neither of us looked away.

Without a word spoken, she gently placed her hand on my face. Tender fingers traced the outline of my jaw and traveled ever so gently over my lips. She arched her body to meet mine and said, "Please, Richard. I want you to be my first." Slowly, her body began to move under me, writhing rhythmically toward me. The hot, fiery fluid seeped between her legs – tempting, enticing, captivating.

I could feel myself drowning in her eyes. No matter how hard I tried, common sense was not going to win the battle between my conscience and my desire. I was physically powerless to hold back. When our lips connected, it was as if we had never been apart – never been divided by time or distance. I tried to move as slowly and tenderly as I could. I didn't want to hurt her. The realization hit me with a sudden and mighty impact. She was my life! Caroline had *always* been my life – there had never been – nor would there ever be – anyone else.

As we united and became one, I could hear her gasp slightly and then she clung to me with the same passion she had been exhibiting earlier. I did not have the experience, the fortitude or the control to slow the process down. I went off like a skyrocket and collapsed on Caroline's body. Both of us were drenched in sweat.

I remained on top of Caroline's warm body – locked in our embrace. We were surrounded by a peaceful silence. Countless minutes passed. My world was filled with the sweetest smells, the softest humming sound, a sense of heat radiating from her, and the taste of her skin still lingering on my tongue: remnants of a perfect union.

"Richard," Caroline whispered. "That was beautiful."

As I propped myself up on my elbow, I leaned to the right and jockeyed for a better position. Wedging myself between the back of the seat and Caroline's body, I found a comfortable spot. Quietly, I watched Caroline. Her jet-black hair, which cascaded in every direction, framed her beautiful porcelain face. With my index finger, I leisurely traced her profile from the top of her forehead to her chin. When I passed over her lips, her tongue magically protruded and sucked enticingly at my fingertip. Goosebumps rushed over my body.

"Tell me something, Caroline." I asked. "Why is it you stopped calling me Ricky, and now you call me Richard?"

"Oh," she smiled in a sensual manner. "I thought you were going to ask me a difficult question." Her eyes left mine and began to roam over my body. With her fingers, she tenderly touched my chest and then her hands traveled to my arms. She stroked the biceps in a feather light fashion and watched as my muscles rippled in reaction to her touch. "When I met you . . . that first day in my father's library . . . I told you … Richard is a big person's name, and you weren't a big person yet. Remember?" She paused long enough to let out a soft chuckle. When she spoke again, there was a mischievous sparkle in her eyes. "But you're not a little boy anymore. You're a man, and you've earned that grownup name." Her words were silky and tempting. "Besides, I knew that moment . . . that instant. It was all crystal clear to me."

I was jolted from the haven her words were creating by a loud banging sound. Someone was hitting the hood of my car. As I sat upright, my instincts went on full alert. There was someone outside. No. There was more than one person. I could hear multiple voices. I couldn't figure out who was there because the windows were so fogged up it was impossible to see outside. Caroline, wide-eyed with a look of horror on her face, grabbed her dress and frantically tried to don it. I shoved my suit jacket in her direction and commanded her to get in the back seat.

"Stay down. Cover your face, and whatever you do, don't talk," I firmly stated as I jerked my pants over my hips and pulled the zipper up. I recognized the voices. They were friends of mine. I could tell they had been drinking. Most likely, the dance was breaking up and the kids were cruising the area looking for a place to hang out. I certainly didn't want to be part of their gathering – not tonight. When I knew Caroline was concealed, I rolled my window down a crack.

"Well, hey there, buddy," one of the boys joked. "I see you've been fogging up your windows. Who do you have in there? I know it's not Dorothy. Last time I saw her, she was fuming because she'd lost you at the dance." His comment generated a roar of laughter from the merry group.

"Can't a guy have a little privacy?" I used my best cajoling voice, hoping I could maneuver them away from the conversation.

"How about you and the little lady come out here. There's plenty of beer to go around."

"Maybe another time," I fired up the engine and used the gearshift on the column to put the car into reverse. The windows were still fogged – I moved backward in an extremely slow manner. The moment I was a safe distance from my friends, I cranked the window down and used my side mirror to maneuver my way out to the main road.

Once I was on the road, I called out to Caroline, "You can come up front now. Coast is clear."

Caroline let out a roar of laughter as she slid into the front seat. "Wow! That was a little unnerving." She chuckled.

I glanced in her direction. To my amazement, Caroline looked completely composed. She was wearing her dress – shoes on her feet – gloves on her hands – her purse in her lap. The white orchid corsage was still pinned on the left side of her bodice. Her face was sparkling and alive as if she had applied a touch of makeup. With the exception of the fact that her hair was hanging loosely, framing her face, instead of bundled on her head, Caroline appeared as if she were beginning the evening's festivities instead of heading home.

"I suppose I better take you home."

Caroline glanced at her watch. It was nearly midnight. "You're right. I can't be late for curfew." Caroline paused. "I hope Jerry didn't call the house." There was a touch of anxiety in her voice.

At the mentioning of Jerry Adams' name, I stiffened. Somehow, during the turn of events of the evening, I had forgotten all about him. Jerry Adams didn't exist while we were in the Chrysler. The last four years had been wiped away and the future had been blocked from my mind. Tonight, while we were in the car, there had been no yesterday – and there was no tomorrow. There was only *this* moment. No past. No future. Only *now* – with Carley!

Caroline sensed my mood swing. She scooted quietly across the bench seat and positioned her body close to mine. Tilting her head, she laid it upon my shoulder and linked her arm around mine. I was speechless – too confused for words. I remembered the Caroline of my youth. She was always confident. This was no exception. She seemed serene yet excited, enthusiastic, and thrilled to be alive. Although I remained quiet, she babbled on about the decorations at the dance, her classes in school, an assignment she needed to finish, graduation day, and her dream of going to Radcliffe in the fall. I made no attempt to speak – I merely listened. A question flashed through my mind. I wondered how Caroline could get married in July and go to college in the fall. Jerry was going to Penn State – Radcliffe wasn't even in Pennsylvania.

I didn't run the car up the winding driveway to Caroline's house. That was a risk neither one of us wanted to take; instead, I parked at the entrance to the property. During the ride to her house, I had practiced in my mind what I wanted to say to her – how I felt – how happy I was she had come with me. I turned the words over and over again inside my thoughts. I wanted to say I would remember this night for the rest of my life. I thought of countless ways to tell her … I didn't want tonight to be an end… I wanted it to be a beginning. Unfortunately, once the car engine was turned off, all of my words took flight. To magnify the silence, Caroline didn't speak either.

When we were kids, Caroline and I were never at a loss for conversation and the moments of silence we did share always felt peaceful and supportive. As I waited for her to break the silence, I noticed she alternated her time looking at her watch and staring at the house.

I finally spoke, "Will I see you again?"

Caroline seemed relieved when I was the first to speak. She turned to look at me – eyes sparkling and a wide smile on her face. "Of course, you'll see me, you silly goose!" For an instant, her voice sounded like the charming little girl in my elementary school class: cheerful, lively, carefree. A slight chuckle emerged from her throat. "There's school, the senior play, the end-of-the-year picnic and graduation. I'm not going to miss any of it. Isn't it exciting! The whole world is waiting. There are no boundaries. Our future is anything we want it to be. She kissed me sweetly on the lips and touched my cheek with great tenderness. Her words were rapidly pouring out of her mouth almost as if a floodgate had opened. "Thank you, Richard. Thank you for tonight. Thank you for being you! You're exactly like I remember – except – you've grown up. I'm so happy!"

Before I could say a word, she kissed me a second time – quickly – opened the car door and left, saying little more than "good-bye" upon her departure. I was flabbergasted and confused.

I didn't see Caroline in church on Sunday, but I did see her in the main lobby at school on Monday morning. She was with Jerry and a flock of their followers. Her demeanor was unruffled, and she appeared to be in good spirits. When Caroline wasn't looking in my direction, I glanced at her left hand. To my horror, there was still a diamond ring on her finger. Anger welled up inside of me – I could barely contain it. As she looked in my direction, I shot her the most hostile expression I could muster. At the exact same moment, the students, who were crowded around her, broke out in hysterical laughter as if they had heard a funny joke. Jerry Adams stared at me with a snide grin. I wondered if I were the subject of their conversation. A cold chill ran down my spine, and my anger mounted. I bottled my rage and walked away.

For the next month, I ignored Caroline at every turn. If I saw her approaching me, I went in the other direction. I refused to have a conversation with her. I may have been born on the south side of town, but no one – *no one* – was going to make a fool out of me.

Two weeks before graduation, I stood by the pot belly stove in my home. Glancing around, I tried to conger up a few of the happier memories with my mother and Calvin, but none came to me. All I saw was extreme poverty and a father who had collapsed in his chair – too drunk to travel the short distance to his bed. I hated my life. I hated this house – and most of all – I hated this town. Graduation couldn't get here fast enough. I wanted to get the hell out of this place.

4

Caroline

"I'm not going to marry Jerry Adams!"
I had been standing in front of my father's desk for more than five minutes, but I knew, until the last sentence, he hadn't heard a word I had said. My father stopped writing in his notebook, put down his pen, took off his glasses and looked at me for the first time since I had entered the room.

"What's this all about, Caroline? Are you having a case of the jitters?" My father truly looked mystified and surprisingly patient. "It's quite common for brides – and grooms – to get cold feet before the wedding."

"I don't have the jitters, Father." I spoke as calmly as I could. "I don't want to marry Jerry. I've *never* wanted to marry Jerry."

"Princess," my father took a deep breath. "You're graduating on Friday. The wedding invitations went out last weekend. People are already responding. Don't you think it's a little late to be having this conversation?"

"I've tried to tell you several times, Father, but you've never listened to me." My voice was beginning to tremble. I was never comfortable talking to my father – this was no exception.

"It's nerves, Caroline. Once the wedding day comes, you will be a beautiful and happy bride." My father pointed to the chair positioned across from his desk. "Caroline, please sit down. You look quite unsettled standing there." After I was seated, he spoke again, "You and Jerry are a good match. It will all be okay."

"No, Father! It's not going to be okay." I fiddled in my seat. Again, I repeated myself. "I don't want to marry Jerry Adams."

"Of course, you want to marry the boy. You've been seeing him for more than two years. While you were away at school, didn't he come visit you several times a month, and since you've been home, you've been inseparable. Of course, you want to marry him."

"I *don't* want to marry him." Unfortunately, although my convictions were strong, my voice was timid. "I want to go to Radcliffe."

"I know Radcliffe was important to you, Princess, and it would have been quite feasible for you to go to that college if Jerry had been accepted to Harvard, but even Bill's money couldn't buy the boy in with his mediocre grades. However, Jerry *is* going to Penn State, and in the future, if you truly want to take some classes at the university, you can enroll."

"I want to get a degree, Father, and I want it to be from Radcliffe." I hated the fact my voice had a whiny quality to it. "That's what I've always wanted."

Would my father ever hear me?

"Girls don't need a college degree, Caroline. What on earth would you do with it? You're going to be a wife. Hopefully, one day you'll be a mother. You don't need a college education." He turned his attention back to his paperwork and wrote something in the margin. As if he were dismissing a disgruntled employee, he tossed out an additional sentence. "You've *always* wanted to marry this boy – college shouldn't be an issue."

"No, Father! *I* haven't wanted to marry Jerry Adams!" Magically, I found an inner strength – a strength I had never had when I was in the presence of my father. I sat defiantly in the chair and continued to speak, this time with a firm voice, "*You* wanted me to marry him."

"Oh!" My father dropped his pen and glared at me.

When I saw my father's anger mirrored in his eyes, I lowered my voice. "I don't love him." I added meekly.

"What does love have to do with this? Many marriages don't start out with love. You build a relationship on common ground. You and Jerry are the same. You come from the same class of people. You have the same interests. You think alike – you have the same goals. And when I die and Bill Adams is gone, you will *own* this town."

"I don't want to *own* this town. I don't give a damn about this town."

"You watch your mouth, young lady." My father's voice bellowed. "You don't know what you want – you're young – you don't see into the future. Of course, you want the benefits this town has to offer. With my money and Bill Adams' influence, you and Jerry will be set for life. There will be nothing you can't have."

"I don't want any of it!" *Why didn't my father understand?* Money never mattered to me. I didn't want it when I was a little girl – and I surely didn't want it now. Money bought false friends. People wanted to know me – be my friend –*solely* because my father had money. Money bought me *things* – things I often didn't want or need. Money bought tutors and boarding school and nannies – when all I wanted was my father. Money was always a barrier – a wall – that kept my father from me. He was always too busy making money – he never had any time for me. I squared my shoulders and lifted my chin in an audacious manner. My goal was to exhibit a sense of confidence. "I am not going to marry Jerry Adams!"

My father slammed his fist on the desk. His voice came across as a boisterous roar. "I've had enough of this rebellious and ridiculous conversation. The wedding is set, and that's final."

My fingers were trembling. I hoped my voice didn't expose my fear. My next sentence could generate a riotous reaction. "When I tell Jerry the truth, he won't want to marry me."

"Nonsense! Jerry will blow it off as pre-wedding jitters."

"It's not the jitters, Father." I paused because I knew I was jeopardizing my life by confessing my quandary. "I'm pregnant."

"Do you mean to tell me Jerry didn't have the courage to face me? He sent *you* to tell me on your own! What a coward! How pregnant are you?"

"Two months."

"You're not showing. Odds are you won't be showing at the wedding either. That's a good thing."

"Jerry doesn't know I'm pregnant. When I tell him, he won't marry me."

"Of course, he'll marry you. I'll take a shotgun to him if he doesn't!"

"Jerry won't marry me because he will know the baby isn't his."

"What do you mean?" There was an expression of shock on my father's face.

"I've never been with Jerry – not in that way." I lowered my head because I didn't want to face the wrath or contempt in his eyes.

"Then who the hell is the father?"

"I won't tell you!" I stuck my chin out. "As soon as I graduate, I'm going to leave town – before I start showing – then no one will know. I'll go to Boston – stay in an apartment. Tell everyone I'm married, but my husband is in the army or something like that. Then in the fall, I'm going to go to Radcliffe – like I planned. And when the baby is born, I'll give it up for adoption."

"You are such a child! How on earth do you think you can pull this off? You're not going to Boston, and you're not going to Radcliffe. You can't possibly support yourself, much less pay college tuition. And I'm sure as Hell not going to condone your disgraceful behavior by paying your way. So! Let's put a stop to this ridiculous escapade of yours and get back to reality." My father stood up and walked around the desk. He towered over me. "Who's the father? Who got you into trouble? I demand to know!"

"I won't tell you!"

"By God, you *will* tell me!" he bellowed.

The force of my father's words pushed me back in the chair. I was quaking inside. All of my courage had vanished. "Richard," I whispered meekly.

"Richard who?"

"Richard Malone."

"You've been with that trash from the south side! How dare you sneak off and be with the likes of him. He is nothing! He is a *nobody*, and he will never amount to anything. What did he say when you told him?"

"I haven't told him. He doesn't know I'm pregnant."

"Trash like Richard Malone will never accept the responsibility of a baby. My guess is – he won't even offer to marry you, which is a good thing. I'd rather see you dead than married to the likes of him!" He shook his head in disgust. "I didn't know I had a trollop for a daughter!"

"Please, Father," I shivered as I spoke. "Please don't call me that. Richard is the only boy. There has never been anyone else." Tears burned my eyes. "I can't marry Jerry Adams."

"You *are* going to marry him." My father paused as he calculated his next words. "There are ways of fooling a man into thinking he is the father. Jerry need never know."

"I won't do it. I won't!" I mustered what little reserved courage I could gather. "I won't marry Jerry Adams! And you can't make me!"

"If you disobey me, Caroline, you can leave this house forever! So help me God! If you so much as speak to that Malone boy again, I will disown you and deny I've ever had a daughter!"

My defiance was completely gone.

2

In spite of the fact it was an absolutely gorgeous spring day, my heart was heavy. I walked slowly across the cemetery. As I expected, Richard was sitting by his mother's grave, hands clasped in silent prayer and head bowed reverently. A cold chill, which was created out of fear, raced up and down my spine. Richard hadn't spoken to me since our birthday – the night of the dance – and I was terrified he would brush me aside like garbage. As I approached, I watched him. Past memories flashed before me – Richard at six years old sitting in my father's library – Richard playing marbles with his friends – Richard at the movies with his hand stuffed in my popcorn bag – Richard sorting through his tackle box for exactly the right hook – Richard gazing at the sky imagining stories from the shapes of clouds – Richard, my champion, racing me to the doctors in that wonderfully protective manner when I thought I was bleeding to death – Richard waving an *Extra* high above his head – his voice ringing through the air – Richard riding his bike – his beautiful brown hair blowing freely – Richard stocking shelves at my father's store – his muscles rippling from the task. Richard standing at the corner of Maple and Main on VE-Day – I could still feel the surge of emotions that raced through me as I ran into his arms. With no effort at all, I could remember the way he kissed me. It was no longer a child's kiss – he was passionate. Kissing Richard felt binding and potent and even lustful – but it never felt wrong. The only time in my entire life I felt like a whole person was when I was with Richard. All of the other hours were empty, futile moments which meant nothing to me.

Even though I didn't make a sound during my approach, Richard turned his head in my direction. It was as if he knew I would be there even before he saw me. For an instant, I could see joy in his expression; then, his mien was masked with blatant hostility. It was agonizing to see he was so obviously intolerant of me. I didn't have a clue what I had done wrong. The last time we were together had been amazingly beautiful – magical. I thought the night we spent in his Chrysler was a new beginning for us, but Richard had quite easily cut me out of his life before I even had a chance to speak with him again.

Perhaps my father was right. I had shamelessly thrown myself at Richard, and I behaved like a hussy – a wanton tramp. Richard was so popular with all of the girls in school. They swooned whenever he was around. A glance or a smile from Richard Malone could make most girls turn into giggling idiots and weak-kneed in his presence. Richard never had one particular girlfriend – he always had a half a dozen of them. *What made me think I was anything special to him?* I was a bony, babbling creature from his childhood. Since I had come home, Richard had barely given me the time of day.

Richard continued to stare at me as if I were an unnecessary disturbance. All of the words I had so carefully rehearsed abandoned me. I was left speechless and overwhelmingly nervous.

"I need to talk to you, Richard." I said as I took the remaining steps between us.

"Sure, go ahead," he muttered. "But make it quick. I need to finish packing. I'm leaving tomorrow after graduation."

"You're leaving?" I paused. "Where are you going?"

"I don't know – maybe I'll go to New York – get a job on the docks – or maybe I'll join the army." Richard glanced toward the sky, then back at his mother's gravestone. "I don't have a clue what I am going to do, but I do know I am never going into the mines, and I'm not staying here."

"But you can't go! I . . . I . . . I have something to tell you."

"Well then – say it and be done with it."

"I can't . . ." I mumbled. "Weren't you even going to say good-bye?"

"No! Why should I?" There was an irritated expression on his face. "When you went to boarding school, you promised to write me every day, but you never bothered – not even one letter! Why, all of a sudden, does it matter if I say good-bye?" His words were strung together in an angry tirade.

"That's not true. I wrote you every day! *Every day!* In fact, I didn't miss one single day for three months, but you never wrote me back."

"I didn't get any of the letters." The irritation on Richard's face changed to a look of bewilderment. "I didn't even know where you were."

"That's not possible – I put the letters in the basket at the front desk."

Like a revelation, I realized – it was highly possible someone took the letters out of the basket before the mailman arrived. Perhaps my father, when he dropped me off at the school, had left instructions regarding my mail. "My father must have told the headmistress to confiscate my mail. If you didn't get any of my letters, someone must have taken them out of the box. I swear to you, Richard. I *swear* to you. I wrote every day. I missed you so much – it broke my heart when you never wrote me back. I thought you didn't care."

"I would have written you. I waited." Richard stared at me as he spoke. "I even asked kids at school if they knew where you were, but no one had any answers. It was like you had dropped off of the face of the earth."

"I was miserable and lonely." I whispered the words. "I missed you so much."

"Then – out of nowhere – you showed up one day last fall – no explanation – no apologies." Richard's words were clipped – laced with antagonism. "And you were with Jerry Adams. *Jerry Adams*! Of all people, why did you have to pick *him*?" Richard's voice elevated a notch, and there was a tinge of exasperation in it.

"That was my father's idea – not mine."

"It doesn't matter whose idea it was – you're still the one who is going to marry that jackass!"

"I'm not going to marry him!"

"Oh, really! Then why are the invitations flying all over town? Every kid in North Side has one! If you're here to give me an invitation – don't bother."

"I told you! I'm not going to marry Jerry Adams!" I paused. "Besides, when he hears the truth, he won't want to marry me anymore."

"Interesting!" Richard said sarcastically as he glanced at my hand and noticed there was no longer a diamond ring on my finger. "Are they printing that tidbit of information in an *Extra*? Maybe I should go down to Maple and Main and sell a few copies. Buy one for myself so I can read all of the details!" His caustic words were biting. Richard paused. "Why are you breaking the engagement?"

"Because I am . . . because I'm going to have a baby." I bit down on my lower lip. Tears burned my eyes. I hadn't meant to blurt it out in such a bold manner. "When Jerry finds out, he'll know he isn't the father."

The entire cemetery was blanketed in silence. Richard's face was ashen: his expression unreadable. "I know there wasn't anyone before me. I know I was the first." His words were slowly spoken – whispered. He paused. "I'm going to ask you this *once*, Caroline, and I want the truth." He took a deep breath. "Am I the father?"

"Yes." When I replied affirmatively, I expected to see anger in Richard's expression, but instead, he seemed relieved – even calm.

Richard looked pensively at the headstone of his mother's grave and took several deep breaths before he spoke again. "Does your father know?"

"Yes!" I glanced away – I couldn't look Richard in the eyes. More than anything in the world, I feared he would simply get up and walk away – deserting me.

"What did your father say?"

"You don't want to know." Again tears burned at my eyes. We sat in silence for several minutes. I could barely control my trembling hands, and my heart felt as if it was going to explode.

Why didn't he say something?

"I've heard there are doctors," I whispered the words, "who help girls like me – and they can make this go away – like a bad dream. I think I can get the money." My words were choppy – barely articulate. "But I'm afraid to go alone."

"I will not be part of *that!*" Richard's words were terse and unyielding. The features on his face were distorted with steadfast defiance. As he tapped his index finger several times on his cheek, his eyes scanned the cemetery. His pensive expression was unreadable. Finally he spoke, "A few years ago, I asked you to run away with me." He paused. His jaw was squarely set in a determined manner, and his steel blue eyes were impassive. "But you wouldn't go with me." He took a deep breath and exhaled completely before speaking again. "If I ask you to come with me now – will you?"

"Yes." I didn't even hesitate.

Richard looked directly into my eyes – his expression was completely blank. Two – maybe three minutes passed in total silence as he continued to rub his finger against his cheek. The area of skin he was tapping turned red from the action. The silence between us was deafening. It felt like an eternity. My heart beat wildly in my chest. The loud, erratic rhythm echoed in my ears; I could no longer hear the birds or the leaves rustling in the breeze. I waited like a statue for him to speak.

Finally words came from Richard's lips. "This is what we are going to do." He stood up and slapped the grass from his pants. "Go home. Don't tell anyone. Pack what's important to you. And keep in mind – if you come with me – we are never coming back here. *Never!*" There were lines of determination etched in his brow. "Tomorrow night . . . after the graduation ceremony . . . we're leaving."

"Where are we going, Richard?"

"I don't know, but I promise you, if you come with me, I will take care of you. I will find a way to support us. If you give me a little time, I swear I will provide for you and the baby. You won't be sorry. I swear! You will never be sorry."

I would have felt better if he had held me or put his arms around me, but he didn't.

5

Richard

We left town a little after ten o'clock. I said good-bye to my father, but he didn't hear me. He had drained a fifth of cheap bourbon and passed out in his chair long before dinner; consequently, he never came to the graduation ceremony, nor did he see me in my cap and gown. When I closed the door, I erased that part of my life forever.

Packed in my car was an assortment of things: my clothes, my bike, my fishing pole and tackle box, eight hundred and fifty dollars I had withdrawn from the bank when I closed out my account, a picture of my mother, my diploma, and Calvin's collection of baseball cards. Those were all of my possessions that held any emotional or financial value. Caroline brought considerably more things: her sewing machine, a radio, two suitcases packed to the max with clothes, a phonograph, a stack of 78-rpm records and a number of 33-1/3 LPs. She also had a shoebox with a bright, blue ribbon tied around it. When I inquired what was in the box, she said, "A few things." We dropped the subject. It took ten minutes of rearranging everything before I finally was able to get it all in the trunk and retie my bicycle to the back fender.

When we passed the post office, Caroline asked me to stop the car. She got out and dropped a letter in the mailbox. I asked her if she were mailing a letter to her father, and she replied, "No, it's a letter to Radcliffe. I want to formally tell them I will not be attending classes in the fall." She said nothing else on the subject. I wasn't sure, but it looked as if there were tears in her eyes. If I had been more confident, I would have reached across the seat of the Chrysler and held her hand, but I did nothing.

When it came to Caroline Sue Miller, I was not sure how to behave.

We drove for a few hours in silence. While Caroline stared blankly out of the passenger window, I focused my concentration on the road. I had no idea where we were going. However, I was certain of one thing – the most important person in the entire world was sitting next to me. I didn't know how it happened – I only knew she was with me and our lives together – our future – began on this day: June 3rd, 1949.

I drove east on Lincoln Highway; then, I turned southeast to Harrisburg. Without any discussion, I decided to forego Chicago or New York City. Instead, I headed toward Washington, D.C. Surely, there was a job for me in the nation's capital. We passed through Harrisburg shortly after midnight. I still wasn't tired, so I pushed further south. I had every intention of spending the night in York and getting a fresh start in the morning, but I missed a turn and ended up in a little town called Dover. By that time, I was too exhausted to drive another mile. Caroline, who had been silently sitting in the passenger seat, pointed to a shabby motel with a neon vacancy sign in the window of the main office. I had no idea what time it was when I pulled into the parking lot. The manager didn't ask for either Caroline's or my name. He wanted $3.50 up front before he gave me a room key. I was overcome by sheer exhaustion. Instead of taking ten minutes to wash up, I crawled into bed. Within seconds, I was sound asleep.

When I awoke the next morning, Caroline was sleeping on top of the sheets, fully dressed with a throw blanket on top of her. She was lying on her back – her face and her hands were the few visible parts of her body. Her fingers were wrapped tightly around the edge of the blanket and positioned directly under her chin as if she were gripping it for security. I watched her for several minutes. She looked extraordinarily beautiful. Although her hands were tense and her body looked rigid under the blanket, her face appeared serene and peaceful. A soft, coal-black curl had migrated from the rest of her hair and was draped over her forehead. It concealed the majority of her left eye and most of her cheek. As quietly as I could, I sat on the edge of the bed and continued to watch her sleep. I couldn't resist brushing the stray strand of hair aside so I could see her entire face. She didn't move.

Of course, no one could tell she was pregnant, but I knew, and the knowledge enhanced her beauty. There was a radiant glow to her skin I hadn't noticed until now. I knew, without question, the child was mine. I didn't need proof – I instinctively knew it – sure as I knew my own name. The idea of being a father was frightening at first, but – the more

I thought about it – the more excited I became. As I watched the steady, rhythmic flow of Caroline's breathing, I promised myself she would never be sorry she came with me, and our child would have all of the advantages the kids in North Side had. I was going to be a good father and a good husband. I knew if I worked hard, I could support us all.

As if a light bulb came on inside my head, I realized Caroline and I had never talked about marriage. It never occurred to me she would say "no." She was the mother of my child. What other recourse did she have? I made a decision. Caroline and I were going to get married. *Today!*

Quietly, I slipped out of the room and walked to the office. The man behind the desk was snoring loudly. When I tapped the silver bell on the front desk, it jolted him awake. He stuttered for a few moments and then asked if he could be of assistance. I inquired as to whether or not Dover had a Justice of the Peace. He replied, "yes" and gave me directions. I went back to my room. Caroline was still in a peaceful slumber. I crawled back into bed, tried to sleep, but realized it was a lost cause. I was too excited to sleep. Instead, I rolled onto my side and stared at Caroline, thankful she was with me. I was – without a doubt – the luckiest man in the world.

Caroline and I were married in Dover, Pennsylvania, at 11:30 a.m. on June the fourth. After the brief ceremony and a quick lunch, we headed south again. As we approached the Maryland State line, there was a small sign for Philadelphia and New York City.

For the first time since we'd gotten in the car, Caroline spoke, "Where are we going?"

I contemplated telling her my thoughts on Washington, D.C., but – for some odd reason – I didn't. Instead, I asked, "I don't have any concrete plan. Is there any place you'd like to go?"

"New York City's nice," she whispered softly.

On an impulse, I took the turn and headed northeast. If Caroline liked New York City, maybe I would too. Outside Philadelphia, we got on Route One. I continued driving until we were so hungry we had to stop.

Although New York City had been our goal, we ended up in a small town south of Newark, New Jersey. I'd like to say there was a reason for choosing our final destination, but there was not. We were simply tired of traveling and stopped at a small family owned diner called Raffaele's Place. The menu had one item on it: pizza. Neither Caroline nor I had ever eaten pizza, and we marveled at the taste.

Mario and Rosa Mancini, the owners of the small café, were native Italians who had immigrated to America in the early 1900s. Since it was too soon for dinner, Caroline and I were the only customers in their establishment; as a result, the couple stood over our table chatting continually. When we told them we had never experienced pizza before, Rosa began to ramble on about Italy, her ancestors, and the origination of pizza. She proudly mentioned – although some people believe pizza was first eaten thousands of years ago by Babylonians and Egyptians – this flat-bread version was initially made in her hometown of Naples in Italy.

"See the colors," Rosa said as she pointed to the pizza. "The mozzarella cheese is white. The tomato is red. And the basil is green. Green, white and red – the colors of the Italian flag! It was legend in our town. In the 1880s – when I be little baby in my mama's arms – a man in town named Raffaele Esposito made this pizza with the colors of the Italian flag so he could impress King Umberto and Queen Margherita when they came to oversee the village. The king and queen liked it so much, pizza became popular to offer family and friends. Raffaele Esposito was a hero in our town – a legend among our people. So! When Mario and I come to America, we think it is a good thing to bring pizza. We start this business, and we name it Raffaele's after the first man who made *real* pizza." Mario and Rosa's pride was written clearly on their faces.

"There's lots of other people make pizza now – but this pizza." Mario perched his fingertips on his lips, kissed them and burst his hand into the air in a grand gesture of excitement. "Delizioso!" Mario smiled enthusiastically. "This pizza – our special recipe – it is the *best* pizza. You'll find no better in America."

The Italian couple seemed relaxed. To our amazement, they sat at the table with us and began nibbling at the remaining pizza on the tray. Part of me was annoyed because I knew money was tight and I wanted to wrap the extra pieces so we could eat them at a later time; yet, another part of me smiled at them heartily because they were truly delightful individuals. Their presence had a calming effect on me, and I noticed Caroline was laughing for the first time since we'd left our homes. There was a twinkle in her brown eyes I hadn't seen since we were kids, and her smile was genuine.

"My Mario," Rosa continued. "He is such a good man. We make a good business. It's not crowded now," Rosa motioned around the empty room. "But it will be – at dinner time – lots of people come. You'll see." Rosa touched her husband tenderly on the shoulder. There was great love in her eyes. "My Mario! He is the best pizza maker in the world. But, sadly, Mario is not a young man anymore. See these big shoulders." Rosa touched her husband's arms. "They ache now. It is hard for my Mario to toss the pizza. It causes him great pain." Sadness washed over Rosa's face. "We thought – when we got too old – we thought our boys would take over the business, and we would not have to work so hard anymore. Our boys – they were good at making pizza – almost as good as their father. But, alas, they are no longer with us. Both of my boys died in the war. God rest their souls." Rosa used her hand to make an intangible cross on her chest. "They were born in America – my boys were *Americans* – and when the United States went to war against Germany and Italy in the Second Great War, my brave boys volunteered to fight. They did not care that Italy was the enemy – they did not like Mussolini." Both Rosa and Mario spat on the floor next to their feet. "Bah! Mussolini was a pig! Thank God he is dead!" Tears sprang to her eyes. "Our boys were brave to fight against him. My first-born – Christopher – what a brave boy he was – never afraid of anything – always a leader. He was a hero. He died in February of 1943 – in Africa – some place called Kasserine Pass. And my baby – Leonardo – he was a quiet soul – tender – gentle with all God's creatures – but when America needed boys – he volunteered – just like my Christopher. He was a brave boy too. He won a medal. Maybe sometime I show it to you. My Leonardo died on that French beach during the Invasion. His captain wrote me a letter and told me how brave he was. Both my boys are buried on the other side of the ocean in countries I have never seen. There is no grave here where I can put flowers. That causes my heart great pain." Rosa used the corner of her apron to dab the tears from her eyes. Afterward, she reached for her husband's hand and squeezed it tenderly – Mario responded by gently patting her hand. "So! You see. We have no sons – no one to help – no one to teach the art of pizza."

Mario interrupted. "We have talked so much – monopolized all of the conversation. Tell us about you. You are too young to have fought in the war against Hitler and Mussolini – but you are a big, strong boy – I can tell you work hard. And your friend," Mario looked at Caroline. "She is such a beautiful girl. You are lucky to have such a pretty girlfriend." Mario chuckled when he spoke.

"Caroline is not my girlfriend." I looked at Caroline. She was blushing. "She's my wife." It was the first time I had said the words aloud. In spite of the fact the statement sounded a little odd coming off my lips, I felt immensely proud when I said it. I glanced at Caroline. She was looking down at her hands.

"This beautiful creature is your wife?" Mario frowned. "No! Cannot be! There is no ring on her finger."

"We got married this morning." I paused. "Caroline doesn't have a ring because we don't have enough money for luxuries." I willed Caroline to look at me, but she did not. "One day, I will buy her a gorgeous ring."

"Young man, you don't understand – 'tis not good for a bride to have no ring. Wives need rings. That's how other men know when a woman is married. You don't want other men thinking this beautiful creature is available. You buy her a ring soon."

"First, I have to find a job and a place to live."

"You have no work?" Mario looked at Rosa. When Rosa nodded, he continued. "You can have a job here. We can't pay a lot, but you and your bride can stay in the backroom. It's not big, but there is a bed." He proudly added, "There is a small bathroom too."

"You can stay for free," Rosa interjected. "Like I said, my Mario is not young anymore. His shoulders pain him all day – he needs help. You seem like nice kids – you help us – we help you."

"I teach you the art of making pizza. I can tell – you are a smart boy – you will learn fast." Mario looked at Caroline. "And your beautiful wife can help my Rosa."

I felt as if I were caught in crossfire. Mario and Rosa were simultaneously speaking in a mixture of English and Italian. All of their words ran together. I couldn't understand either one of them. Their excited voices blended into a string of babble. I looked at Caroline. She was wide-eyed, but smiling. "What do you think?" I mouthed the words so Caroline, who was looking directly at me, could understand. She reached across the table and grabbed my hand. Nodding her head and smiling broadly, she whispered, "Yes."

"Okay, Mario. You have a deal."

Mario and Rosa hugged each other enthusiastically and then embraced both Caroline and me. "I am going to go to the backroom and fix it up for you. Clean sheets. Maybe some flowers. You will like it. Imagine! Newlyweds in my backroom! It's so wonderful!" Rosa blushed. "When Mario and I first bought this place, we did not have enough money for a house. We lived in the backroom like you are going to do. My Mario and I lived there for many years until we had enough money to buy the house." She pointed to the Victorian home adjacent to the diner. "The backroom – it is a good place. My babies were made in that room. Lots of good love is in that room. You will be happy there."

Rosa was right. Although the backroom was small, it was, as Caroline described it, quite charming. It had been originally designed to be a storage room, but Mario and Rosa had transformed it into a functional and quaint room with a comfortable bed, a night stand with a lamp and a Bible, a solid chest of drawers with lace doilies, picture frames, and a vase of flowers on it, two chairs in the corner and a table in between them. I glanced in the tiny bathroom. To my amazement, there was a pull chain toilet and a rather large sink. I laughed to myself. How ironic! I finally had an indoor bathroom – no more out-house in the backyard. To me, this was a mansion, but I knew – to Caroline – it was as if she had moved to South Side. I cringed when I thought the horror she must feel.

Shortly after we put our suitcases in the room, the customers entered the diner. Exactly like Rosa had predicted, the stools at the counter were full. Everything became quite hectic as Mario and Rosa busied themselves with well-memorized tasks. Caroline and I assisted as best we could, but I felt more in the way than helpful. A couple of hours passed; then, as quickly as the frenzy erupted, it was over, and the diner was empty again.

As Mario transferred the money from the cash register to his pocket, Caroline wiped the counter, and I dried the last of the pots. Rosa disappeared. A few moments later, she came in the room holding a bottle of wine. "Normally, my Mario and I would stay and share this bottle of wine with you, but," Rosa winked first at Caroline and then at me. "But because you are newlyweds, Mario and I will go home now and let you two lovebirds have some privacy." She handed the bottle to me and smiled. "You take this. Consider it a wedding present."

Mario slapped me playfully on the back. "You have good time tonight, Richard." He chuckled. "Rosa and I will be back at 8:00 sharp tomorrow morning. Then I teach you how to make pizza dough."

Without another word, the couple disappeared. Caroline and I were alone in the restaurant. For the first time since we had arrived at Raffaele's Place, I felt awkward. I wasn't quite sure what to do or say. When we were kids, I thought of Caroline as such a chatterbox – at times even annoyingly talkative – but for the last couple of days she had been strangely reserved and uncharacteristically quiet. I would have given anything to have her talk incessantly again. I motioned to the bottle of wine. "Would you like a glass?"

"I don't think so. It's probably not good for the baby." She spoke quietly. "But you can have some."

"No. That's okay. I think I'll save it for later." Even though I didn't feel calm, my voice sounded controlled and quite casual. "I'm pretty tired. It's been a long day. I bet you're tired too."

"A little."

"Why don't you go first," I said as I motioned to the bathroom. "I'll unpack some of my things."

"Okay." She took a small bag into the bathroom with her.

Neither of us spoke as we readied ourselves for bed. I didn't know how to behave. I felt awkward and uncomfortable. It was never like this when we were kids – but now – I felt as if I were in a room with a stranger. I knew in my heart, Caroline would never have come with me if she had not been pregnant. Caroline had a destiny. She was going to college. If she chose not to marry Jerry Adams, she probably would have married some other rich guy – lived in a gigantic house like the one on the hill where she grew up – had servants to wait on her every need and desire. She would have had beautiful clothes, new cars, expensive jewelry, a bathtub in her bathroom and a gigantic diamond on her finger. If she had a choice, she would never have picked me, or this one-room bungalow, or the dubious future I had to offer her. Caroline's destiny had been derailed by the actions of one night, and now – she was stuck with me. Recognizing this reality made me anxious – even afraid. I knew – with every ounce of my being – I wanted Caroline in my life – in my future – and I had to find a way to win her respect, her affection, and her love.

Even though I desperately wanted to make love to my bride, I knew I couldn't. Sex would hurt the baby, and the last thing I wanted to do was hurt our child. I knew if Caroline had a miscarriage, there would be no reason for her to stay married to me.

Aside from that, I also knew Caroline didn't want me in a physical way. She made her position perfectly clear last night when she slept rigid as stone under the blanket. She came with me because she had no alternative. Since Caroline had returned home from boarding school – with the exception of the one night – on our 18th birthday – when she had too much to drink and we spent the evening in my Chrysler – Caroline hadn't given me so much as a smile from across the room. Like the other kids from North Side, she thought of me as nothing more than scum she needed to wipe off of her shoe. I was her punishment – her albatross – for a mistake she had made.

When Caroline came out of the bathroom, she was wearing a pink cotton nightgown. With the exception of her head, hands, and feet, every part of her body was covered. Her face was washed clean and her jet black hair was hanging loosely on her shoulders. She looked like a porcelain doll – fragile and beautiful. I watched her as she walked to the bed, turned down the sheets, and crawled to the far side of the mattress. She pulled the blanket up to her chin, clutching the sheet with her fingers. Without looking in my direction, she closed her eyes as if she were going to go to sleep. I felt my heart quicken in my chest, and my breathing involuntarily became erratic. Sweat broke out on my brow. My throat felt parched – every time I swallowed – I thought I was going to choke.

I went in the bathroom, closed the door and quietly released my tension. It didn't take long. Four, maybe five strokes and it was over. The dizziness dissipated, and I began to breath normally again. My God! I thought to myself. How can I possibly sleep in the same bed with Caroline without making love to her? It was torture to think about it. How did other men do it when their wives were pregnant? Nine months of this would kill me.

After washing up, I reentered the bedroom. Caroline appeared to be asleep. I slipped silently between the sheets and turned out the light on the bedside table. As I lay there in the darkness, I tried to control my breathing and relax. It was futile. Although she was nearly a foot away, I could feel the heat coming from Caroline's body. It was tempting – her warm skin seemed to whisper, "Come to me," but I suppressed the urge. She smelled incredibly good. There was a faint lavender fragrance that permeated the air and heightened my senses. It was intoxicating. I felt drunk from it, as if I'd consumed the entire bottle of wine Rosa had given us.

Out of the darkness, Caroline spoke. "Good night, Richard."

"Goodnight, Caroline," I responded casually even though I was far from relaxed. It was too dark to see her expression. "I'm so sorry about all of this. I know you are used to grand things and a big house and servants. I promise things will get better."

"Don't apologize, Richard." Caroline's voice was subtle and sweet. "I like it here. Rosa is wonderful. She's so loving and kind. I can't believe Mario and Rosa opened their lives to us. My father would never have done anything like this for a stranger." She sighed softly. "I think it is a miracle – the answer to my prayers."

3

Throughout the month of June, Caroline and I went about our lives in much the same manner: cordial, quiet, compatible. I opened a savings account and deposited most of my money in the bank. The rest I spent on a ring for Caroline. It was a pretty gold band I found at a second hand store. When I gave it to Caroline, she immediately put it on her finger. I thought it would make her happy, but – to my dismay – she spent the remainder of the afternoon in a melancholy mood.

During the day, we worked diligently with Mario and Rosa, taking care of the diner and the customers, learning how to make pizza, running errands, and cleaning up after a successful day's work. In the less hectic moments, I noticed Rosa and Caroline spent much of their time with their heads together, talking constantly as if they were the best of friends. Sometimes they looked as if they were discussing urgent, personal matters and Rosa wrapped her arms around Caroline in a warm, motherly manner – while other times – they laughed and joked as if their conversations were filled with amusing anecdotes. Caroline seemed so comfortable and cheerful with Rosa. There were even times when I detected a glimpse of a younger Caroline: carefree, blissful, and filled with wonder.

Then, at night, after Mario and Rosa left for the evening and we entered our 12 x 12 bedroom, the laughter stopped, the tension mounted, and a thick silence blanketed the air. Each night, we slept in the same bed together – not a word spoken between us. Her body remained rigid under the sheets, and her silence was deafening. More times than not, I felt as if I were going to explode from the frustration which welled up inside of me. Caroline was so beautiful and so untouchable.

Most nights, I sprang from the bed and stormed out of the room. My stomach was tied in knots, and my head pounded wildly as if it would burst from inner tension. I left the bed and went into the restaurant. Often I spent hours pacing back and forth in the darkness from one end of the diner to the other. I felt like a starving man – dying of thirst and hunger – with food and water dangling in front of me but no ability to consume it. It was an excruciating torture. My body was not the only casualty of my circumstances. My heart ached too. More than anything in the world, I wanted Caroline to love me. *Was that too much to ask?* How could Caroline be so jovial and expressive around Mario and Rosa and so quiet and miserable when she was with me? It was maddening.

As the weeks passed, Mario and I developed a unique bond. We spent hours together laboring over the stove, tossing pizza dough, cooking the sauce until it was – as Mario called it – *perfezione* –and working in his personal vegetable garden behind the restaurant. I'd never known anyone like Mario. He was generous, patient, and exuberant; plus, he talked constantly while using his hands with big swooping gestures. Unlike my father, who had gradually deteriorated into a shell of a man after my mother died and then Calvin, Mario was animated and candid and extremely open about his personal emotions and opinions.

Even though I didn't like to admit it, I was a lot like my father – I never confided in people – my thoughts were my own. I did not want to share them. But I discovered I enjoyed listening to Mario rant and rave about his passions, his dreams and his life. Ironically, Mario didn't seem to mind that most of our conversations were one-sided. I think he appreciated the fact I was a good listener.

The only time I was uncomfortable around Mario was when he discussed marriage – his marriage to Rosa or my marriage to Caroline. It was as if he felt there were no rules of etiquette on those topics, and he would barrel right in without any thought regarding good manners. Nothing was sacred – and certainly not sex. He talked about sex like most men talked about the weather.

One afternoon, while we were outside working on the row of tomatoes in his garden, Mario told me about the "pebbles in the jar" theory. When I said I had never heard of a theory by that name, he roared with laughter.

"Dear boy!" He chuckled. "All men know about the pebbles in the jar." He did not wait for me to respond. "Husbands know if they put a pebble in a jar every time they make passionate love to their wives during the first couple of years they are married, the jar will be overflowing with lots and lots of pebbles." Mario stopped. He took his handkerchief out of his pocket and mopped at his brow. Smiling, he continued, "This makes for a happy beginning to a marriage. Good start makes good marriage!" Mario made a grand gesture with his arms. "But husbands also know – after a few years, if they take a pebble *out* of the jar every time they make mad passionate love to their wives – unfortunately – they will never empty the jar. 'Tis sad but true!" Mario picked three tomatoes off of the vine before speaking again, "My Rosa – we fill that jar up high when we first got married. Beautiful pebbles! Glorious memories! We had a very good start."

I felt a hot blush wash over my face. Mario's candor usually had that effect on me. He was amusing, but I was often ill at ease when he spoke of such personal matters.

"So, Richard! You have such a beautiful wife! So lovely! I bet your jar is overflowing with pebbles!" He chuckled in a boisterous manner.

I was too stunned to comment. An instant image of Caroline lying in bed oozing frigidity and an empty glass jar on the table next to our bed flashed through my mind.

"Oh, my dear boy! I must apologize. I have embarrassed you. Rosa is always telling me my mouth is too big – I talk too much. So sorry!

Some matters are private – I should not talk of it." In a friendly manner, Mario slapped me on the back. "You be good husband – you fill that jar." Without skipping a beat, Mario changed the subject and discussed the benefits of thick versus thin tomato sauce.

I went back to pulling the weeds in my row.

That night, when I came into the bedroom, there was a wonderful fragrance of roses in the air. The phonograph softly played one of Caroline's Frank Sinatra records: *Night and Day.* Its sensual melody was alluring – even haunting – and instantly created a stirring in my loins. The overhead light was off, but there was a candelabrum on the table. The flickering flames from the wicks created dancing shadows on the wall. I could hear Caroline humming in the bathroom. When she opened the door, Caroline stood basking in the light. She was not wearing her traditional pink cotton nightgown. Instead, she was wearing a small white chiffon number, and the backlight from the bathroom made it completely transparent. I could see every detail of her body. The soft curve of her hips. Her firm, round breasts. Her thighs – long and lean. My eyes focused on the beautiful triangle-shaped mass of jet-black hair harbored between her legs. She was beyond perfection.

The breath I had been inhaling caught in my throat. It was a full thirty seconds before I could breathe again. In the meantime, my knees buckled under me. Luckily, I was standing next to the chair – I leaned on it for support.

"Oh!" Caroline spoke bashfully as she crossed her arms protectively over her chest. "I didn't know you were here already." She seemed nervous as she stuttered over her words. When Caroline turned the bathroom light off, her naked silhouette became hidden in the soft chiffon.

Caroline was a vision. Captivating. Irresistible. Her black ringlets cascaded freely around her shoulders and her porcelain skin gleamed in the candlelight.

"Rosa bought this for me." She motion to the chiffon and ran her fingers slowly over the material. Although she apparently meant to be demure, her actions were quite seductive. She looked directly in my eyes until she felt she had my full attention. "Rosa said you would like it."

I couldn't talk. Hell! I couldn't move. I was stunned–startled–

overwhelmed–and I was utterly paralyzed. I sat in the chair, my mouth gaping open. *Was this a dream?*

"Don't you like it, Richard?"

"Of course, I like it!" To my amazement, I spoke the words. They sounded like a frog croaking, but they were still audible.

I was thoroughly enchanted by her incredibly beautiful body; for that reason, I never looked at her face. When my attention finally focused on her expression, I realized there was a steady stream of silent tears trailing down her cheeks. She obviously had been crying the entire time I had been gawking at her.

"Why don't you want me, Richard?" She tried to make her voice sound strong, but there was a tremor to it that echoed her emotions. "We've been married more than a month and you've never even touched me. You won't sleep in the bed unless you think I'm already asleep and you get up in the morning before I wake up. You bought me this ring," she said pointing to her hand, "and when you gave it to me, you handed it to me like it was a sack of cornstarch." She paused to brush the tears from her face. "I'm your wife. Don't you want to be with me?"

"My God, Caroline!" I stammered. "Of course, I do." With a sudden burst of energy, I left my chair and took the paces between us. As I wrapped her in my arms, she melded toward me. There was a fire in the base of my stomach that raged like lunacy and consumed all common sense. I could think of nothing but her as I ran my fingers under the chiffon and pulled it effortlessly over her head. Her face was still damp with tears. I hungrily kissed them away tasting the slight salt residue left on her cheeks. Her skin was hot to the touch. With a fever I did not know we possessed, I seared my hands on her back and then allowed them to travel down her spine and grip ardently on the soft curves of her thighs. Her hips pressed hard against me sending bolts of electricity throughout my body. The room was spinning out of control. With paramount urgency, I stripped off my shirt so my bare skin could touch hers. The feel of her taut nipples pressing against my chest produced an even greater desire inside of me. I was obsessed with feeling her body against me – fire-hot skin against skin.

I buried my lips in her neck, savoring the wonderful smell of Caroline. Her hair enveloped me, and I was drowning in the silky strands. It was glorious. As I picked Caroline up and walked toward the bed, she wrapped her arms around my neck and pulled my lips to hers. I felt her tongue jet across my teeth and plunge into my mouth. She tasted sweet, a hint of peppermint and something else – was it cinnamon? After gently depositing her on the mattress, I hurriedly jerked at my belt and pants until I had stripped them from my legs. My entire body was throbbing with a consuming desire. Waves of tiny needles were marching up and down my spine – but instead of causing pain, it created a splendor beyond my wildest imagination.

Like a child let loose in a candy store for the first time, I sampled everything – every part of Caroline. These were hidden treasures I'd visualized in my dreams. Her breasts were gleaming white in sharp contrast to the chocolate shade of her nipples. When I licked hungrily at one, it grew taut and turned a richer shade of brown. What magic this was – what wonderful tastes and smells, and the sounds coming from Caroline's throat were moans of ecstasy and delight. She thrust her hips against my leg, and I could no longer control myself. I pulled her toward me and positioned her in a manner for easy entry. I slipped into her haven with no effort at all. Her radiating juices encased me. She was tight and hot and wet. I could feel her raging pulse throbbing as it constricted around me, consuming me, swallowing me entirely. Our bodies joined as one, writhing together, thrusting our hips, climbing up, up, up. "Oh, God!" I muttered. "Oh, Carley! Sweet Carley! Hold me! Hold me!" I could no longer hear any sound or feel any sensation other than the roar inside my head and the pulsating sensation that captured every part of my body. I had been catapulted into another dimension as I pounded myself vigorously – vehemently – faster – faster – into Caroline's sizzling nest. The explosion was euphoric, and I began to jerk spasmodically until I collapsed on Caroline's body. I was panting for breath. So was she.

Gradually, I became aware of my surroundings. Frank Sinatra's voice was still ringing clearly in the room. Together – entwined as one – we lay panting on the bed. Minutes passed – finally the album was over – it continued to spin on the turn table, but the needle no longer emitted music. As I began to focus on my surroundings, I noticed the once orderly bedspread was a tangled mountain at the corner of the mattress, as were the pillows. The smell of the freshly laundered sheets filled my nostrils.

It was a pleasant, clean scent. The candles' flames gave off enough light for me to see Caroline's face. Sweat – hers and mine – glistened on her skin. Strands of her hair, damp with perspiration, were matted to her forehead. As I gently brushed them aside, she smiled warmly at me.

"Did I hurt you?"

She shook her head slowly. "No, sweet Richard, you didn't hurt me," she whispered. Her magnificent brown eyes danced with enthusiasm. "You were wonderful." Tenderly, almost reverently, Caroline touched my lips with her fingertips as if she were touching something of great value.

"You are so beautiful, Carley." I kissed her softly, then rolled to my side and scooped her protectively in my arms. Automatically, her head rested on my shoulder. I could feel her warm breath on my skin; her heartbeat drummed a steady melody on my chest. It wasn't long before I knew Caroline was asleep. I closed my eyes and reveled in the moment.

A tormenting thought jolted me. Oh, my God! The baby! I had been so captivated by Caroline – so swept away with my craving for her – I had forgotten about the baby. *What had I done?* Was the baby okay? Did I hurt it? I would never forgive myself if my actions caused Caroline to lose our child.

In the morning, while Rosa and Caroline were at the market, I began my daily preparation ritual in the kitchen. Mario was kneading the dough, and I was flipping the first batch. As usual, Mario carried on a steady stream of conversation, oblivious to the fact I barely spoke unless I had a question regarding our tasks at hand. As was Mario's norm, he often changed topics of discussion without any warning at all. When he reached in the cabinet for another bag of flour, he chuckled aloud. "You are quiet as always, Richard." Mario said, "but today you seem happier. You have – how shall I put this – a special look on your face." A broad grin spread across his lips. "Perhaps you put a pebble in the jar last night? Yes?"

Mario's conversations often had a distracting impact on me. I instantly lost my concentration. Although I tried to keep control of the circling dough, it spiraled slightly to my left and I missed my intended mark, which caused it to cave over my arm. Mario roared with laughter.

"You a funny boy, Richard!" He slapped me playfully on the shoulder. "So silent all of the time, but your face is an open book. My Rosa was right. She knew why you had sour look on your face most of the time. She knew what the problem was. My Rosa – she talked to your Caroline. Problem fixed! Right? You a happy fellow today. Now there will be lots of pebbles in the jar."

I couldn't help but smile. "Yes! I'm a happy fellow."

"Then why do you have a worry frown on your forehead?"

"Mario," I stammered. "It's not as simple as you think." I paused for a second. I knew if I gave Mario an opportunity, he would interrupt my confession. "Caroline's pregnant."

"So soon? How do you know this so fast?"

"Caroline didn't get pregnant last night," I paused. "She was pregnant when we got married."

"Oh, I see," Mario muttered. Surprisingly, he did not have a judgmental expression on his face. However, he did seem perplexed. "Did you marry her because you love her or because you are accepting responsibility for the child?"

Without hesitation, I replied, "Both!"

"Are you happy that you are married to such a gorgeous girl?"

"Yes. Of course!"

"You love Caroline?"

"Yes." I glanced at Mario and smiled shyly. "I think I have loved her all of my life." It felt fantastic to finally say the words aloud.

"Then what is the problem?"

"The baby?" I paused. "I don't want to hurt the baby. I'm afraid – last night – I might have . . ."

"You think passion might hurt the baby?" Mario let out another peel of laughter. "You *are* a funny boy. Didn't your father ever talk to you about anything? Making love to your beautiful wife will not hurt the baby. God takes care of babies." As he spoke, Mario added extra flour to his blend.

"I thought . . . a man should," I stammered. "How should I put it? I thought a man had to abstain while his wife is pregnant."

"What? Husbands would go crazy if they could not enjoy their wives for nine months in a row. It would be lunacy!" Mario stopped kneading the bread and directed his attention to me. "You must make love to your wife – many times when she is pregnant – it makes her feel beautiful.

Pregnant women often do not think of themselves as beautiful – but the truth is that pregnant women are the most beautiful women in the world. Worship your wife. Spoil her. She will love you for it. And another secret I will tell you. Pregnant women make the best lovers!"

"Why?"

Mario's vociferous laughter filled the room. "Because they are no longer afraid of getting pregnant!" He winked at me before he continued. "You put lots of pebbles in the jar before the baby comes. Lots of pebbles." He went back to his task at hand, thrusting his fist into the dough. "And Richard, you have it backwards – it is *after* the baby is born that you must abstain. After the baby is born you must give your wife time to heal. It does not take too long – and it certainly will not take nine months."

"Thanks, Mario."

"I have another piece of advice for you, Richard. This advice is not for now – it's for later – when you've been married a while and you are no longer putting lots and lots of pebbles *in* the jar." Again Mario ceased his activities with his hands and turned his attention to me. "There will come a day when – maybe Caroline is not so perfect as she is when you marry her. Maybe her hips get a little big – maybe her breasts are not so firm – maybe she get a little round like my Rosa. When that time comes, you might look at other gorgeous women and think – ah! I want to sample some of that. And maybe you will – maybe you won't. 'Tis your decision to make." Mario made a grand gesture with his hands waving them high in the air. "It is hard to resist temptation – and beautiful ladies are often tempting – sometimes I think they are little devils in disguise – making a man think – not with his heart – but with other parts of his body. In the old country – 'tis often the case – men have wives and they have – how shall I say it – men have maybe one – maybe lots of other women. But here is my advice and I hope you are listening to me, Richard. Years from now – if you cannot resist other beautiful women, then make a promise to yourself that you will always spend the night in bed with your wife. Always go home! Every day! Because the woman who has your children – she is the one who deserves your respect and your nights. And remember, Richard, there will come a time when you get round like Mario, and your hair go bald like mine, and maybe your poker don't stand up so good and strong like it does when you are a young man. When that time comes, you are going to want the loving arms of a good woman – like my Rosa – like your Caroline. At night, when it's cold, you are still going to want to pull her close and snuggle in bed like spoons. If you don't treat her right, maybe she will not be there when you need her most."

I wasn't sure if I should inquire, but I asked the question anyway, "Are you trying to say . . . you have not always been faithful to Rosa?"

"Ah! I was a little afraid you might ask me that question, and since you did I will be honest." He wiped his hands off on a towel. "I make mistake – two – no – three times. I am not a perfect man. I have no excuse for myself – except – I was not strong enough to resist temptation. I was a fool. The guilt – it ate at my heart – it crippled my soul. I do not wish that agony on any man. I am glad my Rosa forgave me."

"I don't think you understand, Mario." I spoke slowly. "There will never be anyone else for me – only Caroline. I will never want any other woman." I boldly stated my words. "I'm going to do everything in my power to make her happy – give her the things she deserves. She is all that matters to me."

Mario slapped me heartily on the back. "You good boy, Richard. You listen to Mario, you will have a good marriage. For now – you just think about the pebbles!"

The conversation with Mario changed my life. It was as if knowing I could not hurt the baby unfettered me. Without question, every night Caroline and I explored each other with a sexual appetite which bordered on obsession. We touched and tasted and savored each other until we were so exhausted we fell asleep entangled as one. But the nights were never enough. I wanted more. During the day, when there was no one around, my hands were constantly exploring Caroline's body. In the morning when she swept the floor, I would come up from behind her, encircle her in my arms, and allow my hands to roam freely over her breasts. I loved the feeling of her nipples protruding through her bodice. She would press the back of her body against me and move her hips in the most tantalizing manner, rubbing me until I would moan with pleasure. She knew what she was doing, and she loved taunting me.

There were other times when she was on the stepladder putting away the can goods, and I slipped into the pantry to be with her. Before she realized I was in the room, my fingers were traveling up her legs and toying with her silk panties, grateful she did not wear stockings. I could feel the goose bumps on her skin created by my fingertips. She shivered with delight from my touch and gracefully stepped off of the ladder and into my arms, kissing me the entire time and promising me with titillating actions of previews to come.

There were even days when Caroline teased me relentlessly with coy looks and quick, private moments when she would slowly slide her hand over the front of my pants. She giggled when she discovered her actions created a large bulge between my legs, and I squirmed uncomfortably because I could not follow through on my urge. When no one was around, she flirted with me and tempted me shamelessly. More often than not, I was unable to contain my craving, and I propelled her into the broom closet or the pantry or the closest available corner, pulled her dress up enough to give me access to her body and pinned her against the wall. She slipped her hands down the back of my pants and squeezed me with her fingers pulling me tightly to her. Our actions were frenzied and fervent – a kaleidoscope of excitement. Together – in a unified rhythm – we climbed to the summit.

As the months passed and Caroline's stomach grew, my desires were not stymied. I couldn't get enough of her. Often I smiled as I thought of my imaginary glass jar – it was rapidly filling with pebbles.

However, as my joy increased with each moment Caroline and I spent together, there was an equally terrifying notion that nagged at the back of my mind. Flashes of childhood memories invaded my thoughts. I could see my mother walking into the hospital. She was slumped over, supported by my father's arm. It was the last time I saw her alive. Pregnancy had killed her. In addition, I knew Caroline's mother had died while giving birth to her. Although I never spoke of my fears, they still plagued me. I was terrified Caroline might suffer the same fate, and she would leave me – not by choice, but by death.

6

Caroline

"Breathe, Caroline!" Rosa demanded. "Breathe like I showed you. It will help."

I was so tired. The pains were coming every minute, and they seemed to last forever. I could barely catch my breath before my stomach tightened like a cast-iron boulder; during the contraction, it felt like the mass was ripping and thrashing its way out of my body. Rosa said it normally took as much as eight to ten hours for an average birth, and I was lucky the baby was coming so quickly. Rosa also told me of her experience – when she gave birth to Leonardo – it took thirty-six hours.

"Thirty-six hours!" I screamed. "I will never live through thirty-six hours of this." Throughout my pregnancy, I thought about the mother I never knew. *Would I live long enough to see my child?*

Rosa chuckled. "You will be fine, dear Caroline. Your baby will not take nearly as long as my Leonardo did. You have perfect hips for delivering babies. And when it is over, you will forget about the pain. It will become a faint memory. I promise! The moment I put your sweet baby in your arms, the pain will go away."

"Richard," Rosa ordered. "Place the damp cloth on her forehead and give her a small ice chip to suck on while she is waiting for the next contraction. Be quick. It will be coming soon."

I was so grateful Richard was with me. Originally, we had discussed going to the hospital, but Rosa had told us she was quite accomplished as a mid-wife; consequently, we elected to have the baby at home. Rosa reassuringly told me a doctor could come to us within ten minutes of a phone call if there was a need. Aside from the fact it saved money to give birth at home, the added bonus of having the baby in my own bedroom meant Richard could be with me. In the hospital, he would not have been allowed in the room.

At first, I thought I would be embarrassed to have Richard see me in such an unladylike manner, and I feared I might behave like a child with tears and screams, but – surprisingly – with Richard by my side, I felt brave. His quiet strength gave me courage.

"Here, Caroline. Take this." Richard slipped a miniature chip of ice between my lips. His face was riddled with tension, but his smile was warm and loving. As I sucked on the ice, he gently rubbed another chip over my lips. The cold water felt soothing.

"Oh, my God! Here comes another one." I bit down on my lip.

"Push, Caroline! Push!" Rosa's voice filled the room.

I shut my eyes, gritted my teeth, and pushed through the pain as hard as I could. I thought my entire insides were going to rip right through me. Would this ever stop? God! Help me! Please make this stop.

"Caroline!" Richard's excited voice broke through the pain. "Oh, sweet Jesus! Keep pushing, Carley! I can see the head!" Richard's jubilation was in his voice. "You can do it, Sweetheart!" He cheered me on. "Oh my!" Richard exclamation stopped abruptly.

"What?" I cried. "What's wrong?"

"Nothing! Nothing's wrong!" Richard replied softly. He was captivated by the miracle unveiling in front of him. "Oh, sweet Jesus! Caroline! I can see it. The baby has brown hair." Tears of joy misted in his eyes. "You can do it! You're almost there, Honey!" His words were spoken in a whisper, but they kept bouncing off of the walls.

Calmly, Rosa spoke, "Richard's right, Caroline. A couple more! You're doing great. Come on! Give me one more."

I didn't think I had one more push in me, but I focused every ounce of energy I had on Richard. Even though I could no longer decipher his words, I could still hear his voice, and I concentrated on it. Closing my eyes, I thought . . . one more! One more! If he could see the baby's hair color, it was almost over. Suddenly the pain changed. It definitely wasn't gone, but it felt as if it were dissipating. "What happened?"

Rosa, who was normally exuberant with her actions and speech, was incredibly calm. "The head is out, Caroline. The worst is over. You're doing great."

I opened my eyes. Richard was standing next to Rosa, staring at me. Tears streamed down his awestruck face. My husband was spellbound, a complete prisoner to what he was witnessing. He tried to speak, but no words came out of his mouth. His mesmerized eyes reflected an immeasurable love. The anxious lines, which had been etched in his brow moments ago, were gone, and his face shone with enlightenment. "Oh, Carley," he whispered – there was a tremor in his voice. The corners of his mouth turned upward, and Richard added, "He's beautiful! He's perfect!"

"It's a boy?" I asked.

"Yes!" Rosa answered. "You have a beautiful baby boy. Richard's right. He is perfect."

In less than an instant, Richard was at my side, kneeling by the bed with his face on my cheek. "Thank you, Carley! Thank you, darling!" His lips continued to move but the words were barely audible. "Thank you, Lord. Thank you, dear God, for this miracle." Richard buried his face on my chest.

I stroked his head with my free hand, and I, too, began to cry. Moments later, Rosa put our baby in my arms. Richard gently curled up on the mattress next to me.

"Oh, Richard!" I exclaimed. "He looks like you! Look! See the little dimple in the middle of his chin – it's exactly like yours. And he has your eyes. He is beautiful!"

"So! Have you decided on a name?" Rosa asked.

"Yes." I replied without hesitation. "He is named after his father. Richard Malone, Jr." I smiled at my husband. "That's okay with you, isn't it?"

"Of course," he replied. "We'll call him Ricky – like you use to call me."

2

Richard burst into our room – exhilaration written upon his face. I was on the bed, reading *Dr. Spock's Baby and Child Care* book Rosa had given me, and nursing two-week old Little Ricky. My husband's sudden entrance jarred the baby from his task at hand. He pulled off the nipple, looked around for a moment, and then dutifully went back to consuming his morning meal.

Before I had time to say a word, Richard began to speak. "Mario liked all of my ideas. I told him how he could make more money if he offered more variety of foods – not just pizza – but maybe spaghetti and lasagna and rigatoni and – heck – maybe even hamburgers like that McDonald's fellow. I mentioned if he opened the diner in the morning, he could serve breakfast. Route One is a major road between Philadelphia to New York. We get all kinds of traffic – all day long. We don't have to cater to the locals during the dinner hour. I told him about how a breakfast and lunch menu would attract the travelers. The diner is right on the highway. Thousands of people drive by – hungry people!" Richard could not contain his elation. He paced around the room, moving his hands through the air like Mario did when he was excited. The habit was obviously rubbing off on my husband. Richard continued, his voice growing increasingly more excited. "I also told him about my ideas for a new ambiance – put in a few booths and some free-standing tables – white tablecloths and napkins, candles, some flowers. He could even serve wine and beer with the meals. If we rearrange the room, we could fit a dozen booths and tables in that space. Some set for two, some for four and maybe one or two larger tables for bigger groups. I showed him – on a piece of paper – a layout for the room, then I explained to him how he could borrow a little money from the bank – it wouldn't take too much to make all of the changes. He could get rid of the old ice box and invest in a refrigerator, a stove with more burners, a new oven – maybe some nicer flatware to make the tables look a little fancier. Get some music piped into the room – play all of your Frank Sinatra records." Richard sat on the edge of the bed, touched the baby tenderly and then kissed me before continuing. "Do you know what he said, Carley?" Richard didn't wait for a response. "Mario said he would seriously consider all of the changes if I promised to stay and work with him. He said – if the place is going to be open all day and half of the night, he would need lots of help. And if my ideas worked, he'd give us some of the profits."

I had never seen Richard so animated. Even as a kid, when he moved up to my reading group in class or beat Jerry Adams in a marbles marathon or reeled in a big fish on the line, he never exhibited this much jubilation. Richard had always been quietly proud of his achievements – never boastful, nor did he flaunt his victories or successes. Part of me was thrilled for him, yet another part of me was disappointed. In fact, there was a gnawing aggravation eating at my stomach. To my surprise, I was angry with Richard. My husband had promised to wait to discuss these ideas with Mario. I had wanted to be with him and share in the discussion; after all, several of the ideas were *mine*. If I were truly honest with myself, I was jealous Richard had passed them off as his ideas and had approached Mario without me.

Richard did not seem to notice my quiet demeanor. He continued to ramble, "Even though I repeatedly told Mario Sunday's traffic would produce tons of customers, he and Rosa refuse to even consider keeping the restaurant open on God's day – especially not Sunday morning." Richard continued as he paced around the room. He reiterated, "Rosa emphatically said, 'Sunday morning is for church! It is a day of rest and praising our Lord.' I tried to compromise with Rosa and Mario with . . . no breakfast on Sunday – maybe open for late lunch and dinner – but Mario is stubborn, and he 100-percent supports his wife's opinion. If Mario said it once, he said it a dozen times, 'Sunday is God's day!' They refuse to work on Sunday even if it means losing money."

Richard raised his voice in triumph. "But he likes all of the rest of my ideas! All of them! Isn't it wonderful, Carley?" For the first time, Richard noticed I was not as enthusiastic about his news as he had assumed I would be. "What's wrong, Caroline? Is the baby okay?" He peeked at his son, savoring the image of Ricky nursing from my breast. Tenderly Richard touched the baby's cheek. "Our little prince is growing bigger every day! He is such a beautiful boy." Richard smiled. When he looked at my expression, he inquired, "The baby looks content. Why do you look so unhappy?"

"I thought you were going to wait for me before you approached Mario with *our* ideas." I couldn't help myself. I slipped the word "our" into my sentence and pronounced it a little louder than the rest of my oration because Richard had so blatantly referred to all of the ideas as *his*. To my chagrin, Richard didn't seem to notice my choice of words. "Why didn't you wait for me?"

"Sweetheart," Richard stroked my hair as he spoke and smiled pleasantly. "I intended to wait, but this morning, the timing was right. Mario happened to mention he was a little bored with making pizza all of the time, and – before I knew it – the words came out of my mouth. Mario was acutely interested in my ideas, and we discussed them at length." Richard's blue eyes were sparkling. He glanced at the baby and then directed his attention back to me. "Besides, Caroline, you need to concentrate on the baby. You're a mother now. You should be focused on Little Ricky."

"You don't understand," I interrupted. "I *want* to be a part of it."

"Caroline," Richard's voice was firm. "You focus on taking care of Ricky, and I'll concentrate on taking care of our family."

I felt as if I was still in school and the teacher had dismissed my interpretation of a Shakespeare reading. Before I could say another word, Richard had kissed me quickly on the forehead and left the room, humming merrily as he shut the door.

I was fuming inside.

By the end of the day, I had worked myself into quite an emotional state. While Richard was readying himself for bed, I could barely contain my fury. He was still in a wonderful mood – chattering far more than the norm. He even cranked up the phonograph and placed the needle on the LP. When Sinatra's velvety voice filled the room, Richard began to dance as he moved across the floor. It galled me that my husband had brushed my feelings aside so easily as if my opinion was of little importance to him. Although Richard and I had never had a fight, I was ready to do battle, but I needed strategy as to how to broach the subject.

While doing a Cha-cha step, my husband meandered over to the corner and looked in the bassinet. He bent down and tenderly gave Ricky a kiss. His actions did not disturb the baby's slumber. "Hello, my sweet son. You look as if you've had a peaceful day. Obviously, Mommy is taking good care of you." Richard spoke merrily as he undid the buttons on his shirt. He sauntered over to where I was sitting on the bed, reached for my hand, nibbled playfully on my fingertips and then asked in his best Gary Grant voice, "Will you do me the honor of this dance?"

The frustration and resentment – which had been building inside of me all day – immediately vanished. I looked into his eyes and my love clashed head on with my anger. My love won the battle. As I placed my hand in his, my heart melted toward him. From the moment I met Richard, he always had the power to make me smile – even on the inside. I could think of no malicious words to say – they all took flight. I wanted to be in his arms, and I wanted his merry mood to rub off on me. Leaning my head on her shoulder, I joined him. Together we swayed to the music.

3

By our 19th birthday, all of the renovations in Mario and Rosa's eatery had been completed. There was a fresh coat of paint on the inside and the outside of the restaurant. Six booths and six freestanding tables – draped in white linens – were strategically placed in the room. New plates, which had been purchased along with silverware, water goblets and wine glasses, were set at all the tables. The new appliances were in place and functioning to capacity. Richard and Mario had hooked up a temporary sound system so soft music could be heard while customers were dining, and a *Grand Opening* sign was posted on the roof so drivers could see it as they traveled on Route One.

The breakfast crowd was adequate and kept us relatively busy with orders of eggs, bacon, sausage, pancakes and lots of coffee. Most of those customers sat at the counter. I knew before the morning was over, Mario needed to invest in a larger coffeepot; the one he had was definitely not sufficient. The lunch crowd also ordered hastily; most of them wanted to take their food on the road. Then there was a lull for several hours. Richard busied himself cleaning parts of the kitchen – which were already spotless. He continued to wipe the counters, reposition table settings, and wash dishes that were already clean. The more time ticked by, the more anxious and irritable my husband became.

In a whisper, Richard admitted to me, "What if I was wrong? What if people don't come? Mario took out a loan to make these changes. What have I done?" No matter how encouraging I was, Richard wasn't listening.

Then, to our amazement, at 6:00, there were suddenly customers arriving in waves, and every table was full. Mario and Rosa were losing their minds in the kitchen as they madly tried to keep the orders straight. Thankfully, Ricky slept soundly in his bassinet during the entire dinner rush, which allowed both Richard and me the opportunity to greet the customers, take their orders, serve them, and clean the tables when they were finished. The four of us worked like a well-oiled machine. We had reason to celebrate when the last customer closed the door behind him.

Mario and Rosa were hugging each other and cheering with delight. I glanced at Richard. He was beaming.

Weeks slipped by and the restaurant continued to succeed. The four of us worked long, grueling hours. We knew we could never keep up the pace. Mario and Richard decided we needed to divide our time more wisely. Neither the breakfast nor the lunch shifts were as hectic as the dinner shift; therefore, Mario decided Richard and I could handle the morning customers, and he and Rosa would work the lunch hours. Richard's cooking skills for the breakfast menu were quite good, and I was more than able to take the orders and deliver the food. Ricky, who was learning how to sit up, stayed patiently in his high chair. Customers enjoyed interacting with him. Some made faces and prattled in baby talk, while others sang to him and a few even offered to read him a book. Ricky was a delightful, gregarious child. People were naturally drawn to him. By 9:00 each day, Ricky rubbed his eyes – the sign he was ready for his morning nap. Typically, he slept until Mario and Rosa came for the lunch shift at 11:30; at that time, Richard and I would either go for a drive, run errands, take Ricky for a walk in the buggy, or hibernate in the backroom for a couple of hours of quiet before the dinner rush descended upon us. Although I was often exhausted, I was truly happy with my life.

4

In mid-May, Richard and I had our first fight. Because the encounter began in such a pleasant manner, I didn't see the argument coming, which made it all the more hurtful. When I entered the room, I discovered my husband on the bed with the baby. Richard had Calvin's old baseball card collection spread out on the bedspread, and he was flashing cards in front of Ricky, who playfully reached for them as Richard moved the cards around in a circular motion. Richard was captivating his son's attention by rattling off the stats on each player.

"Son! This is Babe Ruth." Richard never spoke to the baby in gibberish. My husband always spoke to our son as if he were talking to an adult. "He was a real power hitter. During his baseball career, *The Babe* hit 714 home runs. That's a record – no player will ever beat it. And do you know what else, my son? Babe Ruth played in over seventy games where he hit *at least* two home runs." Richard elevated his voice when he realized Ricky was enjoying the interaction. "Do you know how hard it is to hit a home run? Let me tell you, it's pretty darn hard! *The Babe* was so good at it – pitchers were afraid to pitch to him. Do you know what happens when a pitcher is afraid to pitch to a batter?" Ricky's eyes widened as his father's voice rose with the question. "Well, son, I'll tell you what happens. The batter often gets a free walk to first base, and *The Babe* had 2,056 bases on balls during his career. How about *that* for a pretty amazing stat?" Richard picked up another card. "Some people say *The Babe* was the greatest man to ever play the game, but my mother liked this guy." Richard held up his Joe DiMaggio card. "Some people call him *The Yankee Clipper*, probably because he moves with incredible grace when he is out in the field catching those fly balls. When I was a little boy – about the time I met your mother," Richard glanced over at me and gave me a wink and a smile. "Joe DiMaggio played baseball for the New York Yankees. He's been playing ball for fourteen years – and he has been with the Yankees for *all* of those years. They'll never trade him." Ricky seemed completely mesmerized by his father's voice. He cooed and gurgled, which were wonderfully warm sounds that encouraged his father to continue. "But *this* card is a real prize." Richard sorted through the stack of cards and pulled another one out of the pile. He waved it slowly in front of the baby.

I leaned against the door jam and savored the one-sided discussion between my husband and our son. From the moment our child was born, Richard was fabulous with the baby. He seemed so natural. I always thought men were ill at ease or even distant when it came to children, but Richard spent every available minute with our son.

"Your Uncle Calvin," Richard spoke as he held up another card. "In 1941, your Uncle Calvin knew this guy was going to be a great player. He listened to his first game on the radio – that was his rookie year. This guy," Richard danced the card in front of Ricky's grasp. "This guy is a great left-handed first baseman for the St. Louis Cardinals. He's still with them. *Stan the Man*! He's been playing nine years, and Musial is still going strong. Do you know what's special about this guy?" Ricky's eyes widened; he let out an enthusiastic coo as he reached for the card. "*Stan the Man* was born in Pennsylvania – like your daddy. Except Donora, the little town Stan came from, is south of Pittsburgh, and Daddy was born in a town north of Pittsburgh." With careful hands, Richard gathered all of the cards in one pile. He patted them until all of the sides were uniform in the stack. "These cards once belonged to my brother, your Uncle Calvin. He was going to give them to his son." Richard's voice no longer had the gleeful glint to it – the jolly inflections were gone, and his words became more somber. "When your Uncle Calvin went to war, he gave these cards to me for safe keeping until he returned." Pensively, Richard exhaled. "But Calvin didn't come back from the war." Richard touched the cards as if they were a priceless treasure. "These cards were my brother's prized possessions. And some day – when you are a big boy – I will give them to you so you can save them for your son." Richard leaned over and kissed Ricky on the cheek.

I chuckled as much to myself as to lighten the mood. "Jeepers! Richard! I've been a mother for five months. Suddenly – you are turning me into a grandmother."

My comment seemed to lift Richard's spirits. He laughed too. "And what a beautiful grandmother your mother will be, right Ricky?"

In response to his father's question, Ricky cooed and spit out a few "da" syllables.

"Richard," I walked to the bed and sat on the edge. "I have a great idea. Why don't we take Ricky back home? We can introduce him to his grandfathers. It would be so nice to go home. I'm sure Rosa and Mario would let us take a few days."

"No!" Richard said firmly. He didn't make eye contact when he spoke the word. Abruptly, he stood up and walked into the bathroom, slamming the door behind him.

I was shocked by his rapid, decisive and negative reaction. Richard's loud one-word response and the equally earsplitting noise the door made when he slammed it startled the baby. Little Ricky began to cry. Too stunned to do anything else, I picked the baby up and tried to sooth him. I could hear my husband banging things in the bathroom. At times, it sounded as if he were hitting the wall with his fist. Finally, he opened the door. Defiantly, he stared at me.

I refused to cower under his gaze. With as much composure as I could muster, I began to speak, "I know things were pretty bad with my father and yours when we left town, but so much time has passed. It's been nearly a year. My father has a horrible temper, and I know he can be intimidating, but I'm sure he would love to see his beautiful grandson. And your father," I paused. "Did you ever tell him I was pregnant? Does he even realize he is a grandfather? Don't you miss him?"

"When I said *no*, I meant no!" Although Richard's voice was steady and he appeared calm, his words were disturbingly stern. "On the day I asked you to go away with me, I said we were *never* going to go back. *Ever*! And I meant it! I won't change my mind." He hesitated a fraction of a moment. "And I forbid you to go alone."

"What?" I shrieked. "You *forbid* me!" I totally lost control of my patience. I carried Ricky back to the bassinet and gently placed him on his back. The baby sensed my tension; as a result, he began to cry again. Comforting my child was a lost cause. I did not try to console him. Instead, I whirled around and faced Richard. "You cannot *forbid* me to do anything!"

"I'm your husband!" Richard's voice was raised in anger. It rebounded off of the walls. "You will do what I tell you!"

I was too shocked to speak. *Who was this man?* Finally, I reclaimed my voice. "If I want to go home, by God, I *will* go home, and you can't stop me." I stormed out of the room thankful it was Sunday evening and no one was in the restaurant.

For a solid week, Richard and I avoided each other as much as possible – even at night. The first time our bodies touched in bed, he cursed and mumbled under his breath. Then, without a word, he jerked a blanket off of the bed, grabbed his pillow, and stalked out of the room. In the morning, I found him sleeping on the restaurant floor. While we worked our breakfast shift, he barked orders at me and grumbled the entire time. When Rosa and Mario arrived for the lunch shift, Richard got in his car and didn't return until 5:00 for the dinner shift. The same pattern continued throughout the week.

I missed watching him play with Ricky. I missed the wonderfully smooth way we worked together during the breakfast hours. It was as if we had been able to read each other's minds, and when the day was over, we both had a fabulous sense of accomplishment. I missed the way he made me laugh even when I was bone tired. I missed sleeping next to him in bed, and I missed the way he wrapped me in his arms, pulling me into the curve of his body. I missed his warm breath on my neck. I missed the feel of his skin pressed against mine. I missed the way he often woke me in the darkness by tenderly touching me in secret places – places only he knew – which created a desire inside of me. Quietly, so as not to disturb the sleeping baby, we moved together as one – reaching the summit simultaneously and then collapsing into each other's embrace – without a word being spoken – then peacefully fell back to sleep again. Most of all – I missed how safe I felt when I was with him.

By Saturday afternoon, I was in tears. Around 3:30, during the hiatus between the lunch and dinner crowd, Rosa found me sobbing into my pillow. I confided in her and told Rosa how terrified I was at the thought Richard might get in his Chrysler and never return. She rejected my fears and gave me her lace handkerchief so I could wipe my eyes.

"You don't understand, Rosa." I blew my nose before continuing. "Richard doesn't love me, and nothing I do will change that. He married me because of the baby." No matter how hard I tried to push them back, the tears returned and trailed down my cheeks. "I've known Richard all of my life – and we've been married almost a year – and he has never said it – not even once."

"Said what?" Rosa inquired.

"He has never said 'I love you.' Never!"

"Words! Bah!" Rosa threw her hands up in the air. "Words are useless. Anyone can say those words! They mean nothing!" Again Rosa waved her hands as if dismissing the need to say it again. "Men are such strange, crippled creatures." Rosa declared. "Often they speak with actions instead of words. Sometimes they do not know how to express from the heart." Rosa reached for my hand and tenderly stroked it. Her voice became calm and reassuring. "I know you and Richard for only a short time, but I know – all of the way to my soul – Richard loves you. I see it in his eyes and in the way he looks at you when you do not even realize he is looking at you. His face shines with pride and wonder and joy. A beautiful glow comes over him whenever you walk into the room. And when you smile in his direction, any fool can see he stands taller, more confident and seems to burst with happiness. I have even seen him tremble when he reaches out to touch you – such a simple gesture, but it speaks volumes. It's as if he truly can't believe such a rare jewel as you has agreed to share your life with him." Rosa patted my hand again. "Can't you hear him? Your Richard screams *I love you* in a million different ways. Maybe he no use his voice to say the words." Rosa gently tapped my chest. "You must listen with your heart, dear Caroline, and you must feel his love through his touch and his actions." Rosa cupped my chin in her hand and gently forced me to look at her. "Maybe – one day – he will say the words, but until then – you should not worry so much about words. You must trust that his heart is yours."

"What should I do, Rosa? I don't want to fight with him. How can I fix it?"

Rosa grinned mischievously. "You leave that to Rosa. I am a good ally." She picked up the handkerchief and dabbed at my tears. "You go make yourself beautiful. Put on a pretty dress. Maybe put on a little perfume behind your ears and between your breasts." She winked.

When Richard returned at 5:00, he found two of Rosa's friends from church donned in aprons and setting the tables for the dinner hour and another one of Rosa's friends singing to Ricky as she tried to get him to go to sleep. My husband was so baffled, he didn't say a word when Rosa shoved a picnic basket in his hands and gave him orders. "You take your beautiful Caroline out for a picnic dinner. It is a lovely day – a glorious May evening. There will be a full moon tonight. It will light up the sky. You go! Find someplace private. There's a bottle of wine in that basket. You drink it. You talk."

"But I need to help Mario."

"Bah!" Rosa waved him away. "You are no good to Mario these days. You are in such a bad mood, you scare the customers away." Again, Rosa waved him toward the door. "You and Caroline have been working too hard. You are young. You need some time for fun. You go out. We will take care of the restaurant and your little Ricky. Everything will be fine. Now go!" Rosa practically pushed us out the door.

For thirty minutes, Richard drove the car and not one word was exchanged between us. I don't think either one of us knew where we were going; in fact, I think we might even have been lost. Finally, Richard pulled into a vacant lot and put the car in park. When I looked out the window, I could see a river. There was no one in sight. Richard got out of the Chrysler, opened the trunk, and picked up the blanket and the picnic basket. He, then, came around to my side of the car and opened the door for me. My husband seemed far more tentative than normal, and his eyes seemed to silently plead for me to join him. I followed him down to the river's edge. He spread the blanket on the ground and motioned for me to sit.

Richard opened the wine, poured some in two glasses, and handed one to me. Still silent, he sat on the blanket, gazed out across the water, and sipped on his wine. In the distant, there was a lone sailboat moving with the breeze. As if in a trance, we both stared at it. An eternity passed before he whispered, "I'm sorry, Caroline." He wouldn't look at me. He continued to stare at the river and watched the sailboat traveling peacefully out of sight. The sun hung in the air slightly above the horizon, and the rays seemed to cast thousands of diamonds over the water. They sparkled vibrantly. The scene was mesmerizing. Richard repeated his words; this time, his voice was clear and slightly louder. "I'm sorry I yelled at you."

I felt an enormous wave of relief wash over me. Softly, I put my hand over his. "It's all right, Richard."

"No," he interrupted. "Please don't talk. Let me finish. I need to say this." He raised his head so his eyes were connected to mine. "When you said you wanted to go home, I felt as if my worst nightmare had come true. I know – if you go home – you'll see your father's house, your father's servants, your father's luxuries, and the grandeur that surrounds him. Our lives pale in comparison. Look at me! I have nothing – I have nothing to offer you. We have no home. Heck! We live in the backroom of a restaurant. For God's sake – you grew up with marble tile floors and mahogany banisters and a porcelain bathtub. Your father is one of the few people in town who owns a television set. I've never even seen one! You were surrounded by luxuries, and I can't even imagine owning things like that – things you took for granted! With me – you have one room and the furniture isn't even ours! Instead of a tub, you have to wash up in a sink. We have *nothing*. And – on top of that – you work so hard – probably harder than any servant in your father's employ." He sighed. "I'm afraid if you go home, you will never come back to me."

"Richard," I interrupted.

Before I could continue, he motioned me to stop. "Let me finish. If I don't say it all at once, I may not have the courage to say it at all." He reached into his pocket and pulled out an envelope. As he fiddled with it in his hands, he continued. "I've thought about you and the baby and the argument we had this week, and I know I was wrong to tell you that you can't go home." He handed the envelope to me. "Open it. There's enough money for a ticket on Greyhound – enough money for you and the baby. If you want to go home – you should go home. I won't stop you."

I opened the envelope. Richard was right. There was a wad of crumpled bills: a five, a couple of ten-dollar bills and lots of ones. I looked at him. Tears welled up in my eyes. I pressed my lips together and took several steady breaths before speaking. "If I go, will you go with me?" I muttered trying to keep control of my quaking voice.

"No," Richard barely whispered the word. There was no anger in his voice, only resignation. "When we left and I told you I was never going back – I meant it. I won't go back there. Not *ever* again."

I handed Richard the envelope. "Then I won't go either." I moved closer to him. "Don't you understand, Richard? *This* is my home now – *here* – with you! I've never been happier in my life. That one room of ours, which you so despondently call *nothing,* is heaven to me. Where you see poverty, I see joy. When you see a lack of luxuries – I see warmth. You and the baby – you're what matters to me. You're what I want – *you're* what I need. Don't you know, Richard? I don't care about anything except being with you." Slowly I wrapped my fingers securely around his hand. "I miss my father. Until you, he was the only family I had. I didn't know any differently, and I'd be lying if I said I didn't miss him." I paused, fearing the mention of my father would throw a dark cloud over our conversation, but Richard didn't react. "Mario and Rosa have been wonderful to us. The longer we stay here, the more they feel like family. They treat us with kindness and respect. I never had a mother – Rosa makes me feel loved – like a mother loves a child. Richard, don't you understand? I have everything I've ever wanted – right here – with you."

Richard turned his face to mine. I could see a mist of tears mirrored in his eyes. He blinked several times to keep them from spilling out onto his cheeks. "Carley," he whispered. "I don't know what I would do without you." Ever so gently, he used his fingertips to brush strands of my hair away from my face. His index finger stroked my cheek and traveled down the bridge of my nose and then lingered on my lips. "Every dream I've ever had is centered around you." The tension, which had been in his voice moments ago, vanished; instead, his words were soft and sweet like a flute playing in the distant. "You're the best thing that's ever happened to me." He kissed me tenderly on the lips. "I can't imagine my life without you."

As was always the case when Richard touched me in that manner, I began to feel a rush of heat spread through my veins. I leaned closer toward him and parted my lips invitingly. Normally, when desire swept over us, I became consumed by a yearning, which originated in the pit of my stomach and spread like a wild fire throughout my body. This was no exception. The faster my heart beat and my pulse raced, the more frantic I became to quicken the pace in hopes of drawing his body to mine as soon as humanly possible. Whenever Richard touched me in this way, there was always such a momentous craving and a sense of urgency for immediate satisfaction. I wanted him to strip my clothes and take me right there on the blanket with the sun's light fading in the distance. Surprisingly, he did not seem to want to hurry the moment. As my breathing began to quicken, his became more stable. I opened my eyes and watched his actions. To my amazement, I noticed Richard's fingers were trembling exactly as Rosa had described. He was slowly and deliberately undoing the buttons on my bodice, and there was a tremor in his touch. My husband seemed fascinated by the curve of my neck and the swell of my breasts as they heaved under the restriction of the garment. Watching him move in slow motion augmented my desire, but I refrained from taking any action. Instead, I locked my eyes to his and savored the moment. Everything Rosa had said to me suddenly flashed through my mind, and all of her words made sense. I had been seeking verbal confirmation of my husband's love, but I was searching for it incorrectly. The evidence was not found in palpable words – the proof of his commitment and his emotions was always crystal clear – even in the beginning. *Richard loved me!* He had *always* loved me. He had been steadfast and unwavering in his devotion. My husband's quiet fortitude was a constant source of strength for both of us. Even when we were kids, he had never run away from me – *I* was the fool who had left him.

"You are so beautiful, Carley. When I look at you, I still can't believe you are my wife." He seemed in a trance as he spoke.

My entire body tingled with an electric pulse that zipped through me like bolts of lightning. His touch ignited me, and I relished the sensations as I watched him tenderly and slowly remove my clothes. As if dealing with a precious, breakable treasure, my husband gently laid me on the blanket. Richard looked at me like he was seeing me for the first time. In awe, he ran his hands over my bare breasts. I was as equally captivated by the expression on his face as I was by his adoring touch. His eyes glistened with elation, and his demeanor was filled with radiant adulation. Involuntarily, I arched my body because I could no longer control my craving for him. Still, he avoided any frantic actions. Determined to treasure the moment like a condemned man savoring his last meal, his fingers moved leisurely over my body.

"You love me!" Although my voice trembled and my words were barely more than a whisper, there was no questioning tone in them. "You really do love me!" I repeated my words more firmly the second time I spoke.

"Of course," Richard smiled. "Was there ever any doubt?"

The urgency enveloped us. Without hesitation, Richard stripped his clothes and encircled me in his arms. To be in his embrace was like being in a magical kingdom filled with my heart's desire. As the sun drifted below the horizon, we made love on that blanket – without apprehension or inhibition.

5

Even though it took several weeks to be certain, I instinctively knew I was pregnant the night Richard and I made love by the river. Two and a half months later, when the doctor confirmed my suspicions, I was overjoyed. It was the happiest news of my life. Our first baby had been conceived in a car on a night of unplanned passion. I had feared banishment and rejection when I had told my father and Richard, but *this* baby was conceived in mutual love and a tender passion on an evening I would hold dear to my heart for the rest of my life.

When I told Richard we were expecting another baby around Valentine's Day, he was instantly thrilled. Rosa and Mario were equally happy for us. As the months slipped by and my pregnancy began to show, I was certain the baby was a girl. Richard and I had already chosen her name. We intended to call her Victoria, after Richard's mother.

The larger I grew, the more Richard wanted to touch me. He had been equally as obsessed with my abdomen when I was pregnant with Little Ricky; however, he was even *more* vocal regarding this baby. My husband talked to the child as if it were in the room. At night, when we curled up in each other's arms, Richard insisted I sleep without my nightgown because he adored laying his hands directly on my stomach. I felt fat and terribly unattractive, but he repeatedly told me I was the most gorgeous woman he had ever seen. When I looked into his eyes, all I saw was love reflected in them. In spite of the fact I was beginning to feel awkward and uncomfortable with my size, his words and actions made me feel beautiful.

Needless to say, we were concerned about our financial situation and the fact we would soon have two children to feed, but our eternal optimism kept our trepidation at a minimum. Richard was saving every penny we made at the restaurant, and he stated confidently that eventually we would have a home of our own and a more financially secure life. My husband continued to promise – one day he would make all of my dreams come true.

7

Richard

A couple of weeks before Christmas, I found Caroline doubled over in pain. She claimed it felt as if a sharp knife was repeatedly stabbing at her spine. I immediately thought she was going into premature labor, but Caroline insisted it didn't feel anything like the pain when Ricky was born. I insisted we call a doctor. When he arrived, the doctor asked me to leave so he could examine Caroline. I took Ricky out of the crib and left the room. It felt like an eternity before the doctor came out to talk to me.

To my horror, the doctor informed me Caroline was – in spite of her refusal to believe him – in premature labor. Thankfully, the doctor said there was very little dilation. He impressed upon me —in order to assure a healthy delivery at the appropriate time – Caroline needed to spend the remainder of her pregnancy in bed. Lift nothing – do nothing – total bed-rest. He also insisted she was not – under any circumstances – allowed to pick up Ricky, who had recently taken his first steps. I was terrified, but I did not want Caroline to see my fear; I concealed my anxiety with a brave façade.

That day, Rosa enlisted a team of her friends from church to assist in Ricky's care, and a *Help Wanted* sign was placed in the window of the restaurant. Before the day was over, there was a waitress hired for both the breakfast and the dinner shifts. We were all relieved.

We developed a routine. Rosa spent the mornings with my wife. She cooked breakfast for Caroline, feed Ricky, read stories to them both, and did light chores. After serving them lunch, Rosa worked at the restaurant while Caroline and the baby took a nap. In the afternoon – if it was warm enough – I played with Ricky in the yard or took him with me when I ran errands. Like clockwork – at 5:00 – I fed the baby, gave him a bath and dressed him in his pajamas. During this ritual, Caroline habitually read the evening paper aloud, and we often discussed the current events of the day. More often than not, the headlines were monopolized by the war in Korea.

Six months ago, North Korean troops, which were ruled by communists, invaded South Korea and were headed for Seoul. The United Nations, which had been formed at the end of World War II, demanded the North Korean troops retreat. When they did not withdraw, the UN asked its members to come to South Korea's aid. The United States was the first to commit troops to block the migration of communism. Sixteen additional countries followed their example, and more than three dozen countries lent their support by sending aid in the form of food and military supplies. The Soviet Union took the opposite stand by sending military equipment to the North Koreans, and China also sided with them.

American's greatest fear loomed over our heads – Communism was spreading.

"Richard, what will happen to us if you are drafted?"

"Don't think about it, Caroline. You know how worked up you get whenever we talk about the war. Try to relax." I kissed her on the cheek and took the front page of the newspaper out of her hands. "So far, we've been lucky. Let's not worry about something that hasn't happened." To lighten the mood, I handed Caroline the comics and asked her to read them. "What does Charlie Brown and Dennis the Menace have to say today?" My wife knew my tactics, but instead of fighting the inevitable, she read from the section and allowed the conversation to drop.

Christmas Day was rather uneventful. Originally, we had planned to join Mario and Rosa at their home for a formal and festive dinner, but Caroline was not allowed out of bed for more than a few minutes at a time, so our celebration was spent crowded in our bedroom. My wife gave Ricky and me matching shirts she had made from remnant material she'd purchased at the local Woolworth's. We gave Mario and Rosa a picture frame for the photograph that was taken last summer of all of us on our trip to Coney Island. Mario and Rosa gave us an oak rocking chair – on the seat there was a soft needlepoint cushion, which Rosa had made by hand. It read, "God Bless Our Home." They gave Ricky a new rattle, a winter coat, and several adorable outfits. Our son had grown so much in the last couple of months, none of his clothes fit anymore. We were humbled by Rosa and Mario's generosity.

After Rosa and Mario left for the evening, I gave Caroline my gift. She slowly unwrapped the package. When she saw the silver-plated brush, comb and mirror set inside the box, she examined each piece and noticed that all three pieces were engraved with her initials. Tears welled up in her eyes.

"Richard," she murmured. "They're beautiful." She stared at them in awe.

I picked up the brush and began to use it on her hair, tenderly stroking the strains. "I noticed you always use my old beat up comb – the one that's missing a half a dozen teeth. I figured, when we left in such a hurry, you must have forgotten to pack yours."

"You're right. I did forget."

"You have never complained." I continued to brush her coal black hair, watching it shine with every stroke. "You never even asked if we could buy a cheap brush or a new comb."

"Richard," she spoke through her tears. "We can't afford this."

"I promised you beautiful things. I intend to live up to that promise." Gently, I kissed her on the neck. I loved the smell of my wife's skin. "You're not to worry about money, Caroline. You relax and concentrate on our baby. Our little Victoria needs two more months to grow inside of you."

Four days later, while I was cooking the breakfast orders, I heard Caroline screaming in the backroom. I left four slices of bacon, two links of sausage, several orders of scrambled eggs, and three pancakes on the stove. After racing into our bedroom, I found Caroline sitting in bed with a puddle of liquid surrounding her.

"My water's broken." Terror covered her face. "Oh my God! Richard, the baby's coming. It's way too soon! What shall we do?"

"It's going to be okay." I tried as hard as I could to remain calm. "Mario's here. He's going to call the doctor, and Rosa will be back in a couple of minutes."

2

Although the doctor often delivered babies at the homes of expectant parents, because of Caroline's premature labor, he insisted I bring my wife to the hospital immediately. He knew our baby was at least seven weeks early, maybe more, and he wanted the best possible environment for the delivery. While Mario and Rosa closed the restaurant, I drove like a madman to the hospital in Newark. The doctor met me at the door. Caroline was placed in a wheelchair and taken from me. I didn't even get a chance to say good-bye. My head throbbed as involuntary memories of my mother's death flashed through my mind. As if it were yesterday, I could see my mother and father walking through the hospital doors. My mother was leaning heavily on my father's arm. Calvin was driving the car, and I was frantically trying to roll down the window of the Chrysler in order to scream out to my mother. The memory washed over me like it was fresh and raw and oh so painful. When I sat in the chair, I laid my head in my hands and prayed. Over and over, I asked God to help my wife. "Please don't let anything happen to Caroline or the baby. Please, Lord! I can't make it without her."

I had no idea how much time passed. Minutes? Hours? Mario and Rosa, with Little Ricky sleeping in her arms, were also with me. It felt like an eternity before the doctor finally came. Upon seeing him enter the room, Rosa reached for my hand and squeezed it encouragingly. As we stood simultaneously, Mario made the sign of the cross on his chest. I could hear Rosa whispering her own private prayer. I thought I'd go insane before the doctor finally spoke.

"The baby is rather small," the doctor said. "A little shy of four and a half pounds."

"She's alive?" I asked.

"I'm afraid your wife was wrong in her prediction." The doctor smiled. "Your baby is not a girl. It's a boy. He's small, but he is a fighter. Your son is going to have to spend a little time in our incubator, but I think the odds are pretty good he will make it."

"An incubator?" I was still stunned by the news. "What's that?"

"It is an enclosed crib which maintains a constant temperature to keep the baby warm. When he is a little bigger and strong enough to come into the real world, we will take him out."

"How long will he have to stay in there?"

"I don't think it will be a long time." The doctor cleaned his glasses as he spoke. "Like I said, your son is quite a fighter. He's a stubborn little guy – came out screaming like he had the lungs of a four-year-old. His color is good. He might be smaller than normal, but he is fully developed."

"My wife?" I knew I would not be able to enjoy the news about our son until I knew Caroline was going to be okay.

"Your wife is doing quite well. She's been asking for you." He patted me on the shoulder. "If you would like, you can go see her now, but don't stay too long. She's had quite a day and needs some sleep."

Rosa began to cry joyful tears as she embraced me, and Mario's laughter filled the room. "God has answered our prayers," Rosa repeated several times as she hugged me tightly. "You go now, Richard. We will take Ricky home – you no worry about him. You go see your baby and Caroline. You give her our love."

After kissing Ricky on the forehead and Rosa on her cheek, I received a bear-like hug from Mario, who grabbed me by the shoulders and planted a firm kiss on both sides of my face. "You give our love to your Caroline and the new baby. We take care of everything else. You no worry about anything." Mario's voice boomed with enthusiasm.

I followed the doctor to Caroline's room. My wife was in a wheelchair waiting for me so we could go together to the nursery and see our new son.

We watched him through the glass. The doctor was right. Our boy was small enough to fit in a shoebox. The doctor's description of his personality was also accurate. Our baby did appear to be a fighter. Instead of resting quietly in his incubator, his arms and legs moved actively and his eyes were alert as he watched us from his protective environment.

Elated tears streamed down Caroline's face. "He's our special child, Richard. He's our child conceived in love." She reached for my hand, pulled it to her lips and tenderly kissed it several times. "Isn't he beautiful?"

"Yes. He is beautiful." I stood in awe. "He looks like you, Caroline!" It was true. Our son did look like Caroline. He had jet-black hair, darker than Ricky's, and eyes the color of chocolate. Most babies are born with blue eyes and the color changes with time, but our son's eyes were already the color of Caroline's. I was certain they would stay that shade. As I watched our infant son, I knew he was a miracle child. I also knew – for the rest of my life – every time I looked at him, I would see my wife, and I would remember the love we shared on that wonderful day in May.

"I'm sorry we can't call him Victoria," Caroline quietly spoke. "I know how much you wanted a daughter so you could name her after your mother."

"Perhaps we can still name the baby after my mother. What do you think of using my mother's maiden name?"

"What is it?"

"Before my mother married my father, her name was Victoria Bradley."

"Bradley." Caroline rolled the name off of her tongue. "Bradley Malone." She smiled. "I like it. It's a good name." She kissed me on the cheek. "That's what we will call him. Bradley Malone. And let's also honor Mario by calling our son Bradley Mario Malone. That's a proud name."

"You're right! That is an excellent idea." I chuckled. "I can think of no one I would like to honor more than Mario. He has been wonderful to us." I leaned over and kissed Caroline on the cheek. "Thank you, Carley. You've made 1950 the most perfect year of my life. You gave me two sons in one year: one born in January and one in December. There is no man who is luckier or happier than I am today."

3

Three months later, tragedy struck. We had no warning, and I didn't see any of the signs. The day began like any other day – up at dawn working the breakfast shift. Mario and Rosa came shortly before noon. In reflecting upon the events of the day, I should have seen that Mario was listless and did not seem to be his normal energetic, talkative self; in addition, when he did speak, his words seemed slightly slurred, and he was a little disoriented, but I did not take note of any of his symptoms.

It happened unexpectedly at the peak of the lunch hour. Mario had a massive heart attack – dying instantly. Our world – as we knew it – changed forever.

Losing Mario knocked the wind right out of me. I was of little help to Rosa or Caroline because I needed all of my emotional strength in order to get through the days that followed. Unfortunately, I offered no support or comfort to the women. It was hard to describe the way I felt about Mario Mancini. He was definitely more than an employer, and he was even more than a friend. I loved the old man like I had wanted to love my father. When my mother died, I had built a protective wall around my emotions – a wall even Caroline had not been able to break through until Mario had made a crack in it. Mario had, somehow, without my realizing it, reopened my heart to the world. His boisterous mannerisms, candor, and enthusiastic encouragement had weakened my defenses, and I discovered – I truly loved him. With our mutual bond, Mario had given me more than love and affection – he had given me self-confidence, which was an emotion I had never known. Losing Mario left a void inside of me – much like the empty whole I felt when I lost my mother and Calvin.

For weeks, Rosa was inconsolable. She didn't eat. She didn't sleep much either, and she often went days without talking. The light in her eyes was gone. She never came to the restaurant, claiming she truly didn't care what happened to it. Rosa said, "The restaurant reminds me of Mario. It pains my heart to go there." Caroline and I worked doubly hard to make sure Rosa was not burdened with any of the decisions or chores. In order to block out the pain, I turned all of my energies toward making the restaurant succeed.

Caroline was the one who found solace with Rosa. Although the connection between them was already binding, their relationship grew even stronger. Whenever there was a pause in customers, Caroline took the boys to Rosa's house. Rosa loved reading to Ricky and rocking Bradley in the same chair she had used for her own sons when they had been infants. The boys and Caroline seemed to be Rosa's source of comfort.

Two and a half months after Mario's death, Rosa called me to the house. She asked that I come alone. Shortly after I arrived, she handed me a stack of papers. They were letters from the bank. When I looked at them, I realized they were foreclosure notices for the loan on the restaurant. Guilt immediately washed over me. I had been the one to convince Mario to take out the loan in order to make the improvements on the restaurant.

Rosa began to cry uncontrollably. "It is not for me that I cry," she sobbed. "The restaurant was Mario's pride and joy, but I don't care about it anymore. Every time I look out the window and see it, I think of him, and it pains me. If I lost it tomorrow, I would not care." She wiped her face with her lace handkerchief. "But Mario wanted you and your Caroline to share in his accomplishment; we hoped one day, we could pass the restaurant to you as we had intended to pass it on to our Christopher and our Leonardo had they lived." Rosa made the sign of the cross on her chest. "God bless their souls." Then Rosa kissed my hand and fresh tears filled her eyes again. "You were like a son to my Mario. You brought back the light in his eyes and the joy in his laughter. The day you and Caroline came to us – it was as if God had given us a miracle. Every night, when he was on his knees in prayers, Mario thanked the Lord for you."

Rosa wiped the tears with her handkerchief. Her voice changed. She seemed to gather an inner strength before she continued to speak. "Mario was a wonderful husband. I will forever be thankful for the time we had together on this earth. He was a kind man – a fantastic cook. He had a green thumb in the garden, and he was good with the customers," Rosa sighed, "but he was a miserable businessman. I know this all of our married life. The restaurant never made much money – enough to put a roof over our heads and a little food on the table. He was not good at making decisions. He did not know how to use his money wisely, and he often forgot to pay the bills. All we ever had was this house and that restaurant, and a little profit at the end of each month. It was not much, but we were happy. The house is paid for – I have the deed, but there is the loan on the restaurant and according to the letters from the bank, Mario missed several payments. Now that Mario is dead, the bank does not want the installments anymore, they want all of the money at once or they will take the restaurant. There is still twelve hundred dollars left on the loan – it might as well be twelve million. I don't have the money to pay." She began to cry again. "It is not for me that I worry. It is for you and Caroline and the boys. The restaurant is your home – and it is how you make your money. What will you do without it?"

After calming Rosa as best as I could, I returned to Caroline. I didn't have a clue how I was going to tell her. According to the letters from the bank, Rosa had two weeks before we were evicted. *Two weeks.* Shortly before Bradley was born, I had saved over a thousand dollars – almost enough money to give Rosa so she could have paid off the loan, but the doctor and hospital bills for Bradley's birth had taken an enormous chunk out of my account. I had nowhere near enough money now.

When both boys were asleep for the night, I mustered up the courage to tell my wife the unfortunate news. She quietly listened as I explained to her the full measure of our plight. I included my desire to pay off Rosa's loan in hopes of having joint ownership of the restaurant. Unfortunately, there was not enough money to satisfy the bank. In addition to losing my dream, I had to tell my wife we no longer had a place to live. For the first time in my life, I felt completely defeated.

Not once during my disclosure did Caroline speak. When I was finished, she got out of the rocking chair, walked across the room, pulled one of her suitcases out from under the bed, and opened it. Inside was the mysterious shoebox wrapped in blue ribbon she had brought with her the night we left town. Slowly, she undid the bow and took the top off of the box. I leaned forward to see what was inside. To my surprise, it was full of pictures, leather pouches and small boxes, all meticulously arranged.

"Do you think any of this might help?" Caroline took the pictures, which were mostly of her father, out of the box and searched through the contents. "These are my mother's earrings. I think they are diamonds." She opened one of the small boxes. "And these are her pearls." To display it, Caroline draped the necklace gently around her hand. "My father gave these to me when I was a little girl. I never knew my mother, but he thought I might like to have some of her jewelry." Caroline opened another tiny box. "This is the gold locket my father gave me when I turned sixteen." She continued sifting through the shoebox. "These are pearl earrings, and this is a cameo that belonged to my father's mother." Caroline opened yet another box. "This is the engagement ring Jerry gave me." She looked at me to see if I was going to react; when I didn't she continued. "*Emily Post's* book on etiquette states if the girl is the one to break the engagement, she should return the ring, but there was no time." My wife shirked her shoulders nonchalantly. Her expression was unreadable as she twirled the ring around in her hand. "I'm sure it's worth quite a bit of money." She shifted the contents around slightly and pulled out a small leather bag. When she opened it, a multitude of bills floated out. "I probably should have confessed this a long time ago." A sheepish grin spread across Caroline's face. "The night we left, I took this from my father's safe in the library. I always felt guilty about it, but I figured he had plenty of money; perhaps, he wouldn't miss these bills." She organized them in her hand and then fanned the bills out in a semi-circle shape. There were tens, twenties, fifties and numerous one-hundred-dollar bills.

"My God! Caroline!" I was shocked by what I saw.

Caroline pushed the box and its entire contents toward me. She smiled unpretentiously. "It's yours, Richard. All of it! Let's go after your dream. Let's start today. Remember what Eleanor Roosevelt always says, '*The future belongs to those who believe in the beauty of their dreams.*' Let's make your dream come true."

Part II

The Turbulent Journey

1

Caroline

By 1956, Richard and I were well established with our thriving restaurant in the new location, but it had not been a smooth journey; in fact, it had been a rather rocky road to achieve our success. At first, in the early 50s, even though we made restitution with the bank by paying off Mario's loan with the money from my shoebox, it still looked as if we were going to lose everything we had. We were young and naïve; consequently, we didn't foresee the impact the completion of the New Jersey Turnpike would have on customer flow. Construction on the Turnpike began during the same month Ricky was born: January 1950. A little more than a year later, when Mario died, we were scrambling to pay off the loan, and our future looked dismal.

For a little while, investing our life's savings in Rosa's restaurant seemed like a judicious decision. In the summer of 1951 – when toddling Ricky was constantly under foot and Bradley was learning how to crawl – Rosa begged us to move in with her and live in the big house adjacent to the restaurant. It was a two-story, three-bedroom Victorian-style dwelling. She was lonely and craved company; for that reason, she offered to watch our boys on a regular basis while Richard and I worked at the restaurant. Because Rosa was so wonderful with our sons, neither Richard nor I hesitated. Ricky and Bradley adored their surrogate grandmother and lovingly called her Nana. The five of us were a family. Upon reflection, I sometimes feel those were the best and happiest years of my life. Ironically, there were times during that period when we held our breath until our books balanced and we often worked side-by-side for 18-hour days, but that was part of what made it so exhilarating because we felt such a mutual sense of accomplishment. Richard and I, with the help of Rosa, were an amazing team.

During 1951, business got progressively better, so we hired additional help. Richard, to my delight, was an incredibly good businessman. Instead of accepting high prices offered for food and beverage from grocery stores and vendors as Mario had done, my husband searched for better prices from local farmers and merchants, which gave us more profit. Unlike Mario, who had wasted a tremendous amount of food on a daily basis, Richard learned how to judge the amount of perishables needed for preparation each day; therefore, the percentage of food that spoiled was small and profits began to rise. My husband also traveled to other restaurants, saw what they had to offer, and checked out the prices on the menu. It became obvious to him that Mario's menu was priced too low. Richard revamped our menu, renamed the items, rearranged the order of those foods, and hiked the prices up fifteen percent. If the customers noticed the elevated cost, they didn't complain about it, and the restaurant remained competitive with the other eateries in town.

Every two weeks, Richard sat down with Rosa in order to look over the accounts. There was no longer a loan to be paid, so every penny earned, which was not spent on the cost of running the restaurant, was profit. To our amazement, the savings account was growing substantially.

Unfortunately, in the beginning of 1952 when the Turnpike opened to traffic, we discovered that the 118-mile-long highway, which ran parallel to Route One, immediately reduced our flow of customers by fifty-five percent. Folks no longer used congested Route One, with all of its stoplights, to travel between Philadelphia and New York City. Truckers, who were the core of our breakfast and lunch crowd, were thrilled to have a 60-mile-an-hour highway on which to drive; as a result, they no longer patronized our establishment. In hindsight, we should have known, but we were too inexperienced to foresee the financial damage the new Turnpike would cause us.

To our dismay, after the completion of the New Jersey Turnpike, there simply were not enough customers to warrant the additional employees, so Richard had to lay off the extra help, and we worked all three shifts. The days seemed endless, and often we barely broke even. For a second time, I offered Richard the remaining treasures in my shoebox. During the first financial emergency, my husband had pawned Jerry's engagement ring and used the majority of the money I had confiscated from my father, but Richard had refused to sell any of my family heirlooms or the gold locket my father had given me when I was sixteen. He claimed they were precious possessions that should be handed down to our boys, and he would not, under any circumstances, sacrifice them; consequently, we were at a financial dead end. We thought we'd lost it all; then, a miracle occurred.

In the fall of 1952, shortly after Dwight Eisenhower beat Adlai Stevenson in the Presidential Election, a well-dressed entrepreneur entered the restaurant. He checked out the building and the land before he approached Richard. My husband was surprisingly calm and quite professional as he listened to the man's offer. The fellow didn't care about the restaurant or the house; in fact, he had every intention of bulldozing both buildings. What he did want to purchase was the fifteen acres of land on which the restaurant and Rosa's house were located. Apparently, he wanted to build a small shopping center for the local population, which would consist of an A & P, a bank, a People's Drug Store, a bakery, and a couple of independent smaller stores. His offer was quite generous. Richard played it cool, explaining he would have to discuss the matter with his partners. Although Rosa was willing to consider the sale of the restaurant, she refused to include the house in any contract. That night, Richard, Rosa and I deliberated the pros and cons of our options.

Within twenty-four hours, the deal was made. The only stipulation was Rosa's house and one acre of land were not included in the contract. With check in hand, Rosa and I agreed we would search for another location – perhaps a little further north – to build a new restaurant, but Richard made an alternative suggestion.

At dinner on Sunday night, Richard pitched his proposal. He first broached the subject by discussing something he had read in the newspaper several years ago. Apparently, in 1947, while he and I were sophomores in high school, two brothers by the name of Alfred and William Levitt had mass produced houses on Long Island. They were Cape Cod-style homes – small and boxy – but affordable to middle income families. After World War II, there had been an enormous demand for housing. Returning soldiers were reunited with their young brides and a population explosion occurred. Growing families were packed into apartments and often multiple families were crammed in a home that could not comfortably hold all of the residents. The veterans – tired of scrimping during the Depression years and armed with the GI Bill of

Rights, which entitled them to inexpensive loans – were clamoring to buy houses. Unfortunately, there were not enough of them.

On Long Island, the Levitt brothers had built a community of thousands of houses that were exactly the same. It was a hugely successful endeavor. In fact, it was so profitable; they did it again in 1951, when they purchased land in Bucks County, Pennsylvania, between Philadelphia and Trenton, New Jersey. The newspaper called it "a self-contained planned community." Not only did they build houses, which cost less than $10,000 each, they also built shopping centers, churches, playgrounds and schools to accommodate the residents. Although it was a suburb of both Trenton and Philadelphia, in actuality, it was its own small town of Levittown. The houses were uniform with many modern conveniences like General Electric stoves, washing machines and refrigerators. Covenants were included in each contract, which specifically stated owners could not have fences or change the color of the house; in addition, every home had a clothesline in the shape of an umbrella for laundry that could only be displayed on Mondays through Saturdays: never on Sunday. Other construction companies were copying the Levitt brother's idea and suburban communities were popping up all over the country.

Richard explained – although we did not have the resources to undertake such a large project as the Levitt brothers had done – we could handle a smaller version. It was a gamble, but he had seen some land that was a good investment for exactly this type of venture. It was approximately fifteen miles north of Rosa's house between Elizabeth and Maplewood. Richard believed we could use the money from the sale of the restaurant and purchase the land outright, borrow additional money, using the land as collateral, hire the necessary workers, and build three or four houses at a time. When we sold those houses, we could reinvest the money and turn over the houses in a leapfrog fashion: build, sell, and build another. In addition, this particular piece of property included a wonderful sloping hill with a winding brook on it. He thought, eventually, when we had saved enough money, we could build a house of our own at the crest. To our total surprise, Rosa agreed.

During 1953, 1954, and 1955, Richard worked on this project. He started with the northwestern corner of the thirty-three acres and sectioned it into half-acre lots. Because he was not going to be able to mass-produce thousands of homes, he wanted to build houses that would attract a different clientele. Richard was certain there were people, who would be willing to pay a higher price for a house, but they would want a little more individuality and more land. He purchased plans from an architect, hired carpenters, plumbers and electricians. Richard worked right alongside the men. At first he was unsure of himself, but eventually he became a proficient foreman by weeding out the unskilled laborers and retaining the talented ones. Six days a week, he was gone from sunrise to sundown, completely dedicated to the success of this endeavor.

While Richard worked at the construction site, Rosa and I continued our customary schedule. On Monday, we did laundry. It took the entire day to wash all of our clothes and hang them on the line. There were generally not many personal items for Rosa or me, as we normally wore the same housedresses and aprons at least twice during the week. In the late afternoon, when we donned our better dresses, pearls, nylons and heels, we rarely got them dirty; consequently, we were able to wear them several times before washing. The boys' clothes, on the other hand, were filthy, and they required changing at least two times a day. I was eternally grateful – thanks to Dr. Spock's suggestions and wisdom – they had both been easily toilet trained before they were two, and I no longer had to wash their diapers. That chore alone took a couple hours. As for Richard's clothes, they were the worst. It seemed to take forever to get the sawdust and dirt out of the material. I dreaded Mondays. Rosa and I often wished we had one of those fancy electric washing machines because the scrub board was brutal on our hands.

On Tuesdays, I ironed the clean clothes while Rosa stripped the sheets and washed the towels and linens. Everything needed ironing, including a minimum of two-dozen handkerchiefs a week. In addition, Rosa insisted on pressing the sheets. She was a fanatic about wrinkles – she would not tolerate them.

On Wednesdays, we beat the rugs, dusted the furniture, swept all of the floors, cleaned the bathrooms, mended any clothes that needed repair and darned the socks.

On Thursday mornings, Rosa made pasta for the week, and I baked homemade breads, buns and cookies. In the afternoon, we washed windows. March through October, we tended to the needs of the garden in the backyard.

On Friday, we went to market and gave the house a good once-over so it would be clean for the weekend.

Every day, except on Sundays, I swept the veranda and the front steps. Once a month, we polished the silver, and twice a year – once in the spring and once in the fall – we cleaned out all of the closets and drawers, washed every wall in the house, took the drapes to the dry cleaners, and polished the hardwood floors.

Dinner was cooked every day at 5:00 and on the table at 6:00. Richard could set his watch to that part of our schedule. By 7:00, the dishes were cleared and cleaned and the kitchen light was turned off for the night.

Unofficially, we prayed for good weather in the beginning of each week, because rain threw our schedule to the wind, and we'd be forced to rearrange the entire week's activities.

While Rosa and I manned the chores in the house, Richard worked assiduously on the construction site. It took six months to do the first five houses; the following six months, ten more were completed. By the end of 1955, he had built and sold fifty-eight homes surrounding the hill, leaving four full acres at the crest. The houses were priced between $15,000 and $21,000 depending upon whether they were three-bedroom ramblers, four-bedroom split-levels or classic colonials. After giving Rosa her share, I had no idea what our profit margin was on each house. Richard had hoped to strike it rich from the enterprise and continue to invest in the same type of speculation; but to our dismay, we had made much less total profit than we had anticipated.

In actuality, we *did* make a significant profit per house, but Richard often spent the proceeds on luxuries instead of rolling the money over into the construction of the next house. After the first two houses were sold, Richard purchased a console entertainment unit. It was a huge piece of blond wood furniture big enough to fit an adult. There were two doors on it. When I opened the left door, I discovered a radio with both AM and FM channels plus a record player that had an adaptor to accommodate the relatively new 45-rpm records and enough shelves for my entire collection of LPs. Behind the right door, I discovered – to everyone's delight – a television set with a 10" diagonal picture screen. Needless to say, it was an enormous hit. I didn't think we could possibly afford such an expensive treat, and when I realized it cost over $800, I insisted Richard return the entertainment unit to the store. My husband refused to listen to my request.

We were the first people in the neighborhood to own a television. Everyone instantly knew about our recent purchase because the unsightly antenna on the roof announced it to the community. To our surprise, people began to drop by, often with no prior phone call or invitation. Rosa welcomingly invited them into her home. A pattern emerged. Monday through Friday, Ricky, Bradley, and their young friends gathered to watch *The Howdy Dowdy Show* and *Clarabell*. During those thirty minutes, I granted myself a break from my daily chores and interacted with the other mothers.

The children were not the only ones entertained by the television. Rosa, Richard and I loved *The Perry Como Show*, *The Jack Benny Show*, and *Your Hit Parade,* but our favorite show was *The Texaco Star Theater* with Milton Berle. Once a week – on Tuesday night – we invited a few couples over – each brought a dish for a *potluck* style dinner. At 8:00, after eating and clearing the plates, we all gathered around the television set to watch Milton Berle's latest antics. It became part of our routine. For the first time in our marriage, Richard and I socialized with friends.

We also invited people over on Sunday afternoons. We'd picnic in Rosa's backyard and let the kids play on the swing set Richard had installed: another one of his spontaneous purchases. Toward the end of the evening, we'd gather in the living room to watch *The Colgate Comedy Hour.* The hosts varied from week to week, but our favorites were Dean Martin and Jerry Lewis. There were not enough seats in the room for everyone; so, Richard and I let our guests have the couch and the armed chairs. My traditional spot was on the floor next to the fireplace curled up in my husband's arms. Of course, in the summertime, there was no fire, but in the winter with the warmth and the crackling of the burning wood, it was cozy in Richard's arms. I lovingly leaned my head against his shoulder, and together we chuckled at the comedians' jokes. The chorus of laughter in our living room could be heard throughout the house.

It was during this time, Richard and I met John and Lucy Harrod.

Their son Martin was a year older than Ricky. Ironically, John was our mailman. They lived within walking distance, which gave the boys the opportunity to play several times a week. If Lucy or I had plans, we gladly helped the other out by watching all of the children. Several days a week, after we had completed our household chores, Lucy and I got together for a cup of coffee or a cold glass of Kool Aid while the children played in the backyard.

Rosa encouraged my budding friendship with Lucy Harrod. Initially, I told Rosa I was perfectly content to have her as my sole female friend, but Rosa was adamant. She repeatedly insisted, "Bah! I'm old enough to be your grandmother – you need young friends – girls your own age."

Lucy's son and my boys got along famously; consequently, Lucy and I rapidly developed a bond. Although her husband John was a quiet, reserved man, Lucy was gregarious and even comical, much like the main character on CBS' comedy, *I Love Lucy*. No one could make me laugh like Lucy Harrod. My new friend even had the same bright red hair and loveable personality as the character played by Lucille Ball. The term "I love Lucy" was a common phrase both John and I said to her and to each other – always with a wink and a smile.

The entertainment unit was the first of many costly items my husband purchased. For as long as possible, Richard had fixed Calvin's ailing Chrysler until it finally broke down one night on his way home from the construction site. As hard as he tried, Richard was unable to permanently repair the problem; thus, he decided to purchase a new car. It tore away a piece of Richard's heart when he finally had to put the old Chrysler out to pasture because – to Richard – it was like saying goodbye to his brother all over again. Thankfully, his mood lightened when he teased me for an entire day by telling me he had purchased a brand new sports car called a Corvette. When he showed me a picture of the two-seater convertible, I was appalled. "Where will the boys sit?" I questioned.

He laughed and responded, "We are going to tie a rope around them and let them run behind us."

I knew he was kidding, but I remained apprehensive about his choice until he came home with the new car. It was not a sporty Corvette as he had teased; instead, it was a shiny, new 1954 black Cadillac.

Richard was immensely proud of the purchase. "Look," he pointed to the windshield. "The glass curves. It's called the panoramic windshield. The first ever!" He raised the hood for my perusal. "It has one of those innovative high compression V-8 engines. Isn't it swell!"

I had no idea what he was talking about, but I feigned interest because he seemed to enjoy talking about the vehicle. The car also had power steering – an extra I had never even heard of until he showed me its benefit. The power steering made driving so effortless. While we were taking the car out for its first spin together, Richard turned on the radio. I was completely floored. *A radio in a car!* How wonderfully sophisticated! Richard said – according to the salesperson who sold him the Cadillac – approximately half of all automobiles made in the previous year had a radio installed in the dashboard; needless to say, Richard wanted the extra feature, and he was willing to pay the additional price to have it included. I adored the car radio, and I especially liked the Alan Freed Show on WINS broadcasted out of New York City. Freed was born in Pennsylvania, which automatically made us feel akin to him, and he played new music with a hip beat. My favorite songs were *Mr. Sandman* by The Cordettes, *If I Give My Heart to You* by Doris Day, and *Unforgettable* by Nat King Cole. The boys liked *Shake, Rattle & Roll* by Bill Haley and the Comets. They would both wiggle their little bodies to the rhythm. During our initial drive, I sang at the top of my lungs to *P.S. I Love You* by The Hilltoppers. I leaned my head on Richard's shoulder. When we were stopped at a light, he kissed me. I blushed like a teenager. After the song ended, I asked Richard how much the Cadillac cost. He quietly responded, "Don't ask." Two days later, I looked in the checkbook and nearly fainted. The car cost almost $5,000. How could we possibility afford it?

The Cadillac and the entertainment unit were not the only purchases Richard made. For Christmas, he gave me a fur coat, a collection of Frank Sinatra records including my favorite song *Someone to Watch Over Me,* which was from the movie *Young at Heart.* We had seen it with John and Lucy. The movie was marvelous, and the song was sensational. I played the record at least a dozen times a day. Richard also gave me a Brownie 8 mm Movie Camera *and* the Brownie Projector, and for my 23rd birthday, he gave me a new wedding band with four perfectly matched diamonds encased in the gold. When he put it on my figure, he

159

pointed to each diamond and said, "See! A diamond for each of us. You, me, Ricky and Bradley." Then he kissed my hand, closing his eyes as his lips met their mark. I was slightly embarrassed because there were only two gifts under the tree for Richard: a tie to go with his gray flannel suit and a Kodak camera because I knew he wanted to take photographs of our family. For his 23rd birthday, I gave him a black derby hat I'd seen him admire on several occasions when we had shopped for the children's birthday presents. I had saved up from my food allowance for three months in order to buy the camera and six weeks for the hat.

Of course, I loved the gifts he had given me, but I constantly worried if we could afford such luxuries; after all, food was so expensive. Milk was over ninety cents a gallon and coffee also cost that much per pound. Bread was eighteen cents per loaf and eggs were over sixty cents for a dozen. In addition, the Fuller Brush Man came by once a month; I purchased all of my cleaning supplies from him. It was necessary to be frugal, because if the money ran out, I wouldn't be able to get the supplies I needed when the salesman arrived. It was hard to make my thirty-dollars-per-week budget stretch for seven days. As an added expense, Richard traveled quite a distance to and from the construction site every day. The cost of gasoline was twenty cents a gallon; thus, the round trip added up to be quite a tidy sum each week.

In June, on our fifth anniversary, my husband surprised me with the most extravagant gift of all. He gave me a 17-foot sailboat, much like the one we had admired on the river the evening we had conceived Bradley. On our anniversary, he'd driven me to a marina, blindfolded me, guided me across the docks and positioned me at the slip before allowing me to open my eyes. When I saw it, I truly believed he was joking. A sailboat! How on earth could we possibly afford such an elaborate indulgence? But I knew the moment I saw the name on the stern – it was definitely ours. Painted in beautiful script was my name: *Caroline Sue*. I instantly fell in love with the boat, and I relished the idea of spending time on it with my husband. I had one secret regret. Although I loved the fact he named the boat after me, I privately wished he had called it *Carley* instead of *Caroline Sue*. It seemed, as the years began to pass, he addressed me as Caroline Sue many more times than he called me Carley, and I missed the nickname he had given me as a child.

Richard was constantly spending money on gifts for the children and for me. He gave me clothes, jewelry, record albums, and fancy French perfumes like Channel No. 5. He bought Rosa a new vacuum cleaner, her first washing machine, and a new winter coat. These weren't special occasion gifts; they were items he purchased on a whim. I didn't have any idea how much the jewelry, the perfumes or the vacuum cleaner cost, but I'd seen the Kenmore semi-automatic washing machine in the store, and I was well aware of the fact that it cost $155. Without any doubt, both Rosa and I appreciated the gift. I no longer dreaded Mondays and hand-washing all of those clothes, but I still worried about the price.

At least three times a week, he bought Ricky and Bradley a new toy; in fact, there were so many toys, Rosa complained she was constantly tripping over them. Sometimes he'd bring the boys an 88-cent slinky, or double holster six-shooter cap guns, or a hand full of penny candy, or a roll of life savers he'd picked up at the five and dime, but – more times than not – his gifts were expensive and purchased for no particular occasion; for example, one day he gave them a $8.75 Red "Radio Flyer" wagon, and another time he purchased matching leather baseball mitts for the boys. I understood my husband's reasoning behind the adorable red wagon, but what on earth were Bradley and Ricky going to do with baseball mitts that were two sizes too big for their hands.

Although our sons were genuinely thrilled with everything their father gave them, perhaps they were most pleased by the coonskin caps Richard brought home the week after Walt Disney aired the "Davy Crockett Indian Fighter" episode on television. Ricky and Bradley were obsessed with Davy Crockett and often insisted on wearing their fur caps to bed. It wasn't until the following fall, when Richard brought them "Mickey caps" in honor of their new favorite program, *The Mickey Mouse Club*, that the boys replaced the now tattered coonskins with Mouseketeer ears. Every day, no matter what outdoor game or indoor activity in which they were involved, all action stopped the moment they heard the show's theme song begin. Ricky, Bradley and several other children who were playing with them at the time would come running into the living room and plop down in front of the television. The group would sing along and spell the letters out. As the tune progressed, Ricky would always chant, "Mickey Mouse!" and Bradley would counter with,

"Donald Duck!" Together they would laugh merrily as they sang the rest of the words in unison. Wednesday – which was "Anything Can Happen Day" on the show – was the boys' favorite day of the week. Although they liked all of the Mouseketeers, my sons each had a favorite: Ricky liked adorable Karen Pendleton and Bradley liked Annette Funicello. While sitting on my lap one afternoon, Bradley said, "I like Annette because she looks a lot like you, Mommy." Then he proceeded to throw his arms around my neck and spread kisses all over my face. There was no doubt about it; Bradley was a mischievous little devil most of the time, but he was also wonderfully charming, and he could melt my heart faster than the summer sun could melt an ice cube.

The Mickey Mouse Club was hugely popular with our sons; thus, most of Richard's gift ideas in the fall of 1955 were centered on the show or other memorabilia relating to Walt Disney's new Disneyland theme park in California. In spite of the fact our children were not yet in school, he bought them Mickey Mouse lunch boxes, which they insisted upon using every day. Rosa made their lunches, packed them in their boxes, and they would sit on a blanket as if they were at a picnic.

One Saturday, Richard promised to take the boys and me to Newark to see *Lady and the Tramp*, the newest Disney movie, but he was so busy finishing up work on a house that had already been sold, he lost track of time. We were sitting on the front step waiting for him, but he neither returned home nor did he call. Needless to say, the boys were crushed. Luckily, John and Lucy Harrod intended on going with their son Martin. When John drove by, he saw us sitting on the stoop and invited us to tag along with them. The movie was delightful, and the afternoon would have been perfect had Richard been there to share it with us. To make up for his absence, Richard came home late that evening with stuffed toys: one shaped like Lady and one shaped like the Tramp. Ricky instantly grabbed the Tramp, and Bradley snatched Lady. Both stuffed animals were necessities at bedtime.

Richard's lavish and frequent expenditures eventually became the source of many arguments. I insisted he should not constantly give our sons gifts; so many presents would surely spoil the boys. I even accused him of trying to buy their love. My husband's argument was, "I want my sons to have all of those things I did not have when I was a child." My rebuttal was, "They don't need *things*, Richard. They would be perfectly happy playing with a wooden spoon and one of Rosa's pans if they were playing with *you*. Your time is more valuable to them than anything you can buy." No matter how often I expressed my personal opinion to him, Richard continued to buy the boys gifts and to bring treats home for me as well.

Also during those three years, we commenced building our home at the crest of the hill. Richard made most of the decisions about the floor plan, but he allowed me to pick the paint colors. There were four bedrooms upstairs and three full bathrooms in the house: two upstairs and one downstairs in the small bedroom beside the kitchen. In addition, there was a "half bathroom" downstairs next to the family room with a sink and a toilet. Richard was so proud when he told people our house was going to have *three and a half* bathrooms. It was luxurious.

Richard told me I could pick between turquoise and black tile or yellow tile with black trim. I chose two of each. It seemed like such an extravagant expense to have four toilets and three bathtubs in one house; even my father's house didn't have that many. The kitchen was another room in which Richard allowed me to participate in the designing. I picked out the refrigerator and stove, both were GE appliances, the light fixtures, and white countertops, which had tiny gold flecks pressed into the Formica surface. At first, I had selected white metal cabinets like those that were installed in all of the homes he had built surrounding ours, but Richard convinced me to pick the more expensive cherry wood. He said the room would look richer and would set it aside from the rest of the kitchens in the neighborhood. Richard also suggested, instead of putting the washing machine in the kitchen, he wanted to design a separate room for the machine with a laundry chute in the upstairs bathrooms that went directly to a bin next to the washer. I was delighted with his idea and instantly agreed.

Unfortunately, construction on our house was halted on numerous occasions because we ran out of money to pay for supplies and labor; consequently, our new home was built in shifts. After three years of construction, it was nowhere near completion. I kept insisting we didn't need such a big home, but Richard wasn't willing to build an ordinary house; he wanted *our* house to be more glamorous, more prominent, and more modern than any of the other houses.

When fifty-six of the fifty-eight houses were completed and sold, we discovered most of the profit had already been spent. Richard, who was entrenched in a stubborn streak like none I had ever witnessed before, was combative and refused to listen to any of my suggestions. Our disputes were heated at times, and our arguments always sounded the same.

At first, they were private conversations between Richard and me when one of us made a subtle reference to our financial situation.

"Perhaps," I said patiently. "It would be better if we found a way to make a more stable income instead of making large amounts of money at one time and living hand-to-mouth for several months to follow."

Richard countered by saying, "There's a lot of money to be made in construction."

"But not if you squander it," I replied.

"You think I squander the money?" he interrupted defiantly. "Don't you like that car? And the television set? You and the children watch it every day. Do you want me to return it? How about the boat? You sure looked happy on it last weekend." He was not gentle in his statement; in fact, he sounded accusatory. "I notice you wear your coat to Sunday service even when it isn't that cold outside. You love it when people ask to touch the fur." Richard squared his jaw like he did when he was a little boy and ready for a fight. "You like what I buy you, and don't even pretend to deny it."

"Of course, I like what you've given us. They're wonderful gifts, but maybe we shouldn't have these things if we don't have the money to afford it."

"I *can* afford it! The housing market is huge, and there's tons of money to be made." Richard obstinately reaffirmed his opinion.

"I'm sure you're right, but if we don't budget it well," I argued, "the money simply disappears. Sometimes, I worry about how we are going to feed the boys."

"You're exaggerating."

"Maybe a little, but there is truth in it."

"I've been poor, Caroline." Richard stood proudly as he spoke. "And

I'm never going to be poor again." Defiantly he added. "We can get rich off of building houses."

I replied. "I don't want to be rich. Have you forgotten? I grew up rich. It's not all that it's cracked up to be."

My comment enraged Richard. "Only a spoiled rich girl would make an idiotic statement like that!" At this point in the conversation, his voice was loud, and his words echoed around the room. "You don't want to take a chance on me," he said accusingly as he pointed his finger angrily in my direction. "You're not listening to me. I can do this! I *know* I can."

Instead of screaming the words back at him, I whispered. "And you're not listening to me."

Richard didn't hear me.

"*You* take care of the house and our sons," Richard stated firmly as he made his exit from the room. "*I'll* provide for our family!"

Our heated debates always left me frustrated and lonely.

Initially, the arguments occurred once or twice a month and in the privacy of our bedroom, but as more of the investment houses sold, our fiery disputes became more frequent and more public. Rosa and our boys were often unwilling witnesses. The children cried and Rosa shook her head in dismay as she guided them out of the room. I knew Rosa disapproved of the way we handled our disagreement, but she kept her opinions to herself.

As time passed, our arguments became more like habits, and there were a couple of days when Richard slept on the couch instead of in our bed. My heart ached.

After the last two houses sold and the profits were deposited in the bank, Rosa stepped in and boldly announced her opinion. "I no like what is happening. My Mario would be sick if he could see you two fighting like alley cats. You should be ashamed of yourselves. 'Tis not good to fight in front of your boys. They need to see your love not your anger." Rosa took the time to stare both of us in the eye. She was not smiling. "I love you like you are my own children, but this is *my* house, and I no let you turn it into a scary place for children." Rosa wiped her hands on her apron and sat in the chair by the refrigerator. She reached into her pocket, pulled out her bank passbook, and placed it gently on the table. "I no invest in any more houses." She stated firmly.

"But, Rosa, I can make you wealthy," Richard declared passionately.

"I no want to be rich." Rosa pouted. "I want to be family again."

Richard and I were stunned by Rosa's sudden candid and heartfelt statement; neither of us said a word.

"I no invest in any more houses," Rosa pointed to her passbook. "But I still want to invest in *you*." Again she looked into both Richard's and my eyes. There was a strong love radiating from her expression. It created an intangible bond between the three of us. The room was quiet for a few moments before Rosa continued, "My Mario and me," she paused. "We were the happiest when we had the restaurant, and we loved it when you came to us. You made our lives joyful – filled with laughter. Sadly, Raffaele's Place is gone – no more. They mowed it down and built a shopping center. Soon, people will forget my Mario, and they won't even remember the restaurant. It will only be alive in our memories." Rosa used the corner of her apron to wipe away the tears in her eyes. After a moment of silence, a smile formed on her face. "Like I said before, I no invest in anymore houses." She pushed the passbook toward Richard. "But if you make a new restaurant, I will invest in *you*." She encouraged my husband to look at the amount inside of the passbook.

Richard's eyes widened when he saw the numbers. "Rosa! You must have saved every penny I gave you."

"I no spend much money." She smiled. "If you use the profits from the sale of the last two houses and put it with my savings, do you think it is enough to make us a new restaurant?"

Richard continued to stare at Rosa's passbook – turning it over in his hands repeatedly, but he remained silent. When he finally looked up, I could see tears glistening in his eyes. My husband looked at me for nearly a minute, almost as if he wanted me to answer for him. He was rubbing his thumb against his forefinger so hard; the sound seemed to echo against the walls of the room.

Richard cleared his throat before speaking. "We can make a nice restaurant with this money. Thank you, Rosa." He crossed the room and hugged her. "I will not let you down."

"And when your big house on the hill is finished, I will sell my house and move in with you." Rosa added, "We stay a family. Yes?"

"Of course, we will stay a family." Richard spoke firmly as he pulled me into their embrace.

The three of us stood locked in each other's arms. Both Rosa and I were crying joyful tears. Richard stroked my hair and kissed me several times on the forehead. "Our restaurant will be grand. I promise." There was certainty, but no passion in his voice.

A month later, Richard purchased a rather large building a few miles north of Maplewood and less than a fifteen-minute drive from the fifty-eight houses we had built. Although the structure was sound, the inside needed extensive renovations. Rosa and Mario's restaurant, even after we had remodeled it, looked more like a fancy diner for travelers. Richard wanted this new restaurant to be the type of place that would attract local customers. He designed it to be a family-style eatery, but also a place where a fellow could take his girl for a romantic evening: low lighting from candles and Tiffany lamps, quiet ambiance, mirrors, upscale menu and a bar. I suggested outdoor seating like I had seen in cafes in Paris while traveling with my father. Richard balked at the idea. It irritated me when my husband didn't think I had a head for business and wouldn't listen to *my* ideas, but I stifled my frustration and continued to make suggestions.

Eventually, I convinced Richard to include a section of tables outside of the restaurant with awnings to protect the customers from extreme sunshine or misting rain. Of course, we all knew this particular seating would be for seasonal use, but I believed it would attract additional customers. Richard, who liked to make all of the business decisions, finally agreed, and a veranda was built on the southwest side of the restaurant so customers could see the sunset. Occasionally, I heard him boast to business associates – the idea was *his*.

When it came to deciding upon a name for our restaurant, Richard jumped the gun and made the decision without consulting me. The word *furious* could not even begin to describe my emotions. I couldn't believe he chose a name for the restaurant and had the sign made without either Rosa's or my input, but I kept my temper in check. Thank goodness my patience won the battle over my irritation, and I remained mute about my fury, because when my husband pulled the tarp off of the sign, I was thrilled to discover he had named our restaurant Carley's Place. Needless to say, my heart melted.

The renovations took four months. Richard hired several outstanding chefs, a couple of reliable managers, and more than two-dozen waitresses and waiters. Although minimum wage was seventy-five cents per hour, rumor had it – as of January – there would be a wage hike to $1.00 per hour. In order to keep his chefs and managers loyal to Carley's Place, my husband paid them $1.15 per hour to start with increases when they earned it; the waiters and waitresses made $2.00 per five-hour shift plus tips. Richard had a great deal of confidence in his staff, but he still intended to remain at the helm and planned to be at the restaurant in order to supervise the employees.

On the first official day of business, reporters from many newspapers including *The Record, The Herald News, Home News Tribune* and even *The New York Times* came to sample the food, the ambiance, and the fluency of our operation. The articles were extremely favorable; in fact, one of the local reporters called Carley's Place the nicest restaurant within a 20-mile radius, and claimed a person would have to go to New York City to get a better meal or a finer atmosphere. To our delight, we had an instant and loyal clientele.

Dependable Rosa watched our boys, so I could help at the restaurant. Generally, I worked as a hostess during the lunch crowd. After the first rush of customers, I drove the Cadillac home in order to do the household chores and spend time with the boys. When Ricky and Bradley were asleep for the night, I'd return to the restaurant until closing; at which time, Richard and I would come home together. Often, the drive to and from the restaurant was the only private time we shared during the day.

Richard had long since given up on the idea of closing the restaurant on Sundays. Sundays, after church, were often as busy as Friday and Saturday nights; consequently, we had no weekends to relax. Instead, Richard and I usually spent Mondays and Tuesdays together – away from the restaurant and household chores. Thanks to the new washing machine, I had more available time on those days, so I was able to enjoy the time with my husband. We often savored lengthy afternoons on the sailboat – sometimes alone – sometimes with our sons – and always with our new portable five-inch transistor radio playing old and current Frank Sinatra favorites. Those blissful afternoons, with the warm breeze on our faces, were some of the most wonderful memories of my life. In fact, our third child was conceived on one such magical afternoon.

Our daughter was born the following spring. She was full term – 8 pounds, 4 ounces and 20 inches long – a beautiful, healthy girl. I had an easy pregnancy and delivery – no complications at all. At the first sign of contractions, I called Richard but he was in a frenzy because his luncheon chef had called in sick and two of the waiters were late to work. I asked him to meet me at the hospital. Lucy Harrod volunteered to drive me, while Rosa watched the boys. I was in labor a little over four hours. Sadly, Richard was unable to make it in time for the delivery; in fact, he didn't arrive until long after dark. Needless to say, I was lonely and hurt. I contemplated naming the baby without my husband's input, but decided against taking such a liberty. I didn't want Richard to be angry, especially now that we had a daughter. However, her name *did* become an issue between us.

I wanted to call our daughter Rosa after our beloved friend, but Richard wanted to name her after me – Caroline – with the intention of nicknaming her Carley. To my surprise, I felt a pang of jealousy at the idea of my husband calling our daughter the nickname I claimed for myself. Although I never mentioned my emotions or my reason, I vetoed his choice. Richard finally found a compromise. With an enthusiastic smile on his face, he suggested calling the baby Rosaline – a combination of both Rosa and Caroline.

"Oh, Richard!" I responded with joy. "That's a perfect name." Tears of jubilation rolled down my face. I gently cuddled the baby in my arms and moved the blanket slightly so Richard could see her face more easily. "She is beautiful, isn't she?"

"As beautiful as her mother." Richard replied as he scanned my face with an adoring glance. "I'm so glad we have a girl."

I pondered my thoughts before speaking again because I knew the subject would probably create tension, and I didn't want to ruin the magic of the moment. "Do you think we could take the children home to Pennsylvania?" I had not mentioned returning to my father's house since that volatile conversation we had shared many years ago; but suddenly – with the baby in my arms – I felt terribly homesick.

Richard didn't speak for several minutes. With his index finger, he stroked his cheekbone and tapped the side of his face – a subconscious habit he often did when he was concentrating. His expression was unreadable, and he avoided eye contact. When he finally spoke, his voice was calm, "Are you sure you want to go back?" he asked.

"Only if you will come with me," I replied tentatively.

Richard silently stared out of the hospital window; it seemed like an eternity before he answered. "Okay," he nodded calmly. "As soon as the restaurant is running smoothly, and I feel we can leave for a few days, we'll take the children to Pennsylvania for a visit, but it will have to be at the beginning of a week; we can't be gone during a weekend. The restaurant's too busy."

"Oh, Richard!" I was so happy I cried. "Thank you, darling! Thank you!"

2

Richard

Eight years had passed since we graduated from high school and escaped the shackles of our respective families. Although I would never admit it to anyone – least of all Caroline – I initially avoided returning home for two reasons. I did not want Randall Miller to think his daughter was married to a failure, nor did I want my wife to revisit what she had left behind. More than anything in the world, I feared she would leave me and return to the luxurious lifestyle her father had to offer.

Even though I still was not a major success, I was far from a failure; in fact, I was beginning to feel less and less like the poor white trash from South Side. The restaurant was an enormous achievement, our three children were healthy and beautiful, and our new home on the crest of the hill was nearly finished with an estimated completion date of August 1st. To an outsider, we appeared prosperous – perhaps even affluent, but I knew I was spending the money as fast as I was making it. I was obsessed with giving Caroline the things she deserved, and if I had to spend every penny in order to do it, then I would. My wife and children were never going to want for anything. However, I did fear Caroline would discover our financial situation was built on a house of cards, which could topple at any moment.

While building the houses, Rosa had seen my financial accounts. I was in partnership with her; I could not avoid her scrutiny. Although, she always received her fair share of the profits, Rosa knew there was no savings account in my name harboring my profits, because my share of the proceeds was already spent.

If it had not been for Rosa, I would have continued to stay in the construction business. A part of me resented her financial stipulations, but the rational side of me was glad she maintained our partnership and invested in our future. To our mutual delight, Carley's Place was an enormous success. Although I wasn't getting large chunks of money at one time, the restaurant was producing a stable cash flow.

After Rosaline was born and Caroline asked me to take her home, I cringed at the prospect. Each time a date was set for the journey, I fabricated a reason why we couldn't go: the restaurant was too busy, or we shouldn't take Ricky out of school because first grade is so important, or I needed to train a new manager, or Rosaline had the measles, or Bradley had a cold. I even blamed the weather a few times. My wife patiently listened to each explanation without saying a word. I postponed the trip at least a dozen times before I finally agreed. A full year passed; in fact, Rosaline had taken her first step three days before we made the journey. Driving through Pennsylvania, I began to realize I could proudly return to our childhood homes, and there would be no cloud of shame hovering over me.

As we traveled up the driveway to Randall Miller's home, I could feel the excitement mounting in Caroline. She was flushed with anticipation. Holding the baby in her arms, she spoke calmly to Ricky and Bradley who were sitting in the backseat awed by the grandeur of the house and gardens.

"This is where I grew up." Caroline said with pride. "I had my own little pony in the stable out back – perhaps there are still some horses. If you are on your best behavior, maybe your grandfather will let you ride one."

Ricky and Bradley, who had been plastered to the window as they viewed their new environment, suddenly began to bounce on the seat with heightened anticipation and squeal with delight. As Caroline and the boys' excitement amplified, my apprehension increased. Randall Miller didn't know we were coming, and I dreaded the meeting. With any luck, he would be out of town on business, and I could postpone the inevitable again.

As I helped my sons out of the car, Caroline mounted the cement steps and was the first to reach the door. She used the large brass knocker to announce our arrival. A servant opened the door. Caroline asked to speak to Randall Miller; her request created a rather startled look on the young lady's face. She motioned for us to come inside and led us to the parlor. After we had taken seats on the couch, the young woman politely excused herself. The boys were in awe. Caroline was pensive. I took advantage of the silence by appraising my surroundings. Although I had only been inside the Miller house once in my life, my memory was crystal clear. To the best of my recollection, nothing had changed. When I leaned slightly to my left, I could see through the foyer and into the library, which was the one room I remembered well. The same two leather chairs were positioned in the exact same manner directly in front of the massive desk. I could see the shelves of books, which covered the entire wall. The portraits displayed in the foyer had not changed, and the magnificent staircase with its mahogany banister still exuded a regal aura. Oddly, it didn't seem as large as I remembered. When I was six, the place looked more formidable – like a castle – but it no longer seemed as intimidating or overwhelming. In fact, I suddenly realized, it was just a house – bigger than most – more lavishly decorated – but just a house all the same. As I sat on the couch with Bradley on my lap, I suddenly felt less disconcerted, and I began to relax. Caroline looked at me and flashed a smile in my direction. In spite of the fact my wife appeared composed, I knew she was anxious, nervous and tremendously excited. I wanted to touch her hand – give her fingers a supportive squeeze – but she was a few inches out of reach; instead, I winked and smiled reassuringly.

Within five minutes, a well-dressed, middle-aged woman entered the room. She was carrying a large, bulky envelope. Although I didn't have a clue who she was, Caroline seemed to recognize her immediately.

"Miss Mavis! How nice to see you again." Caroline stood up. With Rosaline snuggled tightly in the curve of her left arm, my wife extended her available hand in order to greet the woman. Caroline wore a pleasant smile on her face, but the other woman seemed guarded; no smile appeared on her lips.

Miss Mavis summoned the young servant who had answered the door. Upon her entry, Miss Mavis directed her attention back to us. "We need to talk, Caroline. Would it be all right with you if Claire takes your three darlings into another room? You can rest assured, Claire is marvelous with children, and we have a few toys they might enjoy."

Although Caroline was tentative, she agreed. The woman with the starched uniform and the white apron gently took Rosaline from her mother's arms, and the boys happily romped off with the servant. When

173

the room fell silent again, a sense of trepidation washed over me. I moved closer to Caroline and encircled her hand with mine. She leaned gently against me.

Caroline was the first to speak. "Richard, this is Miss Mavis. When I was a little girl, she was my tutor." As the woman shook my hand, she smiled politely but her demeanor was aloof. "Miss Mavis," Caroline continued the introduction. "This is Richard, my husband."

"Your father always wondered what happened to you and that Malone boy." Miss Mavis spoke slowly as if she were pondering her words with great thought. "I see you elected to marry the fellow in spite of your father's wishes." Miss Mavis redirected her attention back to Caroline and her voice became firmer. "For a while, your father searched for you, but you were nowhere to be found. Finally, he gave up." Miss Mavis lifted her chin slightly. "I see you've been busy making a family of your own." Stubbornly, and with a hint of hostility in her voice, she continued. "I presume you read about your father in the obituary section of the *New York Times,* and you have returned in order to collect what you *think* is yours." She glared at Caroline. "You seem to be unaware of an important fact. I'm no longer Miss Mavis. I married your father shortly after you left. I'm Mrs. Randall Miller." She squared her shoulders proudly. "When you were off – God knows where – I'm the one who was here – by his side. When your father had the stroke in the spring of '51, *I'm* the one who nursed him – changed his sheets, put salve on his bedsores, read to him, feed him, and talked to him until I thought I'd go crazy because it was like talking to a mannequin in Macy's Department Store. For six years, I was here – loyal and dedicated to his every need." It appeared as if her eyes were tossing angry, intangible darts in our direction. "Don't think you can come home now and throw havoc to the wind." She stood rigid as she spoke. "After you ran away, he rewrote his will. He gave an enormous amount of money to the church, to the arts, and to build an orphanage in town. We got married – traveled for a while. Thank the Lord we were home when he got sick." She paused a moment as she looked around the room. "The house is mine, and so are the bank accounts." With triumph, she handed the package to Caroline. "This is what he left you. I don't know what's inside that envelope, but I do know what was written in his new will, and don't you dare think you can muscle your way in here and turn my life upside down. I deserve what he gave me, and I don't plan to part with any of it."

I glanced at Caroline. A stunned expression covered her face, and a string of tears trailed down her cheeks. Using her left hand, she clutched my arm. With her free hand and without making a sound, she reached for the envelope. I could feel her body quaking. Desperately, I wanted to console my wife, but I was at a total loss as to what I should do.

My wife opened the package. There was a significant amount of money in the envelope. The bills were immaculately wrapped in bundles. In addition, there were two official pieces of paper. One was a letter addressed to Caroline on her father's personal stationery dated July 1949. The other was a copy of her father's will dated three days after Christmas of the same year. While looking over her shoulder, I tried to read Randall Miller's words, but Caroline was trembling so much, I could barely decipher more than a smattering of what he had written. He used adjectives like disgraceful, ignominious, selfish, and reprehensible to describe Caroline's behavior. In addition, he wrote words like angry, disappointed, disowned, banished and unforgivable to convey his emotions toward his daughter. The final sentence referred to the money enclosed in the envelope and stated it was all she deserved and all she would ever see of his fortune. His letter was brusque and decisive.

It became increasingly difficult for Caroline to mask her feelings. As she allowed her knees to buckle, she sat down on the couch and hung her head in shame. I wanted to wrap her in my arms and tell her everything would be all right – I'd take care of her – but the dominate emotion that surfaced inside of me was guilt. I knew it was my fault. When Ricky was born, Caroline had wanted to go home. She had wanted to face her father again with the hope of reconciliation. Perhaps with time, they could have forgiven each other but my stubborn pride had denied her the chance. She had not asked again until Rosaline was born; even then, I had put off her request until it was too late.

We collected our children and left without telling her stepmother we had been completely unaware of Randall Miller's death. I drove aimlessly through the town; neither of us spoke. Huge black rain clouds threatened to dump torrents upon us. There was even an occasional lightning bolt, but the thunder was far in the distance. Rosaline was asleep in her mother's arms; Ricky and Bradley were bouncing in the backseat begging to return to the big house and ride ponies. I didn't know where to go or what to do; I certainly didn't know what to say. Finally, I drove the car into the parking lot of a motor lodge. I glanced at Caroline; she nodded approvingly. Even though it was still early afternoon, I went in the main office and rented a room for the night.

Caroline gathered the children on the bed and began to read to them from their favorite book: *Fairy Tales by Hans Christian Andersen.* If I were not previously aware of the bombshell which had gone off in our lives, I would have thought the vision of my family, curled up together on that motel bed, was tranquil and beautiful. I was in awe of Caroline's quiet fortitude and calm demeanor. The children had no idea their mother's heart was broken.

I didn't know what Caroline was thinking; her deportment was rather stoic. From the moment we had heard the news, my wife had avoided eye contact. Was she angry with me? Did she feel as if I had stolen her away from the life she deserved and deprived her of seeing her father one last time? All of my insecurities came rushing back. I didn't know what to say to her, and I was afraid of what *she* might say to me. I thought I'd go crazy if I had to stay in that tiny room for another moment. After grabbing the keys, I muttered, "I'm going to get us something to eat." I left before Caroline could reply.

Without giving it much thought, I bypassed the center of town and drove directly to the cemetery, parked the car and walked the short distance to my mother's grave. It was exactly as I remembered it. So much in my life had changed, but that little plot of land – that I had held so sacred – was still exactly the same. It had a calming effect on me. My heart stopped pounding inside my head, and my breathing became more even. I began to relax.

As a child, whenever I had felt the world was crashing in on me, I had always been able to find peace here – sitting by my mother's gravestone. I had given up long ago on the concept I would ever hear her voice again, but I truly believed if I spoke aloud, *she* could hear *me*. I could still remember – as a kid – how much better I felt voicing my feelings – even asking questions out loud.

I should have been worried about the ominous clouds over my head, but I ignored them.

I wanted – no – I needed – to be that little kid again. I needed to be able to speak the words – I *needed* her to hear me. Ironically, it felt therapeutic to talk out loud. With every word I spoke to the wind, I felt stronger. I told my mother about Caroline, about our children, and how much I loved and needed them. I spoke of how wonderful my life had become – better than I ever imagined – and I wished she could be here with me to share it all. The more I talked, the stronger I felt. It was as if huge weights were lifted off of me.

I must have sat there for an hour – maybe an hour and a half – before I noticed the dark rain clouds had vanished; they were replaced with a bright blue sky. As I lifted my face to the sun and closed my eyes, I whispered, "Thanks, Mom." I couldn't hear her voice, but I was certain she was with me. I kept my eyes closed for several minutes savoring the feeling of her presence.

I returned to my car and decided to take a short trip through town. Driving by Maple and Main, I noticed there was no longer a newspaper stand on the corner or a young boy yelling "Extra!" while holding a copy of the latest edition; instead, the newspapers were in a stack outside the drugstore. The town had changed drastically. As I continued to glance around me, I noticed many of the neighboring stores, which had been built prior to the Depression, were gone. Instead, there were newer, more modern facilities. The town was bigger, growing, and far more prosperous than I remembered.

The Grand Palace still stood majestically as a focal point on Main Street. People were already forming a line for the matinee. *Giant,* with Elizabeth Taylor, Rock Hudson and James Dean, who had died in a car crash before the completion of the film, was on the marquee. The movie had been playing in the big cities for a year, but obviously – from the look of the line – it was still hugely popular. While Caroline was pregnant with Rosaline, she had read Edna Ferber's novel and was eager to see the movie. I had promised to take her numerous times, but I was always too busy at the restaurant – we still hadn't seen it. I seriously doubted she would be in the mood to see it at the Grand Palace.

As I crossed over the railroad tracks and drove closer to my old neighborhood, I noticed there were additional changes on the south side of town. I traveled slowly, absorbing the view. The houses in my old stomping ground were gone – demolished – as if they had never even existed. In their places, rows of new homes stood – some finished – some under construction – all small, but tidy and modern. It no longer looked like a slum with rusted fences, broken windows and poverty in every direction; instead, it appeared to be a flourishing community. Apparently – like many places in America – my hometown had also discovered the term suburbia, and the radius of the municipality was spreading beyond the original community.

As I meandered slowly down the unpaved road, I watched as carpenters nailed 2 x 4 boards, roofers applied shingles, and bricklayers prepared concrete. It was a bustling world of activity and growth. Eventually, I came to the home of my youth. To my dismay, the tattered building was even shoddier than I remembered. It was a crumbling shack amongst the thriving community – neglected and shabby as if it were the neighborhood trash heap – it stood as a testament to my troubled past. There was no glass left in any of the windows, and the front door was missing. Scraps from the surrounding construction were strewn around the yard haphazardly with no regard to property lines. The porch had collapsed, and the fence was completely gone. In spite of the fact I instinctively knew my father was not inside, I pulled into the overgrown grassy driveway.

After getting out of the car, I walked to the cabin of my youth. Painful memories flashed involuntarily in front of my eyes. I wanted to wash those thoughts out of my head – erase my roots – but they wouldn't disappear. Instead, I saw Calvin working on the old Chrysler, Mom hanging laundry on the line, and my father sitting on the front porch. I stepped over the piles of trash and walked into the cabin. My God! It was worse than I remembered.

The place was totally gutted. Not one scrap of material or piece of furniture in sight, and the stairs to the loft were hanging by a single dilapidated board. Sadly, that wasn't the worst of it. To look at the shambles was disturbing enough – but the added punishment came when I saw rats scurrying upon my entrance and piles of human excrement in several places. A vile odor permeated the air. I took the handkerchief out of my pocket and covered my nose.

Humiliation swept over me. Thank God I had not brought Caroline or my children with me. I could not bear the thought of my sons witnessing the ugly truth about my family. I never wanted to share this degradation with anyone; I wanted to forget.

"Hello, Richard!" The voice came out of nowhere.

I was jarred by the sound, and I nearly tripped over my feet as I turned to see the intruder. To my horror, framed in the doorway and surrounded by the brilliant afternoon sunshine, I came face to face with Jerry Adams. I was completely taken aback by his presence. The last person I expected or wanted to see under these circumstances was my old nemesis. A mixture of resentment and prior jealousies raced through my blood.

"As luck would have it, I happen to be here today – overseeing the project." Jerry made a gesture toward the yard. "I see you have a new jalopy parked out front. Nice wheels! Nice clothes! You must be doing pretty well." Jerry's voice was steady, relaxed, but not friendly. He took the hardhat off of his head and stuck it leisurely under his arm. After squaring his shoulders and challenging me with a jutting, dogged chin, which oozed confidence, he added. "Is Caroline with you?"

I didn't answer.

"You both disappeared on the same day. The rumor mill figured you were together. Are you still?" Jerry waited for a response.

"We're not going to talk about my wife." The initial shock of seeing my old adversary was behind me, and so were the insecurities of my youth. I stood tall, determined to give a resolute appearance.

"Your wife?" Jerry barely spoke the words. "You and Caroline got married?" There was a stunned expression on Jerry's face.

I stared directly in my old rival's eyes and repeated myself. "I said we are not going to talk about my wife, and I meant it." With a defiant expression, I dared him to broach the subject. I was in no mood to mince words with him about Caroline.

Jerry changed the subject. "And why – pray tell – after all of these years – do we deserve the honor of your presence?" Jerry's voice dripped with sarcasm.

Showing no weakness, I stated firmly, "I'm looking for my father."

It was Jerry's turn to appear surprised. "Sorry, old buddy, I have some bad news for you," Jerry spoke frankly and without compassion. "Your dad died three, maybe four years ago."

"My father's dead?" I whispered. I was too numb to feel the impact of his words.

"Yes." There was no sympathy in Jerry's voice. He didn't even wait for me to digest his information. He continued, "You may be surprised to hear me say this, but I'm glad you've come back. I've been trying to buy this piece of property for more than a year, but with your father dead and you gone – there was no one to sell it to me."

The news of my father's demise caught me totally off guard, and I was unable to grasp the meaning behind Jerry's conversation. "You want my father's land?"

"According to county records," Jerry pointed at me. "It's your land now."

"And you want to buy it from me? Why?" I asked casually.

"I'll give you $700 for it." Jerry's voice was strong. "It's a damn good offer –more than it's actually worth."

"If it's not worth seven hundred, why are you offering that much?"

"You've been gone eight years. For all I know, you will disappear again tomorrow. I've bought the entire area – a hundred acres. I mowed it all down, and I'm building a quaint little subdivision, affordable houses for the miners." Jerry raised his arms and gestured around him. "Your piece of property is dead center in the middle. I'm going to be honest with you, Richard. I need this land. The house is worthless. Any fool can see that! The roof is caving in – there are rats living in it. Hobos squat in the corner." He took a few steps in my direction, gingerly avoiding the feces. "What do you want with this dump? I'm making you a good offer."

For the first time in my life, I felt assertive – perhaps even superior – while in the presence of someone who lived on the north side of town. As I looked around the decaying cabin, I grinned slightly and allowed Jerry to see a fraction of my expression. How ironic! I had something – other than Caroline – that Jerry Adams wanted. With a quiet smirk, I hesitated and kept him in limbo regarding my answer. He was speaking in a casual manner, but I could tell he was desperate to make a claim. It felt fantastic to string him along. I wanted to see him sweat before I relinquished. "I tell you what," I spoke slowly. "I can see you want this

land. And I'm willing to sell it to you, but you have something I want."
I paused to make sure I had Jerry's full attention. "Something that was
originally mine, and I want it back."

"What?" Jerry seemed genuinely confused.

"Baseball cards."

"Baseball cards?" Jerry mumbled. "What baseball cards?"

"You toss in Ty Cobb and Fred Clark," I stated with a definite aura
of assurance. "*And* you throw your Lou Gehrig rookie card into the pile,
I'll sign the deed."

"You mean to tell me this deal hinges on a few juvenile baseball
cards?'

"Yeah." I replied. "That's exactly what I'm saying."

"You're crazy!"

"Maybe!" I replied as the memory of the day I'd lost those cards in a
marble contest, well over a decade ago, flashed through my memory. "It
seems I have something you want." To drive my message home, I added,
"I'd rather see this house rot to the ground before I'll sell it to you. It's
the cards or no deal."

"Jeez, Richard! I don't know where those baseball cards are." Jerry
had a whine in his voice. "Hell! For all I know, my mother threw them
out years ago."

"Maybe she did. Maybe she didn't." I stared at Jerry, calling his bluff.
"But you better hope she didn't throw them away, because this deal de-
pends on it." I steadfastly added, "No cards! No deal!"

"This lot is about the size of a postage stamp! It's nearly worthless!
I'm offering you a good price for the property." Jerry's voice was getting
increasingly louder. "Do you mean to tell me you won't sell it to me
unless I give you three lousy baseball cards?"

"That's exactly what I'm saying." I stared him eye-to-eye and called
his bluff.

"You son-of-a-bitch! You took *my* fiancé, and you left town in the
middle of the night like some kind of thief. Caroline was *my* girl! I got no
explanation – she just vanished. I was humiliated! Years later, you show
up with your high and mighty attitude – driving a Cadillac – acting
like you're somebody special – and you expect me to cow-tow to your
ridiculous requests."

As if it was yesterday, I could see Jerry and Caroline walking in the school's hallways – arm in arm. To my surprise, a surge of adolescent jealousy swept over me. I suppressed my insecurity and focused all of my attention on my anger. "First of all," my voice was oddly serene. "Caroline might have been your fiancé, but she was never *your* girl." I paused long enough for my message to sink in. I savored the moment when Jerry's arrogant expression changed and realization washed over his face. "And secondly, you're the one who wants to make the deal. I don't give a damn! I'll let the rats and the hobos have it for all eternity. If I don't want to sell it; I'm not going to sell it." Without moving a muscle, I eyeballed him. "Live with that!"

"Okay! Okay!" Jerry threw up his hands in defeat. "I won't lose this deal over a few lousy baseball cards. I think I know where they are."

"I figured you did." I smirked. "I'm staying at the motor lodge on North Main. Tomorrow morning – 9:00 – bring the cards and the cash. I'll sign the papers." To my total amazement, once I said the words, I felt relief. Perhaps selling the land would give me closure on a part of my life I wanted to bury forever.

3

Caroline

When reflecting upon my marriage, I realize there have been many peaks and valleys throughout the years. From the moment I met Richard – with the exception of our time in high school – he was my hero, my champion, and my best friend. We were children together – we entered adolescence together – we became adults together – and we became parents together. Our lives were completely intertwined – there were often days when I couldn't tell where my personality ended and his began; *we were one*. In addition, we had a magnetic chemistry that bonded and rewarded us with mutual pleasure. Some of my most cherished memories were those we shared in the dark – those passionate moments when nothing and no one else existed in the world except us.

But we had troubled times too.

Throughout 1957, our relationship seemed out of sync. It was a difficult year – there were a lot of transitions for every member of our family: some of them went smoothly, others did not. In addition, our communication skills were at an all-time low; as a result, Richard and I wrestled privately with the emotional grief caused by the loss of our fathers. We simply didn't talk about it. Our silence compounded our pain.

As the hot summer days passed, my husband spent increasingly more time at the restaurant. Richard read in the newspaper that President Eisenhower was a champion of the small business owner, and the American people were benefiting from the highest wages, the highest employment numbers, and the highest standard of living ever enjoyed by *any* nation on earth. But those facts weren't good enough for Richard; he knew the risk of failure for all business owners. As a result, he became obsessed with being successful and spent a minimal amount of time focused on the children or me.

The first few weeks of the summer, I took the children to the community pool on a daily basis, but it was closed toward the end of June due to an outbreak of polio. With the deadly epidemic of 1956 still fresh in everyone's mind, panic was rampant. The virus attacked children far more frequently than adults, so parents kept their children home. Richard and I had several heated arguments about vaccinating our children, but my husband didn't trust Salk's vaccine. When Richard debated the issue, he vetoed my opinion and cited the incident in 1954 when 200 people contracted the virus *from* the vaccine, and eleven of them died. I countered his argument by reminding him of the article in the newspaper claiming investigators discovered the reason those people became ill from the vaccine was due to an improperly made batch, and I also pointed out – recently – there were two children in our town who came down with polio, and the prognosis wasn't good for either of them. In my opinion, the risk of contracting the virus was greater than the risk of being injected by a bad batch of vaccine.

On more than one occasion, Richard demanded, "Keep the children home, and don't invite any kids over to play." Consequently, for the majority of the summer of '57, Rosa and I were my children's sole playmates.

Several times, I risked my husband's wrath and invited Lucy Harrod and her son Martin over for a visit. We were both starved for adult female companionship, and we talked incessantly throughout the afternoon while the boys played with their toys. Other than the Harrods, I didn't socialize with anyone. I felt like a prisoner – and the house was my jail.

For entertainment, we read a lot of books including Bradley's favorite, *The Cat in the Hat*, which was an innovative children's book by a clever new author named Ted Geisel. The first eight times I read the book, I loved every page, but then I began to dream the words in my sleep. It wasn't long before I dreaded seeing Bradley coming toward me with that book in his hands.

We also played countless board games. I thought I would surely go insane if I had to play *Checkers* or *Chutes and Ladders*, or – God forbid – *Go Fish* one more time.

It would have been easy for me to allow the children to watch television throughout the day, but Rosa kept insisting the black and white tube machine was *the devil in disguise*. Over and over again, Rosa said, "No let that silly thing spoil their minds and weaken their bodies. Television is the devil's playground. Children need to play with toys, run outside – get fresh air." Rosa insisted we limit their viewing to a couple of daytime shows like *Captain Kangaroo* and *Mickey Mouse Club*. While those shows were on, Rosa and I were able to finish our chores; if we were quick, we could occasionally squeeze in a break for a cup of coffee. In the evening, the boys were allowed to watch one show a night: *Zorro, Leave It To Beaver*, and *My Friend Flicka* were normally their favorites choices.

The restaurant closed at 10:00 on weeknights; so, Richard rarely returned before 11:00. Routinely, Rosa retired by 8:30 after the children went to bed, and I found myself alone. It was that stretch of time which was the most difficult to fill. I missed Richard and those years when he and I had worked together – side-by-side – sharing the load. If it weren't for sewing and reading, I would have surely lost my mind.

As much to save money as to fill the hours with my favorite hobby, I continued to make most of the boys' outfits. Brad, of course, wore Ricky's hand-me-downs, until the summer when Bradley grew so much he was wearing the same size as his older brother; after that summer, hand-me-downs became obsolete, and I had to make clothes for both of them.

Lucy often marveled at the boys' outfits and raved at what she called *incredible talent*. "You are an amazing seamstress, Caroline! Have you ever thought about doing it for a living?"

The first time Lucy said those words, I felt as if knives slashed through my heart. I knew she was complimenting me, but to speak so informally about what had once been my dream caused tremendous pain. I wanted to tell her about Radcliffe and my desired career in fashion; but instead, I smiled and said, "It's a hobby to keep me busy."

It was also necessary to make an entire new wardrobe for myself because nothing fit anymore. After the boys were born, I easily lost the weight I had gained during pregnancy; unfortunately, it was not the same after Rosaline was born. Rosaline was well over a year old, and I still had an extra eight pounds pasted on my hips and thighs; therefore, my McCall patterns no longer fit, and I had to purchase an entire new collection. Even though Richard insisted I had – what he so kindly referred to as – an hourglass figure like Marilyn Monroe – all I saw was *chub*, and I hated looking at my reflection in the mirror. He repeatedly told me I had been "too thin in high school," and I looked "better with a couple extra pounds," but I didn't agree with him; in fact, I felt as if he was patronizing me.

It wasn't just the extra weight. I was twenty-six years old, and I could already see tiny wrinkles under my eyes and lines on my forehead. Although I had yet to find a gray hair, I figured it wouldn't be long before I discovered one. It wasn't fair! Richard looked more handsome now than he did when we were teenagers, and he had an aura about him that exuded success. I was acutely aware of the fact that women of all ages noticed my husband. Truth be told, they often gawked at him. Tiny pangs of jealousy cut into my heart. It didn't help my insecurities when Richard's time and attention was totally monopolized by the restaurant; in addition, his female employees fawned all over him. It reminded me of our days in high school when clusters of giddy girls trailed in Richard's wake.

In addition, I noticed my husband rarely moved to my side of the bed at night – not nearly as often as he had before Rosaline was born. All of this was compounded one afternoon when Lucy and I saw Marilyn Monroe in *The Seven Year Itch*, and I wondered who my husband was fantasizing about in his spare time. *Or was he doing more than fantasizing?*

Sewing wasn't my only leisure activity. During the summer of 1957, I devoured at least a dozen books, but three stood out above the rest: Jack Kerouac's *On the Road*, *Profiles in Courage* by a United States Senator named John Kennedy, and *Peyton Place*, which was a tantalizing story about a small town in New England. Those books could not have been more different, and each sparked a distinctive reaction from me; suddenly, I became more aware of my surroundings. John Kennedy's novel inspired a deeper interest in my country's history and made me proud to be an American. Kerouac's novel opened my eyes to the changes in our culture; in fact, I even pointed out to Richard that it had an obvious impact on the clientele and revenue at the restaurant. The café on the veranda, which I had suggested when we renovated the building, was now full of beatnik-type individuals who carried guitars and read poetry most of the afternoon. Although the tables were often full, it was rarely profitable because the customers never ordered more than coffee or an occasional dessert.

But the novel that captured my attention the most was Grace

Metalious' *Peyton Place*. I often blushed as I read the chapters, and I hid the book in my top drawer under my panties so neither Rosa nor Richard would know I was reading it. In spite of the fact the story was quite scandalous, I couldn't put it down, nor would I admit to anyone I owned it. Ironically, part of me identified with two of the characters: Rodney Harrington and Betty Andersen. They were teenagers in love and from different sides of town. Their story touched my heart. In a strange way, the characters and the plot created a fire inside of me that was only quenched when Richard touched me at night in the privacy of our bedroom.

Over the years, I had learned how to read my husband's moods. Most days, he was too tired to talk and would shower then crawl into bed with barely a word passing between us. Other days, he was full of energy and spewed stories of the day's activities. Those were the nights I slipped into my chiffon nightgown and waited for him to show an interest in me. When he did, I instantly encouraged him. After we made love – I would curl up in his arms, and we would sleep in that position until morning. Perhaps it was due to the high temperatures even after the sun went down, which made our bedroom feel like an oven, or perhaps it was because Richard was preoccupied with thoughts of the restaurant. No matter what the cause – it felt as if those *special* nights were occurring less frequently, and I missed his fingers on my skin. I ached to be close to him, but he didn't seem interested anymore.

In late July, John and Lucy Harrod moved into their new home, which was two blocks from the house Richard was building for us at the crest of the hill. The completion of our new home was behind schedule and would not be finished until Labor Day. Neither Lucy nor I had a car; consequently, our friendship was limited to telephone conversations. I missed her. In addition, polio remained a terrifying fear. At Richard's request, I continued to isolate our children from neighbors and friends. My days consisted of household chores, shared coffee breaks with Rosa and entertaining the children.

I was lonely.

By mid-August, I thought I was going to lose my mind. Finally, I took matters into my own hands and had the children vaccinated against polio without telling Richard. When my husband found out, he was

187

furious with me. Richard raised his voice and screamed at me in front of the children. I held my breath and prayed there would be no serious ramifications. Thankfully, there were no side effects from the vaccine. When the doctor gave us the "okay," we found our freedom, left the boundaries of our yard, but I had no car. Consequently, the children and I couldn't go very far.

Richard was rarely home. I continued to feel as if I lived in a prison with invisible bars and nothing to do but mundane household tasks. Each day seemed to be hotter than the last; in fact, it was so hot the ice melted in the boys' Tang before they could consume the liquid. The children didn't seem bothered by the extreme heat, but Rosa and I were constantly damp with perspiration. For days on end, there was no relief.

The movie theater was one place to find refuge. On several occasions, I begged Richard to join us. *Old Yeller* was playing in Newark. I'd heard from numerous sources that Walt Disney had made yet another wonderful movie – a real family film – but I couldn't convince my husband to take the time off from the restaurant to join us.

As he sipped on his morning coffee, Richard smiled and said, "If you go see *Bridge on the River Kwai* or *The Joker is Wild,* I'll join you, but I think you can handle *Old Yeller* on your own." His voice was condescending.

"The boys are too young for those movies. They want to see *Old Yeller.*" I hated the whine in my voice as I added, "The movie is not what's important. It's being together, doing something as a *family.* Please come with us."

"I can't, Caroline. Between overseeing construction on the new house and obligations at the restaurant, my schedule is packed." Richard downed the remainder of his coffee in one large gulp. When he was finished, he donned his suit jacket and gave me a quick peck on the forehead. "I tell you what. When I have a free day, I promise to take you to New York, and we'll see that play you want to see on Broadway – what's the name? *West Side Story.*"

"When you have a free day?" My patience was gone, and my temper flared. "You've been saying that all year. Quit making promises you have no intention of keeping!" There must have been something alarming in my voice that captured Richard's attention because he suddenly stopped.

"I *have* said that a few times, haven't I?" He spoke quietly. "I tell you what! We'll go! This weekend!" He stepped toward the door and reached for the knob. "I'll get tickets for *West Side Story*. I swear!"

"Stop!" I was so angry I thought my head was going to split open. "I don't want to see *West Side Story.*" I caught my breath. "No! That's not true. I *do* want to see it. Who doesn't want to see that play?" I threw my hands up in frustration. After taking a couple of deep breaths, I attempted to start the conversation over again. "Of course, I'd love to go to the play, but – even more – I want to do things as a family." We stood in the middle of the kitchen. Richard looked stunned, and I was shaking from bottled tension. "Do you realize," I paused. "Sometimes days go by and you don't see the children. You barely acknowledge them before you leave for work in the morning, and you're never home for dinner – more times than not – they're asleep before you return. Occasionally, you speak to them on the phone. When was the last time you read them a book or played a game with them or showed them your baseball cards? You use to love to do that! And they loved it when you did." I felt as if I was shrieking, and I hated the tone in my voice. "You're never here! Your children will be all grown up one day and you will have missed it. You won't know them, and they won't know *you!*" I took a break from my tirade. I couldn't believe I was venting in such a fiery way. It was so unlike me. Normally, I behaved in a dutiful wifely manner. *Who was this shrew?*

Richard did not respond to any of my comments. Instead, he lowered his eyes and side stepped around me. Before he reached the front door, he quietly murmured, "We'll talk about this later."

My husband's cavalier behavior made me fume even more. However, the moment I heard the car engine start, my anger melted into tears. I could not control them. Out of nowhere, Bradley appeared at my side silently stroking my arm. His tenderness calmed me.

"Are you okay, Mommy?" He asked.

I threw my arms around him and choked back my tears. "Yes, Bradley. I'm fine. Thank you for taking such good care of me."

Rosa quietly entered the room and put her arms gently around both Bradley and me. The warmth of her embrace gave me much needed fortitude. I finally got control of my breathing. As I was stifling my tears, I could hear Rosa quietly coaxing Bradley out of the room. When he was gone, my brief experience with confidence waned and the tears returned.

"What is the matter with me?" I cried. "Everything is falling apart. I don't recognize myself anymore." Between my sobs, I managed to say, "I wash dishes and change sheets and do laundry and make dinner. I scrub the floors. I change diapers. I iron . . . oh God! I iron and iron and iron! I'm so sick of ironing! Richard goes to the restaurant every day! He seems to thrive from it. He is so happy! *But not me!* I feel like this meek, shallow person who doesn't have an identity. *Who am I?* I'm someone's wife. I'm someone's mother. But really . . . I'm just a maid! Oh God! I feel like I'm dying inside!"

"You sit down, Caroline." Rosa patted the chair. "I make you some tea."

I collapsed in the chair. "I didn't think my life would be like this. Richard is never here. He's either working at the restaurant or overseeing the builders at the new house. I don't care about *that* house. Why does he think we have to live in such a huge house? We were so happy in our room behind your restaurant Rosa. Those were the best days of my life."

"Yes," Rosa interjected. "Those were good days. Good days for all of us." Rosa patted my hand. "But you forget, Caroline. You had *one* baby then. The room was barely big enough for you. How do you think Richard, *three* children and you could live in that one room now?"

"Then why can't we stay here in your house? This is a lovely place."

"It would be okay with me if you stay here – forever. I love that you live with me. I no want to be alone. It has been difficult on me since my Mario died. You and the children keep the loneliness away." Rosa dabbed her eyes with her monogrammed handkerchief. She lowered her voice and looked directly at me. "Your wonderful Richard is a proud man. He wants his *own* home. We know this house is not big enough for all of us. Plus . . . Richard wants the children to have a quiet road. This road not safe for children. Too many cars. Too much noisy traffic." The tea kettle began to whistle. Rosa got up and poured two cups, then returned to the table.

"You don't understand, Rosa. I could have gone to college. I could have had a career – maybe in the New York fashion industry – or Hollywood! I had dreams too!"

"Would you trade those three gorgeous children for some job in the city? Bah!" Rosa threw her arms in the air. "I no believe that! Never!"

"You don't understand, Rosa. You don't understand what happened."

"You think I no understand?" Rosa lowered her voice. "I understand. You no talk about it – but I understand." She whispered her words. "You and Richard make a baby before you are ready to be parents. You are a couple of innocent teenagers – then presto – you have a family. You no get to go to college. You afraid of your father, so you leave your home, and you leave your dreams behind." Rosa paused. "Then you go back to your father's house to find out that he is dead – and has left you very little – a few dollars and a nasty letter. You're hurt and you want to share your pain with your husband, but he is too busy working – working to make *his* dreams come true. His dreams are about *you* and the children – *his family! Your family!*" Rosa paused. "You are a lucky girl, Caroline. Your Richard stand by you. He works hard. He is not a quitter."

Rosa cupped my chin in her hands and made me stare directly into her eyes before she continued, "You do not give up on marriage, Caroline. Marriage is for life. You take the good with the bad . . . it all evens out. Right now is the bad! You not happy. But marriage is not always laced with happiness. Whoever told you marriage is easy? It's no easy. It's work! When one is down the other must be strong. When it's your turn to be down – he will be strong. That's how it works. But you don't give up on marriage – you don't give up on each other." Rosa again patted my hand with gentle strokes. "It's always difficult when children are little – it will get easier with time. I promise. Don't give up on Richard. He is not giving up on you."

2

Richard didn't go with us to see *Old Yeller*; however, the following Monday, we did – as a family – spend the day on the sailboat. Rosa volunteered to stay home with Rosaline, which gave us more time to focus on the boys. It was a glorious day, perhaps the best one of the summer. The temperature was sizzling hot, but there was enough of a breeze to keep the sail robust and the boat moving. I packed an enormous picnic lunch. Roast beef on rye for Richard and me. The kids requested peanut butter and jelly sandwiches made from the new Jif brand. They loved repeating the slogan "Jif is never dry; a touch of honey tells you why," and mimicked "Jifaroo" the blue kangaroo by squatting and jumping on the deck while they ate their sandwiches. If they weren't so adorable, they might have been annoying. Instead of snapping at them, I smiled. I also brought soda pops – which were rare treats for the boys – carrot sticks, pickles, a large bag of Korn Kurls and two boxes of Barnum's Animal cookies on a string: one for Ricky and one for Brad. The idea they might share a box was unheard of in our family. I worried Richard would get upset by the mess the boys made on the deck while they ate lunch, but my husband simply filled a bucket with river water and splashed the crumbs overboard. The boys roared as they, too, were soaked by his gesture.

I packed our portable transistor radio, which provided background music. The songs enhanced the atmosphere. Because it was a weekday, there were not many boats on the water. It was as if we had the entire river to ourselves. Richard showed great patience when he taught the boys how to operate the sailboat. He gave them both small duties, and their faces lit up with pride. It was a magical day, and I thoroughly enjoyed watching my husband interact with our sons. I took an entire reel of home movies – most of the footage was of fishing. When I looked at Ricky with a pole in his hands, it felt as if I were looking at my husband when he was eight years old. The wonderful memories washed over me.

The next day Richard surprised us all when he came home early from the restaurant. In his hand he carried a large box. When the boys inquired, he gently put the box on the floor and let them open it. Inside they found a puppy. It was an adorable dog: part Lab, part Hound, and part Golden Retriever. The puppy looked so much like *Old Yeller*, I was convinced Richard had gone to the movie with us and seen the dog on the silver screen. Needless to say, our sons were thrilled. Ricky and Bradley argued for two days on a name for the puppy; eventually, they agreed upon one: Rex. At first I was upset Richard brought home a dog without discussing it with me, but it wasn't long before the puppy wormed his way into all of our hearts. He was a gentle, loving and fiercely loyal dog. Although Rex was not allowed on the furniture, he behaved acceptably ninety-eight percent of the time. But at night, when the children were asleep, I could inevitably find Rex curled up at the foot of Bradley's bed. Hopefully, my sons were unaware of the obvious; the puppy had chosen a favorite. Rex followed Bradley around like a shadow.

On Labor Day Weekend, we moved into our new house. It was not completely finished, but we needed to be there before the first day of school. In addition, Rosa had put her house on the market, and she had a buyer. It was a move we all made together. Rosa was part of our family.

John Harrod helped Richard while Lucy, Rosa and I stayed behind with the kids, and we did our last minute packing. The process took most of Saturday. When the remaining boxes were loaded and Rosa's house was empty, the kids and I went with Lucy to the new home. Richard met us in the driveway. He was grinning from ear to ear. I'd never seen him so excited. My husband scooped me up in his arms and ceremoniously carried me over the threshold. I couldn't help but chuckle at his sentimental gesture.

Richard smiled proudly as he twirled me around in the foyer. "Is it everything you wanted, darling?"

I was shocked. What I saw was totally unexpected. I hadn't been to the house since before the painters put the finishing touches on the walls and trim. "It's perfect, Richard. I love it." It looked like something I had seen in a magazine. It was beautiful. Custom made curtains. Beautiful rugs. Brand new furniture Richard had secretly purchased and had delivered. Our living room looked like a showroom at a furniture store. It was gorgeous! The dining room had beautiful new furniture too. Stunning! I was impressed with Richard's sense of style and color. The kitchen was a dream come true – all of the modern appliances. There was also a room for doing laundry with a chute connected to the upstairs bathroom so there would be no need to carry the clothes downstairs – what a wonderful luxury! Rosa's comfortable furniture was in the family room along with our television console. It may not have been the prettiest room in the house, but I knew it would probably be my favorite place to spend time with the family. There was a part of me that wished Richard would have included me in making these decorating decisions – it would have been fun to do it together, but I saw how proud he was as he carried me around the house. Therefore, instead of showing disappointment at being excluded from the process, I expressed joy in all of the choices he'd made. He beamed with pride.

When our tour of the first floor was completed, we returned to the foyer. "I can't wait until you see our bedroom. I hope you like it." He kissed me with an urgency that suggested there would be more when the family was in bed for the night.

Hand in hand we raced up the stairs. Although we offered Rosa one of the four large bedrooms on the second floor, she chose the smaller room off of the kitchen, claiming the stairs were becoming increasingly more difficult for her to maneuver. As a result, all three of the kids had their own room, and we had the master suite, which was far bigger than necessary. It was luxurious!

Our new house was fabulous, but it was the four acres of land that made our lives so wonderful. The peaceful environment allowed Ricky and Bradley to roam freely and play in the brook, which flowed through our backyard. It felt like a slice of heaven.

I thought Richard would race off to the restaurant for the dinner shift, but – to my jubilation – Richard spent the evening with us. Shortly before sunset, he opened a bottle of wine. Together, we sat on our porch and watched the boys chase fireflies in the backyard. Rex, with his tail wagging like a metronome, merrily followed their every move. Our new home wasn't like the house we had shared with Rosa. There were no longer any horns blaring or highway traffic sounds from the congestive thoroughfare. Instead, the sounds were pleasant: the chirps of crickets, Rex's occasional bark, and the laughter of our children.

During the evening – after a couple of glasses of wine – Richard reached for my hand. He squeezed it tenderly; then, he pressed his lips upon my fingers. "Are you happy, Caroline?" Instead of his words sounding content and relaxed, they seemed somber.

"How can you ask such a question?" Quite perplexed by his melancholic inquiry, I glanced at Richard. He was not looking at me; instead, he was watching the boys as they scampered playfully through the yard. Richard did not speak for more than a minute. The pensive expression on his face worried me.

"When we went to Pennsylvania," Richard spoke slowly as if he were contemplating every word he said. "And Jerry Adams came to our motel room to give me the check for my father's land," he paused again as he swallowed. Richard looked at me, and then looked away as if he didn't want to see the expression on my face. "When you saw him – did you wish – even for a moment – that you . . ."

"Don't say it, Richard." I interrupted. "Don't give credence to that question." I couldn't believe my husband gave a fraction of a thought as to how I felt about Jerry Adams.

"I built and sold dozens of houses, and I have a restaurant." He took a sip of his wine. "Jerry owns a whole town."

"Do you think I care about that?"

"Don't you?"

"No." I reached for my husband's hand. "Richard, look at those beautiful boys. And our daughter – she's upstairs sleeping peacefully in her crib. Our family. You, me, the children and Rosa. That's what I care about. *Our family*! There is nothing Jerry Adams had or has that I will ever want."

When I looked at my husband, he was staring at the boys with a reflective expression on his face. As he spoke, his eyes remained on his sons, "Thank you, Carley." He gently squeezed my hand again.

His voice seemed so different – unlike any other time I'd heard him speak. I was too spellbound by his mannerisms to make a response.

"I never thought," Richard whispered softly, almost as if he were speaking to himself instead of to me. "I never thought my life could be so perfect." When he looked at me, the corners of his mouth curved upward to form a smile that showed no teeth. There were tears glistening in his eyes. "Thank you, God." His words were barely audible. "Thank you for giving me this wonderful life."

3

The school year began on Tuesday, September 3rd, the day after Labor Day. The previous year, when I had taken Ricky to his first day of first grade, it had been a relatively unemotional occasion. My first-born had been ready and eager to attend elementary school. He left with a smiling face and a quick wave. "Bye, Mommy!" And he was gone: a Mickey Mouse lunch bag in hand and milk money in his pocket. Admittedly, I had a misting of tears at the thought of how easily my sandy-haired boy made the transition. He was growing up. Ricky was able to count to 100, and he already knew his colors, his ABCs, and was able to read the short sentences like those in *Fun with Dick and Jane.* He had done well throughout the entire year, excelling on his report card and receiving complimentary remarks from his teacher.

This year, on the other hand, was not nearly as trouble-free. The day I took my middle child to his first day of first grade, Bradley cried. I had not foreseen the impact the move and the new school would have on my children; unfortunately, I did not explain it well to them. Ricky adjusted instantly, but Bradley was much more tentative. When it was time to go to school, Bradley clutched Rex and sat on the floor, "I'm not leaving, and you can't make me." Tears streamed down his face. "Who will take care of Rex? And who will take care of you, Mommy?" My middle child was not quite ready to let go, and I suppose, I wasn't either. Perhaps he sensed my emotions. In retrospect, I blamed myself.

More than likely, because of the circumstances of their births, I treated my boys differently. The day Ricky was born, he was alert and healthy; whereas, on the day Bradley was born, he was premature, underweight, fragile and frighteningly small. Because I had two children so close in age, I weaned Ricky off the breast early and taught him to use a cup. The moment he could hold a spoon, I taught him how to feed himself, and I encouraged Ricky to walk shortly after he learned how to crawl. Ricky spoke clearly and used full sentences long before he turned two. Even at an early age, my first-born was extremely responsible. I could count on him to be well behaved, articulate, and cheerful most of the time. Ricky, with his sweet disposition, his eternal patience, and his eagerness to please, allowed me to academically push him as hard as I wanted and rely on him to be "my little man" when I needed his assistance.

In contrast – from the day Bradley was born – I coddled him. Bradley was far more stubborn than his older brother and, once he had overcome the obstacles of a premature birth, he suddenly became more physically active by nature; consequently, he wanted to play with his trucks and car, ride his bicycle, or do anything that didn't consist of sitting still for more than five minutes. Instead of being jealous or resentful, my oldest son was tolerant of the attention I paid to his younger brother. He seemed to intuitively understand Bradley needed more care and attention.

As hard as I tried not to, I compared my boys and noticed physical attributes and specific personality traits in both of them that also existed in Richard and me. Even a stranger could tell Ricky looked exactly like his father: chestnut brown hair that turned slightly blonde in the summer sun – same sparkling blue eyes – a warm, friendly smile. He even had a small dimple in the center of his chin: exactly like Richard. In addition, Ricky moved like his father – athletic yet graceful. Confident.

Bradley, in contrast, looked nothing like his father; instead, he resembled my baby pictures to such a degree, Rosa could not tell the difference. Bradley had a broad smile that showed all of his baby teeth. His round dark brown eyes were encircled by a double row of long, thick lashes that matched the jet-black color of his hair. If I let his hair grow too long, it turned to ringlets all over his head. My husband was constantly telling me I looked like Elizabeth Taylor in *Father of the Bride*. I savored the compliment, and when no one was looking, I stared at my reflection in the mirror and made my own judgment. Aside from the fact my eyes were dark brown and Miss Taylor's were violet, we did have some similarities. When I remembered Elizabeth Taylor as a child with her hair cut short in order to play the role and appear boyish in the 1944 movie *National Velvet*, I could see how much Bradley looked like her as well. My husband was constantly saying Bradley was too pretty to be a boy, and he insisted I dress our son in boyish clothes and keep his hair cut short so people would not mistake him for a girl.

When it came to personalities, my sons were the exact opposite. Ricky looked like his father, but he acted exactly like me: academically driven and constantly trying to please people. He was patient. When Ricky felt secure, he showed independence. He moved with poise and had a polished air about him that made him appear refined. Perhaps he was a little timid regarding some issues, but self-assured in most ways.

Bradley, who looked exactly like me, behaved more like his father. Stubborn. Often quiet. Pensive. He rarely expressed his emotions – occasionally brooding. Yet, he was also highly energetic. My middle child would rather go outside and play than look at a book. If I could bottle Brad's energy and market it to others, I would make a fortune. Bradley never sat still, yet – at the end of the day – he was the first to crawl into my lap and ask for a bedtime story. In spite of the fact he didn't speak often about his personal feelings, Bradley was cuddly, affectionate, and incredibly protective. He preferred to express himself with gestures instead of words.

Ironically, although Richard got along better with Ricky and doted on Rosaline because she was the only girl, my husband seemed to gravitate more toward Bradley – giving him more attention than our other two children. For that reason, I made a conscientious effort to devote extra time to Ricky and Rosaline in order to balance the family dynamics.

4

There were many lovely advantages to living in our new home; however, there were a few disadvantages too. The constant autumn leaves turned out to be a huge negative for me. Rosa and I started raking leaves at the end of September and were still not done until the week before Thanksgiving. I never realized the majestic oak and colorful maple trees required so much labor in the fall. Richard wasn't around to help; in fact, he rarely saw the daylight hours at home. Therefore, the job landed on Rosa and me. The boys had small rakes, but keeping them focused on the task at hand was often more difficult than letting them venture off on their bikes to play with friends. One such day in mid-November turned out to be a mental nightmare for me.

Rosa and I worked all day in the yard, but we finished in time to have dinner on the table at the regular time: 6:00. The boys did not come home, which was highly unusual because they both knew when dinner was served, and they both had a Mickey Mouse watch. They were never late. A growing apprehension washed over me.

Concern turned into panic at 7:15. I was about to dial a few familiar phone numbers when the boys and Rex finally came through the back door. Their clothes were filthy, and the dog was covered in mud. Ricky and Bradley didn't even have the decency to look ashamed or worried about being tardy.

The moment I saw my sons enter the room, my fear turned into grateful relief. Within seconds, my initial emotion was replaced with anger. "Where have you been?" I demanded.

"We were playing tag football with our friends." Ricky replied. "Sorry we're late."

"What's for dinner, Mom?" Bradley smiled in his adorable manner.

"Dinner?" I replied with a suppressed timbre of anger in my voice. "There won't be any dinner for you tonight!"

"But, Mom!" Ricky interrupted.

"Don't you dare 'but, Mom' me!" My voice was a notch higher than I would have liked. I was losing control. "You both know when dinner is served. You also know if you are late – you don't get dinner." I could see on their faces they had finally realized they were in deep trouble. "Both of you," I pointed to the door. "Go out back and break off a willow branch – and make it a good one."

Ricky and Bradley were gone less than three minutes before returning with a branch in their hands. Their selections were thin and about three feet long. The boys looked nervous.

"You wait until your father comes home!" I bellowed as I snatched the branches from them. "You boys are going to get it!" I lowered my voice before continuing, "Now march yourselves upstairs and take a bath. When you're done – go to your rooms – and don't come out."

Without a word, the boys vanished. I felt as if I had been holding my breath throughout the entire episode. As I rubbed my forehead with my fingertips, I closed my eyes. I tried to steady my breathing.

A voice broke through the silence. "Don't you think that was a little harsh?" Rosa asked.

I had forgotten she was in the room. "Harsh?" I whispered as much to myself as to Rosa. "They *know* when to come home for dinner!"

"But it is not good to use willow sticks and their father as a threat?" Rosa was using her most gentle tone. "You are too hard on Richard. You make the boys fear their father. It's not fair, Caroline."

"Fair?" I thought I was going to explode. "Stop defending Richard!" I stared directly at Rosa. I was mad! "*Fair?*" I repeated myself. "There is nothing fair about anything that is happening." As hard as I tried, I could not keep control of my voice. It was getting steadily higher and louder. "Richard is never here! He's too *busy!*" The words seemed to be spitting out of my mouth. "It was bad enough when he borrowed all of that money and was general manager for the construction of this community. It was a house of cards. If one thing went wrong, it would all come crashing down. We would have lost everything."

"But you didn't lose everything." Rosa kept her voice calm. "In fact, you didn't lose *anything*. Richard is a smart man. He made it all happen and now you live in this beautiful house – in this lovely neighborhood. He doesn't do the construction anymore. He has a restaurant. He is good at that. He makes a good living for you and your children."

"Yes! One restaurant was good. But now ... now he has *two*!" I cried. "He took the money my father left me." I covered my face with my hands. "He withdrew all of it from the bank and took out an additional loan so he could buy that rundown building in Morristown." Anger welled up inside of me as I remembered the day he told me he had signed the contract. "He didn't even *ask* me about it! He just did it! His defense is that he believes it will be a great location for another restaurant. It's like he wants to create a dynasty of restaurants so he doesn't have to come home to me." Tears streamed uncontrollably down my face.

"Richard is such a smart man. He is gifted in business. I have faith in him. He knows what he is doing. He works so hard . . . he will make you rich."

My voice was quaking, and I was not even certain my words were understandable. "I don't care about restaurants! I don't care about being rich! I want Richard to come home. I want him to be *here* with *us*!" I was sobbing.

"Now! Now! Caroline." Rosa gently patted my back. "You need to be patient."

"I'm tired of being patient. I'm tired of it always being about *him*! He never asks what I think or how I feel." I took a brief moment to look directly at Rosa. "You always say we are 'a team,' but Richard and I never do anything together. It's as if he doesn't even *see* me anymore – like I'm a piece of furniture or something." I waved my arms around the room. "He decorated this entire house without asking me what I wanted. Hell! He didn't even ask me if it was okay if we got a dog. He went out one day and got one!" I stood up and began to pace the floor.

"But you like Rex!" Rosa interjected.

"That's not the point! He did it without discussing it with me! The boat! The car – everything we have. He goes out and buys it like it doesn't matter what I think!" At this point, I was screaming. To steady myself, I took a long, deep breath and stared directly at Rosa. "And I'm tired of you always being on *his* side." I left the room without giving her a chance to respond.

When I rounded the corner to go up the stairs I saw Bradley sitting on the bottom step. His eyes were wide, and his face was ashen. I knew immediately – he had heard the entire conversation. I froze.

Finally my son broke the silence, "Mommy, if Daddy doesn't come home, I'll take care of you." Bradley's voice was so gentle and caring, my heart melted.

I wrapped my arms around him and kissed his forehead. "My sweet Bradley. I love you so much." I kissed both of his cheeks.

5

The following morning, I woke earlier than usual, prepared breakfast for the boys and made their lunches for school. The house was quiet. Richard was sleeping late because it had been another long day for him, and Rosa was uncharacteristically sleeping in as well. I figured she was upset about our argument, and she was avoiding me. I felt guilty. I knew I owed her an apology for my horrendous behavior. As for the boys, there needed to be consequences for their actions, but I would have to find a less severe punishment. Perhaps they should lose their bike privileges for a week or maybe no TV. Rosa was right. I shouldn't use their father as a weapon of punishment, especially when Richard wasn't even home when they misbehaved.

Richard came downstairs after the boys had left for school and before Rosa came out of her room. I was grateful both Rosaline and Rosa were not awake yet. Their absence gave me private time with Richard. We were rarely alone, and it felt good to spend time with him: just the two of us. I chose not to tell him anything about what happened the night before, and I didn't broach any of my personal feelings. Once again, I simply grasped the few precious moments we had together and enjoyed them. We had breakfast and a couple of cups of coffee before Richard kissed me on the cheek and left for Carley's Place.

After bathing, dressing and feeding Rosaline, I looked at the clock and noticed it was nearly ten. I was surprised Rosa was still in her room. It was time for me to break the ice and apologize. I placed Rosaline in her playpen and knocked on Rosa's door. There was no answer. I called out her name. Still no answer.

I opened the door slightly, "Rosa, are you awake?" Still no answer. It was dark in the room, which was odd because it was a bright, sunny day. "Rosa, would you like a cup of coffee?" No answer. I flipped the switch for the overhead light. The hair on the back of my neck stood up. I tried to catch my breath, but it was stuck in my throat. I knew something was wrong – very wrong.

Rosa was still in bed. She wasn't moving.

"Rosa. Are you okay?"

I took slow steps toward the bed. My heart was pounding. I felt sick to my stomach. Perspiration began to form on my forehead and trickled down my face. It seemed to take forever to cross the room. There was no movement in Rosa's bed. When I touched her shoulder, I instantly knew my fears were a reality.

I also knew I was never going to get the chance to apologize to her.

4

Richard

Monday September 15th began as such a wonderful day. I had no idea I was about to be thrown a wicked curveball, and I definitely didn't anticipate the impact it would have on my life or my marriage. To date, 1958 had already been a bit of a roller coaster ride for us. Rosa's death, nearly a year ago, still left my family with a huge void. Our hearts were heavy. The adjustment was difficult for all of us – but even more so for Caroline. That robust, chatty Italian lady, who had opened her home to Caroline and me with no questions asked, had been more like a mother than a friend – to both of us. We not only missed her presence and her love, we missed her help. Without Rosa, Caroline was overwhelmed by our three children and all of the household duties. In addition, my wife seemed distant and quiet most of the time. The restaurants were having a great year financially, but that was because I was constantly on top of every detail. As a result, I was not home much to help out around the house. Caroline carried the load.

On this particular Monday morning, instead of covering my head with my pillow when I heard the jarring ring of Caroline's Big Ben alarm clock, I rolled to her side of the bed and scooped her up in my arms. It had been a few weeks since we'd last made love, and I missed the closeness we felt when we were intimate. Her alarm clock had awoken me from a blissful dream of past memories when we had shared our bed for other things than sleep. The pleasant flashbacks were arousing and inspired me to make a new memory to savor. I nibbled playfully at her ear and nestled my nose in her hair. She smelled wonderful! At first, Caroline tried to wiggle her way out of my embrace, but with a little coaxing, I had her spinning in my arms and ardently kissing me in return.

It felt fantastic to enter her – slowly at first. But the moment I sensed her intensity, mine multiplied. The euphoria swept through me. It wasn't long before I exploded inside of her. She curled up in my arms for less than a minute before attempting to get out of bed.

"Wait, Caroline!" I held onto her. "Stay a little longer."

"I have to get up, Richard. The boys need to get ready for school."

I thought about arguing with her, but I knew it was futile; she was right. Instead, I moved back to my side of the bed where the sheets were cooler. As I drifted off to sleep, I could hear Caroline singing in the shower. It was a Doris Day tune: *Everybody Loves a Lover.* I couldn't remember the last time her voice sounded so cheerful. Her sweet melody was like a lullaby. As I drifted peacefully back to sleep, I mumbled to myself. *Morning sex is the best – especially if I get to go back to sleep.*

I could hear Mario's imaginary voice whispering in my ear. "Richard, don't forget about the jar . . . in the beginning you put lots of pebbles in it – fill it to the top . . . but remember . . . once it is full . . . you must take lots of pebbles out of it."

Mario was right . . . I need to take more pebbles out of my jar!

When I came downstairs for breakfast around 9:30, the boys had already left for school, Rosaline was eating in her high chair and Caroline was cooking scrambled eggs – still singing. This time, she was in harmony with the radio, and the tune was *Great Balls of Fire.* Her toes were tapping and her hips were swaying. A big grin was on her face as she welcomed me into the room.

"You're eggs will be finished in a minute." She added, "Want a cup of coffee? It's ready."

"Thanks." I took the cup from her. With my other hand, I tenderly cupped her bottom in my hand and pressed her hips against me. I could feel her heat through the cotton apron that protected her dress. "Any chance, Rosaline will take a morning nap?"

"Sadly, no." Caroline groaned. "Rosaline gave up her morning naps months ago. She doesn't go down until 1 or 1:30." She smiled in a co-quettish manner. "Want to hang around until then?"

"Not fair. Don't tease me." I hurriedly kissed her on the lips. "I have several vendors coming before noon and a couple of important meetings in the afternoon. It's going to be another long day for me."

"Great." She muttered in a sarcastic manner. She pulled away from me and returned her focus to stirring the eggs. "So . . . what's new!" Her tone was curt, and her disappointment was obvious. The sexual chemistry, which had been palpably hovering around us moments ago, was suddenly sucked out of the room. It was replaced with polite conversation.

I picked up a copy of the *Newark Evening News*. It was a few days old, but I didn't care. Concentrating on the newspaper was better than seeing the antagonistic expression on Caroline's face. I read an article about The National Aeronautics and Space Act Congress had passed during the summer. Some called it "The Space Act" while others dubbed it NASA. It appeared President Eisenhower would sign it into law in the near future. Last October, the Soviet Union had successfully launched Sputnik, the first satellite, into space. In April of this year, Sputnik 2 was launched; unfortunately for the dog on board, it burned up in the atmosphere. Sputnik 3 went up in May. No doubt about it, the Soviets were way ahead of the United States in the race to outer space. Hopefully, this new NASA program would eventually surpass anything the Russians manufactured. The fact our country was talking about putting people into outer space was amazing. *How was that even possible?*

"Did you read the article about The Supreme Court ruling?" Caroline broke the silence.

I was so engrossed in reading about Sputnik and NASA, I'd forgotten she was in the room. "Which article?"

"This one," Caroline pointed to the headline. "The Supreme Court rules in favor of integration in Little Rock. They announced the ruling last Friday."

I scanned the article.

"I think this is a good thing." Caroline spoke quietly.

"It might be a good idea with a lot of good intentions, but people don't like change. And this is probably going to get messy." It was weird to talk with Caroline about current events or politics. I never thought of her as having an opinion on those subjects. She was always so fixated on the children, their needs, and the menu for our next meal. When did she have time to think about anything else?

Catch a Falling Star by Perry Como was the last song I remember hearing on the radio before the disc jockey came on with the breaking news. The tune kept playing over and over again in my head.

"We interrupt this program with the following . . ." The disc jockey paused. He sounded as if he were trying to get a grip on his voice. "A commuter train derailed and fell into Newark Bay this morning. The drawbridge was open and the train did not stop in time." He rustled with papers that kept hitting the microphone. The distracting sound was annoying. His words were disjointed as if he wasn't sure what to read to his audience. The announcer's job was to play music, not report on disasters. "There are casualties but no one knows how many yet." He paused again. "The train originated out of Bay Head, NJ."

The moment the disc jockey said Bay Head, Caroline dropped the frying pan on the floor. The eggs she had been so diligently scrambling flew in every direction. "Oh my God! Lucy and her mother spent the weekend at the shore. They were coming back this morning and going to spend the day in the city. That's the train they would take to get back to Lucy's mom's house in New York. Oh my God!"

I no longer could hear what the man on the radio was saying. I only saw my wife's face. She looked like a ghost. Pale. Horrified. Even though I knew the radio was no longer playing *Catch a Falling Star*, I kept hearing Perry Como's voice inside my head.

I didn't understand why this particular disaster had such a profound impact on me, but I suddenly felt as if everything I had was fading away right before my eyes. Caroline didn't even look like she was breathing. Her hands were plastered on her face, covering her mouth – holding back a silent scream.

"Caroline. Don't overreact." Even though I was certain it was no more than a few seconds, it felt like an eternity before I reached her and surrounded her with my arms. "We don't know anything yet. Where's John?"

"John took Martin to Lake Aeroflex on a fishing trip over the weekend. They should be home by now." She picked up the phone and dialed the Harrods' number.

I took the receiver away from Caroline. "Let me call John." I dialed the number. The phone rang ten times. No answer. Caroline was trembling so badly, she made me vibrate while I was holding her. "Let's stay calm."

Together we walked to the television and turned it on. The horror was on the screen. The Coast Guard and fireboats circled the bridge. Divers were swimming in the water. Multiple sirens could be heard in the distance. An additional passenger car was dangling: part of it clinging to the bridge while the opposite section was already partially submerged in Newark Bay. It didn't look real. *It couldn't be real!*

The announcer was giving details. "Two diesel locomotives and two passenger cars fell into the bay this morning at 10:13 a.m. At least fifteen people aboard have been killed but we fear the number will rise. The Central Railroad of New Jersey commuter train originated at Bay Head, NJ, at 8:28 a.m. and stopped at Elizabeth at 9:57. Normally each passenger car holds as many as a hundred people. The morning rush was over, so there were not as many people on board. Authorities are saying that many of today's passengers were returning from the Jersey Shore after a weekend at the beach."

Caroline whimpered, but she wouldn't look away from the television set.

2

I never did reach John at home. Instead, he telephoned us around noon. John was talking so rapidly, it was difficult to understand him. He was calling from a pay phone on Corbin Street. John said he had spoken to Lucy on Sunday night, and he knew his wife was planning to be on *that* train. His voice was anything but calm as he retold how he had heard the news on the radio and instantly gotten in his car. He was trying to get closer to the accident site, but the traffic was jammed. Nothing was moving. He got off of the Turnpike so he could call us.

John asked if Caroline could meet Martin at the bus stop after school. "Can he stay and play with Ricky and Brad?" John rambled on in a panicked voice. He insisted he wasn't leaving until he had some answers. "If I can't get home, can Martin spend the night with you?"

"Of course, John." I heard Caroline reply on the extension in the living room. "Martin can stay with us as long as necessary. Is there anything else we can do for you?"

"No, thank you." John mumbled. "Just pray." He didn't bother to say 'good-bye.' We were disconnected.

I stayed with Caroline until 1:30. My first two appointments were easy to cancel, but I couldn't miss the meeting at 2:00. It was difficult to leave Caroline in the house alone. She looked like a robot: hollow eyes and a blank look on her face. She insisted she was okay, but all I could see was the exact expression she had worn during the days after Rosa's death. I vowed to return as soon as possible.

3

Forty-eight people died in the commuter train disaster. Lucy Harrod and her mother were among the fatalities. "Snuffy" Stirnweiss, who played second base for the Yankees in the 1940s and Shrewsbury's mayor John Hawkins also died. Investigators could not find any evidence of mechanical failure in what journalists were calling "one of the worst crashes in our nation's history." Many were speculating as to whether or not the engineer may have had a heart attack between the Elizabeth station and the drawbridge to Bayonne. I did not dwell on the reason for the tragedy – I focused on the fact we had lost a beloved friend.

I was inept at consoling my wife. Caroline never left the bedroom; in fact, she never got out of bed. She didn't cry; she rarely talked. Caroline was even more withdrawn and detached. It reminded me of the months after Rosa's sudden death. Nothing I did seemed to help then *or* now. First Rosa – now Lucy – in less than a year's time.

Martin was still with us; it had been a full day since the tragedy. He thought he was having an over-night adventure with his friends and was unaware his mother had died. The boys fixed their own meals – mostly peanut butter and jelly sandwiches – went to school on their own, returned without assistance, and played outside or in Brad's room. They rarely asked for anything from Caroline. Even Rosaline was undemanding for a two-year-old. They seemed to know Caroline was in distress; however, none of them knew why.

Shortly before sunset on Tuesday, the doorbell rang. I answered it. John Harrod stood like a statue on our front stoop. It was the first time we'd seen him since the painful ordeal was announced on the news. Not five seconds after I spoke his name, I could hear Caroline's feet racing down the stairs. She did not say a word as she ran passed me and into John's arms. I stood in the foyer and watched as they clung to each other. John was sobbing. Caroline was rocking him.

As I observed the two of them consoling each other, a pang of jealousy swept over me. I felt handicapped. Although I was completely unable to give my wife or my friend the comfort they needed, Caroline and John seemed to gain solace from each other. The three of us stood in the foyer without talking for at least five minutes. Caroline had silent tears rolling down her face, but John was openly anguished as he cried. I was grateful the boys were unaware of John's arrival. It wouldn't be good for Martin to see his father's grieving state before he was even told about his mother.

John spoke first. He repeated himself twice before Caroline could understand him. "Can you please help me with the funeral arrangements?"

"Of course, I will." Caroline held John tightly. "And Martin can stay with us as long as you need."

"No." John muttered softly as he tried to compose himself. "I need to take him home. I have to tell him what happened." He took a deep breath and wiped the tears away from his cheeks. "How am I going to do that? What am I going to say?" He spoke more to himself instead of Caroline. He squared his shoulders; John appeared to grow several inches as he mustered the courage to address his son.

4

Four months after the funeral, it still felt like I lived in a morgue. When I was home, I never heard laughter. Hell. There were days when my wife didn't even talk to me. She alternated between the same paisley housedress and her favorite cotton nightgown. That was her wardrobe. I had grown to hate both of those outfits.

Caroline was depressed. I tried everything I could think of to help her. I hired a maid who came twice a week, but Caroline didn't like having a stranger in the house. Consequently, I fired the girl even though she hadn't done anything wrong. I bought Caroline a fur coat for Christmas. When she unwrapped the present, she barely looked it, and I never saw her wear it. I even bought her an Edsel. No one in our neighborhood had two cars. It was an unheard of luxury, but I thought Caroline needed to have some freedom to leave the house and be more mobile. I was hoping it would help her get past the mourning stage, but she never drove it. The car was parked in the garage in exactly the same spot as when I brought it home in October.

I was grateful the children were cooperative. Some of our neighbors helped out by inviting the boys over to play several times a week. I hired the lady three doors down to take Rosaline to her house Monday through Friday. I thought it would help Caroline, but I think she spent those days curled up in bed. I didn't know how to reach my wife. I didn't know what to say. Eventually, I spent longer hours at the restaurant because it was easier than going home. It became a routine. When I left each morning, Caroline was in bed; when I returned each night – she was still in bed. I didn't know if she got up during the day or not.

Occasionally, I came home and found Bradley curled up in bed next to Caroline with two or three books tucked under the blanket. Rex was protectively positioned at the foot of the bed. All three of them were asleep. They looked peaceful. If I didn't know better, I might think it worthy of a Norman Rockwell picture on the cover of *The Saturday Evening Post*. But I knew it was an illusion. Bradley seemed to be the one person in our house who had a connection with Caroline. On those special days when I found them together, I would stand over the bed and pray; perhaps, today was a good day. Maybe tomorrow, this nightmare would be over. But the next day – it wasn't. I felt as if I were reliving the same bad dream over and over again.

Ironically, John seemed to be doing better than Caroline. Yes. He was still grieving, but he was moving forward – living his life. He signed up to be a Cub Scout leader for Martin and Ricky's troop, and he was involved with his church. In hopes he could help Caroline, I called John periodically to ask if he could encourage her to get out of the house and become more active in the neighborhood. To the best of my knowledge, that tactic didn't work either.

I missed Rosa and Mario. They would have known what to do to help Caroline. They would have known the right words to say.

Oh God! Please help me. Please help us!

5

Somewhere in my subconscious, I think I realized what was happening; however, I refused to acknowledge any of the signs. As a result, I felt as if I was broad-sided by a Mack truck.

Winter was over. Spring was in the air. The sun was warm. Skies blue. Flowers were peeking out of the ground. Birds chirped – singing their songs. I had a severe case of spring fever. The big news of the day was Hawaii. In January, Alaska had been admitted into the Union as our 49ᵗʰ state, and now Hawaii would soon become our 50ᵗʰ. Fifty stars on the American flag. I needed to buy a new one to fly on the pole in our front yard. It seemed like a good reason to celebrate.

I didn't feel like working. I was tired of spending my days bouncing between the restaurants. I wanted to go home – spend time sitting on my back porch, listen to the babbling of the brook and watch Rex chase the squirrels in our yard. I looked at my wristwatch; the kids would be home from school in an hour. If I left now, I could spend a little time alone with Caroline – coax her into sitting outside with me. Maybe we could have a beer – listen to music. Enjoy the day. *Enjoy each other!*

I knew she was still depressed, but it seemed as if she was getting better. *I have to believe she is getting better.* At the beginning of the year, Caroline had finally agreed to see a doctor. He prescribed pills for her depression. It was a relatively new therapy treatment, and the doctor believed it would help. Sadly, Caroline said she didn't like the way the pills made her feel, so she stopped taking them. I was hoping her decision was a good sign: a sign indicating *she* was more in control and *wanted* to get better without the help of medication. Maybe springtime was the ingredient she needed!

I couldn't wait to get home. *Be with her.*

As I pulled into our driveway, I noticed John's car parked by the mailbox. Good! John often had a positive influence on Caroline's mood. To be honest, I didn't want to share my wife or the evening with John, but I was willing to make the exception if it meant Caroline might have a genuine smile on her face.

When I walked into the house, Rex greeted me – tail wagging. "Some watchdog you are, Rex." I patted him on the head. "You didn't even bark." I scanned the kitchen and peered into the living room. No Caroline or John in sight. I checked outside. No one. Maybe they went somewhere together. *Oh Hell! Was today the day of the school play?* I hoped I didn't miss it. I had promised my sons I would be there. Ricky was playing the lead role in *Rip Van Winkle*, and Bradley had a role too. He was one of the trees in the forest. Apparently, my younger son had a couple of lines, and he didn't want me to miss his acting debut.

"I didn't know trees could talk." I had said to Bradley.

He had laughed at my comment. "Of course, trees can't talk, Dad." Bradley's voice had been completely serious. "This is a play. It's not real, Dad."

It had been hard not to laugh at my son's innocence.

I looked at the school calendar on the bulletin board next to the refrigerator. No play. It was next week. *Good! I didn't miss it.* I was relieved.

As I mounted the stairs, I pulled my tie loose and slipped it off of my neck. I couldn't wait to put on my favorite #7 Yankees T-shirt: Mickey Mantle – what an All-Star! Last year, the Yankees had won their 24th Pennant, and they took the World Series in seven games against the Braves. Now that the Dodgers and the Giants had left New York for greener pastures out west, the Yankees had all my loyalty. Everyone I knew was singing their praises, and I vowed to take my boys to more of the games during the '59 season. Ricky liked Whitey Ford, which made sense because my oldest son wanted to be a pitcher. But Brad's favorite was Yogi Berra – not because he was the catcher, but because "*he has a swell name,*" as Bradley loved to say.

I walked into my bedroom, undoing the buttons on my shirt. I took four steps toward the closest before I saw them. It didn't register right away. *How could it? It wasn't possible!* I blinked several times, but my eyes weren't lying. As I stood frozen in the middle of the room, I focused on the clothes scattered unceremoniously on the floor next to *my side of the bed!* I felt as if I was viewing a movie as I watched them move in unison and listened to their groans of pleasure. I didn't say anything, but I must have made some noise because both John and Caroline simultaneously sprang up in the bed. John covered himself with the sheet, but Caroline was completely exposed. Horror etched on their faces.

I finally found my voice. "Get out!" I pointed to the door. "Get out, John, before I kill you."

Caroline was wide-eyed and terrified as she frantically adjusted the bedspread around her body. John gathered his clothes and left without saying a word. Moments later, the front door opened, and then closed. The house was deathly quiet.

My wife and I were left alone to pick up the pieces of our shattered lives.

As we stood in the silence of the aftermath, distorted images of the two of them – skin to skin – mouths joined – raced repeatedly inside my brain. I took no steps between us because I couldn't bear the *smell* of him *on* her or the thought of him *inside* of her. Rage mixed with horror as the bitter taste of bile creeped up my throat and threatened to erupt. If I didn't leave the room, I was truly afraid of what I might do to her. My whole world was circling the drain, and I didn't have a clue how to react. I turned to leave.

"It didn't mean anything." Caroline spoke feebly. "I swear. It didn't mean anything." Her words were spoken in a timid, quiet manner. "I'm so lonely. I'm so very lonely. John's lonely too. And you're never here."

I spun around to face her. "Don't you dare try to blame this on *me!*" I was shocked at the strength of my voice. "You're the one who has been unfaithful. I have never, *never* wanted another woman. It's always been *you!* No one else!" I was yelling the words. "You've ruined it . . . you've ruined *us.*"

"Richard, please…" Caroline was sobbing; tears streamed down her face.

"I've given you everything . . . everything any woman could possibly want." I paused. "What woman wouldn't want all of this!" I raised my arms high into the air as if documenting the house as a prize. "I gave you everything!"

"I didn't want any of that *stuff!*" Caroline seemed to have found her voice. It was elevated and strong. "I don't care about cars or boats or this stupid house! *You* wanted those things. Not me!"

"Don't you turn this on me! You're the one who had sex with another man in *my* house! In *my* bed! Damn you!"

"You don't care about me!" Caroline yelled. "You only care about those silly restaurants. And . . . all of these things . . . this house . . . the cars . . . that ridiculous fur coat you gave me . . . why do I need *two* fur coats." A sardonic, daunting chuckle emerged from her lips. "Do you even remember that you'd already given me one?" She glared at me. "All of these *things* . . ." Caroline screamed. "They are *your* trophies . . . and they are *my* consolation prizes. You love to flaunt your *treasures* in people's faces. Big, successful Richard Malone." She stared directly into my eyes. Intangible spears darted from her pupils as she spit her words out like toxic waste. "You're exactly like my father."

With rekindled energy, she sprang from the bed. Seconds later, she was dressed. Caroline walked to the closet and pulled out the largest Samsonite suitcase. She tossed it onto the mattress. Haphazardly she scurried around the room collecting articles of clothing and stuffing them into it.

My fury transformed into panic. "What are you doing?"

"You think I can stay here now?" Her composure was totally gone. She was crying so hard it was difficult to understand what she was saying. "I hate this house! I hate it! *I hate it!* I hate everything about it. Nothing in here belongs to me. I didn't pick out one piece of furniture. Hell! I didn't even choose that bedspread."

She stopped screaming and focused on packing. There were too many items stuffed in the luggage, Caroline couldn't close it. She yanked a few things out and then tried again. This time successfully. It was obviously heavy, but she managed to drag it to the stairs. Instead of trying to carry it down to the first floor, she intentionally pushed it off of the top step. It flipped end over end the entire way down the staircase leaving a trail of black marks on the wall. She followed it down, picked it up by the handle and dragged it through the kitchen toward the garage.

"You can't leave!" I demanded.

She stopped and turned around. Squaring her shoulders, she looked directly into my eyes. "Tell me why I should stay, Richard." She seemed to be pleading with me, but I didn't understand. "Tell me why *you* want me to stay."

I was silent.

"I know you, Richard." She looked right at me as she spoke. "I've known you all of my life. You will never be able to forgive me. Nor will you forget." She paused. "It's like you said," Caroline choked on her next words, ". . . *I ruined* us."

"But . . . the children?" For a moment, I think we had both forgotten about them. "What about the children?"

Caroline stopped in her tracks. Confusion was her countenance. After a few moments, she said, "They can't see me like this. I will come get them tomorrow."

214

"You can't leave, Caroline."

"Yes, I can." My wife seemed composed for the first time.

"What will I say to the children?" I stammered.

"Say what I say to them every night when they go to bed and *you're* not here." She sarcastically added, "Daddy loves you. Only this time *you're* going to be the one who's taking care of them and explaining why there is only one parent kissing them good night."

Even though Caroline was the guilty party, she was acting as if *she* were the victim. My anger flared with renewed intensity. "If you leave, I swear I will change the locks on the doors." Why was I threatening her? *Oh dear God!* Why was this happening? How could I put the brakes on this catastrophe?

"Go ahead . . . change the locks." Caroline lifted her chin in defiance. "It's *your* house. It's always been *your* house." She looked around the room. "I don't belong here." A fresh batch of tears sprang to her eyes.

"Where will you go?" I whispered the words.

"I don't know." Her mournful voice lingered in the air. "I don't have any friends. There's no one."

Caroline took the keys to the Edsel off of the hook on the wall. After opening the garage door, she got in the car. I stood there dumbfounded. *This could not be real!* It was a nightmare, and I was going to wake up soon. Caroline backed the car out of the driveway, turned the wheel and drove away.

Somewhere in the dark recesses of my mind, I heard a voice: distant and mocking. It sounded familiar and touched a nerve. I stiffened. It was Jerry Adams' voice, "You can take the boy out of South Side, but you can't take South Side out of the boy. See! *You're not good enough.*"

I was a teenager again. I felt small and inadequate – like I didn't belong! Images of Jerry Adams flashed in front of my eyes. He was standing in the hallway of my high school with his arms draped around Caroline like a coat – smiling in his cocky, arrogant way. My head was pounding! I could *hear* my heart beating violently against my chest and vibrating throughout my body; I thought it was going to explode. It sounded like the ocean's roar magnified a hundred times. Merged with the waves inside of my brain was Perry Como's recurring voice constantly repeating . . . *Catch a Falling Star* . . .

5

Caroline

There are chapters in a person's life that speed by so rapidly you barely have time to enjoy them and other phases that drag on in a painful and infinite manner. During the past year and a half of my life, I felt as if I'd been on a horrendous roller coaster through hell. I wanted to get off of the ride, but I couldn't find a way to stop it. After the initial confrontation, Richard and I couldn't be in the same room with each other without tempers flaring and angry words flying unchecked out of our mouths. We were both wrong, but neither one of us could let go of our own personal agony to find a compromise or a way back to each other.

That first night, I was in limbo with no place to go. I pooled my crumpled bills and found I had enough to get a cheap motel room. After collapsing on the mattress, I proceeded to cry uncontrollably throughout the entire night. Over and over again, I replayed the events of that day. I still could not remember how John and I ended up in my bedroom. It had not been planned. We had never even touched each other in a sexual way. Since Lucy's death, we had spent time together trying to gain solace from each other. There had never been anything physical between us – just a need to console our hearts. I knew Richard would never believe me, but *it had just happened,* and it was the *only* time. Had my husband not walked in on us, I was certain it would never have happened again. How could I ever explain my actions to Richard and make him understand, when I didn't really understand myself.

In hindsight, I admit I was lost long before that disastrous day in the spring of 1959. I was lonely, I was sad, and I felt as if I were living someone else's life. If I thought the first night was awful, I came to realize it was the beginning of a string of bad choices that turned my life upside down. I had no place to go. In retrospect, I could have gone home and tried to patch our broken marriage, but I didn't. Instead, I did the one thing that surely cemented my destiny. I knocked on John's door and asked for asylum. In my mind, it was Lucy's home rather than John's – a sanctuary where I had spent countless afternoons with my dear friend – a place where I felt safe and welcomed. I truly did not think I was doing anything wrong, so I did not try to conceal my actions. As a result, when Richard drove to work the following morning, it was *my* car he saw in John's driveway.

Richard was true to his threat. He did change the locks on the doors, but that wasn't all he did. He filed for divorce on the grounds of desertion, vowed to leave me penniless, and threatened to take full custody of the children if I even dared to take them away from *his* house. The irony of it all was – John and I didn't share a bed or even a kiss for more than two years after that fateful day.

2

I took one day at a time and made a list of goals. First – I had to get my finances in order. I thought it would be easy, but to my chagrin, I could not get my own BankAmericard without Richard's name on it, and the bank I had been using would not give me even the smallest loan without my husband's signature. It didn't take long to realize I needed to get a job – which was no easy task.

I had heard there was a position at the boys' school in the front office, but I didn't know how to type so my interview lasted three minutes. I filled out an application for a waitressing position at Hot Shoppes, but they weren't hiring at the time. The manager of the A & P took my application for checker, but he told me those part-time positions were usually filled by teenagers or college students who were home for holidays or summer vacation. Finally, I received some positive encouragement when I applied at Bamberger's Department Store. They offered me a position at the perfume counter, five hours per day/five days a week. It wasn't full time, but it was a start. My salary was minimum wage: $1.00 an hour - $25.00 a week. Had I thought I needed to live off of that tiny salary, I would have been terrified; however, John came to my rescue.

He didn't give me a loan or a handout; instead, he offered free room and board if I watched Martin after school. John had gotten a promotion at the Post Office; as a result, his hours had changed from a daytime to a nighttime schedule. He was in a quandary as to what to do with Martin in the afternoons and evenings. Martin was old enough to be left home alone periodically for short periods of time during daylight hours, but not during John's graveyard shift. In addition, since Lucy's death, John didn't want his son to be by himself. Part of my decision was based on the fact Ricky and Martin were best friends and spent the majority of their free time together. It seemed like a win-win for everyone.

As it turned out, my hours at Bamberger's accommodated Martin's schedule; in addition, I was close enough to my children to see them on a daily basis. Therefore, John and I made a deal. To me and even to John, it made perfect sense; however, to Richard, the neighbors, and the courts, it looked as if John and I were setting up housekeeping. It didn't matter that John and I were not sharing a bed and rarely even saw each other. It didn't matter that we were both simply trying to function in a busy, crazy time in our personal lives, and it didn't matter how many times I told Richard there was nothing physical between John and me. What mattered was appearance, and it *appeared* as if I had moved out of my home on top of the hill with Richard and into a house two blocks away with John. I could hear the *buzz* on the street, *"and she left her children behind!"*

3

My life was in total disarray and everything was changing. When I read the newspapers, I felt as if America was experiencing a wave of change too. The new decade brought about new issues, dramatic changes, and a young, extremely vocal generation.

Elvis Presley completed his two years in the army and returned home to Rock 'n Roll music, which was evolving on a daily basis. In February, four Negroes sat at a lunch counter at a Woolworth's in Greensboro, North Carolina, and demanded to be served in a *whites-only* diner. Four months later, President Eisenhower signed the Civil Rights Bill of 1960, which was a landmark law allowing the federal government to inspect registration polls at the local level in order to stop discrimination. Eisenhower believed "every individual regardless of his race, religion, or national origin is entitled to the equal protection of the laws." The democrats of the segregated South were outraged. To compound insult to injury, television's nightly news brought the conflict of desegregating public schools into the homes across America. In global current events, Fidel Castro, who commanded the Rebel Army in Cuba, replaced Miró Cardonas as prime minister and aligned his country with Nikita Khrushchev and the Soviet Union. Consequently, the communists had an ally less than a hundred miles from American soil. To exacerbate everyone's anxieties, the Russians shot down an American plane in May, and many people feared The Cold War would ignite into real battle.

On a totally different subject, the FDA approved the use of the birth control pill, and millions of women all over the country instantly felt the freedom the Pill gave them: no more Rhythm Method or rubbers; more importantly, this new drug gave a woman more control over *when* she got pregnant. As for me, I was no longer intimate with any man, so I didn't need the new form of birth control.

Of all of those milestones and people I read about in the newspaper, perhaps the one impacting me the most on a personal level was the presidential election of 1960. Vice President Richard Nixon was running against a young, attractive senator from Massachusetts: John F. Kennedy. I had read his book, *Profiles in Courage,* a couple of years earlier, and it had left a marked impression on me. Even though I had voted for President Eisenhower and felt as if he had done a good job for our country during his tenure, I didn't think of myself as a republican, nor did I feel an allegiance to Vice President Nixon.

The evening hours were often the loneliest for me. Martin was in bed shortly after sundown, and John worked long into the night. Consequently, the house was quiet. One such night in July, I turned on the radio at exactly the time Mr. Kennedy was accepting his party's nomination at the Democratic Convention in Los Angeles. He spoke eloquently; I was riveted and listened to every word.

*We stand today on the edge of a new frontier. The frontier
of the 1960s. The frontier of unknown opportunities and perils.
The frontier of unfilled hope and unfilled threats.*

I felt as if Mr. Kennedy was looking into my soul and speaking directly to me. Sitting up in my chair, I leaned toward the radio, hanging on his every word.

*The new frontier is not a set of promises, it is a set of challenges.
It sums up not what I intend to offer the American people, but
what I intend to ask of them. I believe that the times require
imagination, courage and perseverance. I am asking each of you
to be pioneers toward that new frontier.*

The next day, I went to Kennedy's local campaign headquarters. The
banner above the door stated *For a Strong President, Vote for Kennedy.*
I walked inside and volunteered to help; I wanted to be a part of this
"new frontier". It gave me a great sense of pride to knock on doors and
hand out his campaign brochures. When I talked to prospective voters,
I pointed out my two favorite aspects of his platform; Kennedy believed
a strong military was the basis for a lasting peace, and he promised to
increase the minimum wage. Needless to say, a bigger paycheck would
personally benefit me; I sure could use some additional money. But more
importantly, I wanted my country and my children to be safe.

Some people, John Harrod included, didn't like the fact Mr. Kennedy
was a Catholic. John was constantly saying, "We cannot have a president
who looks to the Pope for approval. I don't think this fellow can win.
Kennedy's too young and too inexperienced. Nixon is not much older,
but he is a lot more experienced. Nixon will win this election in a landslide." John seemed positive about his prediction.

Even though John didn't agree with me, I stood my ground and continued to volunteer my time. In my opinion, the fact Mr. Kennedy had
a beautiful pregnant wife certainly didn't hurt his chances of winning. I
also liked the fact he had a two-year-old daughter with the same name as
I did. When the three of them stood together, they looked like royalty –
the perfect family. Throughout my life, our American presidents had
always seemed to be wise old men. I rather liked the fact Mr. Kennedy
was youthful and was born in this century.

When I wasn't working at Bamberger's or taking care of the children, I was at Kennedy's campaign headquarters. It gave me a sense of
purpose and personal elation. I left Rosaline with the sitter, but I often
took Martin, Ricky and Bradley with me. They were old enough to be
involved and to learn about our political process. The boys helped me

hand out brochures and carry signs. To my surprise, they seemed to enjoy it. However, once school started, they were back to their regular routine.

I finally got into a rhythm of successfully juggling my work schedule at Bamberger's, volunteering at campaign headquarters and running my errands when two things happened. One was fantastic and the other was disturbing.

The positive event occurred at work. The floor manager called me into his office and asked if I would be interested in working in the ladies' clothing department. Needless to say, I was overjoyed. I couldn't wait to get my hands on all of those beautiful fall fashions. Unfortunately, my raise consisted of a meager dime more an hour, but I was still thrilled to be in charge of dressing the mannequins. Clothes! Perhaps I was finally going to get to work with fashion after all. I was ecstatic!

The second event centered on Bradley. None of my children were happy about what had happened to our family. They didn't understand any of it. All three of them were caught in the middle of a power struggle between Richard and me. It was ugly. It was vocal. And the more Richard and I saw each other, the worse it got; consequently, I avoided going to the house when Richard was there. For a year and a half, I took care of the children during the day, cooked dinner, supervised bath time, and did the children's laundry. The moment Richard came home, I took Martin and went back to John's house. More times than not, we didn't speak a word to each other. Part of me felt pleasure at the idea of Richard stumbling as he tried to perform daily parental chores, like supervising the boys as they brushed their teeth in the morning, making their school lunches, or dressing Rosaline before taking her to the sitter. Throughout our marriage, Richard had taken my household chores for granted, as if they were too mundane to warrant praise or even acknowledgement. Needless to say, he had never volunteered to help.

During the summer months, the children had a lot of freedom and roamed the neighborhood; however, during the school year, the schedule was much stricter. Richard was responsible for getting them up in the morning, fed and out the door in a timely manner. The afternoons were my responsibility, and I spent a lot of time with them on schoolwork. I was emphatic about their education.

Ricky seemed to land on his feet with everything he did. My oldest child was making the adjustment, doing well in fifth grade and rarely had a complaint of any kind. He behaved like a "little man," taking on more household duties than a boy his age should have to do. Rosaline was such an easy-going little girl. Even though she was four, she still enjoyed her playpen, smiled ninty-eight percent of the time and was rarely demanding. Brad, on the other hand, was constantly acting out. He had temper tantrums, screaming fits and sucked up more of my energy than the other two combined.

On this particular day in October, Bradley came home from school with a note from his fourth-grade teacher. When I read it, I was furious. Bradley had been caught cheating on a spelling test. Without thinking, I pulled my hairbrush out of my purse and spanked him with it. Bradley didn't even defend himself. After regaining my composure, I sent him to his room. It was a full thirty minutes before I was relaxed enough to discuss it with him. When I entered his room, I found him lying face down on the bed. I sat next to him and rubbed my hand over his hair, gently tilting his head so I could see his face.

"Brad," I spoke softly. "Why did you cheat?"

Tears filled his eyes. "I tried to study the words, Mom, but it was too hard by myself." He rubbed his nose with the sleeve of his shirt. "I was afraid . . . if I got a bad grade . . . you might stop loving me."

I didn't trust myself to speak right away. Tears burned my eyes. I feared they would spill out, and my son would see them. Bradley didn't look like Richard, but for an instant I saw that little boy I had known as a child. A young Richard who had stood in front of the Grand Palace and admitted he didn't know how to read the sign. A wave of loving memories rolled through my heart. There was something in Brad's eyes that mirrored his father's. I bit the inside of my cheek in hopes I could keep from crying.

"Oh, my sweet son," I stroked his hair. "I will always love you. There is nothing you can do that will make me stop loving you."

Bradley threw his arms around me and buried his face in my shoulder. "I'm sorry, Mommy. I'm really sorry."

"I love you with my whole heart, but I *am* disappointed in you. I want you to remember something, Brad. You are not a cheater. Don't ever do that again!" I made him look directly at me. "Think about this . . . If you don't know the answer to the questions on a test, why do you think the person next to you does?" I took a deep breath. "You need to study hard. It's important. If you need help, then I will help you study."

"But you are so busy, Mom. You never have time for me anymore." Bradley was trying hard to be stoic, but I could see his lower lip quivering and tears filled his eyes.

I cupped his face in my hands. "I promise, Brad. I will be here to help you." I kissed him on his forehead. "I will always be here for you."

That night, after Richard had returned from the restaurants and I had taken Martin back to John's house for the night, I contemplated my choices. I wished I had someone to talk to, but John wouldn't be home for hours. I sat in the quiet house and silently debated the issues. It wasn't long before I realized my children needed my time more than Mr. Kennedy. The next day, I went to campaign headquarters and told them I would not be able to volunteer during the last few weeks before the election. I was forfeiting the excitement of being a part of those final days, but I knew in my heart my children needed me more. I was disappointed, but I was certain I was doing the right thing. The specific hours after school and before bed needed to be dedicated to my kids.

The following day, as I walked out of campaign headquarters, I read the poster I'd seen every day . . . *"Give me your voice, your hand, your vote."* I may not be able to give my voice and my hand anymore, but Mr. Kennedy was definitely going to get my vote.

I was true to my decision and turned my attention toward the children. As a result, Brad's behavior was markedly improved. There were no more temper tantrums and no more notes from the teacher.

Even though I no longer volunteered my time to Mr. Kennedy's campaign, I was still interested in the election. I even watched all four debates on television. John and I argued a lot about who won. He had listened to them on the radio, and I had watched them on television. John was adamant that Mr. Nixon won all of the debates. I, on the other hand, believed Mr. Kennedy showed more charisma because he was the candidate who spoke directly to the camera, which made me feel like he was talking directly to *me.* I finally came to the conclusion – the television was a huge factor in this election. Ten years ago, a small percentage of people owned a television. In the early 50s, most people still got their news and home amusement from the radio. Not so anymore. When we had lived in Mario and Rosa's house, we were the one family in the neighborhood who had an entertainment unit. In this new decade, eighty-eight percent of the homes in America had a television set. It was one more mechanical devise that was changing our lives rapidly; until those debates, I hadn't realized the power it possessed.

6

Richard

It had been two years since I had discovered my wife in bed with John Harrod. I would have liked to erase the image from my mind, but it still burned painfully in my memory and haunted me when I slept. I no longer used the luxurious master suite I had designed for Caroline. Instead, I moved Bradley into Ricky's room, and took Brad's room for my own. I couldn't stomach walking into the bedroom my wife and I had shared, so I closed the door and forbid anyone to enter it. I managed to get through each day by focusing all of my attention on the children and the restaurants; Carley's Place was doing extremely well. The Morristown restaurant was building a solid clientele, too, and was making a substantial profit from both locations.

As for the children, I never realized taking care of them was so difficult and time consuming. Thankfully, Ricky behaved more like my partner than my kid. It was hard for me to think of him as a boy because he acted like a grown man. He took charge: mowed the grass, cooked simple meals and helped a lot with Rosaline. If it hadn't been for my oldest child, I never would have been able to get through the initial transition after Caroline left me.

It galled me that John and Caroline flaunted their relationship by living together a stone's throw from me in one of the houses *I* had built. Caroline insisted on being with our children in *my* house during the day and then she spent the nights with John. She claimed their relationship was platonic, but *what kind of fool did she think I was?* Every time I came within fifty feet of her, my rage flared. It had been two years, and I still couldn't control it.

Even though my life was a nightmare, I thought our country was getting on solid ground with the leadership of our new president. Although the Electoral College vote looked as if John Kennedy had won with a solid margin, his victory with the nation's popular vote was incredibly slim: 112,827 votes decided the election – which was less than one tenth of one percent.

On January 20, 1961, President John F. Kennedy got off to a great start with his inaugural speech; he looked like a leader when he passionately stated, *"Ask not what your country can do for you. Ask what you can do for your country."* I was proud I had voted for him.

However, shortly after my 30th birthday, our new president threw the United States into a tailspin with the debacle at the Bay of Pigs in Cuba. What a mess! The covert mission was a disaster, and Fidel Castro won the day making America and her new president look weak and ineffective. Five days later, President Kennedy accepted the responsibility. In his speech, he said, *"There's an old saying that a victory has a hundred fathers and defeat is an orphan."* He did not point his finger in any direction and lay blame; instead, he stated, *"I'm the responsible officer of the government."* I thought it showed two aspects of his leadership: one – perhaps he was too inexperienced in foreign affairs to be president, and two – it showed real guts to stand up and take accountability for the failure. But it didn't solve the problem. Communism and Castro were still a short distance from our shoreline. To add insult to injury, in May, fanatical Castro announced there would be no more free elections in Cuba. If that wasn't dramatic enough news, word was getting out – the city of Berlin in Germany had been cut in half. Almost overnight, there was a wall dividing the two sections of the city: East and West Berlin. Communism seemed to be playing a role in the post-World War II division of land. Trepidation was growing. I could hear the anxiety in the conversations at the bar in Carley's Place. In addition, when I walked by a customer who enjoyed sitting on the veranda at my other restaurant, I heard, "Damn Commies! They even beat us when it comes to putting a man into space. They did it in April, and we didn't get Alan Shepard up there until May." It wasn't just frustration and concern I heard in their voices; it was fear.

In May, I made a major adjustment in our home life. Ricky had been a pillar for all of us, but I noticed how obsessed both he and Bradley had become with baseball. Roger Maris and Mickey Mantle were on phenomenal home run hitting streaks. Yankee fans were screaming for #61 Maris to beat Babe Ruth's record and hit sixty-one home runs in 1961, and it looked like Roger Maris might accomplish the goal. As a result of the Maris and Mantle competition, both of my sons wanted to try out for Little League.

Ricky worked faithfully every day on his skills. When I saw how much time he devoted to his goal, I realized I needed to hire someone to help us around the house. Ricky had never complained, but it wasn't right to ask my son to give up his dream or his summer. After I hired Gretal as a live-in maid, my oldest son approached me and said, "Thank you, Dad. Now I have enough time to concentrate on my pitching."

Bradley was not nearly as dedicated to improving his skills on the baseball diamond as his brother was. Consequently, when tryouts were over, Ricky was selected for a team and Bradley was not. When the draft results were posted, it was painful to watch my sons. Bradley was obviously heartbroken, and Ricky was trying not to show his jubilation because he did not want to rub salt in his brother's opened wound. My first reaction was to wish Caroline were home; she would know what to say to both boys. I, unfortunately, did not.

For two days, we did not celebrate Ricky's success nor did we discuss Brad's disappointment. Finally I addressed both of my sons individually. I came home early from work to find Ricky in the back yard pitching balls into the plywood board I had built for him. I had painted circles on it which measured the diameter of a sweet pitch and a bull's eye hole cut out in the middle symbolizing the perfect pitch. A net behind the wood captured those balls thrown with precision. I picked up a mitt on my way across the yard and squatted in the catcher's position. "Want to throw me a few?" I asked.

Sheer delight covered Ricky's face. "Sure, Dad," he replied. "I'm working on my fast pitch. Let me know what you think." He managed to throw more than fifty pitches before the sun went down. Eighty percent of them would have been called a strike. No doubt about it, Ricky was good.

When we were done, I wrapped an arm around his shoulder and said, "I hope we do this more often." Before he had a chance to reply, I pulled two baseball cards out of my shirt pocket. "I want you to have these." I handed him Ty Cobb and Joe DiMaggio. "These cards belonged to my brother. Calvin was saving them for his son. I think he would have been proud of you, and he would have wanted you to have them to commemorate your accomplishment. Congratulation, Ricky." As we walked back to the house, I pointed to the DiMaggio card. *"Joltin' Joe* was my mom's favorite player." I smiled to myself as pleasant memories of my mother and radio baseball flashed through my mind.

Later the same evening, I approached Brad. He was in his room reading a Hardy Boys mystery. Rex was sleeping at the foot of his bed, taking up nearly as much space on the mattress as Brad. The big yellow lab was never far from Brad's side. The two of them made quite a pair.

All day I had tried to come up with the right words to say to comfort my son, but they still eluded me. I decided to begin the conversation by handing Bradley my coveted Lou Gehrig rookie card. "I want to give this to you, Brad." Of all of the cards I'd collected, this was – by far – my most treasured one. It was *this* card that sealed the deal with Jerry Adams when I had negotiated the price for my father's land. I had used that money, along with Caroline's money, to purchase the second restaurant. As a result, I had come to think of the card as my greatest trophy.

Bradley was awed by my gesture. "Geez. Thanks, Dad." He kept staring at it, flipping it over and over again in his hand. "Where did you get this?"

"I have a box of baseball cards. Most of them belonged to my brother – your Uncle Calvin. I wish you could have known him." I paused for a moment. "Like you and your brother, Calvin and I collected baseball cards." I grinned as I continued, "You probably don't remember, but I used to show you and Ricky the cards when you were little. It was kind of *our thing.*"

"Lou Gehrig! He was an amazing player." Bradley spoke as he scanned the stats on the back of the card.

"Yes, he was. They called him *The Iron Horse.*"

"Thanks, Dad."

"You really love baseball, don't you, Brad?" I didn't wait for his answer. "I'm sorry you didn't make a team this year."

Suddenly Brad's voice became defiant. He sat up on the bed and spoke forcibly, "Ricky got on a team, and I didn't. How did he get so lucky? It's not fair."

"Who told you life is fair?" I felt as if the word *fair* was symbolic of the disappointment in my own life. Nothing had been *fair* for me – it was all hard work and determination. Then when I thought I had everything figured out and life was smooth sailing, it all fell apart. *That* certainly wasn't *fair.* My voice was almost hostile when I said, "You can count on one thing, Brad. Life is *not* fair."

I pushed thoughts of my life aside so I could concentrate on Brad's emotions. With a calm voice, I continued, "Ricky didn't make the team because the coaches were trying to be *fair,* and it wasn't *luck* when they picked him. Sooner or later you are going to figure out . . . it takes persistence, dedication, and hard work to get the things you want in life. They don't just land in your lap. Next summer, you'll be eleven years old, Brad. If you want to make the team next year, you need to work as hard has your brother has. Practice. Practice. Practice. Don't wait for it to happen . . . *make* it happen. Ricky *made* his own luck. Anything worth having is worth working for . . . you remember that, Brad!"

Bradley wouldn't look at me. Instead, he kept staring at the Lou Gehrig card, flipping it front to back over and over again.

"This man," I said as I pointed to the baseball card. "This man is the epitome of grit and determination. Lou Gehrig was born to poor German immigrant parents. He didn't wait for something good to happen to him. Instead, he took his innate talent, honed it and turned it into a stellar career. He broke records. He was humble, and he was a fabulous role model to a generation of boys who loved baseball. When he got sick with that awful disease, he didn't say 'that's not *fair*',"I paused to see if I had Brad's full attention. "The disease took his physical strength, and Gehrig had to retire from baseball. Did he whine and cry about it? No." I lowered my voice. "He gave one of the most amazing speeches I have ever heard. He said, 'I might have been given a bad break, but I have an awful lot to live for.'" I tapped the card in Brad's hand. "The Yankees retired his uniform and the number 4; Gehrig was the first baseball player in the history of the game to have that honor." I smiled quietly for a moment. "I have lots of cards I could have given you, Brad, but I want to give you *this* card ... not because you might turn out to be a fantastic professional baseball player like Lou Gehrig, but because this card represents what you can do if you put your mind to it." After wrapping my arms around my son with a big bear hug, I added, "Don't wait for chance or luck or fairness . . . go out and make it happen!"

Three months later, I drove home in a torrential rainstorm. When I pulled into the driveway, I saw Brad's bike blocking my way into the garage. I was instantly furious. It wasn't the first time he had left his bike outside and in my way. I got out of the car, opened the garage door and guided Brad's bike into the corner away from the rain. Something caught my eye, or was it the sound that attracted my attention? I moved the bike a little closer to the wall. There was the sound again. I looked at the spokes and saw Bradley had wedged baseball cards into the wires so they would make a flipping noise when the wheels turned. I looked closer. To my horror, I saw my beloved Lou Gehrig card saturated and limp. When I touched it, the card practically disintegrated in my fingers.

I walked into the kitchen. Gretal was cleaning up the dinner dishes; the boys and Rosaline were sitting on the couch watching "Wagon Train" on the television. Rex was curled on the couch between the boys.

"What the hell is the matter with you?" I slammed the card down on the coffee table in front of Brad. "Do you have no respect for anything?" I didn't wait for an answer; I immediately left the room. When I passed the liquor cabinet, I grabbed a bottle of Jack Daniel's and a glass. I went directly to my room and slammed the door. *Damn it!* I poured some whisky in the glass and drank it. It burned all of the way down. I turned the radio on and sat in the chair in the corner. After my second glass, I tried to relax my breathing. I didn't drink much, so the alcohol was definitely affecting me.

As I loosened my tie, Elvis came on the radio: *Are You Lonesome Tonight.* I should have gotten up and changed the station the second I heard the familiar tune. That song made me crazy. I was in the car the first time I'd heard it and was still ashamed to admit I'd cried. No. I'd more than cried. I had sobbed. In fact, I had to pull off of the road onto the shoulder because I'd been blinded by my tears.

I didn't want to deal with those emotions tonight. *Damn it!* I tried to get up, but I felt imprisoned in my chair. The lyrics filled the room – invading my mind.

I banged my hands on the side of my head. *"Damn it!"* I yelled the words to the empty room.

I heard a knock at the door. *Was that the second or third time?*

"Dad? Can I talk to you?" It was Brad's voice.

"Go away!" I yelled my words. The last thing I wanted to do was look at my son's face and see Caroline's eyes staring back at me. "I don't want to talk to anyone right now. Go away."

"I'm sorry, Dad." Brad's voice sounded pitifully small and distant.

It was quiet. The song was over. I could tell my son was no longer at the door. *I should get up and go talk to him. No! I can't. I don't want him to see me like this.*

2

The week before Christmas, Caroline called me at the restaurant and made an appointment to see me. *What the Hell!* She made an *appointment!* This was coming from the woman who wouldn't stay in the same room with me for more than a couple of minutes at a time. *An Appointment!* Caroline wanted to talk to me when the children were not around. She said Gretal was taking all of the kids to see "The Absent-Minded Professor" on Friday night, and she wanted to know, "Can you tear yourself away from the restaurants long enough to meet me at the house?" Her tone was condescending. My temper flared, but I managed to agree to the time.

I got home earlier than I expected. While I waited for her arrival, I made myself a stiff drink. *What on earth could she possibly have to say that the children couldn't hear?* She was probably going to lecture me on my skills as a father – or the lack thereof. *Hell! I don't need this crap!* Caroline made it painfully obvious that I was not the better parent. *Did she forget that she was the one who was unfaithful! And she was the one who walked out the door!* To be honest, I had given her next to nothing in our settlement; consequently, I knew Caroline could not possibly afford to financially take care of our children. I had even been able to conceal the money from Rosa's estate; it was wrapped up in the restaurants. She had gotten the Edsel and $3,000. I had gotten the children and everything else. If I were *truly* honest with myself, I had to admit I kept the children at my house in hopes one day my ex-wife would eventually come crawling back to me, but I knew it was a pipe dream. I had finally accepted our situation, and everyone had gotten use to our odd routine.

I was on my second drink when she rang the bell. I left my glass on the desk in the library and went to open the door. Every time I saw

Caroline, I was bowled over by her beauty. Being thirty didn't tarnish even one feature on her face; instead, age seemed to enhance them. Today was no different; she was gorgeous. I silently chauffeured her into the room and took her coat . . . the same fur coat I'd given her for Christmas several years ago. *The one she insisted she hated!*

Her Jacqueline Kennedy hair style was perfect; not a strand was out of place. She wore a little more makeup than usual, and it was applied in a fashionable manner including a slight touch of green shadow on her eyes to match the dress she was wearing. Dark red lipstick magnified the full frame of her mouth. *Damn it! Stop staring at her!* I willed myself to look away, but I couldn't. I was annoyed by the fact I could not restrain the stirring in my groin. *Did she notice?* I didn't want to give her the satisfaction of knowing I was drawn to her. *Why couldn't I control it?*

Spellbound, I watched her every move as she stood in the foyer and took off her three-quarter-length leather gloves. There was an intangible bridge connecting our eyes. We both waited for the other to speak. The silence was deafening. I didn't want to be the first, but I could not stand the muted tension in the room.

"I suppose you are here because of Brad."

"Brad?" Caroline whispered softly. "What's the matter with Brad?"

"He got a couple of Cs on his tests this week. One in science and one in geography."

"I didn't know," she sighed. "I guess we will have to work harder with him," she grimaced sadly. "Nothing's ever easy when it comes to Bradley."

"I suppose you think it's my fault." My chin involuntarily jetted out in deviance.

"I didn't say that, Richard." Caroline took a deep breath. Her words were clipped. She inhaled slowly several times as she contemplated her next sentence. When she continued to speak, the curt tone was gone; her voice was nurturing and surprisingly sweet. "Can't you see how much you and Bradley are alike?" she paused. "He is so much like you, Richard." Caroline looked away. "Sometimes when I stare deep into his eyes . . . all I see is you when you were a little boy." There was a forlorn element to her expression. "He tries so hard to please you. Do you even notice? Bradley hasn't found his talent yet, but he will. And when he does . . . he will be exceptionally good at it." She smiled. "He loves my Kodak and seems to enjoy taking pictures. I got him a camera for Christmas." She paused and stared directly at me. "Please don't ruin the surprise, Richard."

Her little tidbit of news caught me off guard. "That's an expensive gift." The way I phrased my words sounded more like a question than a statement. I wondered where she had gotten the money for it. She must have known what I was thinking because she responded within seconds even though I didn't ask.

"I got it with my S & H Green Stamps. I saved all year." There was pride in her voice.

"I hope he doesn't leave it out in the rain." My words were mumbled; she didn't hear me.

Silence filled the room again. Caroline returned her eyes to mine. There was a message in her expression. *What was she trying to tell me?* I took a step closer. I thought she would retreat, but she did not. To my surprise, Caroline moved toward me. Her eyes were speaking volumes, but I couldn't read a word of her voiceless message. I felt hypnotized by her.

I finally spoke. "Bradley might act like me in a lot of ways," I paused. "But he looks exactly like you, Caroline." We were no more than a foot apart. "Same eyes," I whispered. "Same smile." Neither of us looked away. I felt my pulse quicken, and I could see Caroline catching her breath as if she were trying to control the irregular beating of her heart. Gently I cupped her face in my hands. To my surprise, she did not pull away. "Both you and Bradley have a smile that lights up the room." I traced my fingers over her lips. Her body radiated heat and served as a magnet drawing me closer with every breath. Slowly, I tilted her head up so I could look directly into her eyes. I was lost in them.

There it is! There's that look I always loved. Sweet. Innocent. Tender. *Oh my God!* Gently, I caressed her cheek with my fingertips. It had been so long since I had touched Caroline. We always avoided physical contact of any kind I had almost forgotten how smooth her skin was. All I wanted to do was kiss her. Taste her. Hold her.

We moved at an excruciatingly slow pace toward each other. Lips parted. I was holding my breath; I think she was too. Our eyes were still open; I felt as if I were staring into her soul. Finally our lips touched. I could taste the mint on her tongue as it darted into my mouth and danced with mine. I was captivated. Something clicked inside of me. All I wanted was to be consumed by Caroline. Wrapping her in my arms, I continued to kiss her but with more passion – more urgency.

You've come home! My heart soared. Thank you, God! Thank you!

Joy and lust united inside of me creating a euphoric blend that heightened my excitement. I enveloped her tightly in my arms and savored the moment as I kissed her. I could feel the passion mounting.

Abruptly Caroline pushed me away. "Stop!" she exclaimed in a breathless attempt to regain some composure. "We can't do this." She took several steps backward – a safe distance from my reach.

"What?" I was not even sure I had verbalized the word.

"We can't do this, Richard." Caroline was panting. "I came here tonight to tell you something." She put her hands over her mouth and muffled some words; they were inaudible. Her eyes were wide. She looked terrified.

I was confused – disoriented – and still breathing as if I had run a mile at a rapid pace. Caroline was by the stairs holding onto the railing as if her life depended upon it. *How did she get so far away from me so quickly?* I took a couple of steps toward her.

"No. Don't. We can't do this." Her words were choppy and weak.

"It's okay, Caroline." There was a begging quality to my voice. "Please come to me. It will be okay."

"John and I," Caroline was shaking. "I didn't want you to hear this through the grapevine. I thought you should hear it from me," she paused. She looked like a frightened little girl as she whispered, "John and I got married today."

I felt as if cannon fire went off inside of my head. Caroline's mouth was still moving, but I couldn't hear anything she said. There was nothing but pounding echoes resonating in my brain and drowning out her voice. *Caroline and John got married today! Are you kidding me!*

The shock was replaced with an intense fury. My rage consumed me like the violent winds of a cyclone. Caroline did not anticipate my actions, and she was totally caught off guard. With lightning speed, I took the steps between us and grabbed her by the shoulders. At first, I was shaking her, and she was fighting me. I still could not hear anything she said, but I could feel her nails digging into my skin as she battled defensively against me. Her strength was no match for mine. I easily forced her against the wall and pinned her to it. I pressed myself against her, rhythmically pumping my body on hers. There was no stopping me. When I tried to kiss her, she turned her head. But I didn't give up easily. I used my body to imprison hers and my hands to hold her head still so I could force my mouth on hers. She valiantly held me off during my first several attempts, but the harder I fought her, the more her willpower faded.

I was not sure when or how it happened, but Caroline stopped struggling against me; miraculously, I could feel her move with me. It was as if our bodies were one. I certainly wasn't going to take the time to analyze the moment; instead, I allowed myself to be swept away with the tide. I jerked at her skirt, pulling it up high enough for me to hunt for her panties. Unfortunately, they were underneath her garter belt, which made my ultimate goal more difficult. At least she wasn't wearing a girdle. *God! I hated those things. Why did women wear them?* I thought about striping off her stockings, but I didn't need to because I was able to clasp her panties with my thumb and fingers. Two yanks and they were gone. I wasn't sure if they ripped or I had pulled them down her legs. Either way – it didn't matter; I had a clear passage to my goal.

I shifted my concentration to removing my pants, but Caroline was already committed to the mission. She was equally as ardent as she jerked at my belt and pulled at my zipper. Her hands slid underneath the material and groped me from behind, pulling me as close to her as her strength allowed. I could no longer control myself. I entered her with such a fury; my actions caused her body to slam against the wall. Caroline wrapped her legs around me and locked them behind my back. Together we moved in circles around the foyer. I was subconsciously searching for a place where we could be more comfortable but forfeited the idea because I was too consumed by my passion. Instead I returned to the wall and repeatedly pumped her against it. She wasn't fighting me. Caroline was equally as aggressive in her physical needs.

Panting in unison, we reached the zenith. I was too weak to hold her up any longer. As the roar of the waves in my ears subsided and I could focus again, I felt my perspiration – no – *our* perspiration merging on my skin and trickling down my face. Her heart was beating forcibly; I could feel it pounding through her chest and onto mine. I pressed my lips into her hair and drank in the scent of her.

For as long as I could manage, I blocked out reality. I didn't want to remember. *No! Block it! Don't think about it!* Ever so slowly the truth worked its way back into the present. Caroline had come to the house for a reason. *No! No! Don't think! Hold on to Caroline. Stay in the moment!*

"Oh, Richard," she stammered. "I'm so sorry."

Oh no! I remembered. Caroline came to tell me something . . . she married John. Damn it! Damn her!

"Shut up! Shut up! Don't you dare say another word!" Anger rose inside of me. As if it happened moments ago, I could clearly see John in *my* bed with *my* wife! The memory filled my soul. I struggled for oxygen. It was hard to breath. *How many times had she emphatically stated, "It only happened once!"* Since that fateful day, Caroline had been swearing her relationship with John was platonic. She had stated over and over again . . . "I live in *his* house purely for convenience."

"Shut up!" I demanded because I didn't want to hear anything about the two of them. Caroline came to *this house – our house –* to tell me she had gotten married. My stomach began to churn. I was fairly certain I was going to be sick. I had to get control of myself. I took a couple of deep breaths as reality brought me back to the present.

Caroline and John are married! They could rot in Hell!

I was certain Caroline saw fire in my eyes because she took several steps backward to be out of my reach.

I was not sure how I managed it, but I spoke with a calm and detached voice, "John Harrod slept with my wife." I starred directly into Caroline's eyes and finished my statement. "Now I've slept with his."

Caroline let out a wounded cry.

"Go home, Caroline." This time, I spoke with animosity. "You make me sick!"

7

Caroline

The week after my 31st birthday, the manager at Bamberger's summoned me to his office. I took the elevator up three flights and had to wait ten minutes outside his door. Needless to say, I was nervous. In fact, my palms were sweaty, and I hoped my Fresh stick deodorant was not failing me. After working nearly three years with Bam's, I was making twenty-five cents an hour over minimum wage, which meant I earned $1.40 per hour before taxes. It wasn't a lot, but combined with John's salary, we did okay. I was hoping this meeting with Mr. Phillips was to inform me of another positive annual review and to give me a third raise; however, to my sheer delight, he offered me a promotion.

"We've been watching you, Caroline." Mr. Phillips said. You are an excellent employee. You're prompt, reliable, always courteous to the customers, and you have quite a knack at displaying the garments in the showroom windows." He smiled in a reassuring way. "It's time for us to utilize your talents. How would you like to go into our training program? If you do well, you will be a manager in the Ladies' Department."

"Really?" I felt tongue-tied. "That would be swell."

"You will start tomorrow. Tom Barker will shadow you for six weeks and train you." He paused. "Do you have any questions?"

It was all so sudden, I could barely think. "Ummm," I hesitated. I wondered if it would be okay to ask about a raise. Hesitantly, I inquired, "Does it change my hours and my pay?"

"Of course," he nodded. "It will be a full-time position. You will work eight hours a day, five days a week. Thirty minutes for lunch each day. Keep in mind, you will alternate weeks. When you work Monday through Friday, you will open with the store. When you work Tuesday through Saturday, you will close the store. You're a lucky girl, Caroline, because this schedule will always give you a two-day weekend. Plus you will get a couple of sick days a year and a week's paid vacation." He looked at his watch and then back at me again. "All of this hinges on passing the program. However, I think you will do well. I can tell you have an eye for detail and fashion. It doesn't hurt that you are a looker too." He winked and cocked his lip in a half smile.

"And ... my paycheck?" I asked.

"The job earns $3,536 to start."

"A year?" I could barely contain my excitement. That was a *huge* increase. Of course, I would be working more hours, but the extra money would be fabulous; plus, I was finally getting the chance to prove myself. "Thank you, Mr. Phillips."

As he walked around his desk, he extended his hand. I shook his firmly and turned to leave. He took that moment to tap me softly on my backside. "Congratulations, Caroline." He winked again. "I know you'll do great!"

It was annoying to me when men constantly thought it was okay to touch me in such a personal manner, but I did not want to dampen the moment so I smiled shyly and replied, "Thank you, Mr. Phillips. I won't let you down."

I drove home in a euphoric state. After doing the math in my head, I calculated I would be making $1.70 an hour: a fabulous reason to celebrate. I hadn't been this happy in a long time. Maybe my dream was finally coming true. I wasn't going to be designing fashions for the movie stars, but I was going to be in a position of authority in the Ladies' Apparel department. I could work my way up the ladder. Imagine!

I kept hearing Walt Disney's voice repeating over and over in my mind. "If you can dream it, you can do it." *I know I can do this! I'm going to be great at this job!*

And then . . . I remembered.

I was pregnant. I wasn't showing yet, and I hadn't told anyone, not even John. In fact, I dreaded telling my husband. During all of the times we had made love since we got married at the Courthouse in December, John had used a rubber. One time it broke, and once it slipped off, but he was adamant, "No more kids," and I had agreed. Martin was thirteen, Richard was twelve, Bradley would turn twelve, too, at the end of the year, and Rosaline would start first grade in the fall. It felt as if we were over the hump. No more jars of baby food. No more diapers. No more toilet training. No more holding my breath as they learned how to ride a bike. The hard part was behind us.

In February, when I suspected I was pregnant, I went to my doctor. The results of the *rabbit test* came back the day John Glenn went into space and orbited the earth. Glenn spent four hours and fifty-six minutes circling our planet three times while I spent those hours crying in the bathroom and throwing up in the toilet. For the rest of February and throughout March, I had prayed for a miscarriage, but it didn't happen.

When my doctor had calculated my due date, I had done a quick tally in my head and froze on his examination table. If the doctor was right, I couldn't be sure if my husband was the father of my baby or not. I increased my prayers. *Please, God! Please! I can't be pregnant. It can't be Richard's baby. Please! Please!* But my prayers went unanswered; my hips began to spread ever so slightly and my breasts began to grow. It was not obvious to anyone else, but I knew. This was my fourth pregnancy, and I knew all of the signs.

As I drove the familiar streets close to our neighborhood, I had flash-backs of the day John and I were married. Even now, I wasn't sure why I'd said "yes." John and I had been living in the same house for nearly three years; the first two, we had barely seen each other. John had been in mourning over the loss of Lucy, and I had been adjusting to life without my family. During that time, my world was a complete blur.

Richard had been so angry with me, and I could not blame him for his hostility. What I'd done was unforgivable. I was ashamed. In the beginning, I had wanted to go home, but every time I had been in the same room with Richard, he had shot angry darts from his eyes and had spoken vicious words. I had learned early – there was not going to be a second chance for me – for us. I had been the one to make the mistake, and I was going to be the one to pay the price for it.

Last year, in the fall, John and I had started seeing each other as more than roommates. His schedule at the Post Office had changed, and he had been home more often during daylight hours; as a result, our friendship had grown. John Harrod was not a handsome man, but he was a kind man. And, God knew, I needed kindness in my life. I welcomed the attention he gave me.

When our friendship began to bloom into a physical relationship, we both realized we could not stay in the same house together without a formal commitment. It was one thing to live together as platonic roommates in separate bedrooms, but it was quite another thing to be attracted to each other and have our children witness the personal transformation. As a result, I agreed to marry him.

John and I had gone to the courthouse. When I stood in front of the justice of the peace, I had chuckled pensively at the irony. Most girls get a fancy wedding. Not me! This was my second marriage, and I'd still never had a wedding. No beautiful, white dress. No church filled with loving family and friends. No pretty organ music for me. It felt all too painfully familiar.

When I had gone to the house to tell Richard I was married, I had been engulfed with anxiety. The moment I had seen Richard's face as he stood in the foyer, I had known I had made a mistake. *I would always love Richard Malone.* He had been in my heart since I was six years old, and he would be there for the rest of my life.

When Richard kissed me in the foyer, I truly felt like a teenager again. He magically transported me to a time when we had been young – before life had gotten so complicated. I relished every second of his lips touching mine until reality won the battle, and I had to tell him my news.

Whenever I thought about that night, I was overcome by a combination of fire and ice racing through my veins. Richard had exuded such intense passion; his fury had terrified me. I couldn't believe the gentle sweet boy I had known in childhood was capable of such rage. I didn't like to think about it, and I didn't want to remember the fact his passionate urgency had been contagious, igniting in me a frenzied fervor as he pulled me into the violent physical exchange we had shared. Whenever I reflected upon that explosive moment, I experienced waves of erotic sensations that rippled like electricity throughout my body. Then – like drowning in ice water during a hot day – Richard spoke those venomous words. He hated me, and he wanted to punish me for what I had done to our marriage.

My heart was broken and so was my spirit.

2

During my training, Mr. Barker praised me; I thrived under his tutelage. He was a patient teacher. I learned all about keeping an inventory, when and how to mark the prices down, closing out registers, and evaluating employees. Admittedly, I was tired at the end of the day, but I was also thrilled to go to work each morning. I loved my job. It gave me a sense of purpose and worth – I cherished the feeling.

Several weeks into the training program, I noticed my clothes were getting tight, and it was becoming increasingly more difficult to conceal my growing belly. I wore loose fitting clothes, but I could tell people were curious. Good manners kept them from asking, but the silent question hung in the air.

On Mother's Day, John gave me the soundtrack to *West Side Story*. The movie had come out last year, but I hadn't seen it. Everyone was talking about the film and the music. John told me it was number one on the charts. I graciously accepted the gift, but I silently wondered if I would ever listen to it. For some odd reason, it reminded me of Richard and an argument we'd had several years ago when the play was on Broadway. I stuffed the album at the bottom of the pile; I didn't need additional reminders of Richard in my house.

That night, while John and I were getting ready for bed, he asked me, "Are you pregnant?"

I couldn't conceal it any longer. "I know we said we weren't going to have any children, John, but it looks like we are going to have to make a new plan."

To my surprise, John smiled widely and raced to my side. He gently wrapped his arms around me and kissed me on the forehead. "This is wonderful news. Now we will indeed be a family." He seemed genuinely happy.

I tried to let John's enthusiasm rub off on me, but it didn't work. I could think of nothing but the late night feedings, the baby clothes I needed to get out of Richard's attic and the diapers I would have to wash. I managed a smile, but John didn't know it was not sincere. He was too busy talking about names for a boy or a girl.

Unexpectedly, John changed the subject, "I guess you will have to turn down the position at Bam's."

"What?" I was startled by his comment.

"After the baby is born, you will be too busy for a full-time job." He spoke in an unvarnished manner.

I instantly sat up. With a firm voice, I responded, "I want the job! I'll find a way to do both. We can get a live-in to take care of the baby."

"Stop joking, Caroline. Babies need their mothers. You can't work and take care of the baby too. Besides, we can't afford live-in help."

I pledged to myself, *I will find a way.*

3

It didn't matter how determined I was to juggle my new position and the new addition to our family; it wasn't going to happen. When Mr. Barker found out I was pregnant, he told Mr. Phillips, and I was released from the program. Tom Barker told me I would have made a great manager, but Mr. Phillips stood firm. He looked me directly in the eyes and said, "A manager needs to be dependable. Babies have a way of messing up a woman's schedule. Perhaps in a few years, you might try again." If losing the position was not bad enough, I was told I would be put back on part-time hours. After I heard the news, I went into the ladies' room and cried.

It wasn't fair! I deserved the job! I *knew* I could do it – and do it well.

8

Richard

The day after Labor Day, I walked Rosaline to school. I couldn't believe my little girl was already in the first grade. Gretal had dressed her in a navy blue jumper with a frilly blouse and placed a massive *Pollyanna* ribbon in her hair. It kept falling out, so I took it off and put it in my pocket. Rosaline didn't miss it; she seemed glad it was gone.

I was concerned my adorable daughter might balk at the school entrance and cling to me, but she did not. As we took the final steps, she proudly stated, "I'm going to do great in school, Daddy. You don't need to worry about me." Rosaline let go of my hand, kissed me on the cheek, and proudly walked through the schoolhouse door. My heart involuntarily lurched. Her sweet voice sounded so much like her mother's on the day we met in her father's library. Rosaline also had the same confident air about her as Caroline had at six. I watched my tiny daughter until she disappeared in the sea of other children parading down the hall. Without warning, a wave on nostalgia raced through me, bringing with it a melancholy mood.

I shook my head, and muttered, "Wow! That was more painful than I thought it would be."

The woman next to me chuckled. When I looked in her direction, I could tell she had been watching me. "First child?" she asked.

"No. She's my third. My youngest, but my only girl," I replied, a little embarrassed someone had caught me in such a sentimental moment.

"That's a surprise," she grinned. "You look like a parent who is dropping off for the first time." She paused. "And we don't see too many fathers . . . it's usually the moms."

I looked around. She was right – no other man in sight.

"It's heart wrenching, isn't it?" she interjected.

"What?" I replied as I returned my attention to her.

"Letting them go," she responded.

"I suppose it is," I smiled in a pensive manner. "I certainly didn't expect it to be."

"I have four kids," she paused. "At the beginning of every school year, I'm reminded of something my mother once said to me." She hesitated a moment before continuing. "As parents, the two most valuable presents you can give your children are roots and wings." Again she paused. "We help them build their foundation. But we also have to let them go a little bit at a time, so they can spread their wings – and eventually – they fly away without us."

"Roots and wings," I grinned. "Sounds like your mom was a wise woman."

"That she was." A forlorn smile formed on her lips. "I miss her every day."

"You lost your mom?" I inquired. After she nodded, I added, "Me too – when I was a kid. I wish she could have known my children." When neither of us offered an additional comment, I extended my hand. "I apologize. I have not introduced myself. I'm Richard Malone."

"Yes, I know. I recognize you," she said as she politely shook my hand. "You own Carley's Place. I go there often. Love your restaurant. Food's great." She smiled warmly showing perfectly formed white teeth. "My name's Helen King. It's a pleasure to finally meet you."

We spoke a little longer before I tactfully excused myself, "It was nice talking to you, Helen." I meant it. I couldn't remember the last time I had enjoyed light conversation.

When I turned to leave, I saw Caroline racing up the sidewalk toward me. No! She wasn't racing; it was more like a quick waddle. Pregnancy had always agreed with Caroline. It didn't matter how far along she was in the trimesters; she still glowed with natural beauty. This pregnancy was no different.

When I had discovered Caroline was pregnant, part of me wanted to ask. *Is it my baby?* But I'd never had the chance. Early in the summer, while we had been in the bleacher watching Brad's first Little League game, I had overheard her talking to another woman. She had been sitting up a row and down a few feet, but near enough for me to overhear her conversation when the fans were not cheering a play. Caroline had told the person her due date was October 10th. I had done the calculation in my head. *The baby wasn't mine.*

I didn't know if I was disappointed or relieved by the revelation.

I'd be lying if I didn't admit Caroline's pregnancy drove me crazy. I was still blinded by rage at the thought of John Harrod in bed with her, and now she was married to him and going to have his baby.

Ironically, seeing Caroline today, I wondered if she really had a month left in the pregnancy. She looked ready to pop.

"Did Rosaline do okay?" Caroline was out of breath and a little flustered. "I tried to get here in time. I can't believe I missed it. The new apartment is further away than I thought. It takes longer to get here."

During the summer, John and Caroline had sold their house in my neighborhood. There were rumors John was financially strapped and behind on his mortgage payments; consequently, they moved to the new garden apartments about eight miles from my house. The kids missed her daily visits, but I was relieved she was no longer a constant fixture in *my* home, especially now that she had gotten remarried.

"Your little girl did great," Helen said. "But I think her father is a little sad." It was obvious Helen didn't realize she was poking at a hornet's nest.

Caroline cocked her eyebrow at Helen, scanned her body, and looked as if she were going to say something but changed her mind. She returned her attention to me. "Typical," she muttered.

I chose to ignore her rude behavior and introduced the ladies. "Helen, this is Caroline. Caroline, this is Helen." I smiled widely; Emily Post would definitely be proud of my good manners. The women acknowledged each other; moments later, Helen politely retreated.

I waved and smiled as she left, "Roots and wings!" I chimed.

"Yes! Roots and wings," Helen laughed as she tossed her hair in a coquettish fashion and walked away.

"What does that mean?" Caroline asked. She seemed annoyed.

"Something her mother told her." I responded. "It actually makes sense."

Caroline sloughed off my comment and asked, "How did Rosaline do? Did she cry or hesitate?"

"You would have been proud of her," I smiled. "She's an amazing little girl."

"I can't believe I missed it!" Caroline seemed honestly disappointed. "And Ricky… in junior high school, riding a *bus*. Did he get on the bus okay? When did he get so old?" Caroline was rambling.

2

The following Monday, Caroline delivered her baby. I did not find out until the next day because I was in my office at Carley's Place having sex with Helen King.

There was no question about the fact I was starved for sexual release. I hadn't been with a woman since last December – with Caroline. When Helen knocked on the door to my office, I invited her in with not a thought about her motives. Smiling, she waved a bottle of wine she had purchased at the bar and said, "Want to toast our children's first successful week of school?"

Normally, I was annoyed by unscheduled interruptions while I was working; however, I was done with my bookkeeping for the day and ready for a break. "Sure, come on in, Helen. A glass of wine sounds like a great idea."

We'd finished more than half of the bottle before I read her signals. When Helen placed her hand gently on top of mine, I chuckled to myself at my naivety; I should have seen it coming. She was sitting on my desk, leaning over enough for her blouse to fall open and expose her nicely formed breasts. In response to her gesture, I got up, took the short walk between us, and stood in front of her. Pausing, I waited for her next move. It didn't take long. She gently caressed my tie and slid her hand up and down the material in a seductive and suggestive manner.

Looking directly into my eyes, she softly spoke, "Mind if I take this off?" When I didn't respond, she slowly removed my tie. As she did, our eyes never lost the intangible connection. Even before she touched me, I knew I was bulging with pent up passion and begging for release. With our eyes still linked, she softly ran her hand over the zipper of my pants. "May I?" she whispered the words.

Totally captivated, I was barely able to stand, much less speak. I managed a slight nod, and Helen continued her mission. Slowly, she took the zipper down. I wanted to kiss her, but I was afraid to move for fear my knees would buckle under me. Helen didn't wait for me to make the attempt; instead, she stood up and gently placed the first kiss on my cheek . . . then another . . . and another ... moving across my face until she reached my lips. My mouth was open, and I was breathing heavily trying to steady myself. With her tongue, she slowly circled my mouth as if she were savoring the taste.

I found my strength and surrounded her with my arms. Like a teen-ager experiencing his first time, I groped and fondled her as I battled to get to the prize as soon as I could. I was dizzy and out-of-control, but I still had the good sense to reach for my wallet. As I fumbled to get the Trojan out of its hiding place, Helen muttered, "Not necessary. I'm on the Pill." Those words excited me even more. We both jerked at each other's clothes removing as little as necessary to get to our goal.

I pushed items off of my desk to make room for us. As I swept my hand over the top, I realized I had sent the bottle of ink for my foun-tain pen flying. I knew I had made a horrible mess, but I didn't care. A fleeting thought crossed my mind: perhaps it was a sign I should start using those new BIC pens the waitresses were constantly raving about to the customers. I pushed the thought aside and returned to my quest.

Once I entered her, I was wonderfully rewarded by the fact I didn't have rubber inhibiting my sensation. It was glorious! Together we moved in spasmodic harmony, relishing every moment of the journey. It didn't last long. Like the man in the desert who finally discovered water, I did not waste time – I devoured her and exploded within a few short minutes.

We laid on the desk – panting in unison. Helen finally broke the silence. "I've been thinking about this for a long time."

The thought mystified me. *How could a woman be so enthralled in the desire for sexual release, and I be totally unaware? Furthermore, when did a woman start initiating the act?* During my experiences as a teenager, I knew the girls who were willing, but they always waited for me to make the move. This was all rather bizarre, but I liked it.

As we adjusted our clothing, I noticed her wedding band. I knew she was married. Helen and her husband often came for dinner; some-times, they arrived late and had drinks at the bar. They were frequent customers. I picked her hand up and gestured toward her ring finger. She smiled, "If he can do it, so can I." She spoke in a flip manner and didn't wait for me to respond. "What's good for the gander is good for the goose." Helen chuckled in a flirtatious manner. "And don't worry, Richard. He won't care," she paused. "But let's not advertise it. Okay?"

What the Hell! Damn right! I wasn't going to advertise any of this.

The next morning at breakfast, Gretal told me John had called to let the kids know Caroline had had her baby. "It's a boy," Gretal said – unaware the subject enraged me – she continued, "He is 21 inches long and 7 pounds, 12 ounces. They named him Randall after Caroline's father, but John said they are going to call him Randy. In spite of the premature delivery, mother and child are doing well." She poured more coffee into my cup before adding, "The baby is rather large for a preemie."

3

October was a nightmare of a month for our country, for our families, and for my business. In the beginning of the month, an American U-2 spy plane had flown over Cuba and detected ballistic missiles. The United States formed a blockade around Cuba to prevent the Soviet Union from increasing any military presence on the island ninety miles south of Florida. In spite of the fact Walter Cronkite remained calm as he anchored the *CBS Evening News*, the American people were terrified. War seemed imminent. All across the country, fallout shelters were being built: hordes of food, water and other supplies stored in them. People stayed home, huddled with their families. They didn't patronize my restaurants. I couldn't blame them; I wanted to be home too. Several days I closed early. What was the point of being open, if no one was there and my employees wanted to go home too?

At school, my children were taught how to hide under their desks if they heard the Civil Defense Siren. I knew damn well a desk wouldn't protect them from the blast or the radiation. However, I recognized it was better for them if they believed shelter from a desk could keep them safe. My sons seemed to gain courage because they shared a room, but Rosaline had nightmares. She woke up hysterically crying at least once a night. It took as much as an hour to calm her down and get her back to sleep. I was terrified for my kids.

President Kennedy showed his muster as a leader and stood his ground. Thirteen days later, Khrushchev agreed to remove the missiles from Cuba. The entire country breathed a sigh of relief. The day it was announced, I had a record number of people at the bar. Yes – people were still skittish, but they had finally stopped holding their breath. Everyone was toasting the country's narrow escape and the president's bold leadership.

Helen and Vince King were part of the celebration.

When Helen came to Carley's Place with her husband, she barely made eye contact with me; however, when she came alone, we wasted no time. Helen and I found great mutual satisfaction together. A smile became a natural expression on my lips.

4

Christmas Day was a disaster for me. I had purchased a dozen presents for each of my children, wrapped them myself, labeled some *"From Santa,"* and strategically put them under the tree after they had gone to bed. In the morning, my children had gotten up before the sun and ripped through the packages in less than thirty minutes. Gretal had the day off and was with her family, so I made pancakes and sausage for all of us. I had hoped to have a leisurely morning with my children, but by 9:30, all three of them were clamoring to be with their mother. It broke my heart to watch them happily walk out of the front door carrying their homemade gift in their arms. As they climbed into John Harrod's car, they didn't even turn to wave good-bye.

After they left, I walked the empty rooms trying to think of something to do to fill the void in my heart. Rex seemed to understand my melancholy mood; as a result, he followed me like a shadow. Finally I sat down at the kitchen table, drank my fifth cup of coffee and picked up the newspaper. Rex curled up at my feet. I rubbed him behind his ear, "At least I have you, Old Buddy."

Around noon, I read an article about the movie "To Kill a Mockingbird," which was newly released for the holidays. I couldn't stand the quiet in the house for another moment, so I went to the theater – alone. *Who the Hell releases a movie like that on Christmas Day?* Yes! It was nearly as good as the Pulitzer Prize-winning novel by Harper Lee, but why did Hollywood launch it on Christmas Day? When I returned home, I was more depressed than before I went.

I guess I had my first drink around 5:30. A few hours later when the kids came home, I'd consumed several. Needless to say, I wasn't in a festive mood. My life was nothing like I had envisioned it. *What happened to my family? What had I done wrong to deserve isolation on Christmas Day?*

Shortly after I had heard the front door shut, Bradley came into the library and sat down on the chair across from my desk. He rambled on about the present Caroline had given him: a baseball mitt. Bradley's hard work had paid off for him last summer. He had finally made a team, and he had done it with a worn-out glove that was too small for his hand. Now, thanks to Caroline, Bradley had a new one. His pride was written all over his face. It was obvious he'd had a wonderful time at his mother's house, which galled me more.

Bradley finally ceased his aimless chatter and sat back in his chair quietly staring at me. All of the joy vanished from his face. His brown eyes were following my every move, and I felt as if Caroline was watching me through him. When I looked at Bradley, I often saw Caroline.

It was so unnerving. Even when the clock chimed nine times, we still sat in silence. We seemed to be in a stalemate. *What did he want me to say?*

"Get out of here, kid." I kept my voice flat and apathetic. "Don't bother me." My words were slightly slurred. Instinctively I knew I was being overly harsh. Bradley didn't deserve it, but I couldn't stand his constant appraisal. *Was he judging me?* I stared down at my glass and wished I could magically disappear from the room so my son wouldn't witness my dismal behavior. "Didn't you get everything you wanted for Christmas?" Bradley did not reply; instead, he continued to stare at me with a blank expression on his face. I shrugged. *Neither did I.* Those words were spoken inside my head; I knew if I said them out loud, I would collapse in my grief. Silence filled the room. I felt the tears burning my eyes. There was a knot in my throat; it was hard to swallow. I didn't think I was going to be able to control my emotions much longer.

"Stop looking at me like that!" I waved my hand several times toward the door. "Scram . . . get lost . . . go play with your new toys."

Without a word said, Bradley disappeared. I cradled my face in my hands and stifled the tears. I was not sure how much time passed before

Rick came into the library. He walked directly up to me before he spoke, "Are you okay, Dad?' His words unleashed the last of my composure. With an unfettered response, the floodgates opened and my tears came. I could no longer control my emotions. Without another word spoken between us, my oldest son wrapped his arms protectively around me and let me cry.

9

Caroline

After Randall was born, I asked the doctor to prescribe the Pill for me. One thing I knew for certain, I didn't want any more children. I loved them dearly, but four was enough. The majority of women I knew were using the birth control pill and raving about it. I'd heard them whispering, "it gives me so much freedom," and they'd smile after saying it. I secretly wished I had taken the Pill before I'd married John. *What would my life have been like if I had not gotten pregnant?* Part of me felt cheated. And part of me felt guilty for thinking about what my life would have been like without little Randy.

John loved the idea of having *our* family. Martin would soon be fifteen years old; he was out of the apartment more than he was home. My children didn't live with us, so John liked the idea of having a baby in the house again – our baby. He didn't relate to the aggravation I felt with starting all over again. Of course not! My husband wasn't the one who was burdened. John didn't have to get up in the middle of the night when the baby cried. He didn't have engorged breasts that leaked and dampened his clothes. He didn't change any diapers or have to stand over the toilet flushing the feces out of the cloth. He didn't have a mountain of laundry to do a couple of times a week. He didn't think the highlight of his week was cruising through the aisles of the grocery store, staring at Gerber jars and deciding which vegetables and fruits to buy. And *he* didn't have to quit work and stay with the baby all day staring at walls in an apartment that truly didn't feel like a home.

On the day I had gone into labor, I had quit my job at Bam's. I had instinctively known I couldn't commit to their schedule, and I'd also been told they wouldn't hold the position for me. I had already been replaced. With a heavy heart, I had said good-bye to all of the women I had worked with in Ladies' Apparel. To me, the biggest tragedy had been when I'd realized it was a ridiculous goal to think I could successfully juggle all aspects of my life. Not only had I lost the dream of being a manager and the personal satisfaction it would have given me, I'd also lost the income I'd earned.

Our finances were a mess. We hadn't saved for Randy's delivery or the hospital stay, nor did we have a nest egg to make up for the fact I no longer had a salary. Six months after Randy's birth, we were still playing catch up on the bills. In order to get a little extra money, I elected to watch a neighbor's child for twenty dollars a week. My baby plus a two-year-old was a recipe for exhaustion.

Shortly after I'd married John, I'd discovered two things. The first – our relationship in bed was rather ordinary. There was little chemistry and definitely no passion. My husband didn't seem to notice I did not enjoy our union as much as he did, nor did he attempt to take me with him on the *ride*. I tried not to think about Richard and the magical times we had shared in the dark. When those memories slipped into my mind, I felt unfaithful to John, so I diligently blocked them.

The second discovery was – to my chagrin – our financial situation. John was a couple of months behind in his mortgage payment. Had I been able to work, we probably could have dug ourselves out of the economic hole, but without my paycheck, we were doomed. We had to sell the house and move into an apartment; as a result, I was no longer within walking distance of the children, and they no longer had the ability to visit me on a whim. I missed seeing them on a daily basis, but John did not seem to mind dividing me from that part of my life.

2

Without question, I felt trapped, but it wasn't until the summer of 1963 when I read Betty Friedan's book, that I understood my emotions. The Feminine Mystique took the mystery out of why I was so unhappy. Friedan called it "the problem that has no name," and I instantly related to her words. It seemed unheard of to want more than a husband, children and a home, but I felt as if I were drowning in other people's lives and didn't have one of my own. I was a wife. I was a mother. I was a homemaker. I *should* be happy. I could still hear Rosa emphatically telling me how wonderful my life was. But it wasn't enough. I didn't even feel as if I had an identity.

Who was I? What did I want?

During the children's nap time, I sat on the balcony, sipped on my TaB, and devoured the pages of Friedan's novel. *She was writing about me!* While teenagers all over the world were singing along to the Beatles' *I Want to Hold Your Hand*, I was listening to Lesley Gore's song *You Don't Own Me*, and the lyrics became my motto. It gave me strength. I vowed *my* daughter would have more choices in her life. Independence and confidence were going to be *her* cornerstones. Rosaline was seven, but it was never too soon to plan her future.

Other than reading, I found my personal entertainment centered on my children and their activities. When I watched Ricky and Bradley – who were finally playing together on the same Little League team – I overheard other women in the bleachers openly discussing *the book*. Even though I chose not to voice my opinion, it gave me confidence to know I was not alone; other women – other mothers – other wives – had the same emotions. There was added excitement on the day in June when it was announced President Kennedy had signed The Equal Pay Act. Several of the women stood at the top of the bleachers and cheered "JFK, JFK, JFK!" I wasn't sure why they were so excited because only one of the women had a job; she was a teller at the bank. None of them was getting a raise, but they were celebrating anyway.

In the bleachers – while women talked about Friedman's book and how they felt in their own personal lives – men were discussing the spread of communism in some far-off country called Vietnam or the tragic racial conflicts occurring in the South that we saw every night on the news. During the week, the fathers showed up with drinks – often martinis – in their hands. They called it "happy hour." I could hear them commenting in a jovial way as they toasted their glasses, *"Happy to be home from work, and happy to be spending time with the family."* Except the men weren't spending time with the family, and their attention wasn't totally focused on the game either. By the fourth inning, the conversations were often lively. If they weren't screaming at the umpire about a bad call, they were generally huddled in their all-male group discussing the latest current events.

In the beginning of the season, I'd overheard Richard and several other men talking about the one Negro boy who had tried out. When the draft was over, he had not been picked. I could still remember how badly Bradley had felt – tears streaming down his face – the first year he had tried out and not been chosen. It had crushed him; however, Bradley had not let the failure beat him. Instead, he had worked doubly hard and made the team the next time. Bradley was extremely proud of himself. I hoped the young Negro boy could find the same success as Bradley next year. However, as I listened to the men's conversation, I began to realize the boy had not been chosen because he'd lacked baseball skills; it was another reason entirely.

"It's a shame the coach didn't chose that new colored kid," I overheard one man comment to his peers when our team's short stop overthrew first base on an easy play.

"He would have been an asset in this game."

"Yes. You're probably right." Richard replied. "I watched the boy in tryouts. He might have been the most talented of all of the kids this year. He would've made a great short stop."

"No way!" A third man chimed in – his words slurred from the alcohol. "Doesn't matter how good he is, you can't have one colored kid … before you know it, there will be a half a dozen more wanting to join."

I could see two allegiances forming. Each man stepped toward the side that best agreed with his personal opinion. It was a divisive topic and disturbing to watch as it unfolded.

"Let those colored boys stay in the South where they belong," a heavy-set father piped in. "We don't need them up here. It's the South's mess… let them clean it up."

"They are cleaning it up. I hear they are using fire hoses and dogs." Vince King chuckled in a sarcastic manner. "That'll straighten up those colored rebel agitators," Vince added as he nursed his third martini.

"It's going to get a lot messier since some fellow shot Medgar Evers … did it right in his front yard," the heavy-set father added. "That takes balls with a capital B."

"They'll never catch the guy," Vince replied. "My guess is . . . they won't even try to find him. Those southern crackers stick together."

I noticed Richard had long since walked away from the group. Part of me was proud of him for not participating in such malicious conversation. Without being obvious, I watched him meander to the third baseline where Helen King was standing. Her son was playing for the opposing team. Occasionally I ran into her at school. She always had a Cheshire grin on her face and a glide to her step that radiated poise. Helen looked a lot like that young actress Ann Margret. Helen was older, of course, but she had the same hair and body. I thought it was disgraceful Helen wore similar style clothing as the teenagers in *Bye-Bye Birdie*. She was a grown woman; Helen shouldn't be traipsing around town in skin-tight pants. I wasn't sure why, but it bothered me to see Richard standing next to her. He said something I couldn't hear; his comment inspired Helen to toss her red hair back and laugh loud enough for it to travel across the field.

I tightly cuddled Randy in my arms and turned my attention back to the game on the field. Ricky was at bat. First pitch was a ball. He hit the second one with such force every person in the bleachers stood up to watch it sail through the air. I observed a group of young girls cheering wildly for Ricky as he ran the bases. *My son has a fan club. Isn't that cute!* The ball cleared the fence in left field; as a result, Ricky relaxed his sprint and jogged the remaining way around the bases. Our side cheered exuberantly.

The Wednesday before Labor Day, I watched Martin Luther King, Jr. speak at the Lincoln Monument in Washington, D.C. The picture on our old 17" PHILCO television set flickered constantly, but the sound was good. I was awed by the crowd. Over a quarter of a million people came to hear him. There was a sea of faces: black and white, young and old, men and women: all of them watching Mr. King as he spoke so eloquently, *"I have a dream that my four little children will one day live in a nation where they will not be judged by the color of their skin but by the content of their character . . ."*

I sat in front of the television set, spellbound by his words. Throughout his entire speech, I kept thinking about that Negro boy who had tried out for Little League and not been chosen. Mr. King spoke with such passion and hope. It reminded me of 1960 when I listened to John Kennedy campaigning for president. Both men stirred emotion inside of me: a dream for a better tomorrow.

3

The morning began like any typical day. Martin left for school. I fed

Randy. My neighbor dropped off her toddler and handed me $4.00 for the cost of a day's babysitting. The money instantly went into a shoebox I had hidden in the closest. John sat at the table reading the newspaper as I made him eggs and bacon for breakfast. He was on the night shift, so he was not in a hurry.

I even remembered the conversation we had.

John talked about how well the new Zone Improvement Plan was doing at the Post Office. He called it "ZIP Codes", and he declared it made his job so much easier. He also spoke highly of the two-letter abbreviations for all fifty states they were currently implementing. His singular complaint was concerning the states that began with an M. "Those eight states that start with M drive me nuts," he said as he sipped his coffee.

I complained about the increase in the cost of a stamp, but it was futile to debate the topic with John. He thought a nickel to mail a letter was well worth the price. We sat at the table longer than usual on that Friday in November. Randy was happy in his high chair and the toddler enjoyed the playpen. Finally John stood up, patted me on the hand, and said, "Guess I'll go back to the bedroom and take a nap. If I don't, I won't be able to stay awake tonight."

That was my cue – I needed to keep the children quiet.

It was the Friday before Thanksgiving. I was going to have all of the kids for the holiday dinner, so I was already planning the menu and making my grocery list. If I was organized, I could get most of my errands done before the children's nap time. With luck, they'd be awake and happy by Rosaline's ballet recital after school.

It was a challenge, but I managed to get both children into the car without disturbing John. When it came to driving alone with the little ones, I was truly grateful for my husband's handiwork. He had taken a couple of old high chairs and sawed off the legs. John jerry-rigged a few straps and ropes to keep the chairs firmly attached to the backseat of my Edsel. As a result, the kids could no longer roam all over the car while I was driving. I felt much safer.

Had John been working the day shift, I probably would have heard the news shortly after it happened; however, I was busy laying the children down for their naps and putting the groceries away. I didn't have the television or the radio turned on because I was trying to keep the apartment quiet while John slept. I checked my watch; it was 2:10. If I hurried I could finish making the shepherd's pie for dinner and still have plenty of time to get to Rosaline's school. Normally, she walked home with a group of friends, but today was different. I needed to pick her up at 3:35 and take her to her recital. She was extremely excited. I hoped Richard was able to pry himself away from his precious restaurants long enough to attend. He didn't care about ballet, but Rosaline wanted her father to be there.

Richard always liked shepherd's pie made with mashed potatoes – lots of butter, but John wanted me to make it like his mother did: pie crust and extra sweet corn added to the rest of the ingredients. I had finished lacing the last strips of the top layer of pie crust when Martin opened the door. My initial reaction was to panic. *Had I lost track of time?* Martin was typically not home from school until 4:00 at the earliest. I looked at my watch. It was 2:30. Then I saw his face, and I knew something was wrong.

"You don't know," Martin said as he dropped his books on the couch. "Do you?"

"Know what?"

"I was in shop class," Martin seemed to be speaking in slow motion. "The principal came over the loud speaker and told us we were being sent home early." He paused as he walked over to the television set and turned it on to CBS. "Someone shot the president."

At first, I didn't believe Martin. I thought he was telling some sick joke, but he was such a reliable young man. *Why would he lie?* I turned my attention to Walter Cronkite and instantly knew Martin was telling the truth. Mr. Cronkite took off his glasses and spoke into the camera, "From Dallas, Texas, the flash apparently official, President Kennedy died at 1 pm Central Standard Time ... 2 pm Eastern Standard Time ... some thirty-eight minutes ago." Tears were in his eyes. Walter Cronkite was crying.

"Oh my God! Oh my God!" I looked at Martin. "It's true!" I felt as if the blood was rushing out of my body. I leaned on the arm of John's favorite chair for support and slowly maneuvered myself to a sitting position. Bile worked its way up my throat; I could taste it on my tongue.

I knew it sounded dramatic, but it felt like the walls were collapsing around me. I collected my thoughts and formed a course of action.

"Your father is sleeping," I spoke decisively. "The little ones are asleep too. Can you please stay here? I need to go get Rosaline and see the boys. Make sure they are okay." I grabbed my purse and raced toward the door. "Oh my God! This can't be real."

I drove directly to the school, but all of the children had been dismissed. I could find no one who knew where Rosaline was. I got back in the car and went to the house. As I climbed the hill, I was alarmed by the number of people standing in the road beside the driveway. They were huddled in a group; heads bent down. I saw Ricky right away, but I couldn't see Bradley or Rosaline. A sick knot was forming in the pit of my stomach. There was no clear passage to the driveway, so I parked the car on the shoulder.

When I got out of the Edsel, I saw a teenage girl sobbing next to her car. Three other teenagers were consoling her. All four doors of her Ford Falcon were open. *Why was she crying so much?* Her sobs were resonating. As I approached, the crowd parted. I saw Bradley on the ground. My heart stopped. He was cradling Rex in his arms. Tears were streaming down his face. The big yellow lab lay motionless; blood oozed from his chest. One side of his face was caved in from the impact. *Oh no! No! No! No!*

Bradley saw me. "Mom, you gotta help him." My son could barely speak, and it was obvious his voice was changing. It cracked through every syllable. "Please, Mom. Please help him." My son's chocolate brown eyes were red-rimmed and moistened with tears. Rex's blood was all over Brad's clothes. Splotches were on his face, too, mixing with his tears. He looked so vulnerable.

I knew before I even touched Rex that there was nothing I could do for him. Instead of trying, I sat next to Bradley and wrapped him in my arms. He melted into my embrace and bravely tried to mask his emotions. I knew my son needed me to be strong, so I refrained from tears. I scanned the crowd for Ricky. When our eyes met, I asked, "Where's Rosaline?"

"She's inside with Gretal. I told her not to come out here. I didn't want her to see Rex." Ricky sounded like an adult, calm and in control.

The teenage girl kept repeating the same words over and over again. "I'm so sorry. I'm so sorry," as she cried uncontrollably. "It was an accident. I swear. It was an accident."

I could not deal with her hysteria because I needed to be focused on my children. As gracefully as I could, I stood up and walked over to the group of teenagers. "Is there anyone here who can drive this young lady home?" I asked. Apparently, they all had a driver's license. One of them volunteered. I gained my composure before continuing, "I know this is hard on everyone, but could you please all go home. I need to help my family, and you need to go home to yours."

The teenager continued to repeat, "I'm so sorry. I'm so sorry."

If I weren't engulfed in my personal pain, I might have had more compassion for her; however, my immediate desire was for all of them to disappear.

When the crowd dispersed, I returned to Bradley. He didn't want to let go of Rex. Ricky sat down next to him and together my sons lovingly stroked the yellow fur. I was not sure how long we sat in the street before Bradley finally gave us permission to move Rex. Ricky picked Rex up in his arms and reverently carried him to the backyard. I walked Bradley into the house. Rosaline was sitting on the stairs, wide-eyed. Instead of racing to us, she waited for us to reach her. The three of us sat on the steps in silence for several minutes. Finally Bradley went upstairs to change clothes.

Innocently Rosaline asked, "When are we going to my recital?"

"I think they canceled it, Honey." I said as I recalled Walter Cronkite's solemn expression and the horrible news he had reported. I wrapped my arm protectively around my little girl. I tried in vain to make some sense of the events of the day. "I'm sure they will reschedule it soon."

"Is Rex going to be okay, Mommy?" she asked.

"No, Sweetheart. Rex has gone to doggie heaven."

"I'm going to miss him." Her voice was quivering.

"We're all going to miss him." I wished I could think of something to say that would be profound or helpful, but the words eluded me.

Rosaline toyed with her pink tutu. Gretal came into the foyer and gently took my daughter's hand. "Let's go upstairs and change. You don't want to get your pretty ballet outfit dirty." Rosaline did not resist. Together they slowly climbed the stairs.

I walked to the kitchen and looked out of the window. Ricky was digging a hole near the brook in the far corner of the backyard. He alternated between a pick and a shovel attacking the ground with a vengeance. Rex's body was wrapped in a blanket next to him. My oldest son – who looked like a grown man as he hurled the pick – didn't stop for a single break during his mission.

I didn't hear the door open or close, and I didn't hear any footsteps either. One moment I was alone – watching Ricky in the backyard; the next moment, Richard was standing next to me, placing a gentle hand on my shoulder. The moment I saw him, I melted into his arms and cried. Richard protectively surrounded me with a tender embrace. He stroked my hair and softly rocked me. I couldn't talk. I couldn't think. I could barely breathe. I simply let my body meld into his.

10

Richard

Bradley was never an easy child, but after Rex died, communicating with him seemed even more difficult. Perhaps it was his grief or maybe it was the awkward transition into his teens; either way, the two of us rarely had a conversation that didn't end in Bradley stomping out of the room. Rick, on the other hand, rarely rebelled. He had glowing reports from his teachers; he did his chores without prompting, he was always respectful, and it looked as if he would make the shift to high school in the fall without any trouble. I found myself mentally thinking . . . *Why can't Bradley be more like his brother?* More times than not, I avoided interacting with my middle child. It was simply easier for both of us. As for Rosaline, I gravitated toward my sweet daughter. She struggled in school, especially with reading; consequently, I identified with her. I loved the fact she still enjoyed curling up in my arms when I read to her. In addition, she was always inviting me into her room so I could listen to her "Meet the Beatles" album and have imaginary tea with her. I couldn't believe my eight year old was already listening to Rock 'n Roll.

I was grateful for Gretal. She kept all three of the kids under control, the house clean and meals on the table, which made my life less complicated. The fact she lived in our house also allowed me to be flexible with my schedule. After years of honing the details, my restaurants practically ran themselves; as a result, I had more free time.

I still managed to keep a steady, clandestine relationship with Helen. She and her husband Vince were often customers during the dinner hour. Frequently, I saw them at the kids' school functions and during sporting events, but Helen and I kept our personal rendezvous a secret. No one was the wiser. Vince King, however, was not nearly as discreet as his wife. He boldly brought young women into the restaurant, flaunting an obvious sexual connection. Consequently, I did not feel guilty about being with his wife. Four to five times a month, Helen and I shared a quick interlude in my office or took a ride in my Cadillac. The backseat of my car had plenty of room for afternoon entertainment. I adored Helen. She was uncomplicated, undemanding and a great way to release pent up desires.

My flexible schedule also allowed me to have dinner with the kids several nights a week and to spend time with them on the couch watching our favorite television shows. Often, after I tucked Rosaline in bed, I returned to Carley's Place for a nightcap. The bar had cultivated a rather large and loyal set of customers. After balancing my books for so many years, I understood that drinks – whether they were coffee or cocktails – had the largest profit margin. As a result, I nurtured the bar clientele. Most of them were men, but there were a few women in the circle; Helen, when she accompanied her husband, was among them.

It was an election year; therefore, politics often drove the conversation. I mingled with the patrons and was known as a good listener who rarely contributed an opinion. The 1964 Democratic Convention was to be held in Atlantic City at the end of August, which generated enthusiasm among New Jersey residents. People were still reeling from the Kennedy assassination last fall, so sympathies leaned in Lyndon Johnson's favor. Everyone knew LBJ would ultimately be the candidate for the democrats. His sole rival was George Wallace. Many democrats in the South still opposed desegregation; as a result, they enthusiastically supported Governor Wallace because he adamantly promised, "Segregation now, segregation tomorrow, segregation forever."

As for the republicans, the field was wider and quite diverse. The more drinks ordered at the bar, the louder the volume of the voices. Most republicans supported Barry Goldwater, but a few liked Nelson Rockefeller. Helen, however, steadfastly vocalized her opinion about Margaret Chase Smith.

"She would be amazing!" Helen chimed. "Margaret Chase Smith is the first woman to serve in both the House and the Senate. She's a republican with a lot of experience."

"A woman president!" Vince King, who was an avid democrat, interjected. "I don't think so!" He continued to speak to his wife in a dismissive manner. "If the republicans want to win, they need to run with someone who can beat Johnson, and it certainly won't be the female senator from Maine." Vince was obviously snubbing his wife's comment.

Helen dropped the subject and stopped talking entirely; instead, she quietly sipped on her Manhattan. Instinctively, I knew she was hurt, but I avoided eye contact because I didn't want to draw attention to either of us.

The man at the end of the bar motioned for a refill before commenting, "Johnson wants to fight a war against poverty." The man was visibly drunk as he stumbled on his words. "The government can't fight that war. Roosevelt tried to do it – didn't work for him. He spent a shitload of our tax dollars, and only put a Band-Aid on the problem."

Another customer chimed in on the debate. "The bigger our government gets – the more Americans will become dependent on the government handouts." He raised his voice in frustration. "That gives those politicians in Washington too much power!"

"There will always be people in need," the fellow in the middle bar stool interjected in a more rational tone. "And if you are a good Christian then you should be willing to help the needy. That's what Christians do."

A fresh voice exclaimed, "What we need is to instill drive and motivation in our young people. Instead we are giving them too much freedom and making their lives too easy. We are raising a bunch of lazy, spoiled brats who don't have a clue how to work hard for what they want."

"I agree," said a fellow who was standing in a crowd at the end of the bar. "The churches and the local government should be more involved, because the more involved the federal government gets the more opportunity there is for corruption and waste."

The conversation was jumping around like a ping-pong ball. Was anyone listening to anyone else's opinion or were they simply spewing out their own view without regard to any response.

"Absolute power corrupts absolutely," another man wailed. "Can't remember who said it, but it's true."

"That's a valid point. Perhaps we should let the communities help their own people. Do it at the grassroots level. Don't give the federal government the control."

"These crazy democrats want to play Robin Hood and spread all of the money around," a customer bellowed. "The reality is . . . the demo-crats are doing it to win votes and then keep those voters dependent on them. Take this new Food Stamp Bill Congress is going to pass."

"The government wants to distribute our nation's food surplus," Vince responded. "Sounds like a good idea to me."

"In theory . . . maybe, yes!" The customer replied, "And the government has done this before on a temporary basis – but this new bill will make it permanent. That's a whole new ball game!"

"Who gets to decide what foods are on the list?" One man asked. "Sounds like the farmers might get a perk out of this."

"Food Stamps for the poor." The fellow nearly inhaled his beer and ordered another one. "I don't want anyone to starve, but – just like in the zoo – if you habitually feed the animals they will forget how to find the food themselves."

"What? Are you saying that poor people are animals?"

"No! I'm saying . . . if the government gives them a free supply of food that never stops, they will learn to expect it and will no longer work to earn it."

There was a brief pause in the conversation, before another customer chimed in, "I recently read Michael Harrington's <u>The Other America</u>. It's eye-opening."

A flurry of conversations continued, "According to the census, nine-teen percent of our population is in poverty. We are the richest country in the world. How is it possible nearly one-fifth of us live in poverty?"

"I liked Kennedy. He was a leader I could follow. But this Johnson fellow. He's arrogant and crude. And he keeps talking about a 'Great Society.' We are already a *great nation*. The issue is . . . how can Johnson possibly understand the problem?" The fellow jumped off of his bar stool and paced through the crowd. "He's a rich son of a bitch. How could Johnson know what it's like to be poor?" He paused a moment to wrap his arm around me and continued, "Look at Richard standing here." All eyes were on me as he spoke. "Richard is not as wealthy as President Johnson, but he's got a lot of shit. He drives a Cadillac and has tailor-made suits." The fellow put a tighter squeeze on my shoulder and chuckled slightly as he pointed out the style of my jacket and then waved his arm around in a circle as he spotlighted the room. "Richard owns this restaurant and another a few miles away. He lives in a fancy house. You can't expect a guy like Johnson or a fellow like Richard to understand poverty. They have it all. They don't know what it's like to be hungry and out of work." Jovially, he continued, "You rich guys don't realize how debilitating it is to be poor."

"You're not poor either," another fellow interjected loudly. The alcohol was definitely driving the conversation in a raw and personal direction.

I was glad I was still nursing my first beer. My judgment and behavior were not impacted by it, but my temper was rising. It was becoming increasingly more difficult to keep it in check. As if a photograph appeared in front of me, I could visualize – to perfection – the shabby cabin my parents called home. I didn't remember a day when I went hungry, but – upon reflection – I did remember my mother made every morsel of food count, and there was never any waste. I also remembered the many hours I had collected wood because it was how she cooked our meals and kept the cabin warm in winter. Rarely did I get a new article of clothing. Calvin's clothes were handed down to me. I had three pairs of pants: one for church, one for school and one for outdoor play. When the pants for outdoor play had too many holes in the knees and the material was literally disintegrating, my mother would cut the bulk of the legs off; she turned the pants into shorts, and I kept wearing them. The pattern continued even after she died – only I did the sewing. I wore Calvin's hand-me-downs long after he had been killed in the war. Memories were flashing through my mind. I remembered the freezing temperatures shooting into my clothes as I walked through the snow to the outhouse in the backyard. I would lay a bet that none of these jerks drinking in my bar tonight had a clue what poverty felt like. Part of me wanted to scream at these inconsiderate and ignorant assholes, but I kept my irritation under control. My customers clearly thought I was born to this lifestyle. They didn't know I'd worked and scrimped and sacrificed to build what I had. In their inebriated state, nothing I might say would enlighten them.

"There are still plenty of poor people. There will always be poor people. You want the government to take care of you – go live over in the Soviet Union with the commies," declared a man, screaming. "You can stand in line for toilet paper – and you won't have to pay for it."

It was like someone had poured gasoline on a fire. The debate erupted. It was no longer one conversation among the patrons; instead, it was four and five different conversations jumbled together. Fragmented sentences swirled around me.

"We gotta stop those communist bastards! They are taking over Southeast Asia."

"Johnson is too inconsistent. They are going to roll right over him."

"He won't take a stand because it's an election year, and all he wants to do is win the election! He's not thinking about what's best for America."

"There is all kinds of shit happening in the Gulf of Tonkin. Scary stuff."

"We need a president who can act decisively – no dicking around."

"Where's the Gulf of Tonkin?"

"You are such an *idiot stick*," one fellow replied. "Do you have your head in the sand? It's over in Vietnam. We are going to be in another World War if we're not careful."

At the other end of the bar, the conversation focused on a more domestic issue: James Powell, the teenage Negro who had been killed in Harlem by an NYPD officer named Gilligan. Thousands rioted and looted. There was genuine fear other cities might also fall to agitators and violence. Vince King was waving his hands wildly as he screamed, "Why do those colored people loot and destroy their own neighborhoods? And then – when everything is in ashes – they want someone to come fix it for them."

Two men at the other end of the bar were talking about the three Civil Rights workers who had been missing for forty-four days. They were in Mississippi registering Negro voters. It was announced on the news today – the FBI had found their bodies. They had been murdered. There was no one in the smoke-filled bar who could justify the horror of that event.

Helen calmly tried to turn the conversation to the Civil Rights Act of 1964 that President Johnson had signed into law. She felt strongly it not only benefitted Negroes, it was also for religion and for women too.

Although her voice was not as loud as the men around her, there were a few who listened as she spoke. "This legislation promises to squash seg-regation and discrimination. It will open doors for everyone, and women will have more opportunities."

The man standing next to Helen interrupted, "Do you really think some God-damned politician in Washington can *make* people equal by signing a piece of paper?" He raised his voice a notch. "You get what you *earn* in life."

Vince lit another cigarette and stood up from his bar stool. "Women have to quit rocking the damn boat. Everyone knows . . . men are made to provide for the family and women are made to have babies and stay home." Most of the men erupted in applause. Several raised a glass and cheered.

One fellow piped in, "Women want all of this *equality* . . . they think the grass is greener on *our* side of the fence. Maybe the ladies should have stayed on the Titanic and the men should have gotten in the lifeboats." There was a roar through the crowd. He stared directly at Helen before continuing, "Be careful what you wish for, Little Lady."

The multiple conversations were a thunderous roar. I could no longer decipher what anyone was saying; however, I could see the fire in both Vince and Helen's eyes. Vince was poking his finger into his wife's shoul-der and screaming at her. Helen's mouth was moving, but I couldn't hear even one syllable. Vince and Helen were toe to toe, spitting their words at each other. I moved toward them to try to defuse the situation, but I was too late. Vince hit her. Helen fell backward but was able to catch her balance when she grabbed the edge of the bar.

The room fell silent.

It was hard to believe a second ago I could not hear myself think because of the noise reverberating off of the walls. I walked up to Vince. When I glanced at Helen, I could see a few drops of blood on her lower lip. Tears were streaming down her face.

"Pay your bar tab." I stared directly into Vince's eyes and spoke with a firm voice. "You need to leave."

"What if I'm not ready to leave?" Vince responded defiantly.

I looked at my bartender. "Call the police." He immediately picked up the phone and dialed the number.

"Okay! Okay!" Vince mumbled. He looked at Helen, "Get your purse. We're going home."

Instantly, Helen took a step backward. She looked vulnerable and scared.

"Do you want to go with him, Helen?" I inquired.

At first, she didn't speak. She looked at Vince for ten, maybe fifteen seconds, in silence. "No. I don't want to go with him." When she finished her sentence, she lowered her head and looked down at the floor.

"You heard the lady," I stated firmly. "Get out."

"I'm not leaving without my wife."

"If you stick around much longer, you'll be leaving with the police." Every eye in the restaurant was directed on us. I could see Vince was right on the edge. He was clenching and unclenching his fist. I didn't want to make the first move, but I also wanted to be ready if he threw a punch at me. I stood my ground.

"You think you're hot shit, don't you?" Vince lowered his voice so no one else could hear.

He was so close to me our noses nearly touched. I could smell the bourbon and cigarettes on his breath. "You've had too much to drink, Vince." I was not backing down. "Go home! I'll put Helen in a cab after things settle down."

Vince glanced at Helen who still had her eyes cast downward and then back at me again. "You keep her. She's worn out, and I like younger versions." It was as if he stabbed her with his words. Finally, he retreated and left the restaurant.

I breathed a sigh of relief.

Twenty minutes later, the room was empty except for the employees cleaning their stations and Helen. I picked up a fresh bar towel and a bucket of ice. Quietly, I guided Helen to my office. After she sat on the chair, I gently placed the cold compress on her face. She looked at me with gratitude, but didn't speak. I found it ironic that the song playing over the sound system was Bob Dylan's *The Times They Are a-Changing*. I almost made a comment about it, but I didn't think Helen would find it amusing.

Finally, I broke the silence. "I've heard people shouldn't talk about religion or politics. Guess there's some truth to that."

Helen's lips formed a half smile, and she let out a soft chuckle. "Don't make me laugh. It hurts." As she spoke, a crooked smile remained on her face.

"What a mess," I interjected.

"It could have been worse." The smile left her face. "Thank you, Richard, for standing up for me."

"Is that the first time he's hit you?"

Helen sat in silence for a few moments before answering. "No."

"You should have told me." I spoke softly because I didn't want Helen to think I was reprimanding her. "For crying out loud, we've known each other for nearly two years. I was under the assumption . . . Vince and you . . ." I couldn't finish my sentence because it sounded ridiculous and shallow.

"Vince and I have been married for fifteen years. I don't think we made it to our first anniversary before he had his first affair. I was pregnant. He seemed thrilled we were having a baby, so I pretended not to know about his indiscretions. When he came home late from work or he had to stay in the city overnight, I didn't ask questions. I thought if I didn't confront him, it wouldn't be real and everything would be okay." She shook her head. "As the years passed, I discovered a pattern: lots of other women. So I told myself ... at least, it's not *one* woman. If it had been *one* woman, it would have been worse. Right?" Helen didn't wait for a reply. "We developed a routine. He lived his life, and I stood in his shadow. He always took me to all of the corporate functions and paraded me around like," she paused. "Like I was ... I don't know how to say it ... like I was his *ornament*." Helen wasn't talking directly to me. However, she was verbalizing her feelings, maybe for the first time in her marriage. "Once I did broach his infidelity, he lost his temper and told me it was *my* fault he needed other women. He said, 'if you were better in bed, I would be more satisfied and I wouldn't *need* other women.'" Her voice didn't alter one iota, but thick, round tears rolled down her face. "Vince drinks a lot. Sometimes it makes him happy and even loving, but other times he goes to this dark place and he's mean." Helen inhaled deeply before continuing. "Last year, he didn't get the promotion he had been hoping to get. Nothing has been right for us since then. No matter what it is – dinner – the children's report cards – the way the house looks – everything is my fault. If I say the wrong thing, he gets so angry." She used her fingers to wipe the moisture away from her nose. "There are days when I pray he will hit me instead of . . ." She didn't finish the sentence. It was as if she suddenly realized she was speaking her thoughts aloud. "Sometimes – when he drinks too much – he forces me – he makes me," she kept pausing to find the right words. "He does things to me that a husband shouldn't do to his wife." Helen was crying.

I didn't know if I should go to her, hold her, comment on her statements or merely listen. I elected to stay quiet and hear what she had to say.

"When we first met, I led you to believe Vince and I had," she stumbled on her words. "That we had an agreement." She stopped and looked into my eyes. "You were my first, Richard . . . you are my only . . . indiscretion." She paused. "In the beginning, I approached you because I wanted to punish Vince, but you were so kind . . . so gentle. Being with you made me realize . . . what Vince and I have is wrong." Helen stopped long enough to wipe her eyes and blow her nose. "I was so young when we got married, I didn't understand. I thought marriage was supposed to be that way. I didn't know any differently." Her voice was weak. "I've been thinking about leaving him." She paused. "But how can I? I have no job. I have no money. How will I take care of the children?'""

2

The day after the incident, Helen called her sister in Hagerstown, Maryland, and told her about her plight. Her sister invited Helen and the kids to come to her house. After much thought, Helen accepted. A few days later, I gave Helen enough money to buy bus tickets for her and the four children. I took them to the depot; we said our goodbyes without any emotional display. We both knew her children did not need to be witnesses to our affection. We shook hands, and I kissed her on the cheek. They boarded the Greyhound; I stayed – waving quietly – as the bus drove out of sight.

I knew I was going to miss Helen, but I also knew in my heart that our relationship was over.

I was still baffled I had been so incredibly naïve.

3

After the unfortunate verbal explosion at the bar, business steadily declined. My regulars didn't come. Consequently, my profit margin took a hit. As the weeks rolled by and I balanced the books, I realized I needed to make a change. If I didn't, I would no longer be making any profit. After much thought, I decided to purchase a couple of television sets and place them strategically in the bar area so customers could watch sporting events. The first special occasion I advertised was the Tokyo Summer Olympics, which did not occur until mid-October because of the extreme humidity and heat in Japan during August and the threat of typhoons in September. The timing was perfect for Carley's Place because it was the first Olympics to be televised live instead of delayed and viewed from tapes.

For two weeks, customers were thrilled to watch the games at the bar on the black and white television sets. A few people made derogatory comments about Japan hosting the Olympics after the heinous actions of World War II, but most customers were willing to put the past behind us. Spirits and patriotism were high throughout the games, especially when the USA earned the most gold medals. Even though the Soviet Union won the highest total medals and Japan came in third, the pride for the USA athletic accomplishments in gold created a celebratory mood. Americans dominated in the pool, both swimming and off of the diving board; whereas, the Soviet Union and Japan were the strongest in gymnastics. The largest crowds gathered on the nights our men's basketball team played; they cheered our team to the gold medal. The camaraderie in the bar for our athletes was amazing. The alcohol flowed, and my profits soared again.

It was a good thing I had purchased *two* television sets because there was no way baseball fans were going to miss one single inning of the Yankees' stellar season. On October 3rd, they took their fourteenth American League pennant. The fans went nuts. I kept the bar open an hour past closing so they could continue to celebrate. However, the success did not carry through to a victorious World Series outcome; sadly, the St. Louis Cardinals took an early 6-0 lead in the seventh game and eventually beat the Yankees seven to five. Morale was low, and I didn't sell as many drinks during that game.

I brought both of my sons to most of the evening sporting events. Caroline didn't like the fact our young teenage boys were exposed to so much alcohol and adult behavior, but I wanted them to see how the restaurant operated. I told them, "One day, this will be yours, and you need to learn the business." Ricky immediately latched onto the idea. My eldest constantly asked questions and absorbed even the tiniest detail; Bradley quietly observed. Often he had a furrow on his brow as his eyes darted around the room, but he rarely made a comment.

The next few weeks, there was a trickle of interest in televised sports. A small crowd gathered on Saturdays for *Wild World of Sports*, but Jim McKay couldn't draw a loyal set of customers to my bar. The fact the New York Giants were having a bad year didn't help my bottom line either. The fair-weather fans weren't interested in dedicating an afternoon to such a losing team; however, fans of Johnny Unitas and the Baltimore Colts migrated into Carley's Place each week and drank hundreds of dollars' worth of beer and liquor. Even though I personally liked the Steelers, I found myself hoping the Colts would stay on their winning streak. It was good for business.

By election night, the word had gotten out about the televised events and nearly one hundred people came to watch the results. They all purchased drinks – lots of drinks. I worried the political arena would have a backlash similar to the one in August, but it didn't happen. The election was such a record landslide victory for the democrats and the Johnson-Humphrey ticket that Barry Goldwater supporters kept their mouths shut. To drown their sorrows, they drank double the alcohol.

Between the election and sports, Carley's Place was back in business and running full steam ahead.

4

Ever since Thanksgiving, Rosaline's mood was one of melancholy – even depression. My once happy and enthusiastic eight-year-old daughter was becoming withdrawn and solemn. Notes from Rosaline's teacher came home on a daily basis; all of them spotlighting a negative attitude and declining grades. Her dramatic change in behavior was cause for alarm. Caroline and I became allies in hopes we could figure out what was wrong with her.

Every day, I asked Rosaline, "How was your day at school?" Each day, her response was "Fine, Daddy." But I could tell by the look on Rosaline's face . . . all was not *fine*. At dinner, her dialogue was generally limited to one or two word responses, and rarely did she instigate a conversation.

As the days rolled closer to Christmas, Rosaline was not even interested in decorating the tree. In fact, she refused to help at all; instead, she raced off to her room and slammed the door. Both Rick and Bradley tried to get her to join in the tradition, but even they could not cajole her.

The Sunday before Christmas, we went to church. I saw Caroline after the service, and told her of my growing concern. I was grateful my ex-wife and I had found some common ground. Ever since Rex died last year, I felt as if our relationship had changed. We could be in the same room with each other and not speak maliciously. It was a step in the right direction.

As we stood outside of the church doors, Rosaline asked if she could hold the baby. Caroline handed Randy to her. We both noticed Rosaline had a genuine smile on her face as she wrapped her arms around him. I gently placed my hand on Caroline's elbow and guided her away from our daughter before I spoke.

"That's the first real smile I've seen on Rosaline's face in weeks." I whispered in Caroline's ear.

"What do you think's the matter?" There was great concern in her voice. "It's a little early for puberty."

"Maybe you can talk to her. She's not talking to me." I shrugged. "I don't know what else to do."

Caroline agreed to spend more time with Rosaline during Christmas vacation. We made a plan. Martin would stay at our house with the boys for a few days, and Rosaline could spend the break with John and Caroline.

Later that same day, I walked by Rosaline's room. She wasn't reading a book or playing with any toys. Neither the record player nor the radio was on; there was no music. My daughter looked like a statue stretched out on the bed. When I stopped in the doorway, she glanced in my direction. There were tears in her eyes. My heart lurched. It was obvious my little girl was struggling with an inner demon.

"Are you doing okay, Sweetheart?" I asked.

"Daddy," she spoke quietly. "Can I ask you a question?"

"Of course," I replied as I entered the room and sat on the edge of her bed.

"You have to tell me the truth, Daddy." Rosaline looked directly into my eyes. "No matter what it is, you *have* to tell me the truth."

"Of course, I will," I responded.

Although Rosaline was eight years old, there were days in her short life when she behaved younger than her years and other days when she seemed so much older and wiser. As I looked at her today, she was wearing a mature expression, which led me to believe we were about to enter into a serious discussion. A growing sense of apprehension swept over me. *What on earth was bothering my sweet daughter, and how was I going to help her? Was she finally going to ask the questions I had been dreading since the day Caroline and I separated? Was she going to ask why her half-brother Randy didn't live in the same house with us? Was she going to ask why other families lived together and we did not?* My heart was racing.

Rosaline squared her shoulders and began to speak. "Daddy, I know I can trust you to tell me the truth . . . no matter what it is. I want you to tell me the truth." Her pale blue eyes were huge and round as they stared directly at me.

"Yes. I will tell you the truth. I promise." I replied with a growing sense of trepidation. "What seems to be the matter?"

Without batting an eyelash, Rosaline delved into her question. "Is there a Santa Claus or are you Santa Claus?"

My first reaction was . . . *Oh, thank God! I can handle this question.* I breathed a sigh of relief. But it was short lived. Although Rosaline's question was not the one I had feared, it was still a difficult question nonetheless. I took a deep breath and contemplated my answer. Every parent dreads the day their child discovers there is no magic, no fairy dust, no Rudolf, no flying sleigh, no elves working constantly all year to make the perfect gift. Rick and Bradley had discovered the truth by age seven because the teenage neighbors down the street had told them. However, they had enjoyed playing along for Rosaline's sake.

Those few moments on Christmas morning when the children ripped through the wrapping paper and discovered what was inside

Santa's boxes were the best part of Christmas – I knew I had them for such a short time before they raced off to their mother's for the remainder of the day. Keeping Santa Claus alive was as important to me as it was to any young believer.

Part of me wanted to reinforce the Holiday tradition. Lie – if I had to – in order to keep those precious moments alive for one more Christmas, but I instinctively knew the foundation of our mutual trust tittered on how I answered my daughter's question.

I watched Rosaline for a few quiet seconds. The splashes of freckles on her nose and cheeks seemed to sparkle as I saw the apprehension spread across her face. "Do you really want to know the truth, Rosaline?"

"Yes, Daddy. All of the kids at school are calling me stupid because they say there isn't a Santa Claus. I tell them 'Yes, there is,' but they don't believe me." Tears glistened in her eyes but her voice remained strong. "The kids at school . . . they make fun of me. I don't want to be stupid." She pleaded. "You have to tell me, Daddy. Are they right?"

"Okay, Sweetheart. I'll see if I can clear this up for you." I fluffed her pillow, propped it against the headboard, and leaned against the alcove I created. With my right hand, I motioned for her to lie beside me. After she snuggled into the curve of my arm, I continued. "This is not something a daddy looks forward to telling his child because it is one of the first signs of growing up." I paused and smiled at her. "And you certainly are growing up, Rosaline. You are becoming quite a young lady." Lightly I stroked her chestnut hair and brushed it away from her face. Her cheeks were flushed from tension and her eyes changed to a slightly deeper color of blue as they always did when she was concentrating heavily. "No, Rosaline, there isn't a *real* Santa Claus."

My daughter's first reaction surprised me. I had expected tears or shock or even denial but instead she responded. "You mean, the kids at school are right! *YOU* gave me all of those presents?"

I nodded.

"Daddy," Rosaline said as she gently touched my chest with her entire hand. "*You* gave me my Barbie doll?"

"Yes."

"All of those presents . . . you . . . you gave them to me?"

"Yes." I cupped her tiny hand in mine and gave it a gentle squeeze.

"You never asked for much, Rosaline, and it made me feel wonderful to give those toys to you."

She threw her arms around me and gave me one of her giant bear hugs. It lasted nearly a minute before she spoke again. "I don't understand . . . why then do grown-ups pretend there's a Santa Claus if there isn't one?"

I pondered a moment on the subject before continuing. "It's true . . . there isn't a *real* Santa Claus . . . not one you can touch; not one who lives at the North Pole and flies through the air visiting children on Christmas Eve. But there is a Santa Claus in everyone's heart because Santa represents the gift of giving and the joy you feel when you give a person a present."

"Who is the man I gave my Christmas list to?" she asked.

"He's a fellow who is pretending so he can help little children believe in the gift of giving."

"You mean . . . it's like Halloween. Santa is a man in a costume?"

"Sort of." I responded. I felt like I was stumbling over my words, but Rosaline seemed to understand.

"Well, if there isn't a Santa Claus, then those kids at school must be right about God and Jesus too." Rosaline choked on each syllable as she spoke. "There are two boys who tell me I'm stupid to go to church. They make fun of me and laugh at me, and then all of the other kids start laughing too." It was obvious Rosaline was struggling with her emotions. "Why do we go to church if there isn't a God or a Jesus?"

I felt as if I were in a revolving door – the conversation was changing direction so spontaneously I wasn't sure what to say. "Ah . . . there's another story entirely." I curled my daughter into my arms and gave her a warm embrace. She smiled at me and my heart swelled from the love I saw in her eyes. "Those kids at school are wrong. Jesus *is* real. He is God's son. He was born on Christmas Day and *that* is the *real* reason why we celebrate Christmas . . . because we are celebrating *His* birthday."

The inquisitive look was still covering Rosaline's face. "But, how do you *know* Jesus was really alive . . . how do you *know* there is a God and a Heaven? Maybe they are make-believe too."

For an instant, I was transported back in time, and I was sitting at my mother's grave. The memory of the cold temperature on that day caused a quick shiver; it passed through my entire body. A peaceful calm enveloped me as I remembered the brief warm pocket of air that surrounded me and the sweet sound of my mother's voice telling me, *"I'm okay, Richard. God is taking good care of me."* Each syllable had been as clear as a church bell. The entire foundation of my faith rested on that exact moment.

I didn't go to church every Sunday, and I knew to my soul I often failed when it came to behaving like a good Christian; however, I also knew – with every fiber of my being – I had heard my mother's voice *after* she had died. As a result, I didn't need any more proof. I *believed.*

As I returned my attention to the present, I lovingly smiled at my daughter. "Santa Claus *is* make-believe . . . a fantasy. Santa is a symbol representing the joy of giving. But God and Jesus *are* real." I stared directly into her eyes to reinforce my words. "Those kids at school are wrong, Rosaline. I promise you! God and Jesus live everywhere . . . especially inside of here." I gently placed my hand over my daughter's heart. "Believing in them gives you strength." Rosaline sat quietly. She was transfixed by every word I spoke. "A person can't celebrate Christmas without celebrating the birth of Jesus – just like you learn in Sunday school – and it's wonderful to be able to celebrate such a joyous day with the giving of gifts. That's why Daddy likes to pretend and keep the secret of Santa Claus so the joy of giving can swell our hearts along with our faith in God and Jesus."

"Did it hurt you when you found out there isn't really a Santa?"

I thought about the sparse Christmas celebrations in my house when I was a child. During those years when my mother was alive, there had been a magical aura in our home. There hadn't been many presents on Christmas morning, but I could still remember the sense of wonder and excitement she had created. I tried to remember a Christmas in that dilapidated cabin after my mother's death. I couldn't conjure up a single memory.

I didn't want to share any of my flashbacks with my daughter. Instead, I responded, "Yes . . . I suppose it did hurt for a little while." In order to divert from my own morose memories, I changed the topic a little bit. "But when I had children," I tapped her nose impishly and winked at her. "I realized I could bring Santa Claus back into my life and play along with you and your brothers. It became magical for me too." I smiled at her. "Do you know that you don't have to wait until you have children to get to feel the joy of Santa Claus?"

"What do you mean?" Curiosity was beginning to take the place of apprehension as the expression on my daughter's face transformed from worry to intrigue. She smiled, which enabled me to see those two large adult-sized teeth which had grown in over the course of the last year making her baby teeth look like tiny pearls in comparison. The single dimple on the top of her left cheek was prominent as she encouraged me to go on with my anecdote.

"You see, Rosaline, you have a baby brother." I rarely spoke of Randy or the fact my children were related to John and Caroline's son, but I knew this was an exception to my normal rule of thought. "Randy's two. You can help your mom by keeping Santa Claus and the spirit of giving alive for him. If you do this, it will keep Santa alive inside *your* heart too." I tapped her chest and smiled. "Do you want to keep the secret with your mom so Randy doesn't find out for a long time? Maybe you – just you – can help me put all of the presents under *our* tree this year. Rick and Bradley use to help me after they found out . . . but maybe this year is *your* year to help. What do you think? Want to help me?"

"Yes, Daddy. I'd like that." There was an enormous smile on her face. Then a pensive expression became her countenance. "You know, Daddy . . . thank you for telling me the truth about Santa Claus. . . I wanted to know. I don't feel stupid anymore and I won't let those bullies at school make fun of me either. I'm a big girl now, and I was ready to find out big girl things." Her face glowed with love. "And, I'm glad that God and Jesus *are* real because I really believe in them." She paused as she gave my hand a gentle squeeze. "But, Daddy," she lowered her voice to a whisper. "Don't tell me about the Easter Bunny yet . . . okay? I'm not quite old enough for that."

It was difficult to stifle the laughter erupting in my throat. I wrapped my arms around my precious daughter. As I was hugging her, I noticed Rick standing in the doorway. He smiled and winked. "Good job, Dad."

An hour later, I was on the phone with Caroline. I told her about the entire conversation. We both chuckled. *Kids! Never a dull moment.*

5

Although the United States had been bombing North Vietnam in an operation called Rolling Thunder, U.S. troops had not yet been committed to Vietnamese soil until the month of my birthday. I remembered the day well – for two reasons. First – it was the day I sold my Cadillac and bought the red convertible Mustang. It was a present I gave myself. And second – it was the day I discovered my son in bed with our live-in maid. Needless to say, on that day in April of 1965, the military action halfway around the world was not my priority.

It was a Thursday. I took most of the day off from work so I could hand the title for the Cadillac over to the new owner and pick up my Mustang at the dealership in Newark. I also planned to go to Rick's high school baseball game. He had made the varsity team as a freshman: an amazing accomplishment for a young player. In Little League, Rick had been stellar as a pitcher and a third baseman; unfortunately, there were seniors who dominated both of those positions on his high school team. So far, during the season, my eldest son had seen a few innings of playing time on the mound; however, third base would not be available for another year. Because of Rick's dynamic and reliable bat at the plate, the coach wanted him in the lineup; as a result, he had given Rick a position in right field. His stats were commendable. Rick might be the youngest player, but he had earned respect from all of his teammates.

The weather was perfect for baseball and for putting the top down on my new car. As I drove from the dealership to the high school, I decided to take a quick detour to my house so I could change into a pair of shorts. I proudly drove up the hill and turned into my driveway. There was twenty minutes to the first pitch, so I hurriedly ran in to change. I noticed Brad's school books on the couch, which was odd because he was not usually home at this hour. *My Girl* was playing on the transistor radio on top of the refrigerator. Gretal was a few years older than I was, but her choice of music ran parallel to the teenagers; thus, there was always Rock 'n Roll playing at our house. The smell of cookies baking in the oven filled the air, and I noticed a fresh batch on the counter. I scooped one up and popped it into my mouth. Gretal was a fantastic cook and a great baker. Thanks to her, I was carrying an extra pound or two on my body.

I heard a sound. *What was that?* I heard it again. It was coming from Gretal's room. The door was slightly ajar, which allowed a vantage point to her bed. Gretal had a huge collection of stuffed animals that were normally displayed on her mattress; however, they were currently scattered haphazardly on the floor. As I peered into the room, I saw Gretal straddled on top of Bradley. She was moaning fervidly and calling out "Yes, Brad! Oh yes, Brad!"

Gretal wasn't wearing any clothing. Their bodies had a rhythm that seemed to go with the tempo of the song playing on the radio. The bed's headboard was hitting the wall matching the beat of the base. Their eyes were closed, and there was euphoria all over their faces. My fourteen-year-old son looked like a man immersed in a climax he was obviously enjoying.

My initial instinct was to charge into the room and separate my housekeeper and my son, but a flashback engulfed me. For an instant, I replayed the moment I saw Caroline and John in my bedroom. That personal nightmare felt fresh as if I were reliving it all over again. My heart stopped, and I froze for a second.

Don't overreact! Think!

Quietly I backpedaled my way out of the room, turned and left the house. I thought about reentering and making enough noise to give them a chance to hide their actions, but decided to go another route.

I did and said nothing to Bradley. Instead, the next day, I waited until the children had gone to school. When they left the house, I approached Gretal. I didn't mince words; I didn't want to hear any excuses; and I wasn't going to change my mind. I handed her an envelope with her current salary enclosed plus an extra hundred dollars. It wasn't pay day, so she was curious about the money. I politely thanked her for her service and told her she was no longer needed. I asked her to pack her bags and be out of the house by noon.

She asked, "Why?"

I stared directly into her eyes and replied, "Bradley." I gave no other explanation. She knew by the expression on my face that the decision was final. No excuses. No additional conversation.

Gretal was gone within the hour.

How could I have been so blind? I missed all of the signals about Helen and Vince. Helen had professed they had *freedom* in their marriage. I believed her, especially after seeing so many women on the news protesting for equality. They wanted equal pay at their jobs and equal treatment inside and outside of the bedroom. Helen and Vince's infidelity didn't make much sense to me, but I had gone along with it willingly – especially when I saw how Vince had flaunted his extra-marital flings.

As for Bradley and Gretal! *How did I miss those signs? Who initiated that relationship? How long had Bradley and Gretal been having sex?* Obviously I was spending too much time at the restaurants and not enough time at home. I vowed to focus more on my family. No more live-in help. I still needed to hire a part time lady to watch Rosaline when she came home from school, keep the house clean, and make dinner. It took a few days, but I managed to get everyone and everything back on schedule. I began to relax.

It was two weeks before Bradley asked me what happened to Gretal. He tried to be nonchalant about the inquiry, but I could tell by the expression on his face that he was shaken. I didn't dwell on the subject. In fact, I barely looked up from the newspaper; instead, I calmly replied, "She got a job offer in upstate New York." I casually added, "I'm going to miss her cooking."

There was a quiver in Bradley's voice when he responded, "Me too."

I thought about telling Caroline of the incident and decided against it.

There are some things a mother doesn't need to know.

Part III

The Long Road Home

1

Caroline

I could not count the number of times in the past couple of years I'd taken Rosaline to the doctors. She was constantly sick with a sore throat and fever; as a result, she missed numerous days of school. Her teacher was concerned about her progress. Fifth grade was difficult enough for Rosaline without falling more and more behind because of attendance. Reading was always a challenge and retaining what she read was an even bigger feat. Her confidence was faltering; and it was changing her once-delightful personality. There were even occasions when I found my eleven-year-old daughter sucking her thumb when she thought no one was looking.

Finally our family doctor referred Rosaline to a surgeon, who recommended a tonsillectomy. Richard and I discussed the operation and decided it was in Rosaline's best interest. John's normal sub was out sick; consequently, he could not get the day off and wouldn't get to the hospital until after he had delivered the mail on his route. Everyone said the operation was routine and I wasn't to worry, but the idea of a scalpel cutting into my daughter was terrifying. I wished John could hold my hand through this ordeal.

"Has the operation started yet?" Richard rushed into the waiting room. He was out of breath and had an apprehensive look on his face.

I was relieved to see him. I thought I'd go mad if I had to sit in that room alone.

Eight years had passed since that fateful day when my marriage to Richard had imploded. Our relationship was often turbulent and – some days – the pain still felt raw; however, as the years passed, we had found common ground through our children.

"They wheeled her down the hall about ten minutes ago," I responded.

"Damn!" Richard muttered. "I wanted to see her before she went in the operating room. Was she scared?"

"A little. But you know Rosaline. She wants to be brave."

Richard took the seat next to me and gently patted my hand. "It's going to be okay, Caroline. Everyone says that this is truly minor surgery. Doctors have been doing it for centuries."

"But this is *our* little girl." My voice cracked slightly as I spoke.

"Really, Caroline. It's going to be okay. Rosaline will be up and running like that Kathy Switzer lady who ran in the Boston Marathon last week." Richard smiled in a teasing manner as he tried to bolster my mood. "Can you believe that woman! She signed up using her initial for her first name and no one knew she was female until the day of the race. When the director saw her, he tried to physically pull her out, but she finished it in four hours and twenty minutes. Pretty impressive."

"Guess she broke that long-standing male tradition. Good for her." I couldn't help but smile as I said the words.

"Maybe Rosaline will do the Boston Marathon next year." Richard winked at me when he spoke.

I chuckled softly. "Stop trying to make me laugh." I smiled directly at Richard to let him know I appreciated his diversion. Then I broached the other subject on my mind. "The doctor predicted Rosaline would be back in school in a couple of days, but her teacher claims it's going to take a while to get Rosaline on grade level. She is struggling."

"I still remember how difficult school was for me – especially reading," Richard commented as he leaned back in his chair. "There were all kinds of obstacles. I don't think I would have done well in school without you, Caroline."

I wasn't looking at his face, but I instinctively knew he was smiling. We sat in silence for a moment as we each privately flashed multiple memories through our minds. I could clearly see Richard sitting with me on the bench in the schoolyard as he practiced reading from *More Dick and Jane Stories*. He was always so proud when he finished each chapter – looking at me for approval and verbal praise.

Obviously, he was having the same mental picture when he said, "Remember those days in school when you sat with me during recess instead of playing with the other kids?" Richard gazed into the lobby as he spoke. "You taught me more than the teacher."

I closed my eyes and leaned toward Richard. When he didn't pull away, I gently rested my head on his shoulder. We seemed to be breathing in unison. It was a comfortable, relaxing feeling. Without lifting my head, I chuckled, "Then one day, I discovered you were a far better reader than I was."

"That's because you were a good teacher, Caroline," he said. "Rosaline is lucky to have you for a mother. You will be able to get her over this hump."

"I don't think so, Richard," I sighed. "She fights me. Every day is an ordeal. The harder I try, the worse it gets."

"Maybe Rosaline should have a tutor."

"I thought about going that route," I replied. "But they are expensive."

"I'll pay for it," Richard interjected.

The pleasant mood was instantly ruined. I sat up in my chair. "Why do you always make me feel that John and I are too poor to give our children the things they need?" I snapped.

"That's not what I meant." Richard responded defensively. "I want to help."

I took a deep breath and tried to reclaim the pleasant aura of moments ago. "I'm sorry," I replied. "I guess I'm a bit sensitive. Martin is graduating in a couple of months. John wants him to go to college, but we can't afford it. Martin has decided to enlist in the Marines for a couple of years and then go to college when his tour is done."

"Does he think that's a good idea right now? Vietnam is heating up."

"Without a student deferment," I shrugged my shoulders as I spoke. "He will probably be drafted by the army anyway. John says Martin has always aspired to be the best, and that would be the Marines." I placed my hand over Richard's and squeezed tightly. "You have to promise me, Richard." There was a desperate tone in my voice. "Rick and Brad *must* go to college. Rick graduates next spring. We have to start talking with him about what school he wants to attend and make sure he goes. Same with Brad. I can't bear the thought of them being drafted. Promise me, Richard. Please."

"There's plenty of time, Caroline. Besides, Rick is already talking about college. He wants to go. We don't have to convince him." Richard's voice changed from one of reassurance to one with a more empathic tone. "But I'm definitely not paying for either of our sons to go to any of those damn colleges where the kids put flowers in their hair and do drugs more than study. I'm not buying into all of the hippie bull of this counter-culture generation. All they want to do is get stoned, space out and have sex with anything that walks. None of them has a clue what a hard day's work is all about because they're allowed too much free time and no responsibility. They look like spoiled brats to me, and I don't want some college professor brainwashing my boys into thinking like a commie. If I get my way, Rick will go to a southern school that still has morals and ethics – maybe one of those Christian colleges that has chapel in the curriculum." Richard leaned back in his chair and took several even breaths before continuing, "Rick wants to get a degree in Business or Finance. He is comfortable in the office, and he knows the restaurants. He understands numbers, bottom line, and profit. He has a real head for the business. And he *wants* to do it. But Brad. I don't know about him. He never talks to me. When I try to engage him in conversation, he shuts me down. If I can get two sentences out of him in a week, it's a miracle."

"What are you talking about? Brad is wonderful. I don't have any trouble with him. He comes over to the apartment all of the time and talks up a storm."

"Maybe with you, Caroline, but not with me. With me, Brad is stubborn and rude and defiant. I want him to get involved in the restaurants, but he doesn't seem to care. All he wants to do is take pictures. Brad will never be able to make a living with his stupid camera. The sooner he figures that out, the better off he will be."

"First of all, Richard," I patiently interrupted. "Brad's camera is not *stupid*. He loves taking pictures, and he is quite talented. Did you know he is one of the photographers for his high school yearbook?" I didn't give Richard an opportunity to respond. "And next year – when he is a junior – he will be the photo editor. Apparently Brad is the unanimous choice between both the students and the faculty. That's usually a senior's title. I wish you would give him a chance to prove to you how good he is." I paused before broaching the next subject. "And secondly, Brad says that you never give him anything to do at Carley's Place but bus tables and clean up in the kitchen."

"He has to learn from the bottom up. When he shows a genuine interest, I will give him more responsibilities. Until then, he has to prove to me he is worthy of the job."

"Brad is *not* an employee you hired off of the street," I pounced on the conversation. "He is your son!"

"Yes – he is my son – *our* son. But he is also irresponsible and disrespectful, and I am *not* going to reward his bad behavior." Richard paused long enough to make eye contact with me. "You shouldn't be sticking your head in the sand, Caroline, and pretending you don't know he is hanging out with a bad group of boys. They are running around all over town, and they are drinking."

"Drinking?" I responded in total surprise. "Alcohol? How do you know that?"

"Because I can smell it!" Richard practically shrieked the words. "He waters down my bottle of gin. It took me a while to figure it out, but I did. I have resorted to counting the beers in my own refrigerator. Brad is sixteen years old, and his breath reeks of alcohol."

"Are you sure?"

"Yes! I'm sure."

"What are we going to do?" My head was spinning from all of this new information.

"One thing's for certain, if he keeps acting like this, I'm not going to buy him a car when he graduates, and he's not driving *my* car either."

"Aren't you jumping the gun a little bit? Brad doesn't even have his license yet."

"Typical you, Caroline!" Richard snapped. "You do not think ahead. He has his learner's now. It won't be long before he has his driver's license. I don't want him cruising around in *my* car drinking beer he got from *my* refrigerator."

"How did this happen?" I felt like the wind had been knocked out of me. "Is Rick drinking too?"

"No," he replied. "I don't think so, but he sure sticks up for his brother. I wish that relationship was a mutual one, because Brad doesn't stick up for Rick nearly as much as Rick supports Brad." Richard waved his hands in a grand gesture. "How did they turn out so differently?"

Before I had a chance to comment on Richard's question, the doctor entered the room. My heart raced at an erratic pace. I thought it was going to beat out of my chest. Richard reached for my hand and clutched it tightly with both of his. Even though he didn't speak, I unconsciously knew what he was thinking. *Please, God! Let our little girl be okay.*

When the doctor smiled, I began to relax. I instinctively knew he would not look so calm unless the operation had gone well.

"Rosaline is in the recovery room. She will be waking up soon. There were no surprises. Everything went according to plan." The doctor shook Richard's hand and then mine. "Before you go home, I can answer all of your questions; however, if you would like to be with your daughter when she wakes up, follow me."

Dutifully, Richard and I trailed the doctor down the hallway and into a room. Rosaline was peacefully sleeping on the bed. Richard positioned himself on one side and I stood on the other. As I watched her, I could feel the tension drain out of me. *Thank you, God! Thank you.* I was not sure if I spoke the words or merely prayed them in my mind, but I heard the same words coming from Richard's mouth.

"She's beautiful." Richard whispered. "She looks so much like you, Caroline."

"I've always thought she looks like you. She has your coloring . . . your blue eyes." I debated.

"Yes . . . but look at her face." He spoke reverently as if our daughter was the most precious jewel in the world. "All I see is you! She's an angel. She's *my* angel." He tenderly stroked her hand.

A few moments later, Rosaline's eyes began to flutter. She was extremely groggy.

Her whispered voice sounded scratchy and distant but clear enough to understand. "Don't worry, Daddy," Rosaline muttered. "God is taking good care of me."

My heart leaped inside of my chest. I looked at Richard to see if he'd interpreted Rosaline's words in the same manner. As a child, Richard had told me – many times – he had heard *those exact same words* spoken at his mother's grave on the day she was buried. I could tell by Richard's expression and the tense manner in which his body reacted – he was recalling the same impactful memory. I reached across Rosaline's body and clasped onto Richard's hand.

"Oh my!" I muttered softly as our eyes connected.

"You heard it too, didn't you, Caroline?" There were tears in Richard's eyes. He seemed to be holding his breath.

I nodded as I squeezed his hand. An intangible current passed between us. My gesture helped him relax enough to breathe normally again.

Rosaline finally opened her eyes and managed a tiny smile. First she looked at me and then at her father. "Hi, Daddy."

"Hi, Rosaline," Richard bent over and kissed her on the cheek.

"Daddy?"

"Yes." Richard replied as he leaned closer to her.

"Can you please call me Rosie? I want everyone to call me Rosie."

"If that's what you want, Sweetheart." He kissed her on the cheek a second time and tenderly brushed the hair away from her face.

"Mommy," Rosaline paused until she made eye contact. "When can I have some ice cream?"

Richard and I smiled simultaneously at each other. We both breathed an enormous sigh of relief.

2

Martin's graduation was an emotional event for the entire family. Because Martin had been a star on the football field and a friend to everyone, there was a thunderous applause when he walked across the stage to receive his diploma. His classmates adored him. John's face was radiated joy. Rick, Brad, Rosaline and Randy clapped in unison and cheered so loudly my ears rang for a full minute after Martin returned to his seat.

If I thought Martin's high school graduation was emotional for John and our family, it was nothing in comparison to the day – three weeks later – when we put Martin on the bus to Parris Island. As we said our good-byes at the station, I knew John was doing everything he could to keep his emotions in check. John never wanted Martin to join the Marines. However, Martin was steadfast in his desire to be the best man he could be; in addition, he loved the Marine's motto and he *believed* in The Corps, our country and God. We couldn't help but be proud of Martin; however, that was of little comfort to John because we all knew the war in Vietnam was escalating, which augmented our apprehension.

Even after the bus was out of sight, we continued to wave. I glanced at John and saw a steady stream of tears rolling down his cheeks. I hadn't seen him cry since Lucy died nearly a decade ago. I tried to comfort him by wrapping him in my arms, but he didn't seem to want my support nor did he return my embrace.

3

John, Randy and I were watching summer reruns of *Gilligan's Island* on the television set when the show was interrupted with footage of the riots in Newark. It was the sixth day of total chaos in the streets. Twenty-six were dead, including a policeman who had been beaten to death, and one fireman who had been shot in the back. An estimate of more than 750 people had been injured and over a thousand were jailed.

The colored population was in an uproar because the state of New Jersey had claimed a section of land in the central ward of the city's tenement buildings in order to build the new University of Medicine and Dentistry facility. By doing this, thousands of colored residents were displaced. Even though Newark was one of the first cities in the United States to hire Negro police officers, it didn't appease the residents because only eleven percent of the police force was colored in a city that was fifty percent Negro. The volatile situation was compounded and eventually erupted when two officers were accused of police brutality while arresting a colored cab driver near Hayes Homes.

As the protesters smashed windows and looted businesses, they screamed "Black Power." The National Guard was having great difficulty gaining control of the situation, and there was an estimated ten million dollars in damages to date.

John and I were in awe as we watched the madness on the television. Then I saw something that couldn't possibly be true. I blinked twice and wondered if John saw it too. Before I could ask, he glanced over at me and said, "Is that Brad standing next to the policeman?"

I could barely breathe, much less talk. I sat spellbound on the couch as I watched the police officer snatch Brad's camera from his hand. The newsman who was filming the tumultuous scene was not focused on Brad; instead, he was intent on getting the footage of the men throwing bricks through windows and hitting cars with baseball bats. As a result,

Brad was not the focal point and was not always visible on the television screen, but I was certain the person I saw was my son. He was arguing with the officer as the policeman popped Brad's camera open and ripped out the film. After the officer bunched the film into a ball, he threw it on the ground and stomped on it. I couldn't decipher any of the words being said, but I could tell Brad was enraged and the officer was equally as angry. I held my breath as I watched, hoping and praying Brad would come out of this situation unscathed.

The news story was over and *Gilligan's Island* returned. Ginger and the Professor were in the middle of a conversation but the punch line went dead on me. I didn't hear the words, and I certainly didn't get the joke. I sat paralyzed between John and Randy. I had no idea how much time passed before I reached for the phone.

My figures were shaking. It took two times before I dialed Richard's number correctly. I wanted to scream *why does he have so many nines in his phone number? It takes too long for them to dial around!* Finally, Rosaline answered the phone.

"Rosie," I diligently tried to appear relaxed so my daughter would not sense my turmoil. "Is your father home?"

"Hi, Mom!" Rosaline sounded happy. Obviously, she had not been watching CBS. "I think Daddy's upstairs." She put the phone down. I could hear her screaming, "Dad! Mom's on the phone." I envisioned her at the bottom of the stairs yelling up to the second floor.

A few seconds later, Richard picked up the extension. "Hello."

"Richard." My composure was gone. "Is Brad there?" I was praying my eyes had deceived me, and Brad was home reading a book or listening to the latest Rolling Stones album.

"No, he's not home. I think he went to a movie with some of his friends. It's his night off."

"He's not at a movie, Richard." I was hysterical. I'm not even sure Richard could understand what I was saying. "He's in Newark!"

"What?" Richard questioned. "That's ridiculous. He wouldn't go to Newark. It's too dangerous there. They are rioting in the streets and burning the city."

"I saw him on the television. My God! Richard!" I was trembling so hard I nearly dropped the phone. "Is Rick home?"

"He should be here any minute. He's been working tonight." Seconds after Richard finished his sentence, I heard Rick's voice in the background. "Hang on. Rick just got home. I'll ask him if he knows where Brad is." They had a muffled conversation before Richard returned to the phone. "Rick says that Brad went with friends to see *Wait Until Dark*."

"Richard! That movie is new. There is no way it is showing in any movie theater around here. It won't leave the city for months." I was panicking.

"Caroline. Calm down." Richard was remarkably composed. "I'm sure you are over-exaggerating this."

"I know what I saw!" At this point, I was too hysterical to talk.

John took the phone from me, "Richard," John's voice of reason went over the telephone lines. "I was watching the TV too. It was definitely Brad." He paused. "My guess is that it won't be long before Brad's at the police station. The officer looked teed off." Richard must have been talking because John remained quiet for a few moments before replying, "Yes, you're right. We should hang up the phone. You call the station. I'll keep this line free in case Brad calls us."

Not thirty seconds after John hung up the receiver, the phone rang. I dove across the couch to answer it. "Hello."

"Mom."

The moment I heard Brad's voice, tears filled my eyes. First I was relieved. Then I was *angry*. The two emotions did battle inside my brain. "Where are you?"

"I'm at the police station."

"In Newark?"

"Yes. How did you know?"

"Doesn't matter," I answered. "How did you get to the city, and what the hell are you doing there?"

"I came in with my friends. We wanted to see the action, but when they were rocking the car in the streets, my buddies left."

"You mean the colored boys were rocking the car?"

"Mom, get with the program." Brad answered. "They don't want to be called *colored* or Negro anymore. They want to be called *black*!"

"Right now, I don't give a damn what those hoodlums want to be called." I was shrieking every word. "Why did your friends leave you there?"

"I was trying to get a picture. This is history in the making. I want to capture it." Brad sounded more like a man than a teenager. "My buddies got scared so they left." Brad's voice rose ever so slightly when he continued. "I thought the cop was going to break my camera, but he gave it back to me after he destroyed my film."

"Are you *nuts?*" I was hysterical.

"Don't tell Dad. He'll flip out."

"Too late, Brad. He already knows." My anger kept exploding in waves throughout my body. "Did you really think . . ."

"Mom," Brad interrupted me and spoke with an unruffled voice. "Can you come get me, please? The officer said he won't book me if someone comes to get me within the hour."

"They're going to book you?" I yelled into the phone as I paced the room as far as the cord allowed me to travel.

"Mom! Don't freak out!" Brad was amazingly calm. "I'm okay. Nothing bad is going to happen. I need a ride home – that's all."

John took the phone from me. Completely drained, I collapsed on the couch.

"Your mother is going to stay here with Randy. I'll come get you. Which precinct? What's the address?" John paused as he jotted down the information. "Hang tight. I'll be there in thirty or forty-five minutes. And for God's sake, stay quiet and stay out of trouble!"

4

By the time Brad entered his junior year in high school, things had calmed down a little bit in our family. Brad had been grounded for a month with the exception of working at Carley's Place. As much as it pained me to do it, I took his camera and put it on the top shelf of my closet for the remainder of the summer. I could not believe he had jeopardized his life with a gift I had given him. If something had happened to Brad on that terrible day in July, I would never have forgiven myself.

Also during the summer, Rosaline completed a summer school program that concentrated on phonics. By September, she was not quite on par in reading with her six-grade classmates, but she was a lot better than she had been. I scheduled a tutor to help her on a weekly basis during the school year. The cost was going to cut into my grocery allowance, but I truly believed she needed it in order to succeed.

Rick began his final year in high school as captain of the football team. His leadership skills and talent on the field were spotlighted in the local paper. The reporter predicted the team would have a winning season. I marked all of the home games on my calendar. It was going to be a busy fall.

On Randy's fifth birthday, I vowed to make two changes in my life. First, I returned to Bamberger's and got a part time position. I was able to work during the hours John was home so we did not have to pay for a babysitter. John didn't like the idea. He thought I should be home taking care of the apartment, cooking his meals and putting Randy to bed at night. In addition, John hated those Swanson TV dinners and grumbled on a regular basis about it. I didn't tell John about my ultimate goal, which was to work full time once Randy entered first grade the following September. I still regretted my lost opportunity, and I wanted the chance to prove to myself – and to everyone – I could earn the management position.

The second thing I did was research a new group called the National Organization for Women. Ever since I'd read Betty Friedan's book The Feminine Mystique four years ago, I was enthralled by the wave of change the novel created for women. Apparently, Ms. Friedan was one of the original founders of the organization, and I wanted to be a part of it. This, of course, did not go over well with John. He didn't like the fact that I went to the meetings, nor did he think it was a worthy cause.

"Those women are rockin' the boat," John said every time I left the apartment. "When are women going to figure out they have the best of all worlds. They don't have to get up and go to work every morning. It's the man's job to put food on the table and a roof over their heads." John smirked. "All the woman has to do is take care of the family." He boldly pointed a finger at me when he added, "For whatever reason, you've decided that's not good enough for you." John was angry at the changes I was making in *our* family.

By October, when Martin finished boot camp, I had established a successful routine and managed to juggle my housework, the children, my job, and NOW like an energetic circus act. I felt as if I was running a race and *winning*. It was exhilarating! The unfortunate downside was the fact I often missed Friday night football games and had to read about Rick's successful plays in the local newspaper or see Brad's photographs of Rick's amazing catches on the field. Because Brad was the photo editor of their high school yearbook, he had the best position to freeze-frame the live action on the gridiron. The school paid for all of the film and developing, so Brad gladly took dozens of pictures – most of them of his brother.

Unfortunately – because of *all* of our hectic schedules – I didn't get to spend much time with Rick, Rosaline or Brad – rarely did they come over and crash on my couch – they were too busy. Our free time did not often overlap; however, there was one exception – the day we gathered to say good-bye to Martin.

The night before Martin left for Vietnam, the entire family congregated. I made a massive meal with all of Martin's favorites, and we sat around the table for hours reminiscing. It was a bittersweet night of nostalgic memories, laughter and a few sentimental tears. We even got the photo albums out, including pictures of Martin's mother. It had been a long time since I'd looked at photographs of my dear friend Lucy.

Intuitively, I think those memories might have been too difficult for both father and son; consequently, Martin focused more upon talking about the baseball pictures of the teams he'd played on with Rick and Brad than going down a more personal memory lane with his father. Throughout most of the evening, my husband had a stoic expression on his face. He laughed on cue and smiled when appropriate. John and his son both provided a brave façade for the rest of us.

I enjoyed watching the three boys as they recalled with great accuracy the different plays that won or lost unforgettable games. While Martin, Rick and Brad recaptured their baseball and football memories, I noticed John was lost in thought. He spent most of the later part of the evening staring at old black and white pictures of Lucy. It tugged at my heart.

The following day I had to work; therefore, John and Randy took Martin to the station. That night John was quiet and solemn. He spent the evening gazing blankly at the television set, but I knew he wasn't watching it. I learned a long time ago – if John didn't want to talk about something, nothing I did could make him. I also knew neither of us would be able to fully relax until Martin was back on American soil again.

5

In January of 1968, Richard took Rick on a journey through the South looking at prospective colleges. Rick and his high school counselor had compiled a long list. He applied, sight unseen, to a half a dozen of them. Rick's grades were good enough to apply to Ivy League schools, but he didn't show an interest in any of them. Our oldest son truly felt he belonged on a small campus where he could make friends easily, get a degree in Business, and hopefully – play on a competitive football team. He waffled back and forth about the University of South Carolina and East Carolina University before deciding they were too big for him. He liked William and Mary in Virginia, but wanted to see the rest on the list before he committed to it.

On their road trip, they checked out Guilford, Catawba, Campbell, Brevard, and Appalachian State. Each night throughout the journey, Rick called collect to tell me what they had seen during the day, but it wasn't until the afternoon he saw Elon College in North Carolina that Rick's voice sounded excited.

"Mom," Rick didn't even let me talk before he continued, "I think I found it!" Rick was animated as he spoke. "It's a small campus. Elon looks like something out of a storybook, tucked away in the middle of nowhere. The minute I stepped foot on the campus . . . I don't know how to describe it. I felt like I was *home*." Rick was rambling; as a result, his words were all running together. "I met with Coach Wilson. He was great. He said the team has an All-American tight end named Richard McGeorge, but he has a hole on the other side of the field. He told me that I could fill it. Coach Wilson said he'd been looking at my stats. I think they might even offer me a scholarship." Rick took a deep breath before continuing. "I feel like I *belong* here, Mom. I don't think I need to look anywhere else. They have a good Business program and a good football team. I think this is it!"

Richard took the phone from his son and added, "And guess what,"

Richard chuckled. "They have mandatory chapel." We both laughed in unison.

"So you like it too?" I asked.

"Yes. It's nice. Rick's right. It feels homey. But I think part of the reason he has fallen in love with this school is because every cute little honey who walks by him waves, smiles and says 'hi ya'll.' Makes me wish I'd been able to go to college." Richard continued on a more serious note. "I think it's a good fit for him. It's pretty far away from us, but he'll do well here."

A week later, while I was compiling my monthly care package to send to Martin in Vietnam and watching the evening news, Walter Cronkite announced the fighting had escalated. Mr. Cronkite was calling it the *Tet Offensive*. The images on the television were extremely graphic and created a nauseous stirring in my stomach. John was on the edge of the couch, leaning forward and hanging on every word. I was glad Randy was not in the room to see it; instead, he was playing with his Lincoln Logs in the back of the apartment.

We were completely entranced by the action on the television – we did not hear the knock on the door. Then it was repeated – maybe even a third time. I can't remember who opened the door. Was it John? Or did I do it? We were both standing in the threshold. Everything moved in slow motion. When I saw the uniformed man in the doorway, I knew. I didn't need him to speak to me, nor did I need him to hand me the envelope. I think I stopped breathing for a little while – then, I heard the gasp of pain coming from John's throat.

"Oh my God! Not Martin. Please, Sir. Don't tell me it's Martin." But John knew.

I did too.

6

John and I were later told Martin died during the first days of the Battle of Hue, which was considered to be one of the longest and bloodiest battles of the war. He died with honor trying to save three of his fellow Marines, but that didn't help ease our pain. Neither did the fact we had to wait more than a month to schedule Martin's burial in Arlington National Cemetery.

Even though Martin's body had not yet returned home, we held a memorial service in his honor. Our church was packed with friends and neighbors, but there were strangers in attendance too. In the street outside of our church, a dozen protesters gathered. They paraded up and down the sidewalk carrying signs which read, *We've Lost Another Beautiful Soul, Johnson is a War Criminal, Make Love Not War, and Bring the Troops Home Now.*

During the service, I could hear their loud chants, but after the service – as we walked down the church steps – the protesters stopped shouting their words and proceeded in silence. I was grateful they showed a modicum of respect and courtesy not to approach us. I was also immensely thankful there were no reporters around to capture our grief or to use their microphone and cameras to invade our sorrow. My oldest sons were remarkably strong and flanked both John and me with support; however, Rosaline and Randy wept shamelessly.

On the seventh day of March, we traveled to Virginia for the interment. All of us stayed in the same room at the Marriott. The four kids were in sleeping bags on the floor. John and I were in the double bed. None of us slept, but we didn't talk either. There was a numb silence in the room. I ached for my family.

The following day, we sat through the service at the Fort Myers Old Post Chapel directly outside the gates of the Arlington National Cemetery. There were no familiar faces in the pews – only our family. I don't remember the hymns, the psalms, or even what the military chaplain said. It was all a blur. I do, however, remember how pale John looked and how he pulled away from me whenever I tried to hold his hand.

After the short service, we walked through the hallowed streets of Arlington Cemetery behind a wagon pulled by six perfectly matched white horses. The American flag was draped over Martin's coffin. Eight young soldiers in dress uniforms marched stoically beside the casket. I didn't know any of them, and I wondered if any of them had known Martin.

Although the day was sunny, it was also bitter cold. There were tears in my eyes. Most formed because of my anguish, but some were caused by the biting wind that whipped at our faces. In order to divert my attention away from the sting of the chilly breeze, I focused on the clip clopping sound of the horses' hooves as they hit the pavement. They were in perfect harmony. It sounded remarkably like a sweet song. In different circumstances, I might have enjoyed the rhythmic cadence; however, the rows and rows of impeccably positioned headstones as far as the eye could see reminded me constantly of why we were taking this walk on this bleak, frigid day.

When we reached our destination, the eight pallbearers ceremoniously carried the casket and delivered Martin to his final resting place. John, the children and I sat in the six chairs provided for us. The chaplain said a few short sentences. In the distance, I saw seven soldiers lift their rifles and fire off three shots apiece. The sound jolted me. It was followed by the calming melody of the lone bugler playing *Taps*.

The eight pallbearers picked the American flag off of Martin's casket and held it in the air snapping the edges loud enough to draw everyone's attention. Systematically they worked as a team, folding the flag into a triangle – just the stars were visible. I swallowed hard and took a deep breath because I knew this was going to be the most difficult part of the day. The young soldier approached us with the flag held reverently in his hands. He knelt in front of me and spoke, "On behalf of the President of the United States, the Marine Corps and a grateful nation, please accept this flag as a symbol of our appreciation for your loved one's honorable and faithful service."

I thought he was going to give the flag to John, but he gave it to me instead. I wasn't looking at my husband, but I could feel his shoulders collapsing and the agonizing sound that came from his throat. I accepted the flag and bowed my head.

When the short ceremony was over, the six of us stood up simultaneously. The children headed back to the car while I remained with John next to the casket. My husband knelt beside the coffin and placed both of his hands on it. I joined him. As I prayed and said my final good-bye, I allowed sweet images of Martin's face to flash inside my closed eyes. Even though he had never been comfortable calling me "Mother," he had always treated me as "his family." I loved Martin as if he was my son, and my children always thought of him as a brother. I knew we were all feeling the loss of a special person.

I was not sure how much time passed before John stood up and headed back to the car. I followed. After taking a half of a dozen steps, he stopped and turned toward me. Without a word, he took the flag from my hands and cradled it in his. John finally spoke, "I wish Lucy were here." His words were choppy and barely audible. "I miss her."

My heart wrenched not solely because of Martin's death . . . but also because I missed my dear friend too. And the worst revelation . . . I suddenly knew with great clarity . . . John didn't love me. He was lonely. He had *always* been lonely. Our marriage had *always* been based on the fact that we were *both* lonely.

7

At the end of March, while our wounds were still fresh, John and I watched a televised speech by President Johnson. He declared a halt to the bombing in Vietnam and called for peace negotiations to end the war. It was a lengthy, detailed broadcast. Toward the end, President Johnson shocked the viewers by saying "I shall not seek, and I will not accept, the nomination of my party for another term as your president."

At first, both John and I were too stunned to speak. It was incredible to believe the president was finally backing down. There had been such a swell of negative commentary on the conflict in Vietnam that was compounded by constant footage on the nightly news of the ugly visuals of war. Apparently, the reporters had no filter or rules; thus, they were allowed to bring the death and destruction into all of the living rooms in America.

It was an election year. Four years earlier, Johnson had won in a landslide victory, and most democrats assumed LBJ would be their candidate again in 1968. However, Eugene McCarthy chose to challenge the sitting president. His anti-war platform rallied the youth who eagerly campaigned for him. McCarthy proved to be a worthy opponent.

When Lyndon Johnson withdrew from the race, he threw his support to his vice president; as a result, Hubert Humphrey began his campaign against McCarthy for the democratic ticket.

If that was not enough controversy within the Democratic Party, former democrat George Wallace broke away from his party to form the American Independent Party. He chose Curtis LeMay as his running mate. Wallace campaigned on increasing Medicare and Social Security; in addition, he continued to be in staunch support of segregation.

I was disgusted with the democrats' choices. I was equally unexcited about Richard Nixon, who was probably going to be the republican candidate in November's election. In fact, I contemplated not voting at all this year because I didn't like any of them.

Then, a miracle happened. Robert Kennedy got into the race. I clearly remembered my experience when I was part of the movement supporting John Kennedy.

My heart was so heavy with the loss of Martin, I decided to fill my time by joining Robert Kennedy's campaign in hopes it would lift my spirits. Rick was deep into his final season of baseball before graduation, but Brad did not make the team and had plenty of free time on his hands. Consequently, I encouraged Brad to be a part of this election year. To my surprise, he loved the idea. Brad spent a couple of afternoons a week at the local campaign headquarters. I noticed he always had his camera with him and hoped to eventually meet Mr. Kennedy.

When I heard Robert Kennedy was going to speak in Philadelphia, I asked Brad if he would like to go with me. He jumped at the opportunity. Brad brought his camera and four rolls of Kodak film. I packed a box of *RFK in '68* buttons, 250 campaign flyers plus some *Kennedy for President* posters I'd gotten at our local campaign headquarters; in addition, I had my "Equal Pay for Equal Jobs" sign. Brad was focused on capturing a picture of the event, and I was determined to hand out all of Mr. Kennedy's campaign memorabilia in hopes of spreading his positive message.

We traveled in the Edsel. Originally – during my marriage to Richard – I had hated the car. However, in retrospect, it was the Edsel that gave me the ability to leave. In addition, if it weren't for the car, I would still be a prisoner in my apartment with John. The Edsel gave me transportation to Bamberger's, to NOW meetings, and to this new adventure with my son. Over the years, the car became a symbol of my personal freedom.

I drove the first thirty minutes out of town before stopping for gas. When it was time to get back on the road, I handed the keys to Brad. "Want to drive?" I asked.

"Really?" He responded in a surprised tone.

"You've had your license for a while now." I walked to the passenger side of the car. "Have you had any experience on the highway?"

"No."

"Don't you think it's time?"

He snatched the keys from my hands before I had a chance to change my mind. As Brad slid into the driver's seat, his first instinct was to change the station on the radio. "If I'm driving, I should be able to pick the channel." He glanced at me for approval.

"Okay," I replied as I shut my door. "But you can't play it loudly. That's too distracting." I sat back in my seat and tried to relax. "That's a pretty song."

"*White Rabbit?*" Brad chuckled. "You like that song?"

"Sure. As Dick Clark says, it has a nice beat."

Brad laughed out loud as he put the car in gear and headed for the highway. "I don't think you're listening to the words, Mom. If you were, you wouldn't like the song at all. It's about drugs."

I didn't know if I was more nervous about the topic of our conversation or the fact Brad was behind the wheel of my car. Before responding to his comment, I took a couple of deep, palliative breaths. "Have you tried drugs?"

"You mean like LSD or grass?"

Oh, God! I thought to myself. *He knows the name of the drugs I read about in Time Magazine!*

"Geez, Mom! I don't want to mess with any of that stuff," Brad said as he focused on merging onto the highway.

I felt as if I had opened a can of worms, and I didn't know how to get the lid back on again. "Do you drink alcohol?" I practically whispered the question, and all I could hear was Richard's voice divulging what he had told me several months ago.

"Really, Mom? Am I on trial here or something?" Brad was concentrating on passing the truck in front of us. When I didn't respond, he added, "Do you want the truth, or do you want me to lie to you?"

"Oh," I replied. I definitely regretted starting this conversation.

"Okay. I'll be honest." Brad confessed. "I've tried beer and maybe a couple of other drinks, too, but I'm not really into it. I'm serious, Mom!

I've never been crocked, and I don't plan to be. I like hanging loose with my friends." He looked at me for a moment and then returned his eyes to the road. "It's no big deal, Mom. Don't sweat it."

The topic was obviously unpleasant for both of us, so I decided to change the subject. "When I was at school last week dropping off Rick's check for his cap and gown rental, I saw you with a cute girl."

"Which girl?" Brad said, almost as if he was evading me.

"She was blonde. Long hair. Cute."

"Oh her," Brad said. "She's nice, but we're just friends."

"Looked to me like you were more than friends" I teased.

"Mom," Brad commented as he glanced at me and then back again at the road. "I like lots of girls. They are all great, but there isn't anyone special."

"You're like your father. The girls were always crawling all over him too."

"Geez, Mom." Brad grinned. "You sound a little jealous."

"Sorry. I was remembering my high school days." It was becoming all too clear to me. Brad had my features and my coloring, but his mannerisms, his confidence and his aura all resembled his father. As I watched Brad drive my car, all I could see was Richard as a teenager sitting in his Chrysler with a cluster of doting girls surrounding the car. "Your father had every girl in school chasing after him. Looks like you might be following in his footsteps."

"I'm nothing like Dad." Brad's voice lost its pleasant tone; he was noticeably agitated.

"If you say so," I replied.

"I like going out. I like having fun. I like lots of girls ... but not any *one* girl." Brad seemed frustrated with our dialogue. "Is there anything wrong with that?"

"No," I tried to lighten the mood. "I was curious if you had found the love of your life yet?"

"No, I haven't found her yet . . . but I'm pretty sure I will know the minute I see her." He grinned. "My guess . . . she will be like you, Mom." Brad winked in my direction. "I promise, Mom. When I meet her, you'll be the first to know."

The moment he finished his sentence, the conversation was over.

Brad was done talking about the subject. His father had the same characteristic. We spent the remainder of the trip listening to music on the radio.

When we arrived in Philadelphia, it was extremely difficult to find a parking place and get around the enormous crowd that gathered to hear Robert Kennedy. Finally, Brad and I maneuvered ourselves into a position to see him. When the candidate came to the podium, the people roared with praise and enthusiasm. I held up my "RFK for President" sign in one hand and my "Equal Pay for Equal Jobs" in the other. Brad rapidly snapped several pictures of me. I later discovered my eyes were closed in two of them, but the third was fabulous. I looked like a true supporter for the cause. Brad was also able to take several dozen photos of Mr. Kennedy as he talked about his platform and the things he wanted to change in America. I hung on every word. He spoke of equality for all, and the power of the younger generation to take charge and make changes. I noticed more of the observers in the cheering crowd were closer to Brad's age than mine. I remembered the few gray hairs I'd seen in the mirror that morning, and noticed most of the people standing around me didn't have any gray in their hair.

Robert Kennedy spoke passionately, "I believe in the ideals of this generation of Americans, and I believe we can do far better than we have in the past." Robert Kennedy's voice rallied the people as he eloquently repeated his now famous statement, "There are those who look at things the way they are, and ask *why* ... I dream of things that never were, and ask *why not?*" Brad took the focus of his camera off of the candidate and took pictures of the crowd. They were roaring in applause. There was a palpable magic in the air.

By the time we headed home, it was nearly dark. I elected to drive. Brad and I were both energized from the speech and thrilled we had seen Robert Kennedy in person; we couldn't stop talking about it.

A week later, while I was washing the dinner dishes, I heard the tragic news on the radio: Martin Luther King, Jr. had been shot in Memphis. I prayed for the man who worked for change through non-violent ways, but my prayers were not answered. Walter Cronkite verified on the *CBS Evening News*; Mr. King was pronounced dead at the hospital. *Oh my God!* What a horrible loss for all of us.

That night riots broke out in most major cities across the country; however, I eventually heard Robert Kennedy gave an amazing speech in Indianapolis. There were no riots in that city; some say it was because of his speech. He delivered it from the back of a flatbed truck, which had no protection from the possibility of retaliated violence. He broke the heartbreaking news to the people who had gathered to hear his campaign speech and were previously unaware of the tragedy. Robert Kennedy spoke from his heart as he talked about Martin Luther King, Jr.'s peaceful dedication to equality and justice for all human beings. With an eloquent and reassuring voice he added, "For those of you who are black, and are tempted to be filled with hatred and distrust at the injustice of such an act," he spoke through his bullhorn, "against all white people, I can only say that I feel in my own heart the same kind of feeling. I had a member of my family killed, but he was killed by a white man." Robert Kennedy pleaded to the crowd and said, "What we need in the United States is not division; what we need in the United States is not hatred; what we need in the United States is not violence or law-lessness; but love and wisdom, and compassion toward one another, and in a feeling of justice toward those who still suffer within our country, whether they be white or they be black." His voice of reason continued, "So I shall ask you tonight to return home, to say a prayer for the family of Martin Luther King, Jr., ... and to say a prayer for our own country, which all of us love."

I instinctively knew our country had lost an important and valued life; Martin Luther King, Jr. had touched so many lives with goodness and love. I was in mourning with the rest of our troubled nation. The one comforting thought I held on to was the fact we still had a few great leaders; obviously, Robert Kennedy was one of them.

8

I was headed out of the door and on my way to the grocery store when the phone rang. It was Rosaline. She was crying hysterically. I had difficulty understanding anything she was saying. Thankfully, the school nurse got on the phone and filled me in on the details. Rosaline, apparently, had started her period – her *first* period. She had soiled her light blue A-lined skirt and was more embarrassed than upset. I promised to pick her up immediately.

I took a sweater with me. When I saw Rosaline, I handed it to her so she could wrap it around her waist and hide the spots that dotted the material. She was relieved to be able to walk down the hallway without any of her classmates knowing what had happened.

When we got to her house, I handed her a small box of Kotex and showed her what to do with it. She immediately raced to her room and changed her clothes. I waited for her downstairs in anticipation of having the long overdue *Mother-Daughter Talk*. I vividly remembered when I'd started my period and I had feared I was at death's door. I chuckled as I remembered my naiveté and how Richard had been my hero. It seemed so long ago. Poor Rosaline! I felt badly for her because – like me – she didn't seem to have a close girlfriend who could help her through this rite of passage.

When my daughter came down the stairs, she was more relaxed and wanted to talk. Patting the couch next to me, I invited her to sit down. She told me in great detail about the entire episode; talking about it seemed to make her feel better. During the conversation, she began to confide in me that she was concerned about the changes in her body.

"Sometimes, Mom, my chest hurts." She placed her hands over her heart. She tried to appear sophisticated as she continued, "I know I'm going to grow breasts. All girls do." She paused. "But I think there might be something wrong with me – or with them."

"Why do you think that, Rosie?" I tried not to sound alarmed.

"It's hard to explain, Mom." Rosaline replied without making eye contact. "When I look at myself in the mirror, I can tell that one side is growing." She placed her right hand over her left breast. "But the other side isn't." She looked at me with doubt and fear in her eyes. "I don't understand. What's wrong with me?"

"I'm pretty sure there is nothing wrong with you, Rosie." I think you are growing up, and it doesn't happen overnight. It's not like you are a little girl one day and the next day you become a woman. It's a long process. I think maybe the easiest way to explain it is to remind you about a conversation we had last month. Remember when you told me that you were confused because one day you liked playing with your Barbie dolls and the next day you wanted to put them away because all you wanted to do was listen to Rock 'n Roll? And then the next day you wanted to play with your Barbie dolls again." I smiled assuredly at my daughter. "I think your breasts are a little like that . . . one of your breasts is playing with Barbie dolls and the other one is listening to Rock 'n Roll."

To my complete surprise, my daughter seemed to understand my logic. She threw her arms around me and gave me a giant bear hug like the ones she'd given me when she was a little girl. I savored the moment. We both laughed.

"Would you like to go shopping with me this weekend?"

"For what?" Rosaline asked.

"I think it's time I buy you a bra."

Before I had completed my sentence, the door opened. Richard came into the room carrying a bag of groceries in each arm. He looked perplexed when he saw me. "What are you doing here?"

"It's okay, Daddy." Rosaline came to my defense. "Mom's helping me."

Even though this had once been my home, I still felt uncomfortable visiting my own children in it. There were too many memories: the good ones and the bad. In addition, I rarely stood in the foyer when I didn't remember that fiery night Richard had passionately attacked me and I had willingly succumbed to him. Those images were always followed by his caustic, biting comment, which left me paralyzed with guilt and sadness.

"I'm sorry," Richard responded. His apology was directed to Rosaline. "I didn't mean to snap, Honey." He put the bags on the kitchen counter and proceeded to put the food away. "You're home from school early. Is everything okay?"

"Everything's cool, Dad, but I don't want to talk about it." Our daughter replied happily as she bounced out of the room leaving Richard and me alone.

"Bad grades?" Richard inquired trying to make conversation. "Did you have to go to a teacher's conference?"

"No," I replied. "Her grades are actually improving."

"What then?"

"Our little girl is growing up." I walked across the room, pulled out the stool at the counter and sat down on it. "She got her *period*... first time. Unfortunately, she wasn't prepared."

Richard stopped in the middle of putting cans of Chef Boyardee in the cabinet and turned around with a look of surprise on his face. "After the disaster you experienced when it happened to you, I can't believe you let your daughter fall through the cracks."

"Why are you being so snippy?"

"I don't know," he shrugged. "There's too much happening at the restaurant. One of the cooks quit yesterday right in the middle of the dinner shift. It was chaos." He put the gallon of milk in the cabinet under the sink and the Mr. Clean in the refrigerator.

I couldn't help myself. I laughed.

"What?" He was obviously annoyed.

"Do you know what you did?" I chuckled again.

He looked around the kitchen. "No," he added. "What?"

"You put the milk under the sink, Richard." I walked around him, opened the cabinet, and pointed to the carton.

Richard let out a long, soulful sigh. "Damn!" he muttered. "I didn't even realize." He closed his eyes and took the time to take several long, drawn-out breaths. "This is the first time in three days I've had a free hour to get home for a few minutes. Between the restaurants and the kids' schedules, there is never enough time. I didn't even get to see Rick's game on Tuesday, and I heard he made the winning run."

"It was amazing – a straight shot over the left field fence – two men on base." I said excitedly as I recaptured the final moments. "It was a fabulous comeback in the ninth inning, and the perfect way to wrap up Rick's final regular season of play in high school."

"Thanks for the visual." Richard smirked and then let out a short laugh. "Now I'm even more upset I missed it." He tried to smile, but his disappointment was still etched in his expression.

"If it's any consolation, Brad got a picture of the moment Rick's bat hit the ball. He developed it in the dark room at school." My pride was echoed in my voice. "I have a copy of it at the apartment. If you ask him, I bet he'll make a copy for you."

"I doubt it." Richard replied. "Brad's not talking to me. He's given me the silent treatment ever since I put him on double shifts at Carley's Place on weekends."

"Why did you do that?"

"When Brad has too much time with nothing to do, he gets into trouble." Richard followed his statement with another. "If Brad's working, he doesn't have time for trouble." Richard systematically put the rest of the groceries away; this time without mistakes. "What a mess. I feel like I can't get it all done sometimes."

"Funny." I responded in a whimsical way.

"How so?"

"That's exactly how I feel most of the time."

"Okay, maybe. But you don't *have* to be so busy." Richard jeered. "You can stay home. You *choose* to go off – God knows where – waving signs and walking lines. Plus... you don't *have* to work at Bam's. You're the one who made that choice. Geez, you hardly earn enough money to make it worth your while."

"Stop!" I was truly annoyed. "Why is *your* busy, hectic schedule more important than *mine*?" The tone in my voice was laced with agitation. "Why do you make my choices sound demeaning and insignificant?"

"That's not what I said."

"Yes," I reaffirmed my opinion. "It *is* what you said."

"Damnit! I don't have time for this." Richard stomped out of the room, but not before he added, "You can let yourself out."

9

I was asleep when it happened, and didn't hear the news until the following day. In fact, I didn't have the radio or the television set on because I was paying bills and writing checks including the final payment for the monogramed trunk John and I purchased for Rick's graduation present. I was also putting the finishing touches on the dress I was making to wear to the event next week.

It was Brad who informed me of the tragic news. Tears streamed down his cheeks. I tried to remember the last time I had seen Brad cry – not once since Rex died. Today, he had the same lost expression on his face when he told me Robert Kennedy had been shot in California last night, and he was dead. I felt as if the joy had been taken from both of our bodies, and the hope – which had filled our nation's future – was evaporating. I tried to find the words to comfort my son, but there were none. Martin Luther King, Jr. had been shot two months ago, and now Bobby was gone.

How was our country going to recover from these tragic losses?

10

The following Wednesday was Rick's graduation day. It should have been a monumentally happy day for everyone involved; however, the cloud of despondency from the two assassinations that occurred during their senior year dampened the graduates' celebration. The valedictorian's speech should have been filled with promise for a bright future; but instead, it was a painful oration. We could all sense the sorrow in his voice and the foreboding prediction in his words. What should have been a celebratory, magical day was tarnished with a broken bridge between those who were overwhelmed with sadness by the loss of two brilliant lives and those who didn't mourn their deaths. Everyone lost.

For me, the day's events were compounded with mixed emotions at the "After Party" Richard hosted for our son at Carley's Place. I had waited a month with high expectations for the time I could give my gift to Rick. It had taken most of the spring to come up with exactly the right present to mark this milestone in Rick's life. *My son was going to college!* He was going to experience the dream I had never been able to fulfill. As much as it hurt to know I would soon say good-bye to him and let him go, I was also extremely proud. There were days when I thought my heart might burst with elation, and it was difficult not to shower Rick constantly with my joy.

The monogramed trunk cost a month's pay from my part-time job at Bamberger's, but it was worth every penny. I believed it was the perfect present to symbolize the transition from home to college dorm. I couldn't wait to see his reaction when he opened it.

Unfortunately, I was denied the pleasure because Richard chose *my* moment to bestow *his* surprise gift. He gathered the family and a few select friends around the bar and presented Rick with a small box.

"This is for you, Son." Richard said as he handed Rick his present. "You've worked hard; you've accomplished much in your life to date.

You've showed all of us what determination and tenacity can do. I'm proud of you." Richard put his arm around me and pulled me to his side. "*We* are both proud of you." He squeezed my shoulder to emphasize his words. "I hope you like it."

Richard's grip on my shoulder was evidence of his enthusiastic anticipation. I hadn't a clue what was inside that little box, but I could tell he was immensely excited for our son to open it.

Rick kissed me on my cheek; he, then, firmly shook his father's hand. "Thanks, Mom. Thanks, Dad." Our son had tears in his eyes when he said, "Thank you for everything you have done for me. I know it hasn't been easy. You have both worked hard to give me – to give us – Brad, Rosie and me – all of the things to make our lives better." Rick paused long enough to smile at both of us. "Thank you for supporting me – for helping me with my homework when I was little – for the science projects – for being at my games – for cheering me on – even when I messed up. Thank you for believing in me – even when I failed because – you made me realize I can learn from failure and turn it into a success." He paused a moment to glance directly at Richard. "You did that, Dad. You always made me believe I could do *anything* if I put my mind to it – and I could always *improve* if I tried even harder. Whenever I reached a goal, you helped me see that there are additional goals and none of them are ever out of reach. Thank you!"

I looked at Richard. He, too, had a misting of tears in his eyes.

"When you go to Elon," Richard spoke with pride, "you will have an entirely new set of goals. College will be filled with adventures *and* challenges. Perhaps you will find some obstacles along the way. This time, you will meet those new hurdles without us, but I'm certain you will tackle each new obstacle and reach for each new goal as you have always done." Richard nodded. "All of your life, you have made good choices. I'm certain you will continue to do so." Richard pointed to the box. "Go ahead, Son. Open it."

Rick took the bow off of the box and lifted the lid. There was a key inside. An expression of awe radiated from Rick's face as he held it up. "Dad?" he said. "What's this?"

"It's for your car." Richard stated proudly. "It's not a new car, but I hope you like it."

"A car?" Everyone in the room leaned forward in hopes they could be part of the surprise. "Where is it?"

"It's outside." Richard pointed to his left. "If you look out of that window, you can see it."

"There are four cars, Dad." Rick asked, "Do I get a hint which one it is?"

"It's the red one." Richard replied proudly.

"What?" Rick's mouth gaped open as he stared at the red GTO parked along the street.

"What?" Brad's voice echoed the same word; however, his voice didn't have the same excited tone to it. No one seemed to notice Brad's reaction; they were too focused on the shiny sports car and Rick's astonished expression.

"It's a '66." Richard added, "I'm sorry it's used – a couple of years old and has 23,000 miles on it, but it runs great."

"Holy crap!" Rick was still frozen from his excitement. "Oh my God, Dad! This is incredible."

"Do you want to go look at it?" Richard encouraged.

"Holy crap!" Rick repeated himself. "I don't know what to say." Rick hurriedly hugged both Richard and then me before running to see the car. The crowd followed him.

I shot Richard a look filled with intangible daggers before saying, "You could have at least warned me that you were doing this, Richard!" I whispered the words, but I knew he heard me.

"I told you, Caroline." He repeated himself. "I told you several times."

I took the opportunity to make my case. "No you didn't!"

"I distinctly remember telling you I was absolutely *not* buying Brad a car at graduation next year if he didn't shape up."

"But you never said anything about buying a car for Rick!" I was grateful all of our family and guests were out of earshot. "You could have at least showed it to me first."

"I told Rick it's from both of us!" Richard began to walk away.

I stepped in front of Richard, blocking his exit. It was difficult to keep my anger under control.

"Caroline!" Richard cut me off. "I am going to go outside and enjoy my son's big day. Come enjoy it with me." He veered around me and left me standing at the bar alone.

Now that Rick had seen the car, I knew the monogramed trunk would mean nothing to him in the midst of all of today's excitement. I decided to wait to give it to him another day.

11

Rick left for Elon in early August. He made the football team; as a result, he needed to be at practice weeks before classes commenced. Shortly before he left, I gave him the monogramed trunk. He was delighted and packed everything he needed for college inside of it. As I hugged him, I could tell he was as nostalgic about the moment as I was. A huge knot filled my throat, which made it difficult to breath without choking on my emotions. "Good-bye" was equally as hard for him as it was for me.

Freshmen were not allowed to have cars on campus; therefore, Rick could not take the GTO with him. To everyone's surprise, Rick handed the keys to his brother instead of his father and said, "I trust you will take good care of my wheels."

I glanced at Richard and immediately knew what he was thinking. Calvin had entrusted his Chrysler to Richard when he left for duty. There was a mixture of sorrow, apprehension and pride in Richard's face.

Brad's expression was not nearly as complicated. His was one of sheer delight. He ceremoniously took the keys. "Thanks, Man! I won't let you down."

Richard and Brad made the eight-hour trip with Rick to Elon. Brad wanted to see the college his brother was attending and perhaps he wanted to spend as much time with him as he could before the "cord" was cut. When Brad told me he was going with them, I had to chuckle because I didn't think Brad realized he was going to make the return trip *alone* with his father. I was later told Brad loved Elon and was making it his goal to be accepted to the college next year. I also heard the journey home with his father was long and quiet.

12

The Democratic National Convention was held the week before

Randy started first grade. There was protesting and violence in the streets outside of the International Amphitheatre in Chicago; in addition, there was anger and contempt for the political process. If Robert Kennedy had been a prospective candidate, I probably would have watched every minute of it on television; however, the event no longer held any interest for me, and I wanted no part of it.

Instead, I was focused on my youngest child. The more I looked at Randy, the more I saw Richard. *Was John Randy's father – or was Richard?* It was a question I'd often asked myself since I'd discovered I was pregnant. When Randy was a toddler, I detected personality traits that mirrored John; in addition, I thought my son had John's nose – including the tiny furrow at the tip. However, now that Randy was nearly six, he looked a lot like Richard did on the day I met him – sitting in the library chair at my father's house. Randy's blue eyes were not identical to Richard's, but the resemblance was uncanny. They even twinkled in the same way when he smiled. John's eyes, on the other hand, were hazel and never sparkled – not even when he laughed. It baffled me that no one else saw what seemed so clear to me. I figured the reason other people didn't notice the similarities between Richard and Randy was because no one in our lives today knew either Richard or me when we were children; as a result, they could not see what was evident to me. The question that haunted me . . . *why didn't Richard see the obvious?*

Part of me clung to my secret while another part of me wondered what Richard would do if he suspected. John was completely unaware of my doubts and doted on his son – lavishing Randy with the love and devotion of a fantastic father. My husband had lost one child this year to an ugly war; I knew in my heart it would kill John if he lost another.

I also knew my husband didn't love me, nor did I love him in the way poets professed; however, I did care deeply for John. I also knew he was a kind man . . . a good man . . . a wonderful father. John had rescued me at a time in my life when I was drowning, and I could never intentionally hurt him. As a result, I nurtured my suspicion with constant seeds of denial and pretended not to see. I convinced myself that if I said nothing – did nothing – our lives would remain safe and secure.

I rarely considered telling Richard because I was fairly certain he would not want the chaos that would ensue if I ever told him what I suspected. *Would he even believe me?* In addition, Richard was involved with a woman. To the best of my knowledge, Barbara Powers – the head waitress at Carley's Place – was the first woman Richard dated since our divorce. She was more than a decade younger than Richard and definitely in love with her boss. Their relationship was more than two months old.

I never asked, and Richard never volunteered any information about his private life; as a result, the little I did know about them as a couple, I received second hand from my children. Rick and Brad both thought Barbara was "hip and pretty;" Rosaline confided a little more details, "Dad acts like a lovesick teenager when he is around Barbara." My daughter also mentioned on more than one occasion, "All of my friends think Dad is such a hunk, especially now that he smiles all of the time."

The kids seemed to like Barbara Powers, and they definitely liked seeing their father happy. I, on the other hand, felt tiny cuts in my heart whenever I saw them together.

13

The Miss America Pageant had been on my calendar for two months. In spite of the fact John was adamantly opposed, there was no doubt in my mind I was attending. My intention was not to travel to Atlantic City to view the contestants; instead, I was going to the boardwalk to join several hundred outraged females: some from NOW but most from the New York Radical Women organization. We were on a mission to make people understand women were not cattle or slabs of meat to be packaged and paraded around like a commodity. Our peaceful protest claimed a lot of attention especially when we displayed a *Freedom Trash Can*. Many of us tossed in female items symbolic of the things that imprisoned women. I, personally, threw in three of John's *Playboy* magazines, an apron, and a pair of my false eyelashes I promised myself I would never wear again. I was done spending valuable time gluing those things to my eyelids. Other women tossed in high heels, curlers, mops, pans and other household paraphernalia. One woman took her bra off in the middle of the boardwalk and flung it into the can. After she did it, several other women copied her. The plan was to light the *Freedom*

Trash Can on fire, but we did not have a fire permit for the boardwalk; consequently, we didn't put a match to the bin.

While the pageant was in progress, we distributed Robin Morgan's pamphlet <u>No More Miss America!</u> And carried signs stating *All Women are Beautiful, We are tired of competing for male approval, Let's judge ourselves as people*, and my personal favorite, *Welcome to the Miss America Cattle Auction.* We chanted, "If this is truly a search for "Miss America," why then have we never had a black, an Hawaiian, an Alaskan, a Mexican-American or even an American Indian winner?"

When it was over, and I drove home, I was proud because I felt the barometer had been moved. Perhaps people were beginning to see women were oppressed, and we weren't being silenced anymore.

Could they hear us?

2

Richard

Carley's Place was packed with customers during Richard Nixon's Inaugural Address. The crowd wasn't as large as the one for Super Bowl III the week before, and certainly not as rowdy as those fans who cheered the Jets and Joe Namath on to their unpredicted victory, but it was a profitable group of political junkies who purchased plenty of appetizers and alcohol. Sadly, the conversation was so loud at the bar; I didn't think many of them heard Nixon's speech. I wanted to listen to the new president; therefore, I slipped into my office and turned on the Panasonic portable television that was on the right side of my desk. I turned the dial to ABC and adjusted the rabbit ears to get the best reception. It was a visibly cold, cloudy day in Washington, D.C. In fact, it looked as if it might snow. Everyone was bundled in scarves, gloves and hats. I was frustrated because I had missed the first half of his speech, but I was determined to hear the rest. As I propped my feet up on the corner of my desk, I leaned back in my chair and listened to President Nixon's words. *"We have given freedom new reach. We have begun to make its promise real for black as well as for white. We see the hope of tomorrow in the youth of today. I know America's youth. I believe in them. We can be proud that they are better educated, more committed, more passionately driven by conscience than any generation in our history. . ."*

At that moment, Barbara walked into the room carrying a Coke in one hand and a platter with a chicken salad sandwich and fries in the other. Without saying a word, she placed it on the desk next to me. I flashed a warm smile and a thankful nod. It was amazing how well Barbara knew me . . . she understood me. Barbara was young, but she always seemed to be in sync with my needs. I took a sip from the soda and two bites of the sandwich before returning my full attention to the television.

President Nixon continued, *". . . The American dream does not come to those who fall asleep." Nixon paused. "But we are approaching the limits of what government alone can do. Our greatest need now is to reach beyond government, to enlist the legions of the concerned and the committed. What has to be done, has to be done by government and people together or it will not be done at all. The lesson of past agony is that without the people we can do nothing – with the people we can do everything . . ."*

I clapped my hands together. "That's why I voted for you, Mr. President!" I spoke to the television as if it was a human. "Nineteen sixty-nine is going to be a great year! I can feel it!" I settled back in my chair and returned my attention to the screen. I noticed Barbara looked as if she wanted to speak, but she didn't say a word; instead, she came behind me and circled me with her arms. It felt wonderful to lean my head against her body.

"No man can be fully free while his neighbor is not." Nixon continued to speak. *"To go forward at all is to go forward together. This means black and white together, as one nation, not two. The laws have caught up with our conscience. What remains is to give life to what is in the law: to insure at last that as all are born equal in dignity before God, all are born equal in dignity before man. As we learn to go forward together at home, let us also seek to go forward together with all mankind."*

Barbara finally spoke. "I didn't know you voted for Mr. Nixon."

"Just because I don't talk much about my political opinion doesn't mean I don't have one." I turned to look at her and winked. "Spreading what I think about politics is not good for business, so I listen. I nod. I slap people on the back occasionally and shake hands, but I don't say much. I talk to you, Barbara, because we have a different kind of relationship." I kissed her on the lips as I pulled her onto my lap and cradled her body with my arms. As I gazed into her green eyes, I took a strand of her long brown hair and twirl it suggestively around my middle finger." Our eyes remained connected. "You work here, but I trust you won't go talking to the other employees about what I say to you in private. That's between us. Right?"

"Of course."

"To be honest, I wasn't on board the Nixon train in the beginning. I liked him okay when he was VP for Eisenhower, but – to be honest – I didn't know much about him. Loved Kennedy in 1960 – glad he beat Nixon that year. I would have probably voted for Bobby this time around if he hadn't been killed. I wasn't happy with Humphrey so I thought I'd give Nixon a try." I glanced at the television and watched as Nixon waved farewell to the crowd and proceeded to leave the Capitol steps. "I think I opened the door to considering Nixon when I heard him say during a speech that he was born poor but didn't know it." I stopped myself before admitting to Barbara that I, too, had been born poor. I, too, had scrapped my way out of those meager surroundings. *Part of who I am is a reflection of who I was as a child.* I never talked about it – needless to say, I never shared the information with anyone. Instead of divulging those personal facts to Barbara, I continued by saying, "Nixon is a self-made man. He came from the bottom and made it to the top. That's to be commended!" I paused. "I think Nixon has a good plan. He's a principled man; I admire and respect that quality in a person. He promises to get us out of Vietnam: 'peace with honor.' I think he is going to help fix the crime rate and the violence in our cities. Like his campaign slogan said, I think *'Nixon is the one.'* He's for helping blacks and the poor in our country elevate themselves with hard work and determination. I've always been for that! I don't care who you are. Handouts don't fix poverty – hard work and determination will do that! If you've been given a *silver spoon* in life – good for you – don't waste it!" I paused as I remembered my own personal roots. "And . . . if you've been given a tough lot in life – you have to work harder to make it better. Never give up! I'm a firm believer that sometimes a little struggle in life makes you a stronger person in the long run." I chuckled, mostly to myself, when I added. "That's *my* opinion!"

"I happen to like your opinion, Mr. Malone." Barbara's voice had a soft, purring quality to it as she cupped my cheeks with both of her hands. First she kissed me on the forehead, and then she left a trail of tiny kisses on my face before reaching her ultimate destiny. Prior to our lips touching, she slipped the tip of her tongue into my mouth. It danced around my teeth teasing me and creating sensations that rippled like an electric current all of the way to my toes.

I'd had sex with a variety of women before and after Caroline, but none of them could compare to Caroline and none of them had the ability to make me forget the memories she and I had shared. Barbara came close to freeing me from that mental bondage; as a result, I craved every minute I could get alone with her. Until Barbara had come into my life, the sexual act had become nothing more than a release of bottled tension. Barbara helped me feel the joy of foreplay again.

Barbara's shift did not start until the dinner hour, so she was not yet wearing her Carley's uniform. Instead, she was donned in a colorful paisley empire dress with a yellow sash around the bodice. It was low cut, exposing a hint of swollen breasts. The hemline was short like the popular mini-skirt length the teenagers wore. Barbara was young enough to pull it off; her legs were long and lean. I ran my fingers on her thighs and noticed her skin was silky smooth; she had recently shaved them. As my fingers traveled to her hips, I was rewarded by the discovery Barbara wasn't wearing anything underneath her dress. *Oh Man! This is going to be a good day!* As I maneuvered myself in the chair, I adjusted her body on top of mine. At the same time, she began to undo my zipper. Slowly! Everything was leisurely measured. Barbara liked it better when the pace was gradual in the beginning and mounted to a fever as the actions increased. Perhaps that was why I enjoyed her so much. The pleasure was augmented when the act was built with waves of indulgence.

My hips instinctively moved toward her. I couldn't control the action; the steady spasmodic movement was completely involuntary. Closing my eyes heightened my senses. I could smell the sweet scent of the Chanel No.5 perfume I'd given her for Christmas. When I licked her neck, I could taste it on her skin. *Glorious!* The tiny, soft hairs behind her ear were standing on edge prickling my lips as I kissed the heated area. Barbara let out a yielding groan. Her enjoyment heightened my excitement. I moved my hands to her breasts and felt the taut nipple of pleasure pressing through the material of her dress. I couldn't wait to reach her flesh. I began a mental strategy to get to my goal.

A distracting thought popped into my mind. Did Barbara turn the latch and lock the door when she entered the room? I didn't have time to ask. The sound of the knob turning echoed like a trumpet playing *Reveille.* Even though I knew the action barely made a sound, the noise alerted me. I twisted in my chair and bolted upright, still holding Barbara in my arms. Both of us snapped our necks toward the door anticipating an employee with a work related question. I didn't want to advertise my relationship with Barbara to my staff; as a result, we had both been cautious about our affair, especially while we were in one of my restaurants.

To my horror, the person standing in the doorway was *not* an employee. It was Caroline. My heart stopped. I knew there was no reason to feel guilt, but the embarrassment still swept through me and took my breath away.

"Oh my . . ." Caroline didn't finish her sentence. Her face was as white as a ghost, and her eyes screamed volumes. Her initial syllables hung in the air for what seemed like an eternity before she added, "I'm so sorry. I knocked and . . ." She began to back pedal out of the room. Caroline was gone before I could get a word out of my mouth.

"Wow!" Barbara muttered with a nervous undertone in her voice. "I guess it could have been worse. You could have still been married."

"Stop!" I held my hand up between our faces. "Don't talk!" My head was pounding. I didn't have a clue why I was so upset. I had been dating Barbara since last spring. Over the July 4th weekend, I had introduced her to my children and was fairly certain at least one of them had told their mother about Barbara by now. In addition, the children and I had shared Thanksgiving dinner with Barbara, and she had even given each of them a present at Christmas.

"Was Rosaline standing next to her?" I questioned.

"No, Caroline was alone. No one else was there."

"Oh, thank God! At least I can be grateful for that."

Barbara lifted herself off of my lap and adjusted her dress back into place. "Sorry," she grinned. "I guess the mood's been shot all to Hell."

"It's not your fault." I smiled back at her trying to lighten the aura in the room. "Maybe after dinner tonight?" I gently rubbed the hem of her dress and lifted it ever so slightly in the air.

"I don't think so," Barbara teased. "I'm working until closing – won't get off until 11." She grinned. "Unless my boss wants to give me the evening off." She hung her words in the air like a question.

"No can do," I replied sadly. "We're short-handed today. Guess we will have to pick up where we left off tomorrow."

After my comment, Barbara left the room. I was relieved.

A few hours later, I gathered the courage to call Caroline. When she answered the phone, I asked, "Was there anything you needed?" I tried to keep my voice steady. To my surprise, I felt like a kid who had been sent to the principal's office. I was nervous.

Caroline made no mention of the afternoon's encounter; instead, she curtly replied, "No. It's nothing important." After a few seconds of awkward silence, she added, "It will hold until another time."

Neither of us spoke of the incident again.

2

My 38th birthday fell on a Tuesday. Tuesdays were almost as slow as Mondays unless there was a specific sporting event televised, which augmented the crowd at the bar. There was nothing monumental happening on my birthday; consequently, I didn't have any trouble scheduling a day off for both Barbara and myself. I left the assistant manager in charge for the evening. Barbara mysteriously said she had "special plans" so I needed to make sure Brad and Rosaline were taken care of for the entire night.

Barbara took me to dinner at a local Italian restaurant; it was not expensive and the food was merely adequate, but the setting was nice and I liked being alone with her. After the meal, we went to see *The Thomas Crown Affair*. The movie was originally released last summer. Barbara loved it, but I hadn't gotten a chance to see the Steve McQueen film. Thankfully, it was making a second-round appearance at the local theater. As I watched the movie with Barbara, I understood why she wanted me to view it with her. It was tantalizing, and I had to admit the chemistry between McQueen and Faye Dunaway was extremely provocative. Barbara spent much of the movie with her hand in my lap. *Perhaps that is why I enjoyed the movie so much.*

But that wasn't the best part of the evening. Barbara's present to me was a room for the night at the Holiday Inn. It was a fantastic surprise. We didn't have to fumble around in my car or worry someone would interrupt us in my office. We paced ourselves and even enjoyed a bottle of wine between climaxes. Definitely the best gift I could imagine. After we had sated our sexual appetite, we fell asleep. It was the first time since my divorce that I'd slept in a woman's arms.

When I woke up the next morning – for a few seconds – I forgot where I was and whom I was holding. In those misty moments before

I was fully alert, years of suppressed memories of Caroline plagued me. Even though I could vividly see her face behind my veiled eyes, I was truly thankful I didn't say Caroline's name. That, of course, would have ruined the mood and the subsequent morning *tango under the sheets*.

All in all – it was great to be thirty-eight!

3

A few weeks later, I got a phone call from Caroline. I was busy closing out my monthly books and wasn't in the mood for chitchat. "What's up, Caroline?" I was bordering terse.

"Now that both boys are going to attend Elon in the fall," she hesitated. "I'm a little worried about the cost."

I didn't want to admit to Caroline that Brad hadn't told me about his acceptance to Elon or any of the other colleges. For two months, I'd been waiting for the news. I'd even tried to get to the mailbox before my son in hopes of finding the letters first. Apparently, he'd known for a while and hadn't told me. *Typical!* I had stopped wondering why the two of us could not communicate; instead, I was thankful we could at least live in the same house without declaring it a combat zone.

"Don't worry, Caroline." I said. "I've got it covered. Between Rick's football scholarship and the money I've set aside, we'll be fine."

"Ever since I got the position as floor manager at Bamberger's, I've been able to save a little bit," she paused. "John and I can pay for their books and their meal plans."

I could tell she was in one of her defensive moods, so I walked the fine line between not offering too much and calming her financial fears. "Sounds like a good plan."

"I think Brad's going to live in the new boys' dorm in Harper Center. Moffitt, I think it's called. That's where Rick is. For the life of me, I don't know why they want to go to the same college. But I'm okay with their choice because Lord knows I'm glad they aren't going to Cornell or Columbia or Berkeley. There is nothing but chaos on those campuses these days."

"I know," I interrupted. "If either of them had chosen one of those schools, I would not have given them a dime for tuition." I paused. "I heard Governor Reagan in California might have to call in the National Guard to Berkeley. It's been all over the news."

"When you send your kids to college, you think you are sending them to a safe place where they can learn and grow." There was apprehension in Caroline's voice.

"These crazy hippie anarchists are brainwashing a generation with their communist agenda." I could feel myself getting worked up. "Sometimes I wonder who's in charge. It's like the animals are running the zoo." I laughed, but – in truth – I didn't think it was funny. I tried to defuse our growing sense of trepidation. Taking the edge off of my voice, I continued, "It's rough times, Caroline. But the boys are going to be okay. I have faith in them."

"Thank God, Elon is a peaceful place," Caroline replied. "I've not heard of anything bad happening on that campus."

"Maybe they will actually get a good education and a job when they get out." I smirked. "One can only hope."

Caroline cut into my tirade. "I am going to need a check when Brad finalizes his commitment to Elon. The rest will be due in August."

"We have four more years of this and we will be done." I thought the conversation was over, so I returned my attention to the figures in my book and added the column of alcohol purchased in April.

"What?" Caroline questioned. "We won't be done in four years. We need to pay for Rosaline to go to college too."

"Why?" I was surprised by her statement. "She's a girl. She doesn't need a college degree."

"Rosie has every right to go to college – just like the boys." Caroline's voice stepped up a notch. "And *we* are going to pay for it."

"You mean *I'm* going to pay for it." I corrected her knowing the irritation it would cause.

"Damn it!" Caroline spit the words.

"Rosaline's in seventh grade. Can we please talk about this later?" I didn't wait for an answer. "Let me know when you want me to write the check for Brad." I hung up the phone.

4

For graduation, Caroline gave Brad a monogrammed camera bag

and a telephoto lens that could focus on a ladybug across the yard. He was overjoyed with the gift. Needless to say, even with her employee's discount at Bam's, I was certain it took her a couple of months' salary to pay for his present.

When I gave him my gift, I sensed his disappointment. Brad opened the small box and discovered a wallet. I was inspired by Caroline's sense of nostalgia and had Brad's initials monogrammed on the leather. Inside the wallet, Brad found three one-hundred-dollar bills and my coveted Babe Ruth baseball card. Folded inside one of the pouches was a slip of paper. On it, I had written my favorite Babe Ruth quote.

It's hard to beat a person who never gives up.

I watched Brad as he mouthed the words. I was not sure why, but for a moment, I feared he was going to rip up the card or crunch the piece of paper into a ball – but he did neither.

Brad stood a long time staring at his gift in silence. He didn't even make eye contact with me when he muttered, "Thanks, Dad."

I glanced at Caroline. She was not looking at Brad; she was watching me. There were tears in her eyes. Caroline took the half a dozen steps between us and whispered, "That's beautiful, Richard." The expression on her face was difficult to read. "I know in my heart the day will come when Brad will appreciate your gift." She touched my face with so much tenderness; I almost forgot we were no longer married.

Rosaline broke the uncomfortable awkwardness in the room by gleefully saying, "Brad, open my present." She handed him a tin of cookies. "I made them myself in Home Ec Class. They are your favorites: chocolate chip!"

Brad laughed in his charming way and threw his arms around his sister. "Thank you, Rosie. I know if you made them, they are going to be delicious!"

Rick, who had finished his first year at Elon and was home for the summer, handed Brad his gift. He chuckled as Brad took it from his hand.

"What's this?" Brad asked as he looked at the maroon and gold cap.

"It's your freshman beanie," Rick replied. "You'll need it the first week of school." Rick proceeded to slap his brother on the back in a con-gratulatory manner. The gesture prompted laughter; even Brad chuckled when he placed it on his head.

"I predict today is the *only* day I'm going to wear this thing." Brad said as he glanced at himself in the mirror over the couch. "And I'm wearing it now because *you* gave it to me."

Caroline called everyone to gather around her dining room table so Brad could cut his cake. Our graduate was flanked by Caroline and me. We were both radiating our pride. John used his Kodak instamatic to capture the moment. Before the cake was served, Barbara – who had been invited personally by Brad – offered to take a picture of the entire family. All of us, including John and Randy, stood together – arms locked and smiles beaming. I was certain it was the one and only time we were all photographed together.

5

There are times in a person's life when something so powerful and significant happens in the world, a person will forever remember where he or she was when it occurred. For example, when the Japanese bombed Pearl Harbor or when President Kennedy or Martin Luther King, Jr. or Bobby Kennedy were shot. Those were all traumatic and painful dates leaving a black mark on memory. However, July 20th of 1969 was also a day that would forever be imprinted on the minds of all Americans; thankfully, this date would not be tarnished with death. This date would sing forever with awe in the minds of those who watched it.

I was at Carley's Place in a room full of excited patrons as we waited patiently for Neil Armstrong to come out of the capsule. Conversations were popping up all around the bar. Many were talking about the Mets, and how the "Lovable Losers" were having a good season, but the most popular topic of the day – aside from the lunar landing – was the bizarre news about Teddy Kennedy. Apparently, two days earlier, Senator Kennedy was in a car accident on Chappaquiddick Island in Massachusetts. He'd driven his car off of a bridge, but was able to get out of it. The girl with him, Mary Jo Kopechne, drowned in the accident. The clamor during the conversation was the rumor that Kennedy was drunk, left the girl to die, and didn't report it for hours. I overheard one fellow say, "Guess that's one Kennedy who won't be running for president." Another responded, "I bet the guy doesn't even go to prison." I worried the conversation would turn ugly, and was thrilled when there was movement on the television screen. All eyes turned and conversations stopped. No customer placed an order. Everyone watched – even the cooks and the dishwashers came out of the kitchen and stood with the crowd. It was so quiet in the restaurant; I think the people were holding their breath. Not a sound could be heard.

Barbara stood next to me with a firm grip on my arm. Her fingers were laced tightly in a semi-circle around my bicep, and her head lay gently on my shoulder. Neil Armstrong came slowly down the steps of the lunar module and put his foot on the moon.

"One small step for man; one giant leap for mankind."

The entire room erupted with joyful cheers and boisterous applause as we watched Mr. Armstrong place an American flag on the surface of the moon. Less than ten years ago, John Kennedy's dream seemed impossible; now, this amazing accomplishment was a reality!

July 20, 1969 was also the day Barbara first mentioned marriage. It happened hours after the moon landing. The crowd had thinned out. The *Smothers Brothers Comedy Hour* was on the television set. No one was listening to it because the sound was turned down too low. Instead, the music piped in from my system was playing in the background. We were sitting at the bar. I was nursing a Budweiser, and Barbara was drinking a Tom Collins. We were both savoring a good day of business. She'd made a record $73 dollars in tips, which was more than double what she usually made. I hadn't yet figured out my profits, but I knew it was a stellar day.

Barbara's shift was over – we were both relaxing. She didn't come out and say anything about *us* getting married. She did, however, ask, "Do you think you will ever get married again?"

I was not sure what prompted Barbara to ask the question, and I was equally unsure what answer she wanted to hear. The one thing I was certain about was the song playing on the sound system at the time: *These Eyes* by The Guess Who. I had a love/hate relationship in my heart for that song. The first time I had heard it, I was in my Mustang, and

I had to pull off to the side of the road. The lyrics had drawn so much emotion from me – I had not been able to concentrate on driving my car.

Was Barbara listening to the song? If so, was she unaware of the words or was she focused on them? I pretended not to hear her question, and she didn't ask twice.

6

Carley's Place was pulling huge crowds to watch The World Series on our dual television sets. The Mets had a remarkable regular season of play. They had jockeyed for first place throughout the year, but didn't officially earn the position until they pulled off a sweep of victories against the Braves led by Phil Niekro and Hank Aaron at the end of regular season play.

No one was calling the Mets "Loveable Losers" anymore.

I had originally planned to go to Elon for their Homecoming game, but decided to postpone my trip to a later game on their schedule because I didn't want to miss the opening game of The World Series between the Mets and the Orioles.

As it turned out, neither of my teams won.

Elon's Fighting Christians lost, and it was a rainy mess. I spoke on the phone with Brad, who was in a foul mood; he didn't have much to say about Rick's performance on the field, the game in general, or the Homecoming Weekend. Our call lasted less than a minute.

In addition, the Mets also lost: 1-4 to the O's. The disappointment from my customers was painfully obvious, and some "fair-weather" fans were already throwing in the towel. There was no post-game victory party because the customers went home shortly after the game ended.

The following day, loyal Mets fans returned to the bar to watch the second game played at Memorial Stadium. They were not disappointed. A 2-1 victory renewed the fans' dreams of winning the title. The chemistry in Carley's Place was beyond intense. The dining area and the bar stayed packed until closing.

On the 14th, when Baltimore had to play at Shea Stadium, the tide truly turned. With home field advantage, the Mets spanked the Orioles 5-0. It was a Tuesday and, perhaps the busiest and most profitable Tuesday I had ever experienced at the bar. I was congratulating myself multiple times for making that initial decision to mount televisions in the bar area.

Wednesday's game was a squeaker. It took ten innings to bring the victory home for the Mets. The aura in the bar surpassed rowdy. More than a dozen glasses were broken: some accidentally and a few on purpose. In addition, two of my mahogany bar stool were ruined – not intentionally – simply because there were too many people packed together and the energy, at times, bordered destructive. It was Barbara's night off. She was not a baseball fan; consequently, she was nowhere to be found. I missed her company, mostly because I wished I could vent to her instead of scream at my bartenders for losing control of their area. It wasn't their job to keep the fans from being unruly.

The fifth game of the Series was – in short – simply amazing. No one had predicted the comeback or the final outcome. Orioles' pitcher Dave McNally shut out the Mets in the first five innings; as a result, our team was trailing due to their pitcher's two-run homer followed by Frank Robinson's homer – both in the third. Spirits were glum, but loyal fans were still purchasing beverages. Miraculously, in the bottom of the fifth, the energy shifted. Cleon Jones was hit in the foot by a pitch. It was a controversial call, and the umpire didn't confirm his decision until Mets Manager Gil Hodges showed the umpire the shoe polish on the ball. Jones walked to first base. With one man on, Donn Clendenon hit a two-run homer taking the score to within striking distance of victory. The noise factor in the bar was a constant roar; I could barely hear myself think. In the bottom of the seventh, Al Weis' home run tied the game. Ron Swoboda's double hit Jones home for the go-ahead run in the eighth; Swoboda also made it to home. The final score was 5-3.

No one who was in my bar for any of those games will ever forget the adrenaline rush they received from those *Amazing Mets*.

In November, I finally made it to one of Rick's football games; Barbara came with me on the trip south. It was Elon's last game of the season. The 63-7 victory over Gardner-Webb was anti-climactic because it was such a romp; however, the final win gave the Fighting Christians the Carolinas Conference Football Championship. It was the first time Elon had earned the title since 1964. Rick was happy to take some of the credit, but he insisted the victories were largely due to Coach Wilson's strategy and the record-setting passing duo of Jimmy Arrington and Richard McGeorge. Quarterback Arrington set records for best completion percentage and most successful touchdown passes during a season. After McGeorge's senior year record successes catching passes on the field and in the end zone, it was a good bet he would earn his second All-American title and an odds on favorite to be drafted into the pros.

Of course, we included Brad and offered him a ride to the game; however, he was in a sour mood. Brad seemed more interested in a cute co-ed in the stands than his brother's achievements on the field. I tried to talk with him, but he wasn't interested in communicating with me. Later that night at dinner, I noticed my sons barely spoke to each other. They were normally thick as thieves; I found their discord disturbing. When I was alone with Rick, I asked him. "What's up between you and your brother?"

"Nothing, Dad." Rick smiled confidently. "Nothing we can't handle. Don't sweat it."

I dropped the subject and vowed to ask Caroline when I returned home; perhaps, she knew what was going on between our sons.

On Sunday, Barbara and I headed back to Jersey. We decided to turn our trip into a small vacation by stopping in Washington, D.C. to see some of the monuments and museums. I'd never been to the nation's capital. Being with Barbara amplified the experience. She was a huge history buff and knew countless facts about everything we saw. We stayed three days, which gave us enough time to walk through the entire American History Museum. I loved the Civil War memorabilia, plus the exhibits on transportation and technology. Barbara enjoyed the First Ladies' gowns; she prattled on about her favorites.

We walked 897 steps to the top of the Washington Monument. As we looked out of the window, Barbara mentioned, "Did you know that you are in the tallest stone structure in the world? It's over 555 feet high." It was a gorgeous day, and the view was amazing. We could see for miles in every direction.

As my thighs burned from the climb, I asked Barbara, "Maybe we should have taken the elevator."

She laughed, "Did you see the line for the elevator?" She had a point.

Waiting in that line would have taken most of the day, and we wouldn't have had enough time to see Jefferson or Lincoln's monuments.

When we left the Washington Monument, we journeyed across the Mall to the Capitol. As we stood in the Rotunda, we were completely awed by the sights and sounds filing the enormous room. I could feel the power exuding from the walls. Barbara had gotten passes from New Jersey's Senator Clifford Case, which allowed us access to the Senate chamber. We watched the proceedings for nearly an hour before moving on to the next tourist attraction.

We spent several hours in the Natural History Museum. I liked the massive elephant at the entrance; Barbara liked the gems. When we saw the Hope Diamond, she teasingly said, "Are you going to buy me one like this?"

I didn't take the bait; thus, I answered with a witty, but non-committal response, "I can't afford anything like that stone."

On our final day, we drove across the Memorial Bridge to Arlington National Cemetery. For me, that was the most impressive moment of the trip. The rolling grounds were majestic. Most of the leaves had already fallen from the trees, but the immaculately groomed grass was void of the remnants of autumn foliage. Thousands of white tombstones symmetrically aligned as far as the eye could see. It took nearly an hour, but – with Caroline's directions and help from the sentry – Barbara and I finally found Martin's headstone. Although not every soldier buried at Arlington died in battle, they had all served our nation. Standing at Martin's grave gave me a reverent respect for every life that had been sacrificed in the name of duty, honor and freedom – heroes who had chosen our country first.

Throughout our trip, Barbara was the one who took the majority of the pictures. She must have snapped at least four rolls of film. However, as I stood at Martin's grave, I felt compelled to freeze the memory. I took the camera from Barbara and proceeded to capture a half a dozen pictures of Martin's grave and the surrounding site. I included a wide-angled shot that captured the massive oak tree sheltering the area. John had told me there were no pictures of the day Martin was buried. In fact, he had never even seen the marker with his son's name on it because the gravestone had not yet been made on the day of the interment.

My children meant everything to me; I could not even begin to imagine the pain John felt at the loss of his son. I said a quiet prayer before we left – for Martin – for all of the soldiers – for our country – and for John.

The three days of sightseeing was informative and even entertaining, but my favorite part of our trip was the nights. We stayed at the Old Colony Inn on the outskirts of Alexandria. It was a little cheaper and a lot less congested. On the final night, we had a quick dinner at the hamburger joint around the corner and then saw *Butch Cassidy and the Sundance Kid* at the Virginia Theater, which happened to be next door to the motel. I loved the movie. The music was sensational; plus, Paul Newman and Robert Redford were the best duo on the screen I'd seen in years. Barbara wasn't impressed. She fell asleep twenty minutes into the movie. She didn't even budge during the explosive gun fights. At the end of the movie, I woke her up by gently massaging the inside of her thigh. She purred like a kitten and smiled in her sleep. When she finally opened her eyes, I teased her by saying, "It must have been those 897 steps."

She replied in an equally teasing manner. "I've had a nap." She brushed her lips across mine. "When we get back to our room, I hope you don't fall asleep on me."

I didn't.

7

Rick and Brad were home for Spring Break. My oldest son spent every available minute focused on Carley's Place; however, Brad spent his time dedicated to avoiding me *and* my restaurants. I knew Brad was home because I'd seen his bag full of dirty laundry sitting next to the washing machine, but I still hadn't seen him.

With hopes of spending time with her children, Caroline stopped by unannounced. I told her neither Rick nor Brad was home.

"Is Rosaline home?" Caroline asked as she presented a small wrapped gift in her hand. "It's her birthday present. I want to give her my locket.... You know the one. It was my mom's. Rosaline has been working so hard in school – her grades show it. I am proud of her. Plus she is doing such a good job in her role in the spring play. Who knew she was such a good actress." Caroline chuckled.

"And who knew she'd get the role of Emily in *Our Town*." I smiled.

"I can't believe schools are still recreating that production a generation later. Remember when Calvin had a minor role in that play?"

"Yes – I remember – feels like it was yesterday," Caroline responded. "*Our Town* has such a fabulous message. When we were kids and watched Calvin on the stage, I don't think I was old enough to truly understand the play or its lessons." Caroline's facial expression shifted. She looked lost in thought – even sad. "Makes a person realize how precious and fleeting life is."

Caroline was still standing in the doorway. I took a step toward her. As I gently touched her arm, I quietly said, "Are you okay, Caroline?"

She turned the small wrapped package around with her fingers – staring at it in silence for several minutes before she responded. "Yes. I'm fine. I guess I'm a little nostalgic – a side effect of turning thirty-nine. I'm not looking forward to that birthday." When she looked up at me, there was a misting of tears glistening in her eyes. "Where have all of the years gone?"

"The years do seem to fly, don't they?" I barely whispered the words as a paused a moment to study Caroline's face. The years had been kind to her. Perhaps she didn't look like a teenager anymore, and the innocence was wiped away from her expression. However, she still radiated a natural and mature beauty – the kind a person usually found on a magazine cover or a Hollywood poster. Truth be told, Caroline had a few tiny lines at the corner of her eyes, and some thin creases on her cheeks caused by smiles, but there was no question about it, Caroline was beautiful.

She blushed slightly and glanced down at the gift in her hand. "I thought Rosaline might be able to wear my mom's locket in the play. It sort of fits the fashion of the time period."

"Rosaline hasn't come home yet." I felt awkward. We were still standing in the doorway. "Would you like to come in?" I inquired as I glanced at my Rolex. During the last few years, Caroline and I rarely had a conversation that didn't involve the children. We were cordial, but – more times than not – slightly standoffish. I stepped to the side and welcomed her into the house. "Drama practice will be over soon, and she should be home in twenty or thirty minutes."

Caroline's eyes glanced passed me and then darted around the foyer.

She hesitated several seconds before taking the steps into the house. In silence, she looked at the wall adjacent to the stairs. She seemed guarded. I could not read her expression.

"Why don't you come into the library and have a glass of brandy with me?" I gently touched her elbow. She didn't agree or disagree with my suggestion, but she did allow me to guide her down the hallway.

When we entered the room, The Beatles newly released song *Let It Be* was playing on my radio – softly and in the distance.

After Caroline took a seat in the wing-backed chair across from the desk, I proceeded to pour brandy into two crystal glasses. I handed one to her. She didn't sip it – she gulped it. I offered her another. She didn't speak, but she did nod as she handed the glass to me. I poured her an encore. Caroline cradled the second serving in her hand and swirled the liquid around as she watched it circle the edges. She seemed to want to speak – but didn't know how to form the words.

The end of the Beatles song drifted off into a muted calm. I wanted to break the silence, but didn't know how. With a feeble attempt to disrupt the uneasy quiet, I addressed a popular teenage topic. "Song's good; however, rumor has it The Beatles are breaking up."

"That's what I hear from the kids. Rosie is devastated," Caroline sighed. She didn't look up from her goblet.

"She plays that *Abbey Road* album you gave her for Christmas all of the time; I've contemplated hiding it from her." I couldn't help but chuckle. Caroline rewarded me with a small return smile. "There's something I've been meaning to give you." I pulled open my desk drawer and took out an envelope of pictures. "Barbara and I took these photos last fall while we were in Washington. I won't bore you with the whole stack of the monuments and floral pictures, but I thought you and John might like a copy of the pictures we took at Arlington Cemetery." I sifted through the dozens of pictures before handing her the few I selected. "Sorry it took so long for me to give these to you. I didn't get the final roll developed until last month."

Caroline took the pictures and slowly flipped through them. I could see her catch her breath as she looked at the one of Martin's headstone. Slowly she ran her fingers over it as if she could pour love into the photo.

Finally she looked at me, "Thank you, Richard. This is very kind of you. John will appreciate it."

"It's peaceful there." I barely whispered the words.

Caroline continued to look at the pictures as she spoke, "It's been over two years. I'd hoped time might lessen the pain, but it doesn't." Caroline looked up for a moment. There was sorrow etched on her face. "The cemetery is so far away; John can't visit his son – can't take him flowers – can't sit by his grave. However, I do think he does find some comfort in knowing Martin is resting with heroes." Caroline continued to look through the pictures. There were a half a dozen that were taken of Martin's gravesite and the surrounding grounds in Arlington Cemetery. "Brad will like this one," Caroline said as she flipped it around so I, too, could see it clearly. "He would claim it has good composition. See the way the tree arches and frames the top and the left side of the picture. The angle highlights all of the headstones – they seem to form a wing-span. The shadows from the sun are a subtle accent. I can hear Brad now . . . he would say this picture talks to him."

"Brad and his camera," I smirked. I didn't mean to sound dismissive; however, Caroline definitely interpreted my words in that manner. I visibly saw her shoulders slump as she broke eye contact with me.

Instead of responding to my comment, Caroline shifted to the next picture. I could see the startled expression on her face. When I glanced at the picture in her hand, I immediately noticed it was not a shot of the cemetery. The photograph was of Barbara and me. I had my arm draped protectively around her – we both had enormous smiles on our faces as we pointed up toward the top of the Washington Monument. I had asked a stranger to take the picture of the two of us together after we had made the arduous journey up and down the 897 steps. Caroline continued to stare at the photograph without saying a word. Finally she placed it on the desk and put the others in her purse. "Thank you, Richard. I'll give these to John. I know he will be glad to have them."

Quietly, Caroline glanced around the library. "I haven't been in this room for over a decade. It's exactly the same – almost as if the room has been frozen in time." She made a second perusal checking out every painting, bookcase and corner. She sipped quietly on her brandy before adding, "Looks remarkably like my father's library – I don't think I ever noticed that before. Even the chairs are the same style and color." Caroline leaned forward in her chair; she had a look of concentration on her face. "What's that?" She pointed to the tiny jewelry box sitting next to the pencil holder under the desk's lamp.

I realized what Caroline saw. On high alert, I snatched the tiny box in my hand, scooped it out of view and stuck it in the desk drawer. The last thing I wanted to do was have a conversation with Caroline about the diamond ring that was in that jewelry box. I had bought it for Barbara a month and a half ago with the anticipation of proposing to her on Valentine's Day, but I didn't do it. In fact, I still wasn't sure I wanted to make the final commitment. Caroline was definitely not the person with whom I wanted to debate the subject.

Caroline seemed startled by my actions. Ironically, her bruised expression cut into my heart. I watched her as she gathering her purse and the wrapped gift in her hands. She stood up. As she turned to leave, both of us heard Rosaline's sweet voice in the kitchen.

"Dad! I'm home."

"I'm in the library, Rosie," I responded.

Moments later, Rosaline entered the room. She looked thrilled to see her mother. I elected to leave and let them have some privacy. An hour later, Caroline was gone – without saying good-bye – and Rosaline was proudly wearing the locket. It looked beautiful on her.

I reentered the library with the intention of getting a little paperwork completed so I could have a free weekend for a change. Shortly after finishing the first page, Neil Diamond's voice came on the radio. The lyrics to *Sweet Caroline* filled the room. The song had been popular for months and every time it came on the radio, I turned the channel. That song grated on my nerves. I stomped across the room and turned the radio off. Instantly, a bad mood enveloped me. I walked to the corner cabinet, pulled out the decanter of bourbon and poured myself a stiff drink.

"Damnit to Hell!"

I went back to my desk and took out the jewelry box I had previously concealed in the drawer. The diamond ring sparkled in the dim light. I opened and closed the hinged box at least a dozen times before I finally snapped it shut and returned it to the desk drawer. I had no idea how much time passed or even how many fingers of bourbon I'd consumed before I drifted off to sleep in my chair.

Hours later I heard the front door open. I was in a fog from the alcohol, but I could still tell someone was tiptoeing across the foyer. I leaned across my desk and peered into the hallway.

"It's almost four in the morning!" I bellowed as I saw Brad deliberately sneaking past the library door and stealthily trying to go up the stairs without seeing me.

"Jesus, Dad," Brad chuckled in a half-hearted manner. "I didn't know I had a curfew."

I stood up, walked around my desk and took the necessary steps between us. It had been a hell of a day. The alcohol I had been drinking and the nap I'd taken at my desk around midnight hadn't absorbed the edge off of my foul mood. As I reached Brad and we stood face to face, I spoke harshly, "When are you going to grow up and start acting like an adult?" I was close enough to him to smell the alcohol on *his* breath. "Look at you! You turned nineteen a few months ago. You think you know it all, don't you? You think the entire world is your personal playground and life's one huge fun game with you being the center of it all."

Brad turned away from me and went half way up the stairs in an open disrespect for my conversation.

"I'm not through with you yet, Brad! You get your tail down here and listen to me. I'm still the one paying the bills around here, not to mention the fact that I'm flipping the tab for the education you seem to take for granted. You spend most of your time partying instead of hitting the books, and your grades show it."

"I bust my ass in those classes." The cocky tone in Brad's voice was gone. "I didn't want to take most of that shit anyway. I would have been perfectly happy going to a vocational school and taking nothing but commercial arts courses. But no! You wanted me to get a degree in Business." Brad's suppressed anger was obviously at a boiling point. He approached me with squared shoulders. His jaw was tight – locked in a stubborn mode – and his eyebrow was cocked. Even as a child, when Brad was venting his anger, he had the same defiant expression. "What the hell's got your shorts in a knot, Dad? Bad day at the office?" Brad's rebellious tone oozed with cynicism.

"You impudent, young punk!" I pointed my finger and jabbed it at him. "I'm sick and tired of your back talk. I'm fed up with you carousing all night long, sleeping with every bitch who'll spread her legs for you and doing nothing . . . nothing about planning any kind of a future. You've been sowing your wild oats – to coin an antiquated phrase – since you were fourteen years old. It's about time you cut all of that shit out and start acting like a man."

"And what exactly do you consider a man to be?" Brad, who was approximately my height, stared directly into my eyes, refusing to yield under my scrutinizing stare. "Is a man someone who slaves his life away for some stupid business nobody gives a shit about? Someone who's so damn busy his wife gets fed up with it all and leaves? Is a man someone who is so fucking selfish that he separates a mother from her kids and so damned tight that his ex-wife can't squeeze a dime out of him? Is that what you consider a man to be . . . someone like you?" Brad screamed the words.

It took me a second to realize what I had done. As a knee-jerk reaction to my son's painful words, I had lashed out at him – not with malicious words but with my fist. I'd hit Brad. He reeled from the impact, but he didn't react. He stood stoically still and brazenly raised his chin in defiance.

Shame washed over me.

We both stood in a controlled furor – eyes boldly locked in silent battle. Finally I lowered my face wishing I could relive the moment. There was no excuse for my actions. "I'm sorry, Brad. I shouldn't have done that." I closed my eyes and shook my head despairingly. "You don't know what happened between your mother and me." My tone was more reserved, and the words cut like a knife as they came out of my mouth. I took a few steps toward the stairs, turned and faced Brad. This time with renewed strength, I spoke. "And don't you ever . . . *ever* accuse me of neglecting your mother again."

Brad did not respond, but he still wore a defiant expression. We both stood frozen – locked in our own personal emotions.

I broke the silence. "You *will* stop screwing around. You *will* take your Business courses more seriously. And you *will* go into the business with me, Brad. I created all of it for my sons. I will not stand by and watch you waste your life freeloading off my money. Money *you* make a point of not wanting – but you don't mind spending it – do you? You *will* finish your education. I'll give you one year after graduation to try and make it in photography, if that's what you think you really want … but after that, you come back here. In the meantime, you work off your debts during the summer in one of my restaurants." I steadied my voice. "I'm a fair man, Brad. You can decide to work in whichever one you want . . . but you *will* work in one of them during all holidays and summer vacations. You're through getting a free ride. I'm being reasonable with you. I'm giving you a choice. Don't be a bigger fool than I picture you right now. Think about my offer because I'll throw you out on your ass if you don't comply." When Brad remained silent, I continued, "I want what's best for you, Son."

I turned and proceeded to go up the stairs. I held tightly to the railing because I didn't think I had the strength to make it to the top without support. I had never felt so old. Next month, I would be thirty-nine – but I felt double that age. My body, my mind, my soul and my heart were out of sync – leaving me lost and terribly confused.

As I climbed the steps, I muttered the words, "Why can't you be more like your brother?" The moment I said it, I knew I shouldn't have. It was always the comment that circled inside of my head whenever I was frustrated with Brad. I hoped he didn't hear me because I truly didn't mean it! If I was guilty of anything, I was guilty of loving Brad more. I pushed him harder, and I never let up on him. I wanted him to excel. And when he looked at me with those chocolate colored eyes that were exactly like Caroline's, my heart wrenched with the intense love I felt for both of them.

3

Caroline

In the spring, when the New York Postal Service workers went on strike for two weeks and multiple other cities joined their fight, we both thought John's local branch would get involved. My husband agreed with their arguments stating conditions were bad in those downtown buildings: too cold in the winter and too hot in the summer; but their biggest beef was their salaries. The catalyst occurred when Congress raised postal workers wages a mere four percent, while increasing their own pay by forty-one percent. It was like pouring fuel on smoldering embers. Although John would have joined the fight had his fellow branch employees decided to strike, he hoped the movement would not spread to our town. For as long as I had known John, there was one thing I knew rested in his core; John was a rule follower. He would not cross *their* picket line, but he didn't want to be party to their wildcat strike either.

In March, a couple of days after the strike began, President Nixon spoke on television and ordered the strikers to return to work. His words did nothing to ameliorate the problem; instead, hundreds of other locations across America joined the fight. As a result, mail delivery came to a virtual standstill – especially in New York City. The stock market dropped dramatically. Tax returns did not go out as scheduled nor did thousands of draft notices or countless other business and personal letters. It was bedlam for two weeks.

President Nixon declared a national emergency and ordered the National Guard and military reserves to deliver mail in New York. Over 1,800 military personnel were assigned to seventeen New York Post Offices. When the strike was over, not one worker was fired. Those in charge of negotiating settled on a six-percent wage increase that was retroactive to 1969. The framework for the Postal Reorganization Act began. Consequently, there was – going forward – an eight-percent increase in pay. It also allowed postal workers to reach the highest pay scale in eight years. These changes were applicable across the country.

As a result, even though John had not been involved in the strike, he did get the raise. We were relieved to have an unexpected pay increase in our pocket.

We pooled the extra money and decided to take our first week-long vacation. In July, after researching our options, we chose Asbury Park. The popular beach resort had been John's favorite as a child, and he wanted to share the experience with Randy. I cajoled my husband into including Rosaline. We made a compromise. Rosie could have her days free for the boardwalk and the beach, if she promised us two evenings of babysitting. I wanted both Rick and Brad to join us too, but I knew they could not take the time away from Richard's arduous work schedule at Carley's Place. Their father was unyielding when it came to his restaurants and the boys' commitment to them. Rick and Brad didn't seem to mind. It was almost as if they were relieved to avoid a vacation with John and me. I suppose they had outgrown family excursions.

As we packed the station wagon for the trip, Randy asked, "Dad, can I sit on your lap and drive?"

"Trip's too long, son." John grinned. "Besides, you're getting big. I don't think you will fit between me and the steering wheel anymore."

I confirmed John's statement by adding, "You're almost eight years old, Randy. It won't be too many more years before you can get a learner's permit."

John had often allowed Randy to sit on his lap and steer the car while we drove through quiet neighborhood streets. They both enjoyed it. It was a little sad to realize Randy was outgrowing the tradition.

Randy looked disappointed. He crinkled his brow in the exact same manner as John did when he was frustrated. I glanced back and forth between my son and my husband and concluded they looked identical when they were pouting. Both Randy's and John's mouth turned downward in the same manner. Their lips were *exactly* the same. *How could it be I never noticed their similarities?* Although Randy's eyes were the exact same shade of blue as Richard's, they were shaped more like John's. I jerked my head to the side and focused on the passing terrain. *I did not want to think about who Randy looked like: John or Richard? Very disturbing.*

We got to the Flamingo Motel with enough time to enjoy the sand

and the surf before the sun went down. As luck would have it, July 4ᵗʰ and the fireworks festivities fell on a Saturday; consequently, our first night was destined to be celebratory for all of us. John purchased hamburgers and fries on the boardwalk. We laid our gigantic beach blanket on the sand and waited for the sun to go down. Once it was dark, the explosion of fireworks began. I watched the awe on Randy's face. My youngest child had never seen *real* fireworks before. In Fourth of Julys past, his celebrations had been limited to neighborhood gatherings with fountains, sparklers, helicopters, and Whistling Jupiters purchased by neighbors and set off in the parking lot of our garden apartments. It was evident by the wonder in his eyes. Randy was thoroughly enjoying the firework display and the reflection of color in the ocean.

When the festive spectacle was over, we walked back to our motel room. I could hear fire engines in the distance. "Looks like smoke over there." I pointed to my left. "Can you smell that?" I asked. "The firework residue has been gone for a while. That smells like a fire."

John took note. "Yes it does. I wonder if one of the embers from the fireworks caused a real fire." We continued toward the Flamingo – each of us lugging a day's worth of beach supplies in our arms. "I'm sure it's fine." John spoke casually. As always, he was calm.

On Sunday, we ate brunch at Michal's on the corner of Ocean and Second Street. As the waitress took our order, I overheard several men talking about the raucous event that had occurred the previous night. Apparently, after a dance at the West Side Community Center, some of the young people had been disruptive and had broken windows. It had been a tense night for the police and the fire department.

"They are a rowdy bunch of black kids," one of the three men in the booth commented.

"They're frustrated because white kids come from out-of-town and get all of the good summer jobs." His companion responded.

"Plus, it's unbearably hot this summer, and those kids have too much time on their hands." He added, "Idle hands are the devil's workshop."

"I think it's probably a little more than that. There's a lot of hostility over there on Springwood Avenue. It's like a pot of water that's simmering hard and about to boil over." The man put another spoonful of egg in his mouth.

"Could get real messy," one man predicted as he shook his head in despair.

John and I were both listening to the men's conversation in the booth next to us. I leaned toward my husband and whispered, "Do you think it's safe?"

"Oh, it's fine, Sweetie," our waitress, who appeared to take our order, interjected reassuringly. "A couple of the local kids were on a bit of a rampage last night, but the police have it under control. There's nothing to worry about." She turned to Randy and said, "What would you like to drink with your meal?"

"Can I have a Mountain Dew, Mom?" Randy begged.

"It's a little early in the day for pop, Honey." I responded.

John jumped into the conversation. "Oh, let the boy have it, Caroline." His voice had an annoyed ring to it. "We're on vacation. Lighten up a little bit."

I was surprised by John's surly tone, but I did not want to have an argument with him in front of the children; consequently, I responded, "If you drink your milk first, I suppose you can have a soda."

"I'd like a Fresca, please?" Rosaline asked the waitress.

After we'd placed our order, John inquired, "So . . . what's the plan for the week?"

I was the first to respond. "I would like to go to the Mayfair and see *Airport*. Arthur Hailey's book was great."

"I don't know, Caroline. I heard the story is good, but Dean Martin and Burt Lancaster aren't that great in it. Besides, I'd rather see *Patton*."

"But you love Jacqueline Bisset."

"She's in it?" He smiled. "I'm warming up to the idea."

"I want to go to the *Palace Amusements*," Randy interrupted. "I want to ride the carousal fifty-five thousand times."

"What?" John, Rosaline and I spoke in unison as we laughed good-heartedly.

"Well maybe three or four times a day." Randy's energy level was intensifying. "I want to build a giant sand castle with you, Dad. You brought the big shovel, right?"

"Yes," John replied. "And all of the buckets and molds too."

"Rosie," Randy turned his attention to his sister. "Will you ride the paddle boat with me?"

"Sure, Randy," Rosaline replied.

"What is on your list of things to do, Rosaline?" I asked.

"I'd like to go listen to that singer we heard when we were walking back to the motel last night."

"What singer?"

"Bruce something . . . Bruce Springfield," she replied.

As the waitress placed Rosaline's Fresca in front of her, she interjected. "His name's not Springfield, Honey. It's Springsteen, and he's pretty well known around here. I saw him sing at The Stone Pony a few times. He's good. I wouldn't be surprised if he doesn't cut a record one of these days. I'd buy it."

"Can I go, Mom?"

"Rosie, you can't go into a bar by yourself."

"Maybe you and John could go with me."

"We'll talk about it."

Our brunch was delivered, and we began to eat.

2

By Monday evening, we were all a little tired of the heat and the sun. I had read <u>Love Story</u> cover to cover while John and Randy road the waves on the rented rafts and built a giant sand castle near the high tide line. Rosaline had covered herself in baby oil; as a result, she had large patches of sunburn all over her body and her eyes were slightly swollen from too much exposure.

Around 4:30, I took the kids back to the Flamingo and got a quick shower. John picked up some beach fries, lemonade and hotdogs for the kids. Rosaline was tired after two full days in the sun; she was easily convinced to babysit for Randy while John and I went out to dinner and a movie.

I wore my favorite print dress and put on my mother's pearls. John and I hadn't been out together without children in so long – I'd almost forgotten what it was like to be alone with him. We went to the Howard Johnson's on 5th Street, more for the view than the food. To my disappointment, we sat through our meal in silence. It seemed that, without the kids, we didn't have a lot to say to each other. I was grateful when John paid the check and we headed toward the Mayfair Theater.

The good thing about movies is – there's no need for conversation. The film does the entertaining. *When did John and I stop communicating?*

Airport was okay, but far from fantastic. After the movie, as we walked through the lobby toward the exit doors, John was the first to critique the performances, "The rumors were right. Dean Martin's acting was horrible and Burt Lancaster should retire from Hollywood."

I agreed.

John mumbled, "Lancaster may have been good with Deborah Kerr in *From Here to Eternity* in the early 50s, but he is awful in this movie."

I tried to think of something positive to say, "Helen Hayes was amazing. She's still a shining star."

John was grumpy. "I should have insisted we go to *Patton*. I know I wouldn't have been disappointed with George C. Scott."

A wave of regret washed over me because I had pushed John into seeing *Airport*. I was about to apologize when he opened the theater door and the smell of fire filled my nose. Sirens were wailing in the distance. The night's sky in the southwest seemed to glow shades of orange and yellow. "What's that?"

"Looks like a serious fire – and a big one."

Anxiety began to trickle up my spine. Apprehension and fear merged with it. "Something is wrong, John. We better get back to the motel as soon as possible."

"Don't over-react, Caroline." John said. "It's not the motel. The fire is further away than the Flamingo."

My maternal instincts were in overdrive. John took hold of my elbow and steered me to the car. Originally, we had talked about walking, but I was thankful we had chosen the station wagon as our means of transportation. "I hope the kids are okay."

We got back to our motel as quickly as we could. When I entered our room, the first person I saw was Richard.

Richard? Why was he here?

I was shocked. In a stunned voice, I inquired, "What's wrong? What are you doing here?" I glanced around the room, saw the children and returned my attention to Richard. He was tossing Rosaline's clothes in her suitcase.

"What am *I* doing here?" Richard bellowed. "The question is what the hell are *you* doing here? You should have gotten out of Asbury Park yesterday. I couldn't believe it when I called the motel desk and found out you were still checked in. As soon as I hung up the phone, I got in the car and drove here." Richard stopped what he was doing and glared directly at John. "What the hell's the matter with you? Haven't you seen the news?"

Using a defensive, guarded tone, John muttered, "We haven't read a paper or watched any television since we arrived."

"They are rioting in the streets and burning buildings a few blocks from here. Springwood Avenue is on fire. It's a matter of time before they cross the railroad tracks and head this way." The agitation in Richard's voice was clear. "I'm taking Rosaline home right now." He glanced at me and then glared at John. "If you're not taking Caroline and Randy out of here tonight, then I will."

"The hell you will!" John's normally controlled voice flared. "They are *my* family! I will take care of them." Both Rosaline and Randy were in tears.

"Daddy, stop yelling." Rosaline cried.

Richard ignored his daughter's plea. "I cannot believe you left them alone in this motel room."

John fired back. "Rosie is fourteen years old. She babysits all of the time. How were we to know . . ."

"Shut up, John." Richard closed the suitcase and headed for the door. "Come on, Rosie. We're leaving."

"But, Dad, I didn't get to see Bruce Springsteen."

"Rosie, the mayor has ordered a mandatory curfew. We've got to get out of here, and we've got to get out of here now." Richard glanced at me. "Do you and Randy want to ride home with me?"

The entire room fell silent. Even Randy, who was sitting on the bed, stopped whimpering. There were intangible darts coming out of John's eyes. I had never seen him so angry.

"John," I finally spoke. "Are we going home tonight?"

It felt like an eternity, but I knew it was less than a minute before my husband finally answered. "Pack our bags. We'll go home too."

Instead of walking out of the door, Richard crossed the room and knelt by the bed in front of Randy. He cupped both of Randy's hands in his and stared directly into his eyes. "Randy, you need to be strong, and you need to look out for your mother." Richard's voice was simultaneously sympathetic and persuasive. "Can you do that, Little Man?"

I was surprised to see Randy's tears instantly dry up. He squared his shoulders in a determined manner, and a confident expression appeared on his face. "Yes, Mr. Malone. I can do that."

As I watched Richard and Randy's connection – perhaps for the first time – my heart swelled inside of my chest. It was difficult to breathe, and I definitely couldn't move. I felt as if I were watching a movie instead of *real life*. To me, it looked as if Richard was staring into a mirror at himself. Randy was a genuine replica of Richard as a little boy. *Did Richard see himself? What was he thinking?* Richard had a firm hold on Randy's hands. Their eyes were locked in silent communication.

Oh my God! Did John see what was the obvious? Or was it all in my imagination?

Moments later, Richard stood up, took Rosaline by the hand and walked toward the door.

As a last word of advice, Richard spoke directly to John, "When you leave, don't take a left on Main Street. That will run you right into the thick of it. The road is littered with fire hoses and it might even be blocked by now. Besides, it's too dangerous. Go right and go the long way out of town."

Richard stood in the doorframe and stared directly at me. There was a palpable longing in his eyes. An involuntary urge washed over me; I wanted to run into his arms because I subconsciously knew he would keep me safe. A moment later, the spell was broken. He closed the door. Richard and Rosaline had left the room leaving an ominous void behind them.

3

We made it home from Asbury Park without incident. Throughout the week, I read the newspaper and watched the television. *The New York*

Times reported firebombs and looting. The rioters destroyed countless buildings and businesses on Springwood Avenue with damages in the millions. On Thursday night's *ABC Evening News,* Howard K. Smith reported that the seaside town of Asbury Park had become a battleground of rioting and was now on the list of national riots in 1970. The pictures on television and in the newspaper were devastating – charred buildings, some with smoke still drifting into the air. Broken glass and battered cars lined the sidewalks and streets. Homeless black families wandered aimlessly with dazed expressions on their faces. It looked like a war zone.

Richard was right. We shouldn't have been there. I got on my knees and thanked God we all made it home safely. Unfortunately, even though we were not physically hurt by the actions during the riot, the family did have battle scars from the experience. The lines of communication between Richard, John and me were damaged. We consciously avoided each other, and if we did accidently cross paths, we didn't speak.

Shortly after our disappointing vacation, I discovered a painful truth: John had multiple pictures of Lucy in his wallet. It was not my habit to open my husband's billfold; however, one morning while he was sleeping, I needed a couple of dollars for the paperboy. I didn't have enough in the cookie jar, and I hadn't yet cashed my paycheck from Bamberger's. I wanted to let John sleep in on his day off; consequently, I opened his wallet in search of two dollars. As I flipped through it, I noticed a picture of Martin in his cap and gown at his high school graduation, two of Randy and one of Martin in his military uniform. It was taken the day he left for Vietnam; the last time John saw him. There was a corner of a photograph sandwiched between the two pictures of Randy. My curiosity got the best of me. When I pulled on it, I discovered three black and white photographs concealed between the pictures of the boys. Lucy was in all of them. The first was of Lucy alone. She was wearing a wedding dress. The second was of Lucy holding Martin when he was a baby. The third picture was of John, Lucy and Martin. I had not seen this particular picture in a long time, but I definitely knew it well because I was the person who had taken it. Martin was young – maybe six years old. The three of them were standing on Rosa's front porch. In the background of the picture, I could see the modern stores where Raffaele's Place had once been. Lucy was beaming with her wide, inviting smile. Martin's expression was one of excitement. If I remembered correctly, he was about to go with his parents to see a Walt Disney movie and was thrilled for the opportunity. And John . . . John looked wonderful. Happy. Proud. His arms wrapped protectively around his wife and their son. I couldn't remember the last time I had seen that loving expression on John's face.

As I stared at the pictures, a mournful sadness swept over me. I quietly returned the pictures to their hiding place and handed the paperboy two dollars. Normally I would have given him a pleasant smile and a thoughtful "thank you," but I didn't trust my voice enough to speak nor could I manage a smile. I was simply grateful when the door clicked shut, and he was gone.

A few weeks later, Brad dropped by my apartment. He wanted to say good-bye before he left for his sophomore year at Elon. Brad rattled on with various conversations ranging from summer reruns of *The Mod Squad* to Rosaline's remodeled bedroom. He even discussed at length his experience working at Carley's Place. To my surprise, he didn't seem as bitter about working there as he had in the past. He spoke about ideas he had to enhance the restaurant. Even though he avoided mentioning his father's name, Brad's voice had the same enthusiastic tone as Richard's did whenever he was considering a new concept or strategy for the restaurant. If I closed my eyes – father and son sounded identical.

Throughout the conversation, I was getting an unspoken message that seemed to have a common thread woven in each of his topics. Normally, I could easily read Brad's verbal cues, but I was evidently missing the significance of what he was trying to convey.

Finally, I interjected, "Brad . . . Sweetheart . . . is everything okay?"

"What do you mean, Mom?"

"I do not have to be a rocket scientist to see that you are trying to tell me something . . . spit it out."

"It's not that easy, Mom." He had a melancholy expression on his face.

"Are you in trouble?"

"No, Mom. I'm fine."

"Girl problems?"

"There's no one in particular, Mom." Brad mumbled without making eye contact. "I wish you would quit asking about girls. It's annoying."

"Is everything okay at the restaurant with you and your father?"

"Yes. It's all cool there." Brad muttered. "I kind of like working in the bar area. Dad's given me more responsibilities. It's not so bad."

"Then what is it?"

"It's Barbara." My son did not look at me; instead, he kept his eyes down. "Did anyone tell you?"

Of course! I thought to myself. Barbara was the *common thread* in all of Brad's conversations. My son had said *Barbara* watched all of those television shows with them. *Barbara* was the one who helped redecorate Rosaline's room into a teenage girl's dream. *Barbara* was always at Carley's Place either working or hanging out with Richard. Brad had strategically inserted Barbara's name into every topic.

"What about Barbara?" I asked. "I thought you liked her."

"She's okay." Brad was mumbling again. He stood up and began to pace the room. "But I don't want her for a *mother*! Besides . . . she's about a minute and a half older than I am." Sarcasm oozed from his words. "Geez! She's closer to my age than she is to Dad's!"

Brad continued talking, but I didn't hear anything he said. I was still fixated on his initial statement. I practically whispered the words, "Your father and Barbara are getting married?"

Brad froze. "You didn't know?" When I remained silent, he continued, "They got engaged about a month ago. Ever since she put on that mega diamond ring, Barbara thinks she lives in our house. She redecorated Rosaline's room . . . took her shopping with Dad's credit card . . . and now they are *best friends*! She's remodeling the kitchen and replaced all of the old appliances with avocado ones. I think I'm going to barf. Who the hell wants a green refrigerator?" Brad threw his arms up in the air to accent his words before continuing. "Dad doesn't say anything. He lets her do it."

I sat silently on the sofa. I didn't trust myself to speak. Somewhere in the dark recesses of my mind, I knew Richard and Barbara were serious about each other; however, I never dealt with the possibility that they might get married. There was an enormous weight on my heart. It was hard to breathe. I could still hear my son's rants, but they were drifting off in the distance.

"Love sucks!" Brad spewed the words. "I'm never going to fall in love!"

4

Richard

In October, I convinced Barbara to travel with me to North Carolina for Elon's Homecoming game. Carley's Place was keeping us extremely busy as was my other restaurant, but I had promised Rick I would make at least one game during the season. Last year, the Fighting Christians had a superior run with Richard McGeorge carrying the ball, but many of those players graduated. This season the team was young and riddled with injuries. They lost the starting quarterback Jackie Greene in the first conference game against Guilford. In addition, the back-up quarterback, freshman Alan Parham, was injured in the Presbyterian game. As a result, they hadn't won any of their first five games. The team was struggling, but Rick was still optimistic. I wasn't sure I wanted to travel so far to see Elon play without a viable quarterback, but Rick claimed his team still had a few secret weapons to watch, including stellar players Mike Lawton, Eddie Williamson, Nick Angelone and Ken Morgan.

To my delight, the game was exciting and worth the journey. Field-goal kicker Grover Helsley put the Fighting Christians on the board in the second quarter; however, they ended the half trailing the Indians 3-7. While the Homecoming Court was announced and Gena O'Berry was crowned the queen, Brad introduced me to his date, a cute blonde named Cindy Wilder. She was clearly enamored with my son, but Brad's attention was distracted by a gorgeous co-ed a few seats away. I invited Brad and Cindy to go out to dinner with us after the game, but Brad declined. Apparently, my son was more interested in going to a fraternity party than spending time with Barbara and me. I saw Brad less than ten minutes during our entire visit.

The second half of the game was filled with bittersweet athletic excitement. Elon lost a *third* quarterback, Steve Rumley, who injured his collarbone during a play, giving Jimmy Twisdale his time to shine. In the final minutes of the game, the novice freshman quarterback threw a fantastic 39-yard pass to David Rudder who scored, and gave Elon its first victory of the season. The crowd was overjoyed; Barbara and I were swept up in the enthusiasm.

Rick was ecstatic with the outcome of the game and thrilled to spend a few hours with us. Unfortunately, his date had gotten the flu, which left Rick without a partner for the weekend's festivities. Apparently, he liked the girl and wanted to introduce us, but she was too ill to leave the dorm. In spite of the situation, Rick was in a positive mood, and a steady stream of conversation came from his lips. He predicted he'd make the Dean's List again this semester; he loved his courses, especially Professor Anderson's Economics and Sander's Business classes. The more my son talked about his academic schedule, the more I knew he had an excellent intellect for the major he had chosen. After graduation, my oldest son would be the perfect asset for my restaurants.

Also during the evening's dinner table conversation, Rick told us a little bit about Brad and his current girlfriend; there was nothing in Rick's dialogue that I didn't see for myself in the few minutes I'd spent with Brad and his date. The cute blonde was another one of Brad's flings. However, as I listened to Rick talk about *his* girlfriend, I could tell my eldest son was madly in love. He was wearing his heart on his sleeve.

"I wish we could have met her," Barbara injected. "Seems pretty clear that you are wild about this girl?"

Rick blushed. "That obvious?"

"Yes. It's pretty obvious," I responded. "Is there a future for the two of you?"

"I don't know, Dad." The gleeful expression, which had been on my son's face, vanished. "I don't know how she feels about me."

"Have you bothered asking her?" I said in an almost teasing manner.

"No," Rick replied softly. "I get a little tongue-tied when I'm around Lori. I think *she* thinks we are just friends." Rick glanced up at me and smiled. "Right now, I'm good with that. I'll take friendship. I'm hoping we can build upon it."

"That's a good attitude, son." I spoke. "The best and lasting relationships are built on friendship."

"Maybe – one day – you can invite her to New Jersey," Barbara added, "and we can meet her."

"I'm working on it." The grin returned to Rick's face.

It was nearly 10:00 before Barbara and I got back to the motel room. I was exhausted, but Barbara wanted to rehash her favorite subject: *When are we going to pick a date for the wedding?* I tried to cajole her away from the topic, but she was relentless.

"We've been engaged for three months." Her voice had a bit of a whine to it.

"Are you serious?" I said. "Can't we enjoy this motel room – this bed!" I patted the mattress. "We don't get a lot of time off together. We're alone – no one here but you and me. Let's savor it!" I cocked a crooked smile and motioned for her to join me.

My strategy worked. I remained seated on the bed, and Barbara took the steps in my direction – I let her bridge the gap between us. To my delight, she enjoyed initiating the first move. Edging toward me, she straddled my lap with her legs and wrapped her arms around my neck. While humming softly to her favorite Carpenters' tune *Close to You*, Barbara ran her fingers tenderly through my hair. "I long to have you close . . . and inside of me," she whispered into my ears as she rhythmically rubbed her pelvis against me to the tune she was humming. Using her tongue, she left a moist trail from my cheek to my lips.

I decided I couldn't be teased any longer. After pulling her sweater over her head, I tossed it across the room. The bra was next. I cupped my hands on her breasts. Her skin was hot; her nipples were hard. Forcefully, I rolled Barbara onto the bed. We both fought with the zipper on my pants as I simultaneously pulled her skirt to her waist with my other hand. Barbara was aiding in the task. Together we managed to remove most of our clothing before I climbed on top of her. It had been nearly a week since we'd last had sex, and I was ready for it. We initiated our union face to face, but she rolled underneath me. Turning her head slightly so I could see her expression, she gave me a coy smile. I came from behind and entered her warm, juicy nest. We developed a rhythm that heightened my senses. Even though I was certain she was no longer humming, I could still hear the melody in my head. It was slow and methodical . . . the same lyrics repeated a dozen times. I couldn't have turned it off inside my head even if I tried: over and over – each time – a little faster – our breathing quickened with the accelerated pace. I could feel it building. *Here it comes!* My fingers dug into her skin. Barbara didn't seem to mind. She groaned with pleasure. I could tell she was riding the wave with me. I tried to slow the pace a little so the excitement would last longer, but it was out of my control. Barbara was already peaking, and I was right behind her. With the explosion came total blackness, then complete contentment. As reality came back into focus, I could feel Barbara's arms tightly around me and hear her humming the song again.

It was exhilarating to know we could spend the entire night together without worrying about interruptions or planning strategies to avoid my children. Although Barbara and I spent most of our time together, rarely did she stay in my house overnight. I didn't think it was appropriate for her to share my bed while my daughter was across the hall. But occasionally, I couldn't resist. There were times when I would sneak Barbara into my room like a teenager in heat. On those days, we quenched our sexual appetite without making a sound. That wasn't easy! But the biggest problem was the bathroom. Unlike the master bedroom in my house, which I rarely entered, my bedroom did not have a private bathroom. Consequently, if Barbara needed to use it, she had to go into the hall and around the corner. It was the same bathroom Rosaline used. We were careful.

On numerous occasions, Barbara tried to coax me into staying at her apartment, but I was not willing to leave Rosaline home alone overnight. As a result, most of our sexual activity occurred in my office and were hampered by my busy work schedule. All of these details added to Barbara's argument for why we should set a date for our wedding. Rarely a day went by that my fiancée didn't bring up the subject.

I wasn't sure why I was dragging my feet about setting a date for the wedding because I adored Barbara. She was fun and kind. She enjoyed sports and loved my restaurants. We shared similar views on politics and life in general. She had a good head for business. We had a lot in common. The kids liked her – especially Rosie. Barbara was gorgeous, and most importantly, she was great in bed! But still . . . I hesitated.

Barbara was humming Karen Carpenter's song again, and I was

relishing the warmth of her arms. Our breathing had returned to normal, and I was savoring the peaceful feeling of bliss.

It was Barbara who spoke first, "That's the song I want."

"Want for what?" I replied.

"That's the song I want to dance to at our wedding reception."

"Oh," I replied. *Way to kill the mood.*

2

Christmas came and went; so did Brad's 20th birthday. *Heaven help me!* My second child was no longer a teenager. *Now that was a scary thought!* Also while the boys were home for Winter Break, we rang in the New Year and celebrated Rick's 21st birthday. It was difficult to believe my boys were so old. Adults! Rick constantly rose to every challenge and rarely let me down. Brad, on the other hand, still acted like a spoiled, irresponsible child. Caroline was always coming to his defense, but I wasn't buying Brad's bullshit. He was a constant thorn in my backside. My middle child was obsessed with his camera and taking pictures. He showed little interest in my restaurants and no respect for my authority. Having Rick home for a few weeks was a joy, but having Brad home tossed the dynamics in the house all to hell. Every night when I came home from Carley's Place, I was in a foul mood. Brad repeatedly shirked his duties and produced the minimum effort. His attitude *steamed* me!

Barbara was of little comfort because she was completely focused on preparations for our wedding. There were days when Barbara and I barely saw each other, and even then – the conversation centered upon color schemes and flowers. We had finally picked a date: Saturday, April 10th. I chose the day because the boys would be home for Spring Break, and it wouldn't interrupt their courses.

An additional thought flashed through my mind . . . *on our wedding day, I will have just turned forty years old and Barbara will still be a couple years short of thirty.* The thought gnawed at me. *Forty-years-old!* It was incredible to believe it was 1971. *Where did the years go?*

When Barbara was not engrossed in planning our wedding, she was focused on redecorating rooms in my house. She'd already transformed Rosie's room. That was her first project and a relatively smooth transition. My daughter loved the attention and was one hundred percent on board with the change. The kitchen was completed last summer. Barbara had wanted to gut the entire room, but I had convinced her that the solid-wood cabinets were still in fabulous condition and I wasn't willing to change them. Therefore, Barbara was forced to leave the floor plan as-is, and made the renovations by purchasing new appliances, countertops, fixtures and knobs. In addition, she hired a person to put up wallpaper. I wasn't crazy about the zany pattern, but everyone else seemed to like it. She repainted the family room a pale green and rearranged the furniture so the television was on the other side of the room. It didn't make a lot of sense to me – more steps from the sofa to the kitchen – but she thought it looked wonderful. Barbara turned Rosa's old room next to the kitchen into a craft room. She replaced the single bed with a small sleeper sofa. Foldout tables ran along one wall, and her boxes of art supplies were on the other. I figured, after we were married, I'd be able to find her in that room most of the time. Barbara left the living and dining rooms relatively the same. She said, "They look like showrooms, so why change them?" The first time she mentioned my library, I nipped her ideas instantly. She backed off by saying, "That's your room. I suppose you should have it the way you want it." Several times during the holidays, Barbara mentioned she wanted to work on the upstairs in January.

I tried to dissuade her. "Everything looks fine. Thank you for all of your time, but you have done enough. It all looks great." Regrettably, nothing I said stopped her.

"I think you need new carpeting, especially on the stairs and in the hallway."

I finally conceded. By early February, we had new gold carpeting. I was willing to overlook her zealous attitude toward transforming my house so it would feel more like *her* home when we were married, but then she crossed the line.

The day before Valentine's Day, I found Barbara in the master bedroom. She had sample paint strips, remnants of material, and magazine pictures strewn all over the bed. I had been in a relatively good mood until the moment I saw her standing in the one room in the house I'd forbidden anyone to use.

Trying to keep my anger in check, I steadied my voice. "Barbara, you are *not* changing this room." My voice and my expression were un-yielding. "In fact, we are not going to use this room."

"Richard," Barbara stopped what she was doing and turned her at-tention toward me. "This room is magnificent, and it's huge! Why should we sleep in that tiny room in the back of the house, when we can have *this* room?"

"I thought I made myself clear a long time ago. This room is off limits!"

"Richard, please let me redecorate it. I know this room has bad memories for you, but I can change it – and *we* can create new memories here – *good* memories. All I need to do is change the way it looks."

"No!" My single word was firm and terse.

"This is ridiculous. Why are you being so stubborn?" Barbara's voice went up a notch as her frustration became visibly apparent. "Do you expect me to live in this house with Caroline's ghost?"

"Ghost?" I muttered. "Caroline's not dead."

"Exactly!" Again Barbara's voice rose a little louder. "She's still alive – and she is living in *this* room. You still have pictures of her on the night-stand. Some of her clothes are in the closet. Her robe is on the back of the bathroom door. There's a stack of old 45 records sitting on the dresser," Barbara pointed in that direction as her voice elevated sharply. "There are at least a half a dozen of Frank Sinatra's love songs in the pile – my God, Richard – do you still listen to them? How are you ever going to move forward if you won't clean the memories out of your house – get rid of the past."

"I've had enough of this conversation." I left the room.

On Valentine's Day, instead of celebrating our love, Barbara returned her engagement ring to me. Along with it, she gave me an ultimatum. "Sell the house – let's buy another one *together*." Her words were spoken with a serene composure. "If you can't do that – then I can't marry you." Tenderly she kissed me on my forehead. It was a sweet lingering kiss that rippled through my veins – not with lust, but with a gentle comfort much like the kiss a parent gives a child. "Think about it." She left.

I spent Valentine's Day alone watching *Ben Hur* on my television and sipping approximately a gallon of iced tea.

The next day, I made a feeble attempt to change Barbara's mind, but I refused to agree to her terms. She was equally as steadfast and committed to her way of thinking. Part of me believed she would falter and renege on the ultimatum if I simply ignored her challenge. We spent several days avoiding each other and denying the obvious. A week later, Barbara resigned her position at Carley's Place and said "Good-bye."

I could see the tears in her eyes, but she did not succumb to my conditions.

"You're still in love with Caroline and hanging on to your past. The tragedy is – we could have been happy, Richard, – if you had been willing to let go of her."

5

Caroline

Even though my marriage to John was lukewarm on our best days, the rest of my life was evolving in a vigorous and positive way. I had done well as the floor manager in the Ladies' Department. Last fall, I received a promotion, which meant an additional increase in salary, but it also meant a transfer to the Bamberger's at Brunswick Square. My position was in the new indoor mall in East Brunswick, and Bam's was one of the two anchor stores. Connecting all of the stores with a covered, climate-controlled setting was the latest craze in retail shopping. The customers loved the concept and flocked to the indoor mall. Bam's' regional manager believed my leadership skills and dedication could help make the new mall even more successful. I didn't wait to discuss it with John. I took the offer. Brunswick Square was a shorter distance to travel than the Newark store, which meant less gasoline needed for the Edsel and more money in my pocket. In addition, I'd put a lot of miles on that old car. I didn't know how many more years I was going to get out of her.

My increase in salary paid many of our monthly bills. We were no longer financially strapped, and I was even able to save a little extra in the cookie jar. If I put enough aside, perhaps, I could buy a new car. My achievement gave me a strong sense of pride. Unfortunately, my bubble burst when I discovered – quite by accident – that the fellow who held the same position in the Men's Department and had fewer years' experience, earned significantly more in his paycheck than I did. I was furious, but not angry enough to confront my boss. I stewed in the knowledge.

During the fall, I met a single mom named Joyce Anderson. We had a no-dent fender bender in the parking lot of our garden apartment complex. She lived in the building adjacent to mine. During our initial conversation – which was quite amicable considering we spent the first few minutes perusing potential damage to our cars – we discovered our mutual interest in NOW. We also realized we'd attended many of the same local meetings and rallies. As the months passed, we commuted together to some of the events and developed a friendship.

Joyce was more than a decade younger than I was and gravitated toward me because she called me her "substitute mom." The nickname pierced my heart because it made me feel old – especially since I was approaching my 40th birthday in April. I enjoyed Joyce because she reminded me a little of Lucy. Even though Joyce did not have quite the same shade of red hair as my beloved friend, she did have an auburn tone in her strands, and Joyce did have the same friendly expression on her face. I truly enjoyed spending time with her. By January 1971, Joyce and I had developed a strong bond.

When Randy met Joyce's freckle-faced daughter Karen for the first time, my son instantly recognized her. They rode the same school bus and were in the same third-grade class. Joyce and I spent a lot of time together; as a result, so did our kids. At first they complained loudly about "*cooties.*" It didn't take long for Joyce and me to figure out they were flirting with each other – it was their personal strategy for building a friendship. Before long, they were begging to spend time together. That was an added bonus for all of us: one babysitter – one shared price – equaled extra time away from home for two women on a mission. Joyce and I were able to attend more NOW events.

During the car rides to and from the meetings and rallies, I learned a lot about Joyce. She had gotten pregnant shortly before her 17th birthday. She and her boyfriend dropped out of high school and got married. There was no emotional or financial support from either side of the family because their parents disowned them. Joyce had not seen her mother in over nine years. As Joyce retold her story, she confided that her husband left the apartment one day – years ago – on the pretense of buying milk and bread, and he never returned. A couple of years later, an envelope came in the mail. He had petitioned for a divorce. Joyce received no financial aid from Karen's father. He simply evaporated into thin air. As a waitress at the local Hot Shoppe's, Joyce managed to keep herself and her daughter financially afloat. She joined NOW in the late 60s because the organization gave her a sense of purpose and a feeling of belonging. The women embraced her; she willingly accepted their support. As she became more and more involved with NOW, she campaigned adamantly for two of their goals: to legalize abortion, giving the woman the right to choose, and equal pay for equal work.

One day, after Joyce had consumed a couple of beers, she admitted to me that – although she loved her daughter dearly, she often wondered what her life would have been like had she not gotten pregnant as a teenager – or subsequently, "What would my life be like if I had chosen *not* to have a baby?" Choice! The moment she said the words, I could tell she was embarrassed about stating her innermost thoughts; consequently, I did not pursue the subject. Joyce didn't bring it up again.

I considered telling Joyce about Richard and me and how our teenage story ran parallel to hers. I thought about my elusive childhood dreams and all of my missed opportunities because of the choices I had made and the roads I had chosen. *What would my life have been like had I not gotten pregnant in the backseat of Richard's Chrysler?* When I reflected upon the potential conversation; somehow, those alternate options didn't seem so important anymore. I elected not to divulge my personal secrets.

I could not imagine my life without my children – all four of them.

During one of our many road trips in March, we traveled to Pittsburgh to protest the sexual segregation of the "Help Wanted" ads in the *Pittsburgh Press*. NOW was attacking the newspapers for using "Help Wanted: Female" or "Help Wanted: Male" in their classified employment advertisements. It was a long-standing tradition in all newspapers, but *Pittsburgh Press* was this week's target. Our organization did not think it equal to specify which gender should apply. *Why is a man more qualified than a woman for certain jobs? Why are some jobs only suitable for women? And others only for men?* NOW was determined to make newspaper employment ads generic.

"I like how NOW is branching out even more for our rights." Joyce said as she drove the car. "Did you hear the speaker last week at the meeting?" She didn't wait for my response. "The message is to embrace our sexuality, and they are supporting our right to choose our own lifestyle." Joyce paused to see if I was listening. "NOW is committed to helping lesbian women keep their children if they don't want to live in their closet marriages: women no longer have to suppress their secret and stay married to men they do not love – living lives they do not want. Isn't it wonderful?"

When I didn't respond, Joyce changed the subject, "Have you read Sexual Politics?"

"No," I replied. "Who wrote it?"

"Kate Millet," Joyce replied. "I can't put it down. Millet shows how male authors have made women look like sex objects. It's degrading and disgusting."

Instead of listening, I analyzed my personal thoughts on sex. I had not read many books on the subject. Joyce mentioned Kate Millet denounced a list of novels, including D. H. Lawrence's Lady Chatterley's Lover, which was the one book I had read, and I liked it.

Joyce turned the conversation to Hollywood and how movies depicted women as sex symbols. She bellowed, "Makes me *sick!*"

I thought about the movies I'd seen, and the way men and women interacted in them. To me, the story lines didn't seem to depict women as sex objects. Many of the movies had a sexual tension that was palpable like in *Two for the Road*. I loved the movie and would never forget the enticing way in which Albert Finney and Audrey Hepburn looked at each other. Always with a yearning – the sexual act was left up to the imagination. It was tantalizing. Furthermore, how could anyone forget the yearning and desire in Omar Sharif's eyes when he looked at Julie Christie in *Doctor Zhivago*? I didn't interpret the underlying message in those examples in the same way as Joyce did. I saw them as true love stories, but she viewed them as sexist and demeaning. It was odd that we saw the same movies and took opposing views analyzing them.

Besides – I shrugged it off – they were movies – not real life.

When I privately scrutinized my own life, I realized I didn't have a lot of personal experiences; there had only been three men. Jerry Adams – when I was a teenager – that relationship had never been consummated. Then there was Richard and now John. I had never so much as kissed anyone else.

If I remembered correctly, there was nothing about Jerry Adams that inspired any true emotions – either from my heart or from my body. He was the "easy road" to nowhere that my father wanted me to take. Richard, on the other hand, was a totally different story. He ignited flames inside of me similar to the ones I saw on the silver screen. Richard stirred magic in my soul – and it was beautiful.

Ironically, when I thought about John, I began to see Joyce's claim. With John in the equation, Joyce's argument made more sense. If I was honest with myself, I did feel like sex with John was part of my "job" as a wife. A few times a month, he rolled toward me in bed and pawed at my nightgown. On the days I didn't respond immediately, he became a little more forceful until I finally yielded. If I was honest with myself, I had to admit I didn't enjoy having sex with John. It had never been special or exciting or even pleasant. It felt more like a duty than a joint adventure. In the beginning of our marriage, our physical union left me sad and unfulfilled, but as the years passed, I stopped thinking about the sexual aspect and was merely grateful it didn't last long.

As we traveled west on Interstate 80, I couldn't help myself. My mind began to wander to those remarkable nights with Richard when we kissed and teased each other's bodies. I vividly remembered – when we'd finished making love – I had always felt completely exhausted and quite satisfied. Being with Richard had been exciting and wonderful – much like the beguiling way Hollywood depicted it. I brushed the thoughts of Richard away. It felt like adultery, and a part of me didn't want to rehash those old, lost memories. It hurt too much to remember.

Richard and Barbara were getting married next month. She would be *his* wife. She would be the one sleeping in *his* bed. I forced their images from my mind.

As I leaned my head against the window and watched the country-side go by, I let out a sigh. When I left my father's home – all of those years ago – there was no Interstate 80 – only back roads. Apparently, President Eisenhower's goal of connecting America with a network of highways was truly a good idea. Sure made traveling easier. If it weren't for this road, I wouldn't even consider this trip with Joyce.

Shortly before we saw the sign to go south to Pittsburgh, I saw the exit to my old hometown. Joyce was talking about a song on the radio, but I didn't hear her. I kept staring at the sign. I didn't move my head; however, my eyes followed it until I could no longer keep the sign in sight. I considered asking Joyce to take a detour. For a split second, I longed to see my father's house. I wanted to stand on the corner of Maple and Main. See the Grand Palace. Maybe go to the river. Stand on the shoreline. Smell the grass. Traces of spring were in the air. The memories tugged at my heart. Then I realized. *What's the point?* Nothing will be the same.

I shifted my attention to Joyce's conversation. She was rambling about the history of Interstate 80. "Did you know that this road goes all of the way to San Francisco?" She sang along with Scott McKenzie's song on the radio. A few stanzas later, she paused long enough to look at me. "Maybe we can put flowers in our hair and go to a love-in." Joyce paused. "Want to stay on I80?" She questioned with a hint of laughter in her tone. "Drive right past Pittsburgh . . . keep going . . . go all of the way to San Francisco?"

"You're kidding, right?" For a moment, I wasn't sure if Joyce was going to take the exit to Pittsburgh or not, but ultimately, she did.

At the rally, we both held signs. Many of the protesters carried the same tattered *Equal Pay for Equal Work* and *No More Sex-Segregation* signs. But I'd made a new sign for this rally. Mine read, *Women unite! You have nothing to lose but your kitchen sink.* Joyce's was slightly shorter in words. *Free our sisters! Free ourselves!*

As I waved my sign, a tiny voice whispered in the back of my mind. It was John's challenging words whenever he and I debated my activities with NOW. John's ultimate comeback to any of my positive arguments for equality was always, *"Be careful what you wish for, Caroline. You want everything to be equal? What about the draft? You want your daughter drafted? You want her to fight in a war like Martin did?"* John knew the moment he said those words, I had no rebuttal.

A week after the rally – while at an encore NOW meeting – I heard the courts had given *The Pittsburgh Press* thirty days to change the way they wrote their classified ads. After the meeting, Joyce and I celebrated with a glass of wine. Sadly, our victory was short-lived. The newspaper appealed the court's decision.

I was so busy with my new job, helping Randy with his homework, and the NOW meetings, I rarely saw Richard and didn't hear the news until Rosie told me. She came over to babysit for Randy and Karen so Joyce and I could go to a PTA meeting at school.

My daughter blurted out the news within seconds of entering the room, "I can't believe Dad and Barbara aren't going to get married."

When I asked her "why", Rosaline didn't have an answer. I could tell she was disappointed. She liked Barbara, and she had been looking forward to including her in the family. I was too stunned to be of much help to my daughter. Shortly after Rosie's burst of information, Joyce and Karen knocked on the door. The subject was dropped, but my mind was still spinning.

The boys came home for spring break as scheduled. Because there was no longer a wedding, they had more free time on their hands; as a result, Brad came over a lot. He told me a little bit about his current girl-friend. During the conversation, I asked him, "Is Cindy the one, Brad?"

Brad glanced away. His expression didn't change and his voice didn't alter. "No! Cindy isn't the one," he paused. "She's nice. I like her okay, I guess." Brad was quiet for a long time. He stared at his hands in his lap as if he were contemplating his next words. Brad finally looked directly at me; his beautiful brown eyes laced with melancholy. "I have already met *the one*, Mom. But she didn't want me."

My heart lurched. Brad looked more vulnerable and more grown up at that moment than at any other time in his life. Even though his expression conveyed a stoic façade, it was clearly evident my precious son harbored a broken heart.

"What's her name?"

"It doesn't matter," he muttered. "I don't want to talk about it."

And the subject was dropped.

2

I thought I was going to spend the day cleaning the apartment, but my daughter had other plans for my time. She dropped by unannounced and was sitting on my couch. Tears streamed down her face. She'd grown so much during her freshman year in high school. There were days when I had to look at her twice to recognize her. My little girl wasn't so little anymore; she was spreading her wings, and pushing the envelope.

On the last day of her freshman year, Rosaline pierced her ears with-out either Richard's or my consent. Two weeks later, she purchased a box of Clairol frost & tip. Apparently, a girlfriend – not a professional – put blonde highlights in Rosie's hair. To be honest, it looked good, but – to my chagrin – it made her look much older than fifteen.

On this particular day, Rosie applied way too much blue eye shadow, which was distracting from her innocence and her natural beauty. Admittedly, strong make-up around the eyes was the current fashion; however, on my little girl, it made her look more like a circus clown. She had no idea how to apply it correctly. In addition, the tears pouring from her eyes created long black streams with sparkling blue glitter that rolled continually down her cheeks. If that wasn't enough of a mother's nightmare, Rosie was wearing a see-through blouse with no bra underneath. I was glad it was navy blue instead of white, but the color still didn't camouflage the fact that her breasts were playing peek-a-boo through the flimsy material whenever she moved.

Everything about my daughter screamed – *Look at me!*

I didn't know whether to reprimand her or cradle her in my arms. Instead of reacting or even talking, I simply held her hand and listened.

"I like him so much, Mom!" Rosie wailed uncontrollably. "I've tried everything, but Paul doesn't even know I exist!" She threw herself in my arms.

I returned her embrace, holding her as tightly as I could. *There are times in a mother's life when she realizes a Band-Aid will no longer fix the problem.* Sadly, this was my moment with my daughter. Rosaline's pain was my pain, and I ached for her. As I continued to embrace Rosaline in my arms, a fleeting notion crossed my mind . . . *I thought getting them to sleep through the night – toilet-training them – teaching them how to tie their shoes – were difficult challenges. In hindsight, those were the easy days.*

As Rosaline's tears began to subside, the phone rang. My daughter took several tissues out of the box and blew her nose. "It's okay, Mom. You can answer it."

I leaned across her body toward the side table and picked up the receiver. It was a collect call from Rick. He was going to be a day late coming home from his summer school session at Elon.

"I'm stopping by Lori's house in Virginia – it's on the way." Rick's voice was filled with excitement. "I'll meet her parents, and then I'm bringing her home with me. I want you to meet her, Mom. Can we come by on Thursday or is another time good?"

At least one of my kids was happy!

A few days later, Rick and his girlfriend were sitting on my couch in the exact position as Rosaline and I had been. Truth be told, I wanted to like Lori. As she sat next to my son, I studied the petite, charming girl. Admittedly, she was adorable – every bit as pretty as Rick had proclaimed: beautiful smile – sparkling personality. But something was missing, and it was obvious Rick didn't see it. There was nothing but adoration in my son's eyes. Even though Lori's face was kind – even sweet – there was no love in *her* eyes. Within minutes of inviting them into my apartment – I knew – this girl did not share the same emotions as Rick, and she was going to break his heart.

It seemed all three of my children were struggling with love.

6

Richard

I thought 1972 might be a calmer year for me, but I was hugely mistaken. The boys were home for spring break, and the house was in total turmoil. Rosie was in a distracted and foul mood. I wanted to blame it on that mysterious monthly female cycle; however, she had been on the same emotional roller coaster ride since shortly after Christmas. Whenever I approached her, she clammed up and refused to talk to me. Most of the time, she was barricaded in her room, crying into her pillow. Barely a week went by that I didn't call Caroline on the phone and ask her to stop by the house. She couldn't get any answers either, but at least Caroline seemed to comfort Rosie enough to quiet the tears. It was all quite confusing. I never did understand teenage girls, and mine was perhaps the worst of them all.

Brad was his typical belligerent self, which annoyed the hell out of me. His midterms were disgraceful, and he had no excuse for his mediocrity. He was closed off and irate most of the time. The irony of it all was at Christmas, he had been dancing on clouds and amenable; I barely recognized him. Brad had broken up with Cindy Wilder last fall and had been dating another girl at Elon. He seemed crazy about her. Then – with no warning at all – he was back together again with Cindy. However, I was certain the relationship couldn't be a full commitment because whenever Brad was working at the restaurant there was a good-looking number sitting at the end of the bar waiting for him to get off of work. Typical Brad. There was always a merry-go-round of girls parading in and out of his life. He couldn't commit to anyone or anything. When it came to women – the boy made no sense at all! I would have thought his relationship with Cindy Wilder would make him a happier person; but apparently, it did not. He didn't want to talk to me about his grades, his gloomy disposition or his love life.

Most of the time, Brad sat in his room and listened to the same maudlin song on his record player. The lyrics tore holes in my heart.

Isn't Life Strange? I wanted to ask Brad why he chose to continually play *that* song. The melody was embedded in my brain. Over and over again! The forlorn Moody Blues lyrics made me think of *my* life. It conjured up images of Caroline and days long past. The tune gnawed at me; I even considered throwing Brad's record player out of the window. Instead, I banged on his door and shouted, "Turn that damn thing down!"

Rick, on the other hand, was in a jubilant mood during the entire spring break. He was able to balance some of the negative karma in the house. Last summer, my eldest son had his heart broken by a cute little co-ed at Elon, but thankfully, he mended quickly. Rick was wrapping up his last semester of college and completely committed to his relationship with a lovely sophomore named Valerie. I'd never seen him happier.

I spent as much time as possible with Rick, because his joy rubbed off on me in a medicinal way. There were days when I thought his happiness was my lifeline; consequently, I enjoyed our time together. Rick openly talked about his dreams and his future. President Nixon had significantly reduced the number of troops in Vietnam and there was rumor of peace on the horizon. Thankfully, neither of my sons needed to worry about being drafted. Their lottery numbers were high enough to avoid concern and the threat was behind us.

After listening to Rick talk endlessly about the restaurants, I knew he was ready after graduation to take the managerial position at the Morristown restaurant. Rick was up to the challenge, and I was ready to divide the responsibility of my two locations. I had to admit – juggling my restaurants was getting old. I was tired; therefore, I was glad and grateful to hand over the baton and share the duties.

As for my personal life . . . I was still numb. It had been over a year since Barbara had broken our engagement. At first I was hurt, and then I felt *relief*. I could have married Barbara. Perhaps I could have been happy with her. However, in retrospect, Barbara was right. If I searched my soul, I knew the truth; I didn't love Barbara – not in the way she wanted – and not in the way she deserved, but losing her did leave a void in my life. My evenings were lonely, and my bed was empty. All I had were my restaurants and my kids – both hugely rewarding but not completely fulfilling.

My mind lingered on thoughts of Caroline, but I knew they were futile. She was flourishing. Caroline had a firm harness on the career she had always wanted. She'd been promoted a few times. I'd be willing to bet she'd be in the corporate office before much longer – running the business from a desk. She was the epitome of the *modern woman* the female population was so fond of spotlighting– and from my vantage point – she wore it well. In addition, she was constantly on the move with her protesting signs and her passion for change. I had to admit – I never saw that coming. Caroline – holding signs and marching for a cause! *What a surprise!*

Even though I longed for days in our past, I knew there was no room in Caroline's life for me.

To fill my loneliest hours, I periodically went to a neighboring bar and sat on a stool nursing a bourbon and water. On those nights, it didn't take long before a random lady sat next to me and smiled in my direction. After an hour of aimless conversation, she would hint at "extra-curricular activity." At first I thought the girls were 'professionals'; however, it didn't take long to realize they were equally lonely and on the prowl – looking for the same physical release I needed. There were times when we didn't even exchange names; we simply shared a quick sexual release. Trust me – I wasn't complaining. Those random, nameless women served a purpose and filled a void.

What an odd and interesting world we live in. I hardly recognize it anymore.

2

Toward the end of the boys' spring break, I came home to what I thought was an empty house. As I sat in my library sipping on a light bourbon and Coke, I noticed muffled sounds from the second floor. I strained to decipher the noise. I knew it wasn't Rick because I'd left him at Carley's; he was scheduled to close. I was equally sure it wasn't Brad because he mentioned going to see *The Godfather* at the theater after his afternoon shift. Process of elimination . . . it must be Rosaline.

As I ventured up the stairs, the sounds got louder. It was definitely tears. Rosie was crying again. My heart lurched. *God! Please help me – give me some guidance – give me some answers – so I can help my little girl.*

I tapped at the door. "Rosie," I spoke softly.

She didn't respond.

I cracked the door a little bit and poked my head inside. "Can your old dad come in and sit with you for a while?"

My daughter buried her head in the pillow and did not answer. I decided "no response" was as good as an invitation to enter, so I walked in and sat on the edge of the bed. Quietly I scanned the room searching for the right words of comfort. As I glanced around, I silently commended Barbara for doing a nice job transforming Rosie's childhood bedroom into this lovely teenage girl's dream. It was such a pretty, cheerful room. What teenage girl wouldn't love it? *Why, then, was my little girl so unhappy in this arena?*

"Sweetheart," I broke the silence. "Is there anything I can do for you? I'm a good listener."

"You can't help me, Daddy." Her words were muffled in the pillow.

Rosaline moved so quickly, I barely had enough time to open my arms to welcome her before she flew into my embrace. I automatically encircled her with as much love and comfort as I could muster.

"No one can help me, Daddy. It's too late," Rosaline cried. "He doesn't care about me. He never cared about me. I thought he loved me. I thought . . . I thought . . ." Rosaline was sobbing uncontrollably; her words were no longer coherent.

"I'm going to call your mother."

Rosie nodded slightly and managed to whisper, "Okay." She nearly choked on the second syllable.

I didn't like leaving my daughter in such a state, but I needed to get to the phone in the hallway to make the call.

"Caroline," I said when she picked up the phone. "Any chance you can come over right now?"

"What's the matter?"

"I don't know, but Rosaline is hysterical."

"I'll be there in fifteen minutes."

Caroline was upstairs with Rosaline for nearly an hour before she came into the library. I felt as if I had been holding my breath the entire time. The expression on Caroline's face when she entered the room did not give me even a modicum of relief; in fact, my anxiety multiplied the moment I saw her.

"Oh, God help us," Caroline whispered as she sat in the chair across from me. Her eyes were leaden with sadness. She stared at me for what seemed like an eternity – the connection was so tangible it felt as if we could touch the energy between us. Caroline took a long, slow breath before speaking, "She's pregnant."

Neither of us moved. A world of memories flashed back and forth between our eyes. No words. No sounds – only waves and waves of memories crashing around us. I could see all of them reflected in Caroline's eyes.

"Did she tell you who the father is?" With all of the questions and emotions swirling around inside of me, those were the first words that emerged.

"Paul Winston." Caroline's voice was as robotic as mine.

"The guy who took her to the Homecoming dance last fall?"

"Yes. Rosaline has had a crush on that boy for a long time."

"He use to come around . . . but I haven't seen him since . . . geez – I can't remember – since before last Thanksgiving – no – longer than that – last Halloween."

"Halloween?" Caroline repeated the word. "Rosaline told me Halloween was the last time they were together." She took a long, laborious breath. "If that is true then she has been pregnant for five months." Caroline gasped. "*Five months!*" she choked on the words. "I didn't know." Caroline's entire body sagged in the chair. "How is it possible that I didn't know?" She kept repeating the sentence over and over. "This can't be happening." Caroline's voice became increasingly weaker. "Rosie doesn't look pregnant. Yes – maybe she has gained a few pounds – her face is rounder. She's been wearing baggy clothes. But I thought it was because she was *sad* and she was eating too much." Caroline cupped her face with her hands. "Oh, God! How is it possible that I didn't know?"

Caroline collapsed in front of my eyes. I moved on sheer instinct and rushed to her side. All I wanted to do was hold her. I didn't know what to say or how to fix any of this . . . but I wanted to start by holding Caroline in my arms. "It's going to be okay, Caroline. I promise – it's going to be okay. Lean on me. We can help Rosie together."

I cradled Caroline as she cried.

My mind was racing as I weighed all of our daughter's options. *Five months!* Was there a chance Rosaline's boyfriend would do the right things and marry her? With all of the tears I'd heard from my daughter in the last several months, I suspected Paul Winston might not be interested in doing the honorable thing. I had to suppress the anger because there was no time for my personal wrath.

Through rumors, I'd heard of places where girls could get abortions, but *that* was *never* going to be an option. *Five months!* Visuals of Rosaline lying on a dirty table in some back alley room kept strobing in my mind. I envisioned a man with a knitting needle or a coat hanger standing over her. *Oh my God!* She was too far along to even consider that illegal option. It could kill her or at the very least destroy her chances of having kids in the future.

An idea began to take shape in my mind. A couple of years ago, one of the waitresses at my restaurant confided in me that her daughter had gotten pregnant. She had asked for an advance in her salary so she could take her daughter to a home for unwed mothers. She later told me the baby had been delivered safely and been given up for adoption. Perhaps that was a viable avenue to explore.

As if in a verbal loop, the same words kept repeating inside of my head. *Rosaline would not be sixteen for three more weeks! How did this happen?*

I spoke before I thought about the details. "Do you think that Winston fellow will marry her?" I continued to comfort Caroline in my arms.

Caroline buried her face in my shoulder. "That boy doesn't love her . . . he will never make her happy . . . marriage will make her miserable." Her voice was quivering with each word.

"We need to be realistic," I interjected. "Marriage seems to be the viable alternative."

Caroline's head snapped to attention. The tears miraculously evaporated and her voice was firm and concise. "I don't care if she is pregnant!" Abruptly, Caroline pushed me away as she frantically waved her arms and spoke with a shrill, determined voice. She continued, "I will not stand by and let her ruin her life."

"Caroline," I interrupted. "What if she wants to marry him?'

"It doesn't matter. She's not eighteen years old. She may be legal age in a court of law to have sex, but she isn't legal age in this state to get married without parental permission. I won't stand for it, Richard! I mean it! I won't let my little girl destroy her life the way I did." Caroline lowered her voice slightly. "Rosaline will not make my mistake."

If it were possible for words to cut into my heart, Caroline's did. *Destroy her life the way I did! Make my mistake!* I was transported back in time. The memories pictured in my mind were as clear as if they had happened yesterday. Caroline and I – sitting at my mother's grave – her head bowed in shame and her beautiful face wrenched in emotional agony as she whispered – *"I've heard there are doctors who help girls like me – and they can make this go away – like a bad dream. I think I have the money, but I'm afraid to go alone"* – verbally implying that an abortion was her *first* choice. Caroline – standing next to me as I packed her possessions in the trunk of my Chrysler. The silence as we traveled through Pennsylvania spoke volumes, and the forlorn expression on her face pierced my heart. That motel room in Dover – oh my God! That night – Caroline clutched the blanket tightly under her chin – as if it were the one thing protecting her from me.

She thought of our marriage as the mistake that ruined her life!

Caroline continued, "I wanted an abortion . . . but you wouldn't let me! No! Not you! You wouldn't think of such a thing. I simply *had* to marry you and do the 'right thing!' But what you really wanted was a free ticket to my father's money."

"Come off it, Caroline," I finally found my voice, and I fired back at her. "You *know* that's not true." *Why was Caroline rewriting our history together? Or did she always wish she had made another choice instead of coming with me?* I elected another line of attack, "and besides," I calmed my voice before I added, "would you rather that Rick was never born? For that matter, would you rather none of our children was ever born?" I was screaming.

"Richard! How can you say such a thing?" Caroline truly looked wounded. "You are always twisting my words. I hate it when you do that. You know I love my kids. I love them more than you ever could. You don't love them. You never have!"

"That's not true! And you damn well know it!" I was furious. *How could she say such horrible things? How did we get side tracked from the real issue? Why was she attacking me?*

"You seduced me with your pretty words. You conned me into sleeping with you, and what did I get for my weakness? A baby and a marriage I never wanted."

There! She said it! My greatest fear spoken out loud! The words reverberated throughout the entire room. My pain merged with my anger – I was not going to let her tear at my heart any longer. "That is *not* how it happened, Caroline!" I was shouting. *I never seduced Caroline.* She came to *me* that night.

"Shut up! I'm sick of listening to you. You and your declarations! You and your stubbornness! You wouldn't let me go! You wouldn't let me have my own life. No! You had me cornered, and you knew it! You saw the easy way to get rich – old family money. And you – so smug – thought you could walk right in and take it. How I hated you, Richard! I hated you for stealing the best years of my life. I wanted so much more than you could ever offer me. I had a boyfriend who was twice what you are. My father approved of him. Everything would have worked out perfectly. But he wouldn't touch me with a ten-foot pole after you'd ruined me."

What? That's not how it happened! In what fantasyland was Caroline living?

"Caroline," I was screaming too. "I never wanted your father's money. After all of these years, you must have figured *that* out by now!"

"Don't you try and talk around me anymore. I'm through with your flowery speeches! Rosaline will *not* make my mistake. I know what it's like to have a child when I was little more than a child myself! And I still remember what it was like to live with a man when there is no love. I wouldn't wish that hell on anyone . . . least of all my own child."

Caroline and I had had a lot of verbal fights over the years, but no battle was as vicious and destructive as this one. It was obvious Caroline was speaking from suppressed emotions. I had no idea she hated me so much. I had always hoped – *prayed* – we could find a strong bond during our marriage. When that didn't work, I had tried for common ground so we could share the rearing of our children. Unfortunately, verbal skirmishes were a steady part of our lives.

I returned the focus to Rosaline and our current dilemma. "An abortion isn't that easy to get, Caroline." I steadied my voice. "You can't waltz her into your doctor's office and ask for one!"

"I know a place where it can be taken care of – a safe place – but it's going to cost a lot. I want the money, Richard, and I want it now . . . or it will be on *your* head if she goes to some butcher for a cheaper price."

"I will not be party to this, Caroline!" My voice was stern. "I can't believe that you are encouraging our daughter to do this. This is unbelievable!"

"I will not listen to you! You are through running my life!"

"Damnation, Caroline! This isn't about you and me! This isn't about what *we've* been through. This is about our daughter!" I paused long enough to make sure I had her full attention. "For God's sake . . . this is about our grandchild!"

Suddenly it was quiet. Neither of us moved. Caroline's expression transformed from complete anger to total defeat. Tears began to roll down her face, and there was a pitiful whimpering sound coming from deep inside her throat.

"This is what we are going to do, Caroline." To my surprise, even though my heart was breaking, my voice was calm and reassuring. "I've heard of a place in Illinois. It's a home for girls who are in trouble like Rosaline. When she starts showing, Rosaline can go there and stay until the baby's born. They even handle the adoption. It's safe and private." I paused. "You and I will go check this place out. If we don't like it, we will find another place."

Caroline resigned. She had no fight left in her. She walked the steps between us and leaned her body next to mine. Without saying a word, I wrapped her protectively in my arms. I could feel the moisture of her tears through my shirt.

"I'm so sorry, Richard. I didn't mean anything I said. I swear. I don't know why I said those awful things. You have always been there for our kids. I don't know what I ever would have done without you. Please forgive me." Caroline was choking on her words. "Please, please forgive me."

"It's okay, Caroline." I held her in my arms, rocking her as if she were a child. As I drew her closer to my body, I stroked her hair and pressed my lips into the loose strands that covered her forehead. *My Caroline. My beautiful Caroline!*

3

I wondered if all parents feel like they are perpetually riding on the string of a yo-yo. The ups and downs. The highs and lows. The successes and the failures. Never feeling sure-footed or confident – waiting for the next misstep in their child's life.

In April, Caroline and I took Rosaline to a convent in Illinois. It broke my heart to say good-bye to my daughter and to watch her in my rearview mirror – standing between Caroline and Sister Teresa.

I questioned everything I said aloud, everything I felt in private, and everything I believed. Nothing made sense to me anymore.

Caroline took three weeks of unpaid leave to stay with Rosaline; then, she flew to Greensboro. I picked her up at the airport, and we drove the thirty minutes to Elon so we could watch our son graduate from college. Rick was the first person in our family – on both sides – to attend college and earn a degree.

For one sunny afternoon in May, the sorrow in my heart for Rosaline was replaced with the elation I felt for my son as we watched Rick accept his diploma. When he walked across the stage, Caroline leaned slightly on my arm. Without any words exchanged, I reached for her hand and gently wrapped my fingers around hers. She looked up at me and smiled that charming, beautiful smile of hers – the one that lights up her face – it was the same smile she shared with me on the day Rick was born. My lips quivered slightly as I smiled in return. Tears of joy misted both of our eyes.

7

Caroline

Rosaline's baby was not due until August 2nd; however, with my history of delivering early and the fact my mother had died from complications at childbirth, I was not surprised when I received a concerned phone call on the morning of July 20th. It was Sister Teresa; she told me Rosaline was in labor.

I was ready with a packed suitcase and another lie to tell my husband and my boss; in actuality, it was two different "stories." I told my boss I needed to visit my sick mother in Pennsylvania. The irony – anyone who knew me at all – instantly realized my words were a fabrication because they knew I had no extended family. The tale I spun for John was a little more elaborate. I told him I was in line for another promotion. Part of me wanted to tell John the truth, but a small voice in my head kept whispering *the fewer people who know, the better it will be for Rosaline.* After all, even my sons were unaware of Rosaline's pregnancy. It seemed wise to keep my husband out of the loop too.

Once again, I was taking unpaid leave – another fact John did not know. I hoped I still had a job when all of this was over.

The moment I hung up the phone, I dialed Richard's number. He wasn't home, so I called his office number at Carley's Place. He answered on the third ring. I frantically told him the news.

"It's going to take us too long to drive. I'll get us on the first available plane and we can rent a car when we get there." Richard's decisive tone and take-charge attitude had a calming effect on me. "I'll pick you up as soon as I've made the plane reservations."

The moment I hung up the phone, I dialed Joyce's number. She, too, was unaware of our situation, but she was willing to take care of Randy while I was gone. Randy was almost ten years old. The idea of having a babysitter annoyed him, but he was thrilled to be able to hang out with Karen at Joyce's apartment while John was working. All of my ducks were in a row, and I was ready to leave. I prayed we would make it to Illinois before the baby was born.

2

Getting a flight was not easy, nor was the trip in the rented car to the convent a quick journey. Consequently, it was nearly nine hours before we found ourselves standing in Sister Teresa's office. Much to our chagrin, we did not arrive in time to help Rosaline through her labor, but the sister insisted Rosaline's delivery was routine: both mother and baby were doing fine.

"Follow me," Sister Teresa's words were gentle. "I will take you to Rosaline."

"Can we see the baby?" Richard asked.

Sister Teresa, with her hands clasped in front of her, bowed her head and spoke softly, "I do think we have a little time. The nurse will bring the baby into Rosaline's room. You can see him there."

"A boy?' Richard whispered.

"Yes," Sister Teresa smiled, "a beautiful boy. Even though the little fellow made his debut a few weeks early, he will be fine because he's a fighter: a healthy, strong boy."

When we entered Rosaline's room, we saw her curled up in her bed, staring out of the window. The moment she saw us, she wept uncontrollably.

"Mommy," her single word brought tears to my eyes. I rushed to her side and encircled her with my arms. "I'm so glad you are here. I've been so afraid. It was awful, Mommy. It hurt so much."

"You are going to be fine, Sweetheart." I spoke the words into her ear. "Yes, it does hurt, but you will forget about the pain soon. The doctor says you will be okay – and you will heal quickly."

"Daddy, I'm so sorry." Rosaline choked on her words. "I know you are ashamed of me. I'm so sorry."

"I'm not ashamed of you, Rosie." Richard clasped her hand and kissed it tenderly. "You made a mistake, but you will always be my precious girl. I love you."

I love you. I could not believe my ears. It was the first time I had ever heard those words come from Richard's mouth. He spoke them clearly:

I love you. Not once during our entire marriage, did he say those three words to me. *What I would have given to hear them!* Silently I watched the interaction between Richard and our daughter. The man, who always appeared to be in total control and confident, looked vulnerable and lost.

Sister Teresa walked into the room carrying the baby. Rosaline instantly reacted by recoiling in the bed and turning her head away.

"I can't see him, Mommy." Rosie whispered. "I don't want to see him. I can't! I can't! Take him away." She pulled the sheet over her face.

"Are you sure?" Sister Teresa said. "This is your chance to hold him."

"No, I can't! Please don't make me," Rosie begged. "If I touch him, he will become *real*. If he is *real* – I won't be able to . . ." she firmly added, "Please, please take him away."

Sister Teresa, still holding the baby, turned and left the room. Richard followed her, and I stayed with our daughter.

When the room was quiet again, Rosaline returned her attention to me. She finally spoke, "Sister Teresa says he already has a new home." Rosaline stared at the doorway. "Somebody wants my baby. It's a good thing, right?" Her eyes were glued to the place where Sister Teresa had been standing. "The sister told me she met the couple. She said they are nice. They live in Peoria. They are in their early thirties. Sister Teresa told me that they had been trying for ten years to have children, but they can't have any of their own." Still gazing at the doorway, Rosaline continued, "They think I am their angel." Fresh tears emerged. "Mommy!" Rosaline choked on each syllable. "I don't feel like an angel." Rosaline could no longer hold back the tears. They gushed from her eyes. "Sister Teresa says they are kind, and they will be wonderful parents. I can't meet them – Sister Teresa said it's against the rules, but she did tell me that they thanked me for giving them a child, and they promised to be good parents." My daughter used the sheet to wipe the tears from her eyes. "They will be better parents than I would have been – won't they, Mommy? I wouldn't be a good mother, would I?" A constant stream of tears flowed from her eyes.

Are we doing the right thing? Is God ever going to forgive us? Will I ever be able to forgive myself?

"Sister Teresa says that I will be all right.... She said time will heal my wounds. She said I will move on and find a good life. Sister Teresa told me that God has already forgiven me, and I made the right choice because I gave my baby life." Rosaline tried to steady her voice, but to no avail. She sobbed with each word. "Sister Teresa said that an earth angel will come to me – and that person will help me through this time in my life – she promised me I will have joy in my heart again someday." Rosaline looked directly into my eyes. "Mommy," she struggled to speak through her tears. "Am I ever going to be happy again?"

I was crushed by the weight of my daughter's sorrow. *If only I had the answer.* I crawled onto the bed and wrapped my arms protectively around my daughter. I stifled my tears as best I could and let Rosaline sob into my chest.

Thirty minutes later I found Richard in a vacant room, holding the baby. He was gently rocking in the chair gazing at the infant humming a tune I didn't recognize. I slowly entered the room and sat in the chair next to him.

"Do we know his name?" I inquired.

"No," Richard replied without looking at me. "Apparently, he does have a name, but they can't tell us – or won't tell us." Richard slowly traced his fingers over the baby's face as if he was making a template with his fingers. "His adoptive parents are on their way. Turns out – our painful nightmare is their happy ending – or should I say – beginning." There was grief-stricken agony in each of Richard's words.

"May I hold him?" I asked with a timid intonation.

"Not yet," Richard's voice had a guttural, pleading element to it. "I don't think I can let him go, Caroline. He is part of *me*. He is the best part of *us*. How can I let him go?"

"Sister Teresa said the couple is coming to pick him up in about fifteen minutes. They are almost done with the paperwork. The decision has been made."

"How can you be so calm?" He glanced up for a moment before returning his attention to the baby.

"I'm not," I replied. My voice sounded more serene than I felt inside; in actuality, I was anything but calm. "Trust me, I'm not. But I am trying to help you because throughout our entire lives –*you've* always been the strong one." I gently placed my hand on Richard's shoulder. "I think it's my turn to help you."

384

Richard ran his fingers lovingly over the baby's eyebrows and tenderly down his jawline. "He looks like Brad." He bit into his lower lip fighting back his tears. "Remember when Brad was born – we were so worried about him – but he was such a fighter. Strong willed. Stubborn. Always had a never give up attitude." Richard chuckled for the first time. "God help us . . . Brad's still like that."

"Like father like son," I whispered. For the first time in a long time, there was no malicious edge to my tone when I spoke those words. Normally, the comparison would have inspired a caustic response, but this time Richard simply glanced in my direction and smiled.

Richard shifted the baby in his arms enough to allow him to pull his wallet out of his pocket. He fumbled with it until he could open it with one hand. I wasn't sure what he was doing until I saw him lift a baseball card out of it. Stan Musial.

"This is *Stan the Man!*" The baby opened his eyes and looked alert. Richard flashed the card in front of the baby's face, and he followed the movement with his eyes – or perhaps it was simply Richard's voice that captured the infant's attention. "This is a special card – this is Stan Musial's rookie card – it was in my brother's collection of favorites. Calvin knew Musial was going to be one of the great players of all time – in his rookie year – Calvin knew. My brother was always good at spotting talent." Richard's voice cracked with emotion. He hesitated a moment to regain his composure. "Musial had quite a career in baseball – an amazing player. He played twenty-two seasons with the St. Louis Cardinals, but he actually grew up in a town not far from where I was born." Tears streamed down Richard's face, but his voice never wavered. "He was inducted into the Hall of Fame a few years ago." Richard elevated his voice, and the baby reacted with what looked like a genuine smile. "Over his entire career, Musial batted .331. He was a left-handed slugger. It takes determination and talent to have such an outstanding batting average. And did you know . . . he was the National League's Most Valuable Player *three* times; plus, he was a huge reason why St. Louis won *three* World Series. *Stan the Man* owns the record for playing in the most All-Star games." Richard hesitated a little before adding, "I think Willie Mays – maybe even Hank Aaron – might tie his record someday – but right now – *Stan the Man* – owns that title. He's a champion!"

There was a frailty in Richard's voice as he spoke. "One day," he gently stroked the baby's cheek. "There *will* be a day – I'm sure of it – *you* will be a champion." With each word, Richard's voice became stronger and more confident. "You will find what *your* talent is – maybe it is baseball – maybe it's something else – but you *will* find your talent – and you will go for it! Be determined like Stan Musial. Be the best man you can be and *never* settle for less." The baby was mesmerized by Richard's voice. Eyes wide opened. "I want you to have this card." Richard placed the baseball card in the folds of the infant's blanket and kissed his cheek. He tapped it twice, and then tapped the baby's heart. "You will never know me, Sweet Baby Boy," Richard's voice cracked slightly; he paused for a few moments to collect his composure. "But I want you to have this card so you will always know – you *are* a winner! You can be anything you want to be." Tears filled Richard's eyes. They spilled out onto his cheeks and rolled down his face. Like a waterfall, the tears fell onto the baby's forehead. The infant didn't seem to mind – he was cooing and gurgling in a sweet way almost as if he were trying to carry on a conversation with Richard.

Sister Teresa walked into the room and stood quietly in the corner. Richard didn't see her, but I did. Her mission was clear. *It was time.* I could barely contain my emotions, but I knew in my heart that Richard would never get through the next few minutes without my help. I knelt by his side and placed my hand over his as he lovingly stroked the baby's cheek.

"It's time, Richard." I whispered the words.

First he looked at me, then at Sister Teresa in the corner – then returned his gaze to me again. There was such a deep sadness in his eyes. The normally crisp blueness of his irises appeared translucent as they filled with tears. I felt I could see all of the way to his soul – and his pain was monumental.

"If Rosaline can do this . . . we can do it too. We have to be strong for our daughter." I spoke the words as soothingly as I could.

Sister Teresa crossed the room and gently took the baby from Richard's arms.

"You must tell me the names of the people who are adopting him," he begged.

"I can't do that, Mr. Malone. You know I can't do that." Sister Teresa spoke with kindness but she was also firm. "The adoption is *closed*. Rosaline will never be able to find out; however, when the child turns twenty . . . if he wants to know, he can have his records unsealed by the court."

"Please, Sister Teresa, please give this baseball card to the parents." Richard pointed to Stan Musial's Rookie Card that was nestled in the folds of the blanket. "Please ask them to keep it for the boy. Give it to him when he is older. I'll never see him – he will never know us – but I want him to know we were with him – we held him –and we love him."

"I will make sure they get the card, Mr. Malone." Sister Teresa stood in the doorway with the baby in her arms. "Trust me – trust in God – this is a good match. These are loving people, and they will give the baby a wonderful home."

Sister Teresa was gone. It wasn't until the sound of her footsteps faded down the hallway that I realized . . . *I never had a chance to hold my grandchild.*

8

Richard

By the first of September, there was a calmer façade in our house. Brad had returned to Elon for his senior year. Rick was living at home – saving his salary – and successfully tackling his new managerial position at my restaurant in Morristown. As for Rosaline – I saw a glimmer of hope that she was coming out of her depression.

In August, my daughter had approached her high school guidance counselor. Even though Rosaline had missed the last two months of her sophomore year, the counselor suggested testing to get her back on track. Thanks to the sisters at the convent, who believed education to be a priority, Rosaline was able to pass all of the necessary tests to keep her on grade level. She was scheduled to start her junior year.

It wrenched my heart that Rosaline never had any visitors. Most homes with teenagers had a revolving door of friends constantly going through the house, but not so in mine. No giggling girls sharing the latest gossip, no teenage boys calling on the phone, no groups of kids congregating in the yard. Rosie was withdrawn from the social scene, except for one fellow. His name was Tony Anderson.

Tony's family lived around the corner from our house. His parents were original owners – they had personally designed and purchased one of the houses I had built in the 1950s. I knew them fairly well. In addition, I knew Tony too. He was a couple of years younger than my sons, but he was a talented enough athlete to occasionally play up on the same team with Brad and Rick when they were in Little League. In addition, Tony made varsity his freshman year in high school and played on the same team with Rick when he was a senior. The guy was a great centerfielder: fast as lightening, strong at the plate and a real team player. I never saw him out with groups of kids; instead, he had a reputation for being studious, polite and a bit of a loner. If I remembered correctly, Tony was the valedictorian of his high school class and would soon start his sophomore year at Bucknell University. Normally, I would have banned the boy from our home because he was too old for my daughter, but something convinced me otherwise.

I couldn't remember one single time when I had seen Tony so much as glance in Rosaline's direction – much less carry on a conversation with her – until one day – in the middle of August – she was in the driveway with Rick helping him wash his GTO. My daughter was wearing cutoff blue jeans and a t-shirt that was perhaps a little too tight for my liking. As I watched my kids from the window, it was hard for me to think that Rosaline was anything but a normal girl enjoying her Sweet 16th year. She and her brother were spraying each other with the garden hose more than they were spraying the car, and I heard a flurry of laughter floating in the air.

I was about to return to the library to get some work done when I saw Tony Anderson pull up in his yellow Chevy Vega. He spoke to Rick; however, he was intermittently glancing at Rosie. Within minutes, all three of them were washing the car. I noticed Rosie wasn't participating in the conversation, but she was smiling. I was pleased. It was good to see my little girl smile again!

Tony stopped by a couple of times before he left for college. On his last visit, he brought Rosaline a gift. It was a poster. That evening, when I went into Rosie's room to kiss her goodnight, I saw the new poster on the wall.

"Cool poster," I commented as I nodded in its direction.

Today is the first day of the rest of your life.

"Tony gave it to me." Rosaline blushed. "He asked if he could write me while he is in college."

"What did you say?"

"I told him 'yes'." She paused. "Do you think that is okay, Daddy?"

"Do you like him?"

"He's a little shy, but he's nice." The edges of her lips curled upward to form a grin. "And he's nice to me."

"Then, of course, it's okay if he writes to you."

2

A month later, while I was watching the local news at 11, I heard about the fatal car accident. Paul Winston was the driver; he had wrapped his car around a telephone pole. Paul and three other boys were pronounced dead on the scene. Apparently, alcohol and marijuana were found in the car. *I wondered if Rosie knew about it.*

I didn't want my daughter to hear the tragic news at school; therefore, I walked up the stairs to her room. *I dreaded being the bearer of bad news – especially when I was certain it would upset her.*

9

Caroline

Joyce and I were at a NOW meeting on a Monday in January when the news came: The US Supreme Court legalized abortion. Roe v Wade was a landmark case that was destined to change our society as we know it. The entire room erupted in celebratory applause. Although I was surrounded by euphoria, I did not feel their excitement. I backed away from the rejoicing women.

For years, I'd been holding signs and protesting for this cause, but today I felt neither triumph nor satisfaction for the victory. All I could think about was my insane tirade as I'd tried to convince Richard last year that an abortion was the right choice for our daughter. It was my immediate knee-jerk reaction, and for a few moments, I'd even believed it. That was before Richard's consoling resolve influenced me.

And . . . before I saw my daughter's baby.

I no longer knew what to think anymore. It pained me to realize I would never see my grandchild again – but at the same time – I felt relief to know the baby was alive. My guess – he was sitting up at this point. Maybe even pulling himself up to a standing position. Making happy sounds. Smiling. Clapping. In a few months, he would learn to walk – one tiny step at a time.

Joyce, who was unaware of my melancholy mood, threw her arms around me. "Isn't it wonderful!" She kissed me firmly on both cheeks. "What a fabulous victory for all women! We did it! All of us! We made this happen!" She didn't seem to comprehend that I was not joining in the celebration or sharing her enthusiasm.

On the ride home, I was quiet, but Joyce was chatting up a storm. *You're So Vain* was playing on the radio.

"I love this song! It's kick ass!" Joyce hooted as she clapped along with the beat. "She's singing about an obvious jerk," Joyce howled. "Who would want to be *his* partner? Who would want to be with *any* man," she hesitated before adding, "like that?"

How appropriate! I thought to myself. *Let's trash men a little more today.* The entire evening had been about the mighty woman; *hear me roar!* Helen Reddy's song was the anthem of the day. The spokeswoman and all of the speakers had focused on women's freedom, independence, and equality! Because – Lord help any woman who might need a man! All of this *beating up on men* was giving me a headache! As I drove the car, I focused more on the road than the song or Joyce's voice or even rehashing the evening's events. In fact, I blocked it all out as much as possible.

After the song was over, a news alert came over the radio. The DJ reported, "Lyndon Johnson has died. He was pronounced dead at Brooke Army General in San Antonio, Texas at 3:39 Central Time." I glanced at the clock on the dashboard. Noting the time, I realized he had died three hours ago. I wondered if they knew at the meeting and elected not to tell anyone because it might dampen the celebration.

The DJ continued, "Within two months, our nation has lost two past presidents: Harry Truman in December and now LBJ. This leaves our country with no past president to hold in esteem."

"Oh Sweet Jesus," Joyce bellowed. "That leaves us with Nixon. God help us all!"

"I don't think Nixon is a bad president." I finally spoke. "He's ending the war in Vietnam – like he promised; plus, the POWs are coming home, and he is the first president *ever* to go to China." I paused. "The economy is doing well too. Did you see the stock market at the end of last year – the Dow Jones closed over 1000 for the first time in its history." Unfortunately, John and I didn't own any stocks, but Richard did and he was definitely doing the *happy dance* as the numbers rose.

"When did you start going all *republican* on me?" Joyce smirked.

"I'm not a republican!" I responded. "But I'm not a democrat either. I'm for the best man for the job."

"Man?" Joyce frowned. "Why can't the president be a woman?"

"Okay . . ." I replied. My voice sounded slightly annoyed because Joyce's unwavering slant was beginning to frustrate me and grate on my nerves. "I'm for the best *person* for the job. And right now . . . that person is President Nixon. And I'm not the only one who thinks so," I took my eyes off of the road for a second and glanced at Joyce before continuing,

"Last November, Nixon was reelected in a landslide victory. Didn't you notice – McGovern took one state. *One state!* A presidential candidate needs 270 electoral votes to win. President Nixon got 520 – almost *all* of them." I paused. "So someone in America – other than me – thinks Nixon is doing a good job! Hell! My boys even voted for him."

"Of course, they did," Joyce interrupted with a sneer in her voice. "Most boys voted for Nixon. Congress passed the 26th Amendment lowering the voting age to eighteen."

"My sons were already twenty-one on Election Day. They could have voted without the Amendment." I argued.

"Yes, but Nixon courted the young male vote by telling them he was stopping the draft. What boy wouldn't vote for him – it beats going to war."

"Why is it, you can't see the good?" My ire was increasing. I pulled into our parking lot, turned off the ignition and opened my door. "I'm tired. Let's call it a night."

"Caroline," Joyce was practically whining. "Please don't be mad at me. This is such a glorious day. We've worked so hard. We've moved a mountain. We are changing the world!"

"For the better?" I questioned in a soft-spoken voice.

"Of course, for the better! You *know* we are."

"Please," I mumbled as I dropped the keys in my purse. "Let's please put this day behind us."

"Caroline," Joyce reached for my arm. "I'm sorry. I've upset you, and I don't even know what I did. Please forgive me. Why are you so mad?"

"I'm not mad at you. I'm tired."

"Please don't shut me out. We're a *team* – you and me. We're the dynamic duo! Nothing can beat us! We've traveled so far together." Joyce held my hand more tightly and encouraged me to look at her.

"I don't know, Joyce." I muttered. "It's been pretty difficult lately."

"What do you mean?"

"John and I haven't been getting along very well – not since last summer."

"What happened?" Joyce asked. "Why didn't you tell me?"

"It's kind of personal."

"Trust me – I'm your friend." Joyce patted my hand in a soothing manner. "We can help each other."

It was painful to think about the chaos in my life – talking about it was unbearable. "I lied to John, and he caught me in it. He lied to *me,* and I *saw* him."

"*Lied?*"

"I told him – because of my promotion to the main office at Bam's last year – I was being groomed to be a buyer for Ladies' Apparel – which as you know – isn't a lie," I paused. "However, I told John my new position required that I go to a training conference in Illinois."

"And?"

"There was no conference. I was with Richard."

"You're ex-husband?" Joyce was flabbergasted. "You're having an affair with your ex-husband?"

"No!" I rubbed my forehead. "I'm not having an affair with anyone. It's not like that at all. Besides, Richard would rather walk over a bed of hot coals than be with me again."

"Then what were you doing with Richard?"

"We were . . . we were . . ." Flashes of memories popped into my head: Richard holding our grandson, Rosaline's hysterical tears, Sister Teresa's footsteps fading into the distance as she took the baby out of our lives forever. "It doesn't matter what Richard and I were doing. The problem is John called Bamberger's looking for me. They told him there was no conference. When I got home, John confronted me. He was self-righteous and indignant. He jumped to the same conclusion you did. John accused me of horrible things, and he demanded a divorce on the grounds of adultery." I smirked. "The irony of it all is," I took a deep breath before finishing my sentence, because I had never said the words out loud. "John is the one who is having an affair – not *me.*"

"John's having an affair?"

"Yes," I sighed. "I was so busy juggling all of the issues in my life; I never noticed he wasn't at home much."

"Are you sure?" Joyce inquired with a sympathetic voice.

"Yes," I replied. "I saw him with her in a restaurant. They were holding hands. He even kissed her – and not on the cheek." I paused. "She looked familiar. When I scanned my memory, I realized she is a mother of one of the kids in Randy's school. You probably know her. Nancy. Nancy Smith."

"Bryan Smith's mother?" Joyce looked completely flabbergasted.

I nodded.

"Wow! I never saw that coming," Joyce muttered.

"Me either."

"Are you going to leave him?" Joyce asked.

"My salary won't pay the bills. By the time Uncle Sam gets his cut in taxes, I get to take home a little short of $7,000 a year. If I do well as a buyer, I have the potential of making a pretty decent salary; however, until I prove myself, I'm stuck at this level." I paused. "I've done my budget. I see where the money goes. My rent is nearly $200 a month. I spend $50 a week on groceries – sometimes, I go over," I laughed in a sarcastic manner, "but it's never less. Then there are utility bills and clothes and doctors and God help us if we ever get sick or injured." I slammed my hands on the steering wheel. "Crap! Have you seen the cost of gasoline; it's over forty cents a gallon. I have to drive all over the place now. I hold my breath every day, praying the Edsel will make it from one destination to the next. This car is on its last leg. I don't have any money in the bank, and I certainly don't have four grand for a new car. I'm a prisoner. I can't afford to leave." I paused. "The worst part about it is, when John caught me in the lie, he thought he had a weapon to use against me because he wants custody of Randy. He constantly threatens to take him from me." I groaned sadly. "I can't let John have my son. I *won't* let John have my son." I began to cry. "I'm trapped. I don't want to stay, but I can't afford to leave."

"Men! They are all scum!" Joyce pulled me across the car and into her arms. "I'm so sorry, Caroline." She tenderly stroked my hair. "Perhaps there is another option." She paused. "We can leave this place. You and me – and we can take our kids with us." Joyce commented. "There is something I've never told you, Caroline. I led you to believe my husband walked out on me when Karen was little – I painted a picture of him leaving one day and never returning. It didn't happen like that. My husband didn't leave me – I left him." Joyce hesitated. "I didn't walk in on *him* in bed with another woman. *He* walked in on *me* in bed," Joyce paused for several seconds before adding, "with another woman." She stopped talking long enough to let her statement take credence. "When he saw us . . . he threatened to take Karen away from me. I was so afraid the courts would look at me as a freak – instead of a mother – and they would give custody of Karen to my husband. I couldn't let that happen. I took my daughter and ran."

It was difficult to digest all of the information in my friend's confession; as a result, I remained silent.

Joyce stared at me with confidence. Her words were decisive and crisp. "I know how to disappear, Caroline. Trust me." She stared directly into my eyes before adding, "We can leave and never look back. Disappear." She spoke the words slowly to let the meaning resonate. "We can raise Karen and Randy together – someplace else – the four of us can be a family."

I felt like a statue. I could not move. I was not even sure I wanted to move.

My world was turned upside down *again*! Every aspect of my life felt like a train wreck. Joyce had been a stabilizing factor for me, and I had clung to her on many occasions – grateful for her friendship. It was incredibly difficult to process any of the words she was saying. Nothing made sense anymore.

Joyce looked deep into my eyes. For the first time, I saw desire – a yearning – I had never seen in her expression. *Or had it always been there, and I simply didn't acknowledge it?*

"Come with me." Joyce spoke softly but with conviction.

I blinked.

"No!" My single word was pronounced quietly. I was not certain Joyce heard me.

"We can do this together, Caroline." Joyce cupped my hand in hers.

"I'm not going to run away with you, Joyce." I sat up in the driver's seat and square my shoulders. "No. This is not going to happen."

"I can help you, Caroline. We can be together. You and me. We can build a life with our kids."

"No!" I said firmly. "I'm not running away. And I can't choose you, Joyce."

"Stop!" There was a begging quality in her voice. "Don't leave."

"These last few years – I don't know what I would have done without you, Joyce. Your friendship is so important to me. You came into my life when I needed you the most, and you gave me strength when I didn't have any." I looked directly into her eyes. My voice was calm but also firm. "I can't be with you . . . nor am I going to run away. I have to change my focus." I peeled Joyce's fingers off of my arms. "I have to think about my children – especially Randy and Rosie." I got out of the car. So did Joyce.

I was certain of one thing . . . I could not *disappear* with Joyce and leave Rosaline behind, and I couldn't take my daughter with me either. I could not – would not – rip her from her father and the only world she knew. Rosaline was fragile – she needed both of her parents.

And my little boy – Randy was too young to be uprooted and separated from his home. My sweet son idolized John and would never understand. There were days when I looked at Randy and saw Richard – those sapphire blue eyes – so similar – were a constant reminder of that *one* night – years ago in the foyer of Richard's house. Yet there were other days – when I saw John and Randy together in the same room – playing Monopoly, talking about sports or laughing at a comedian on television. They had the same mannerisms. The two of them had many shared features. If I looked at their profiles – they could be twins.

Would I ever be certain – which man was Randy's father?

I waffled back and forth on a regular basis about my youngest child. Often I wanted to scream my frustration and doubt. Instead, I remained mute – never confiding in anyone.

To my horror, John often hinted at separation and his desire for custody. John truly believed he was the better parent for Randy. He often bellowed, "You are so busy with your personal crusades! You barely have time for our son!"

Perhaps there was some truth to my husband's words. Perhaps I did have my personal priorities in the wrong order. I needed to readjust and rectify that aspect of my life. In addition, I needed to figure out a way I could financially support myself and Randy if John ever followed through with his threats of divorce.

My concentration needed to be on what was best for *my children.*

That day was the last time I attended a NOW Meeting. I was

determined to concentrate on *my* life – not *changing* the world – but fixing *my* world.

That day was also the last time I saw Joyce. Several days after the NOW meeting, a police officer knocked on my door. He was looking for Joyce *and* Karen. Apparently, there was an outstanding arrest warrant. Karen's father had official custody of his daughter, but Joyce had snatched her years ago. According to the papers the policeman showed me, the courts were on his side.

The officer had knocked on Joyce's apartment door and discovered the landlord inside – the apartment was nearly empty. The furniture was still there, but the clothes, the personal items, Joyce and Karen were gone. *Vanished*. I never saw either of them again.

Suddenly, the conversation we had in the car made more sense to me.

2

In May, Richard, the kids and I traveled to Elon for Brad's graduation. John refused to go. It was probably for the best. We had not said more than a dozen words to each other in months. In fact, John was rarely at the apartment when I was there. He spent most of his free time with Nancy – at her place across town. To my total surprise, I didn't harbor any jealousy; if truth be told, apathy was the predominant emotion I felt toward John. I finally figured out the reason his actions didn't hurt – it was because I didn't love him. It was as simple as that – the tragedy was deciding which was more unfortunate: the fact I didn't love him or that John didn't love me? The answer didn't matter because we remained together – in a farce of a marriage. We chose not to confront each other about our situation; John and I went on with our lives – status quo.

My husband's absence from the apartment was easily explained to Randy – John simply told him he was working the graveyard shift. No one, not even Randy, was aware of the sham John and I called a marriage. To an outsider, we were happy – the perfect example of the new face of the nuclear family of the 70s: two working parents and a child who had his own key to the apartment attached to a chain hanging around his neck and tucked inside of his shirt.

John and I attended school functions together. We rallied around Randy whenever he was involved in an activity, and we even went to church periodically as a family. But it was all a façade to create as much stability for Randy as possible.

I had thought about leaving Randy behind with John instead of taking him to Elon for Brad's graduation, but decided against it. First, because I wanted Randy to witness Brad's accomplishment, and second, because a tiny fear gnawed at me; maybe, John and Randy would be gone when I returned. *What if John did to me what Joyce had done to her husband?* The thought terrified me.

We all traveled together in Richard's new Gran Torino. The car was enormous, and it had *air conditioning.* I found it ironic that Richard had two cars; he still owned his convertible Mustang – which looked brand new – and now he also had a gold four-door Gran Torino. *Must be nice to be able to afford such luxuries.* I continued to drive my Edsel – which *didn't* have air conditioning – and I didn't trust it more than a thirty mile radius from home.

The night before the ceremony, Richard took all of us out to dinner at The Cutting Board in Burlington. Rick brought his girlfriend Valerie. The seven of us sat at the gigantic round table in the center of the restaurant. Brad was constantly distracted by his peers who were also with their families. He spoke more to them than to us. Our graduating son might have graced us with his presence for a few hours, but his attention span wavered and his manners toward his father were anything but polite. Rosaline kept Randy occupied by playing "hang-man" on a paper napkin; she was definitely bored. Rick and Valerie were periodically whispering into each other's ears like *lovebirds* do, and Richard was scoping out the restaurant for its attributes and defects. From the vantage point of a stranger, we probably looked like a *normal* family, but I could easily see all of our flaws.

After we ordered, Richard directed his attention to Valerie. "So," he said. "When will you graduate?"

"I have two more years," Valerie responded, "then I will have my teaching degree."

"What grade do you plan to teach?"

"I will be qualified to teach K-3."

"Where would you like to teach?" Richard inquired.

Valerie and Rick simultaneously glanced at each other. "I'm not sure, Mr. Malone," she responded. "I suppose that's still up in the air."

From where I was sitting, I could see Rick reach over and squeeze Valerie's hand under the table. She blushed. He smiled.

Richard changed the subject and directed his attention to Brad. "We are so proud of you, son! You've worked hard. I know it wasn't always easy, but you made it. You crossed the finish line. Good job, son!" Richard continued, "When are you coming home. I have a position at Carley's with your name on it."

"You want me to come home so I can bus tables and serve drinks? No thank you, Dad." Brad jutted his chin out defiantly. "I'm going to New York." Brad didn't wait for his father to respond. "One of my professors gave me a few contacts. I'm taking my cameras."

"You're not coming home?" Richard truly sounded wounded.

"I've been telling you for years – I'm not going back to Jersey! I'm not interested in working for you, Dad! I'm not going to be your lap dog. I have plans – I have dreams!"

I could tell Richard was crushed, but he stopped debating with Brad. As if admitting defeat, he finally added, "If you ever want to come home, I'll find a place for you."

"Don't hold your breath, Dad. It's not happening."

3

Brad did not come with us back to New Jersey; instead, he packed his bags and hitched a ride with a friend. They went directly to the Big Apple. Our return trip was quiet – even somber at times. Randy slept most of the way; Rick was lost in thought because he knew he would not see Valerie again for two months, and Rosaline was in her own world.

Instead of listening to music, Richard had the station tuned into the first days of the Watergate Hearings. There was little conversation in the car. Occasionally, Richard made a comment directed at the radio. "What a can of worms this has turned out to be."

There was one diversion during the trip. It occurred as we passed South Hill in Virginia, and it was Rosaline who instigated the conversation.

"I'm working on this extra-credit history project at school. If I do it, I can raise my grade in History to an A."

"History, I love history." Rick, who was sitting in the front seat with Richard, perked up with interest. "What's it about – maybe I can help."

"It's kinda like merging my life with American history." Rosaline was stumbling on her words as if she were hesitant to pursue the subject. "I need to do a timeline."

"Well, that should be fun," Richard commented as he turned the volume down on the radio. "A lot sure has happened in America since you were born."

"Yes," Rosie paused. "But it's not just about the years since I was born. The timeline needs to go back further – it needs to include my parents' lives and my grandparents' lives." She paused to see if her comment would create a reaction.

The conversation in the car fell silent. I was sitting in the middle of the backseat, between a sleeping Randy and a fidgety Rosaline. I glanced at the rearview mirror and saw Richard's blue eyes reflected in it. He was looking directly at me through the mirror. Our optical connection locked for several seconds before he returned his attention to the road. My pulse skipped at least two beats, which caused me to forcibly breathe slower to regain my composure; I felt as if my heart was going to pound right out of my chest. The harder I tried to calm the pulsating rhythm, the faster it raced.

Richard spoke first. "What are the requirements of the project, Sweetheart?" His voice was surprisingly gentle and encouraging.

Rosaline fumbled with her purse and pulled out a small tablet and pen. Her demeanor was more confident. "I need to know birthdays and compare those dates with what happened in America at that time. I need to interview at least one family member from each generation and ask that person what they think about the changes that occurred during their lifetime. Pictures are not mandatory, but the teacher said it would help." Rosaline looked first at me and then at her father before she spoke again. "Every kid in my class has at least one grandparent they can interview, but I've never met any of mine. Can you tell me about them?"

Richard's and my eyes locked again in the rearview mirror. This was a subject my children had never broached – and certainly never when Richard and I were together. *How on earth are we going to answer our daughter's questions? Do I tell her about my mother who died giving birth to me? Do I tell her about my father who was too busy building his fortune, he didn't have time to build a relationship with me. How was I to describe Richard's mother? She was the kindhearted woman who cleaned my house every day until one day she died giving birth to stillborn twins. And Richard's father? How do I describe him? Do I tell Rosaline about the handsome man in the immaculate suit with gold braids on his shoulders who welcomed me with a smile every time I went to the Grand Palace to see a movie or do I tell her about the disheveled individual who stood on his front porch – beer in hand – slurring his words and looking tragically unkempt?*

Richard took command, "Unfortunately, our parents died when we were young."

"Do you remember anything about them?" Rosie asked.

"Yes," Richard replied firmly, but he didn't continue to speak for several moments. "My father was born in 1899."

"Oh, my," Rosie muttered excitedly as she wrote on her tablet. "That is a long time ago – practically the Dark Ages."

Richard's chuckled. He even smiled for a moment, "Yes, I suppose that does seem like a long time ago for you." He glanced in the rearview mirror again and grinned. "You might want to mention in your timeline that my father – your grandfather – fought in the First World War. He was a brave soldier, but he came home early – before the war was over – because he'd lost an arm."

"Oh," Rosie spoke softly as she scribbled words on the paper. Even Rick was on high alert, paying close attention. This was interesting news to both of them. We all sat silently waiting for Richard to continue his story.

"My mother was born in 1905. She and her parents came from Europe via Ellis Island. My mom and dad fell in love when they were young." Again Richard looked in the mirror; he looked more like a teenager at that moment than a grown man –as if reflecting upon the memories of his youth wiped away the small wrinkles on his face and the dusting of gray in his sideburns. "My father and mother were completely committed to each other – even during the Great Depression – my brother and I lived in a house that was so full of love we didn't even realize we were dirt poor." A melancholy expression covered Richard's face.

We all waited for Richard to continue, but he remained silent for so long, Rosie finally asked, "You were poor, Daddy?"

"Yes," Richard replied in a robotic manner. "We were extremely poor."

"What happened to your family?" Rosaline innocently inquired not realizing the sensitive subject she was addressing played havoc with her father's mood.

Richard, as he drove 65-miles-an-hour north on I85, took in a long, labored breath. He whispered the words softly – I wasn't sure anyone else heard them – but I knew what he'd said.

"What, Daddy?" Rosaline asked as she feverishly wrote on her paper.

It was Rick who spoke first. He looked at his father, who was noticeably showing his grief, and then repeated the words for his sister. "They died." Rick continued, "Uncle Calvin died in World War II at the Battle of the Bulge. You should include that in your timeline, Rosie. Your teacher will know exactly when that occurred." Rick returned his gaze to his father and added, "When I was a kid, Dad talked about Uncle Calvin all of the time."

"You remember that?" Richard glanced at his son.

"Of course, I do," Rick replied. "You talked about your brother a lot. And I still have his baseball cards." Rick stared directly at his father. "But you never talked about your parents, Dad. I have a faint memory of going on a long trip in the car – all of us – to meet our grandparents. There was a winding driveway to a big house – and stables with horses in the backyard – we were going to meet your dad," Rick turned around in his seat and stared at me. "Or was it *your* dad we were going to meet?" No one responded to his question. Rick added with a soft voice, "If I remember correctly, we didn't meet anyone. Instead, we turned around and went home. You never talked about it again – until today."

"That wasn't *my* parents' house." Richard muttered. Our eyes connected in the mirror again. The look on his face was no longer youthful. It was forlorn and distant. "My family lived in a small cabin. My mother and father had a hard life. Both died too young. Poverty is an ugly thing."

"How did they die, Daddy?" Rosie innocently inquired. She obviously did not realize she was treading on an emotional tidal wave.

"I think I've done enough talking in this interview." Richard tried to make his voice whimsical, but it definitely had a terse quality to it. "It's your mother's turn to talk." Richard did not look in the rearview mirror; instead, he kept his eyes fixated on the road.

"Mom," Rosie changed gears easily. "When were your parents born?"

"They were born at the end of the 19th century. I don't know very much about my mother. She died when I was," I paused not wanting to tell the truth about her death – I still felt guilt at the thought it was my fault she died, ". . . when I was . . . little." *That wasn't an actual lie – she died on the day I was born – I **was** little.*

"So, you never knew your mom?" Rosie asked.

"No. I didn't."

"But you kept her jewelry and you've given some of it to me."

"It's our legacy." I kept my eyes focused on the road.

"How about your father?" Rosaline inquired as she busily jotted down tidbits of information.

"I never knew him either. He was a busy man." My answers were clipped.

Rosalie instinctively knew she was losing ground on that subject, so she changed directions, "You and Daddy were both born on the same day in 1931. Right?" Rosaline didn't wait for a response; our mutual birthday was one fact our children did know.

Rosaline jotted the date down on her paper before asking, "When did you and Daddy meet?"

I was completely caught off guard by her question; as a result, I remained silent for so long, Richard finally answered the question, "We were six."

"Six?" There was a gleeful intonation in Rosaline's voice. "You were little kids."

Richard and I exchanged another glance in the rearview mirror. I was stiff with apprehension for the next question. It came seconds later.

"When did you and Dad get married?"

"In 1949," I replied quietly hoping she would not ask for the day and time. I noticed my eldest son sitting quietly in the front seat, head cocked slightly to the left as if he were straining to hear every word.

"Isn't that when you graduated from high school?" Rosaline continued to write feverishly on her tablet.

"Yes." I responded but included no additional information.

After Rosie had written the latest personal facts down on the paper, she sat up straight and said, "So, Mom," she paused. "What do *you* think is the most important thing that has happened in America since you were born?"

A sense of total relief flooded over me. I had been afraid we were going to delve into emotional subject matter that was simply too painful to discuss in a car with three of my children and my ex-husband. I could see by the way Richard seemed to relax behind the wheel of the car that he, too, was relieved.

"Wow!" I replied, "Let me think about that for a second." I was taken aback by the entire conversation, and I was having difficulty concentrating on the current question or a viable answer. Finally, I said, "Perhaps . . . landing a man on the moon."

"Oh – that's good, Mom." She frantically wrote on her paper.

As I watched my daughter writing on the notepad, it was difficult to think that she was the same girl Richard and I had taken to the convent a year ago. The despondency was fading. She never talked about it anymore, and Richard said he didn't hear her crying in her room like she had been doing. Every once in a while – I could see fragments of that sweet little girl she had been before Paul Winston.

"Dad? How about you – what is the most important event in your lifetime?"

"There are so many possibilities . . . it's hard to pick one thing. Your mom's is good."

"You have to pick something else, Dad"

"Okay – can you give me a second?" We drove in silence until Richard said confidently, "I think the most important thing was defeating Hitler."

"I thought you might say the television." Rosie giggled.

Richard and I both laughed, which broke a lot of the tension we had been feeling. "No. Not the television," Richard replied jovially. "I remember our dear friend Rosa use to say the television was the devil's playground." After a short pause, he continued with a more somber tone, "Sometimes – looking back – I think she might have been right."

"What do you think would be your parents' answer?" Rosaline inquired as she continued to write down our comments.

Richard didn't even hesitate before responding, "Flight," he said decisively. Then added, "Think of how far we have come since 1903 when the Wright Brothers got that first plane in the air. It lasted twelve seconds and covered 120 feet. Sixty-Six years later, we put a man on the moon. If we can do that in less than seven decades, imagine what life will be like in the next seventy years."

"This is great stuff!" Rosie happily spoke as she continued writing on her tablet. "I'm sure I'll get an A."

4

Summer seemed to drag on forever. I saw Brad twice in the city, but he never ventured out of New York. He was struggling. A career in photography was a little more difficult than he had anticipated, but he was determined to make it. He admitted the money he had gotten as graduation gifts was running low. Each time I saw him, I slipped him a couple of twenty-dollar bills. He tried to push them back in my direction, but it was with a half-hearted attempt. I knew he needed the money; I wished I could have given him more.

Valerie spent a couple of weeks in the beginning of August with Rick. He seemed truly happy when she was with him. The more I got to know Rick's girlfriend, the more I liked her. Valerie was definitely a good "fit" for my eldest son; much better than that other girl. I asked him if he had any *serious plans*. He always smiled, but he never answered me. "I'm not ready to talk about it, Mom. But it's looking good."

During the summer, Rosaline turned into a real beauty. By the first day of her senior year in high school, her hair had grown nearly to her waist. She parted it in the middle like Cher, except Rosie's had a little bit more of a wave to her strands than the popular singer's hairstyle. My daughter had become more skilled with make-up and chose to apply it in a manner that enhanced her features instead of over-exaggerated them. Her bell-bottom jeans were a staple in her wardrobe as were a collection of mini-skirts and empire dresses. Her outfits looked much like most of the girls her age; however, the tops she wore were more demure and flattering than those I saw on her peers. *Thank goodness!*

Richard said boys called on the phone and a few even dropped by the house, but Rosie showed no interest in any of them. She spent the majority of her time with Tony Anderson. According to Richard, he came over to the house four or five times a week throughout the summer. Sometimes they went to the movies, but mostly they sat on the couch and watched TV.

It worried me that Tony Anderson was the only person in Rosie's life. He was a rising junior at Bucknell University in Lewiston, Pennsylvania. *Why was he interested in a high school girl?* I'd be lying if I didn't think about what had happened between Rosaline and Paul Winston; I was apprehensive it could happen again. In fact, I spoke to Rosie about it. Her eyes widened, and she became defensive.

"You don't have to worry about Tony, Mom!" she insisted. "He's not like that!"

"Honey!" I tried to be sympathetic and supportive. "Sometimes boys can't help it."

"Tony is religious," she said defiantly. "He does not believe in *doing it* before marriage." The second she said it, she froze. The expression on Rosaline's face affirmed the fact that Tony was unaware of Rosaline's past. She glanced down at her hands as she muttered, "I haven't told him about Paul, and I've never told him about the baby." Rosaline let out a wounded cry. "Tony is so special, Mom. Remember when Sister Teresa said an earth angel would come to help me – help and guide me to find joy inside of me again? I *know* Tony is my *earth angel*. God sent him to me." A tear formed in her right eye; she wiped it away before adding, "I don't know what I would do without him. I love him. I mean, I *really* love him. It's nothing like the way I felt for Paul. That was so childish and small. Tony is different. And I think he loves me too . . . no . . . I *know* he loves me." She spoke with true certainty, and then her voice wavered. "I don't know if he will be able to forgive me when he finds out that I'm not a virgin like he is . . . or if he ever finds out about the baby." Rosaline fell into my arms. "What will I do, Mom? I don't know what to do. Tell me what to do."

"There may come a day when you have to tell Tony – but until then, enjoy his friendship and his commitment to his faith." I paused as I thought how Richard and I had gone to great lengths in order to limit the number of people who knew about Rosaline's situation last year. By keeping her secret confined to a few individuals, we truly believed we were protecting her from the gossip and the stigma.

"Isn't that the same as lying?" Rosie brushed the tears from her cheeks and rubbed the material of her sleeve across her nose.

"Has he actually asked you?" I inquired.

"No," Rosaline replied. "When Tony talks about his celibacy, I listen, but I never say anything."

"Then you aren't lying to him," I stated firmly. "However, if he ever point blank asks you," I looked my daughter in the eye before continuing, "then you must tell him the truth, because if you don't . . . then you *are* lying, and lies will eventually catch up with you." I held my daughter for a full minute before adding, "If you ever think your relationship with Tony is evolving into something more," I searched for the correct word, "something more *physical,* and you think you are tempted," I paused again. "Come to me first, Rosaline. I can take you to the doctors. There are pills girls can take . . ."

"Mom! Stop!" Rosaline was adamant. "You don't understand. Tony doesn't believe in all of this *free love* stuff. He believes a person should wait until the wedding night. He is not going to push me into anything. I *know* it!"

Wedding night? Has this young fellow been talking about marriage with my daughter? Rosaline is entirely too young for that discussion. "Why don't you give your relationship time to grow?" I paused recognizing the subject was sensitive. "Why don't you wait and see how you both feel about each other in a few months. You have your senior year ahead of you. While he is away at college, why don't you start concentrating on which colleges you want to apply to for next year?"

"I don't know if I want to go to college, Mom."

"Of course, you want to go to college. Your brothers loved college life, and it's more than memorizing what's in the textbooks. It's learning about life – gaining independence. There are so many wonderful colleges in North Carolina and Virginia. We can go on a trip and you can visit as many of them as you want."

"If I do decide to go to college, Mom, I'm not going south. I'll go someplace in Pennsylvania. I want to be close to Tony."

"You shouldn't apply to a college because of a boy." I tried to be as gentle as I could with my coaxing. "You don't know how your relationship will be a year from now." I stopped belaboring the subject because – I knew from one glance at my daughter's expression – she had already tuned me out.

5

I spent the entire day in Manhattan's Garment Center picking clothing for Bamberger's spring collection of Ladies' Apparel. I loved my job. This was my fourth season in this position; as a result, I felt comfortable in it. For the first two seasons after my promotion, I'd lived in fear I would make a multi-million dollar mistake for the store. Constant butterflies tied my stomach up in knots. It was exhilarating and terrifying at the same time. To my delight, I had an innate intuition when it came to foreseeing fashion trends. Over the years, I'd spent a lot of time watching the women while they shopped, analyzing what girls wore in Rosaline's school and observing the co-eds at Elon when I visited my sons. As I accumulated the images in my mind, I developed a sixth sense for what was coming in and going out of style.

I advocated for the sale of trousers for women even before I got the promotion to buyer. My boss thought I was insane to suggest it because women wore dresses – not pants. In his mind's eye, there was the "housedress" for cleaning and cooking and the "nice" dress for all other occasions. The mature woman might have a pair of jeans for gardening or capris for the hot summer months, but *trousers*? He was convinced pants would never sell. I stood my ground and reminded him that First Lady Pat Nixon had been seen in public wearing pants. She was the *first* first lady to dress in such a manner – she set the stage. In addition, I argued that with the passage of Title IX of the Education Amendments of 1972, girls were no longer forced to wear dresses – they had a choice.

I could see the trend before it became fashionable and felt validated the first time I saw the *Charlie* ad by Revlon perfume in a magazine. The model wore pants – and she looked professional, sexy and confident. Our stores sold racks and racks of pants – flared, bell-bottom, hip-huggers, cuffed and no cuffs, plaid and solid colors – the variety was enormous. The trend was on my radar before women even realized they wanted to buy them. It was a "feather in my cap" at the office. To my delight, the men began to look at me for my opinion and advice.

Dresses were equally as popular. The mini length was still the fashion, but now there were additional choices: the midi and the maxi. Even women in their forties and fifties were sewing their hemlines up several inches above the knees while the younger girls were donning the midi and maxi length. I didn't put a lot of stock into the midi. In my opinion, it wasn't flattering on women unless they were stick-thin like Twiggy. I was fairly certain the average woman would not buy into the trend; consequently, it was not high on my priority list.

Halter tops, bodysuits, platform shoes and the "wet look" boots were a must in every female's wardrobe. But the biggest seller was the pantsuit. Be it jacket and trousers or tunic and trousers – it mattered not – the pantsuit was the best seller. Working women, who had finally earned the right to wear pants in the workplace, jammed their closets with the merchandise.

After a long day of making fashion decisions, I tried to reach Brad. I hoped to see my son during my business trip into the city. Unfortunately, he was working at the one job that gave him a consistent paycheck: dishwasher at a restaurant near his apartment. He earned minimum wage; thankfully, a buck sixty an hour was putting a little money in his pocket.

I was disappointed we couldn't get together. Truth be told, I wanted an excuse *not* to go home to an empty apartment.

I knew John and Randy were not home. They were on a Boy Scout camping trip in Sharpsburg, Maryland where the Civil War Battle of Antietam had been fought 111 years ago. Randy loved that number: 111. My son was infatuated by the triple digits because he had recently turned 11 and there were 11 members in his Boy Scout Troop, all of whom were also 11. John planned the entire trip for the boys in hopes of teaching them camping skills while also blending a little history into the adventure. To his chagrin, Randy seemed more mesmerized by the irony of the number 111 on his 11th year and his 11-member troop than the fact the Battle of Antietam was considered by historians to be the bloodiest single-day battle in American military history.

As I walked to the subway, I was surrounded by a despondent aura. I had my job. I had a few acquaintances at work. And I had my children – all of whom were busy with their own lives. John and I were still officially married, but we weren't even friends, much less husband and wife. I was virtually alone. I felt empty inside. Not one friend I could call. Rosa . . . Lucy . . . Joyce . . . they were all gone. I felt like I did as a child – sitting alone in my room in that massive house – a building full of servants – but no one to talk to – no one to confide in – no one who might care or even listen and pretend to care. *No one.* I was all alone.

In order to avoid going home to the lonely apartment, I elected to go into a movie theater. It was an early release preview of a Robert Redford and Barbra Streisand movie: *The Way We Were.* The film was scheduled to be officially released in October.

If I had had previous knowledge of the storyline, I would never have chosen to see the film. From beginning to end – it tore at my heart. In the final scene, when Barbra Streisand put her gloved hand on the back of Robert Redford's neck and her fingers ran through his blond hair, tears welled up in my eyes. My personal memories collided with Hollywood's latest romantic tearjerker. The tune alone – without the words – was haunting and heart-wrenching enough, but with the lyrics and Streisand's incredible voice, I could barely breathe and I certainly could not contain my emotions – it hurt too much. Through my tears, all I could see was Richard's face . . . the years and years of wonderful memories. For some reason – at that moment – I could not conjure up even one bad memory during our marriage – only the good ones.

What happened to us? How . . . Where . . . When did we go wrong?

Even though I knew it was in my imagination, I believed I could see fragments of our lives flashing across the movie screen: Richard holding our first child in his arms – looking up at me with a beautiful and doting expression on his face. Richard dancing around the room to one of Frank Sinatra's songs and pulling me into his arms so I could dance with him. Richard making love to me under a tree on that glorious night when Brad was conceived. Richard holding me in his arms by the fireplace in Rosa's house – a room full of friends watching television and laughing. Richard and I – in bed – curled up in each other's arms. Richard and

I – sailing on the river – savoring each other's company on a gorgeous summer day. I felt so safe – I felt so wanted.

If I asked him for a second chance . . . would Richard give it to me?

When I finally dried my eyes, I noticed everyone in the theater was gone. The room was empty – I was alone.

10

Richard

I got home from work shortly after 8:00 on Tuesday. Rosaline was sitting on the couch watching *Happy Days* – a TV dinner on the coffee table. At quick glance, I estimated two or three bites had been eaten. It looked cold. She didn't even acknowledge my arrival. I walked across the room with an armload of groceries. As I put them on the counter, I glanced at my daughter then turned my attention to the mail on the counter. Flipping through it, I spotted the phone bill. After ripping it opened, I saw the amount and gasped in shock. This was the highest one yet. Rosaline and Tony's long distant phone calls were going to bankrupt me. I counted the number of calls: twenty-three in one month. *Twenty-three!* And he'd been home a couple of times during the last four weeks. *Twenty-three times!* I looked at the length of the calls. Not one of them was less than ten minutes; the longest was over an hour. *Holy Crap!*

"I thought I had made myself clear last month, Rosaline." I was using great restraint to keep from screaming. "You are supposed to limit your phone calls to once a week and less than fifteen minutes." I waved the phone bill in my hand. "This is ridiculous! For God's sake, Rosie, can't you use a pen and paper – write him a letter?"

I received no reaction from my daughter; in fact, she didn't even look in my direction. She simply continued staring blankly at the television set as Fonzie and Richie generated another round of laughter with their antics. Rosaline didn't even chuckle.

It wasn't until I put all of the food in the fridge and threw the bags away that I noticed the letter next to the stove. It was addressed to Rosaline Malone – from the Admission's Office at Bucknell University. I glanced at the short paragraphs and understood the woeful expression on my daughter's face; it was *not* an acceptance letter.

I walked to the couch and sat beside my daughter. "I'm sorry, Rosie." She looked at me and immediately collapsed into tears. I wrapped my arms around her quaking body and tried my best to comfort her. When her sobs stopped, I spoke, "This is not the end of the world, Honey. There are other colleges . . . in fact, you've already been accepted to York College and Lafayette and Gettysburg College. Those are three good choices."

"But Tony's at Bucknell." Rosie wiped her tears with the sleeve of her blouse. "If I can't be with Tony, then I won't go to college."

"Please don't be rash, Rosaline. This is all going to work out."

"Why do I have to go to college? I don't care about college!"

"It's an opportunity most kids dream about and never get to do. Your mother and I didn't get to go to college. Mom wants *you* to have the benefit she never had."

"Then why doesn't Mom go to college and let me live my own life?"

It took most of the spring to convince Rosaline that college was her best option for the future. Thankfully, Tony was of the same opinion and convinced her to pick a school. In the beginning of May, she decided on York College of Pennsylvania – a co-ed, private college with a beautiful campus. Neither the size of the school nor the majors it had to offer were primary reasons for making her decision; instead, my daughter picked it solely because – of the three colleges – York was the closest to Lewistown and Tony's campus. Her reasons didn't matter. Caroline and I were elated our daughter had finally committed to a college.

2

I had a staff meeting the Monday before Rosaline graduated from high school. After the other employees left, I motioned Rick to stay. He had moved out of my house and was living in a one-bedroom apartment a few blocks from the restaurant in Morristown; consequently, I didn't see him nearly as much as when we lived under the same roof. I had tried to convince Rick to stay with me – after all – there was plenty of room – but my son wanted his own place. He liked the short commute to his job, but – even more – I think he wanted the privacy when Valerie came to visit him. I couldn't blame him. After all, they were in love.

Rick claimed the rent on his apartment was low, which allowed him to bank a good portion of his salary. He was saving for a diamond ring and a down payment on a house. Valerie had one more year of college to complete. The two of them had a concrete plan.

"Have a seat, son." I motioned to the chair. It's been ages since we've talked. "I want to touch base – see how you are doing."

"Everything's great, Dad. My people are running like a well-oiled machine."

"I knew I could cut you loose and you'd sail through the job. I'm proud of you, Rick. I always knew you could handle the restaurant all by yourself. You're a good manager – great leadership skills, son. Your employees *want* to please you and do their best. That's the mark of a good boss."

"Thanks, Dad."

"I was wondering," I paused. It always felt awkward to broach the subject. "Have you heard from Brad?"

"Yeah, occasionally we talk."

"Is he doing okay?" I asked. It had been a year since Brad had graduated, and I hadn't seen him one time since his milestone – not even at Christmas. Brad had gone to Caroline's apartment for the holiday, but didn't bother to stop by my house for even a minute. "I was wondering; do you know if Brad is coming home for Rosaline's graduation?"

"Sure. He'll be there."

"Your brother has been in New York for a year. Has he been able to make any money with his cameras?"

"He's struggling, Dad. It's not as easy as he thought it would be."

"Nothing ever is." I tried to make light of a conversation that seemed awkward for both of us. "Do you think he might come back to Jersey?"

"I don't know, Dad. He's pretty determined to stay in the city."

"Rick," I spoke slowly. "I am so grateful and happy you are with me. You have a head for this business. You are detail oriented – you understand numbers and how to make a profit. You are a great manager. I'm proud of you, son. But if Brad could join us . . . he is the one with the creative mind. He has vision and imagination. He can see beyond the bricks and mortar of a building. We need Brad to keep this business fresh. The three of us would make such a fantastic team." I used a persuasive tone in my voice. "When Brad comes for Rosie's graduation . . . try to talk to him. Try to convince him to come home. I know in my heart that he belongs here – with us."

"Sure, Dad," Rick replied. "I'll do what I can."

Three days later, I watched my baby girl receive her diploma. The bleachers were packed; as a result, the proud spectators were jammed shoulder to shoulder in the stands. I was sitting between Rick and Tony. His parents were behind me. Caroline, Brad and Randy were four rows down and over twenty feet to my left. *Where was John?* Periodically I saw Caroline glance in my direction, but she never made a move toward me. As for Brad, he managed to avoid me during the entire day.

Why did he hate me so much?

3

Thursday morning on August 8th, Rick left for a long weekend to visit Valerie in Winston-Salem. He had the engagement ring in his pocket. That evening, I sat alone in my family room in front of the television waiting for a summer rerun of *Ironside* when the show was preempted by President Nixon. He was speaking from the Oval Office.

Reading the words directly from several sheets of 8 X 10 white paper, President Nixon addressed the nation with a somber face and a stoic voice. I leaned forward on the couch and turned all of my attention to his speech. It had been a grueling couple of years for Nixon. The Watergate scandal had taken a toll on his presidency.

During the first few sentences of Nixon's speech, Rosaline and Tony came into the room and sat on the couch next to me. Neither spoke. We were glued to the television set.

"I have never been a quitter." President Nixon said: his voice devoid of any passion. "To leave office before my term is completed is abhorrent to every instinct in my body. But as President, I must put the interest of America first. America needs a full-time President and a full-time Congress, particularly at this time with problems we face at home and abroad."

Oh My God! I mouthed the words more to myself than to Tony or Rosaline. *He's going to resign! He's actually going to do it.*

"Therefore, I shall resign the Presidency effective at noon tomorrow. Vice President Ford will be sworn in as President at that hour in this office."

The phone rang in the middle of Nixon's sentence. At first I ignored it, but then it became too annoying; therefore, I picked it up in order to stop the irritating sound. I suspected it was someone who wanted to talk about what the nation was watching on TV; however, the person on the other end of the line surprised me. It was Rick. He was apparently unaware of the historical event taking place on the television. His voice was filled with exhilaration. Rick and Valerie were both talking at the same time. I could picture their faces cheek to cheek as they spoke simultaneously into the phone.

"I asked her, Dad," Rick spoke gleefully, "and she said 'yes'."

"We're getting married!" The excited couple screamed in unison. The energy they generated could be felt through the phone line.

11

Caroline

Rosaline and I were walking the aisles of the toy store searching for the perfect Christmas gift for Randy. I waffled between a regulation-size football and a new bike. I was fairly certain the Schwinn Stingray was going to win the debate, which meant I had to decide between flamboyant red and school-bus yellow. But I wanted to give Randy the football too. At twelve, he was showing quite an interest in the sport. According to John, he was a talented receiver.

I was proud of the success I was having at my new position at Bamberger's and thrilled the raise in my salary finally gave me the flexibility to pick either present – I was no longer limited to *one* choice. Maybe – I thought to myself – *this* Christmas – I might buy both of them. Perhaps *this* year, I could pile numerous presents under the tree.

"What do you think about inviting your father to Christmas dinner?" I asked nonchalantly as I inspected the spokes on the bike. To my surprise – as I waited for my daughter's response – I felt as if butterflies were doing the quickstep in my stomach. I was apprehensive about her answer. I'd been thinking about including Richard at our table for two reasons. John had already told me he did not plan to be home for Christmas dinner. After presents in the morning, he was going to go to Nancy's place. I was still trying to figure out how I was going to explain *that* to the children. My second reason for inviting Richard concerned Brad. Richard and Brad had not spoken to each other in well over a year. I thought it was time they mended their fences.

Truth be told – there was a third reason. *I wanted Richard to join us.* I had not seen Richard in months. Once Rosie left for York College last summer, there wasn't any reason for Richard and me to connect. To my surprise . . . *I missed him.*

"Normally," Rosaline replied. "I would say . . . 'great idea, Mom.' I always feel badly for Dad. He's home alone, and by the time we get back in the evening, I can tell he's in a bad mood. I think Dad hates

Christmas." Rosie paused as she, too, examined the bike. "I honestly think Dad would have liked a dinner invitation; however, I don't think he can come this year. He told me yesterday that he is going to a movie with Sandy. They are going to see *Godfather II*. It came out this week, and Dad is psyched about seeing it."

"Who's Sandy?" I inquired. I didn't realize Richard had a new girlfriend.

"Dad's dated her a few times." Rosie left the subject hanging in the air.

"Really?" My curiosity was running rampant, but my voice remained casual. "I suppose your father is dating another one of his young waitresses."

"No," Rosie responded. "Sandy doesn't work at the restaurant. I think she is a secretary in a law office. And she's not young. She looks more like your age."

I felt two stabs in my heart. One because Richard was involved with a woman *again* and . . . two . . . because Rosie said . . . *not young* . . . *more like your age* . . . which was another way of saying . . . *old.* My goodness, I was in my early forties . . . *is that old?*

"Well," I muttered more to myself as I picked through the merchandise. "Glad to hear your father won't be alone for the holidays."

Rosie glanced at me in an inquisitive manner but she didn't respond. I let the subject drop. "So," I said with a little enthusiasm in my voice. "Would Tony like to join us for dinner?"

"Tony and I are going to church on Christmas Eve, and he will go again with his parents on Christmas Day, but I think he would love an invitation for dinner. What time?"

"The usual," I replied. "Around 5:00."

"Perfect," she responded. "I'll ask him and let you know. Thanks, Mom!"

"So – what are you getting Tony for Christmas?"

"I got him *Pretzel Logic*." Rosaline responded with glee.

"What's that?" I was truly mystified.

"It's the Steely Dan album. Tony is crazy about them."

I *almost* asked *who or what is* Steely Dan? But I did not want to show my naiveté; I let the subject drop. After deciding to purchase the red bike, I began to wheel it down the aisle. Rosaline still had the football in her arms. I didn't tell her to put the pigskin back on the shelf because I intended by buy both gifts. It felt wonderful to know that I could afford it.

As my daughter and I walked toward the cash register, I addressed what I knew was going to be a sensitive subject. "About your first semester grades," I stated. Richard had told me they'd come in the mail: one B, three Cs, and one D. They weren't good; in fact, Rosaline was bordering on Academic Probation.

"Mom," Rosie's voice was strong. "None of those courses interest me. I've told you over and over again; I don't care about going to college."

"Are you trying to fail?" I didn't mean it, but there was a sting in my voice.

"Of course not," she replied. "But you know school has never been easy for me."

"I really want this for you, Rosaline. It's imperative to get an education. It will matter in your future. A good education will help you get a good job."

"Mom," she debated. "I've never been good at school. It's always been a struggle for me. Dad has said many times that I can work at one of the restaurants. He'll train me with the books. I'm decent with numbers."

"Then why don't you take a couple of business courses?"

"My student advisor said I have to take my core courses first."

"Do the best you can, Honey. Trust me. It's important. In the long run, you will be glad you did." I sounded patronizing.

"Okay, Mom." Rosie was exasperated. "Can we drop it? It's nice to be home. I don't want to think about school, and I don't want to fight with you."

2

Christmas Day was totally monopolized by Rosaline. Rick was in Winston-Salem with Valerie. They were spending the Holidays together and cementing the plans for their wedding next fall. Brad was in a solemn mood and unwilling to talk about anything. He spent the majority of the day sitting in the recliner and staring at the TV. I threatened to turn the set off, but decided not to after seeing the leer on his face whenever I approached the television. Randy spent most of the afternoon riding his new bike around the neighborhood, and John's absence didn't even inspire questions from the kids.

All things considered . . . it was definitely Rosaline's day.

Tony had surprised her with an engagement ring on Christmas Eve, and they were both walking on clouds. Rosie kept talking about a small May or June wedding – after Tony's graduation. I bit my tongue to refrain from speaking. Tony noticed my lack of enthusiasm about picking a date and did not contribute to any conversation regarding the subject.

I spent ninety percent of my time in the kitchen avoiding conversation with everyone in my family.

All-in-all, it was not my favorite Christmas.

12

Richard

"**D**addy," Rosaline said. "Please talk to Mom about letting me get married *this* summer. If anyone can talk her into it – you can!" There was not a hint of childish whine in her voice – only determination. "I promise to finish my spring semester as planned – but once Tony graduates in May, we want to get married."

"I don't know, Rosie," I replied as we sat at the kitchen counter eating the pizza I'd ordered from Dominos. "Your mother can be stubborn when it comes to *your* education."

"Good point, Dad!" she bellowed. Her blue eyes flashing with frustration, she continued to speak. "It's not *her* education; it's *my* education. A college degree is *her* dream; not *my* dream."

"Your mom's right, Sweetheart," I added. "With a degree, more doors will open for you."

"I don't need any doors to open. I don't want a career. Tony and I plan to have a family. We are both emphatic – I'll work for a while – maybe in an office. I can type seventy-five words a minute – I ought to be able to get a job somewhere with that skill alone. Then – once we have kids – I am going to stay home with them."

I put my pizza down on the paper plate, wiped my face with my napkin and took a deep breath before inquiring, "Did you ever talk to Tony?" I didn't need to add anything else to my initial question; my daughter knew exactly what I was asking.

"Yes, Dad. I told him about the baby last summer."

"And?"

"It was pretty bad. For a while, I was afraid Tony was going to break up with me. He said it was probably a good thing Paul Winston died in that car accident, because he would have killed Paul himself. I'd never seen Tony so mad; he is normally kind and strong and reliable. Like a pillar! But after I told him, he yelled . . . and he cried … and then he prayed. He asked if he could talk to his pastor about me, and I said he could. Tony told me that his preacher helped him see what happened in our past can be left in our past." Rosie paused long enough to look directly at me. There was an unwavering confidence in her expression. "Tony told me the only future he wants – is a future with me in it." She smiled. "Daddy, Tony loves *me* – even with my mistakes. He knows all about it – and he loves me anyway."

Tony Anderson was earning more and more of my respect every day. I was enormously impressed when he came to me last December and asked for my daughter's hand in marriage. It was becoming increasingly more apparent – each time I saw them together – Tony was totally committed to Rosaline. I smiled at her. "I will talk to your mom. No promises. But I will try."

"Daddy?" she said in an inquisitive way. "Can I ask you a question?"

"Anything, Sweetheart."

"It doesn't take a rocket scientist, Dad," Rosie looked directly into my eyes. "I can do the math. You got married because Mom was pregnant with Rick."

My spine stiffened. "I know you think you're a grown up, Rosie, because you're out of high school and you're engaged." Irritation was evident in my voice, "but you're on sensitive ground here, and I don't think we should be talking about this."

"Daddy," she interrupted. "With what happened in *my* life, how can you think I will sit in judgment of *your* choices?" Rosie sighed. "Daddy, not one day goes by that I don't think about my baby. I wonder what he is doing." There was a vulnerable yet mature tone to my daughter's voice. "If I saw him, would I recognize him? What's his name? Where is he? What is he doing?" She bowed her head ever so slightly and whispered, "He will haunt me for the rest of my life." Rosie closed her eyes for several seconds – then they fluttered opened again. "I pray God will forgive me – and I hope – someday, I can forgive myself." She paused. "You and Mom had Rick when you were kids. You stayed together long enough to have Brad and me too. You must have been happy for a little while."

Holy crap! I picked up my pizza and gnawed on it. Didn't matter how many times I chewed, I couldn't taste a thing. Rosaline continued to stare at me. *Why did my daughter look like a little girl and a grown woman at the same time?*

"When you got married, did you love Mom?"

Now that was a question I could answer!

"Yes," I replied. "Very much."

"Why did you and Mom get a divorce?"

I rubbed my forehead. *Nuts!* When I had said she could ask me *anything* . . . I wasn't expecting *these* questions. I didn't want nor did I know how to answer them. One thing was certain; I wasn't going to tell my daughter I'd caught her mother in bed with another man. That information wouldn't be good for anyone. In addition, I'd come to realize a long time ago . . . infidelity had not been the reason our marriage imploded – but it was the final straw that broke the camel's back.

Rosaline kept staring at me in silence waiting for my answer.

"Your mother thought the grass was greener on the other side of the fence." I wasn't thinking about my comment – the words simply flowed from my mouth. "I tried to make her happy, but her definition of happiness was different than mine." I spoke slowly. "When your mom was young, she had dreams – big dreams. She was never happy staying at home. She was restless and – I suppose – unfulfilled." I paused long enough to take in a deep breath. "I didn't see it at the time. I was too busy trying to keep a roof over our heads to notice that your mother was questioning *what else is out there. What am I missing?*" I didn't look at my daughter as I spoke. Instead, I stared directly in front of me and focused on the half empty Pepsi bottle on the counter next to the refrigerator. I was mesmerized by it. "Your mother keeps searching for something magical in jobs, in political campaigns and crazy woman's organizations. In my opinion – I don't think she can find the answers there."

Again, I paused. My daughter did not contribute to the conversation; as a result, I continued. "Your mom and I are living in a generation that really shook the trees and rattled the cages of the traditional family. She wanted to have a career in a time when women didn't have careers. Caroline wasn't content staying home. It's difficult to see and accept the way people's roles in life are changing – right before our eyes." My shoulders slumped as I continued, "I was guilty of not supporting her – of keeping her in the stereotype role I wanted her to be in. I loved my life – I loved what we had . . ." I inhaled slowly before continuing, ". . . but she didn't. If I had it to do over again – I'd try harder. Maybe if I had tried harder . . ." I was whispering the words, and didn't realize until Rosie wiped my cheek with her napkin that a single tear was rolling down my face. I was embarrassed. After clearing my throat, I stood up and left the room.

A few minutes later, I returned. My daughter enveloped me in her arms, "I'm sorry, Daddy," she said as she squeezed me tightly.

I returned her embrace. Not quite confident of my voice, I remained silent for a few moments. Finally, I commented, "I'll talk to your mother about a June wedding – but I'm not making any promises."

"Thank you, Daddy." She kissed me on the cheek. "I love you."

"I love you, too, Baby." I whispered as I made a note to call Caroline tomorrow; however, tonight, I was going to call Sandy. I needed to get laid, and I could count on Sandy to take my mind off of today's conversation with my daughter.

13

Caroline

There was no doubt about it – 1975 was going to be an eventful year: two graduations and two weddings. I had to merge them all into my incredibly busy work schedule, plus juggle Randy's sporting events. No doubt about it – the year was going to be a roller coaster ride.

Richard spent the better part of the winter convincing me that our daughter should be allowed to make her own decisions. He was an obvious ally for Rosaline, who wanted to quit college and get married after Tony's graduation in the spring. We had several heated arguments.

In our first dispute, Richard approached me at my apartment – unexpectedly – and he caught me by surprise. Initially, he sounded like a diplomat and spoke with a neutral, rational voice, but before the evening was over, we were in a screaming match. I empathically stated, "Rosaline *must* finish college. I want *more* for my daughter. I want her to have options and to do better than I have done – dream bigger than I did."

Richard's frustration showed in his voice as he fought back by saying, "Maybe she doesn't want what *you* want. Maybe Rosaline sees that you had it all but you lost it because you threw it away looking for something better." Richard's caustic tone had a cynical element to it as he challenged me with his biting words and his mordant expression. "Did you ever find it?" His question hung in the air.

Neither of us spoke; however, our eyes were screaming volumes about our combative emotions. It was obvious Richard was deliberately trying to control his breathing and regain his composure. I, too, was battling built up tension.

I had no response. His conversation felt more like a direct interrogation of my life instead of an allegiance to our daughter's. Tears sprang to my eyes, and my voice escaped me. I felt as if I had lost the battle, but I was determined not to lose the war.

Richard verbally attacked me on more than one occasion. The

second round occurred a few weeks later at his office when I showed up unannounced. I had all of my reasons in order and felt confident because I had memorized them well enough to make my point. I initiated the debate by offering a compromise. "Perhaps Rosaline can get an Associate's Degree. That will take one more year."

Richard was busy with his monthly paperwork. Irritated by the fact I had interrupted his hectic schedule, he went back to repeating his typical argument in hopes I would concede so he could get back to his business. "You cannot make your children live *your* dreams, Caroline!" He was dismissive in the way he spoke.

I fired back – using his argument against him. "Isn't that what you have always done to Brad? You've always demanded he work in *your* restaurants when he wanted to go after *his dreams* of a career in photography. What makes *you* right and *me* wrong?"

Richard paused a long time before answering, "Touché."

The room fell silent. Neither of us spoke for a full minute. Instead, our eyes connected, and we communicated through them. Richard seemed to relax slightly. His shoulders no longer held the stubborn stiffness they had seconds ago. Even his incredible blue eyes stopped flashing those angry darts and began to sparkle as they often did when he was lost in thought. The right corner of his mouth cocked upward, and a dimple appeared on his cheek. The tiny lines around his eyes softened and were no longer visible. As Richard relaxed, so did I. I could feel the blood begin to flow more evenly throughout my body and the tightening in my chest, which had been steadily intensifying to the point of pain, gradually decreased. Both of us began to breathe more calmly.

We held each other's attention until the phone rang. When Richard picked up the receiver, our intangible link was broken. "I have to take this call, Caroline." He covered the mouthpiece. "Can we talk about this later?"

The next time Richard broached the subject, he was composed. So was I. There was no rage in our sentences and no fire in our debate. In the end, it was Richard who swayed me with his objective and insightful words. "We cannot live our children's lives for them, Caroline. We can listen to them – support them – love them, but ultimately they are the ones who have to live with the choices they make."

It was an extremely difficult transition for me, but I eventually bent to my daughter's will and gave her my blessing. She had her father to thank for that!

2

Once I decided to support Rosaline and Tony's decision to get married, the new discussion became *who, what, where, when and how*. Rosaline picked the date for *when* the wedding would occur: May 17th. Tony's graduation was scheduled on May 10th, and his job at the DA's office in Harrisburg, Pennsylvania, started on May 21st. Rosaline insisted on sandwiching the wedding between the two dates so they would have at least a couple of days for a honeymoon.

The groom chose *who* and *where*; there was no debate as far as Tony was concerned. The pastor at his church was going to perform the ceremony. *Where* was not an issue either. Richard and I were thrilled Tony and Rosaline wanted to say their vows in a church instead of on a hilltop surrounded by a meadow of flowers and singing birds like so many of the young people of their generation.

When the subject first came up, Tony made his plea to both sets of parents by saying, "I know there is a wave of people who believe in the *God is Dead* movement; but Rosaline and I do not buy into that philosophy." Tony took the time to reach for Rosaline's hand before he continued. "Rosie and I are firmly committed to our faith. We want the church to be our foundation, and we want to pledge before God that we are going to spend a lifetime together."

Richard leaned over and whispered in my ear, "I like this fellow more and more every day." We smiled at each other.

The *what* and *how* of the festivities fell on Richard and me. Rosaline and Tony wanted complete control of the simple ceremony at the church; however, I insisted on planning the wedding reception. I had never had the chance to have my own wedding – or should I rephrase and say – weddings – however, I had one daughter and I wanted to pour my ideas into her celebration.

Richard concurred by saying, "You and Tony plan the wedding ceremony, but the reception is *our* party to celebrate and honor *you*. All you have to do is show up." Richard winked at Rosaline as he blew her an intangible kiss. "We will host it at Carley's Place. I'll close it down for the day. The whole place will be all yours." Richard glanced at the bride and groom and added, "You can choose the music – I know how you young people love your Rock 'n Roll, but let your mother and me take care of everything else." Richard, once again, leaned over in my direction. With our shoulders touching, he whispered in my ear. "You plan it, Caroline, and I'll pay for it."

I automatically stiffened at the thought of him – once again – making me feel inferior when it came to finances. My temper flared, "Why do . . ."

Richard blocked my retort by saying, "She's *our* daughter, Caroline. Let's spoil her together without any of our negative baggage." He patted my knee in a condescending manner before dropping the subject.

During Rosaline's spring break, we went shopping for her wedding gown. I had anticipated it would be a time-consuming ordeal that would monopolize most of the week as we traveled to malls, perhaps all over the tri-state region in search of the perfect dress; but I was wrong. We began our quest in Conshohocken, Pennsylvania, at a lovely David's Bridal Shop. One of the many benefits of being a buyer for Ladies' Apparel was having first-hand knowledge of fashion and where to go for it. The boutique was out of our way, but well worth the trip.

Between the two of us, we collected twenty dresses off of the rack and carried them to the fitting room. Most of the gowns looked lovely on Rosaline, but dress after dress was tossed aside for one reason or another. The second to the last dress created magic. I knew before the zipper was pulled up and the buttons were done – we had found the perfect wedding gown. I didn't say a word. I simply sat back and watched as Rosaline looked at her reflection in the mirror. She was beautiful. Even though her hair was not styled . . . even though she wore no make-up or jewelry . . . even without stockings and shoes . . . I knew we'd found *the dress*! She looked like a fairy princess. It was as if the gown was designed solely for her.

Rosaline knew it, too. My daughter didn't say, "This is the one." Nor did she say, "Can we buy this one?" Rosaline simply looked at me and said, "You know it, too, don't you, Mom?"

I replied, "You look gorgeous."

"Why are you crying, Mom?"

It was true. I had huge tears in my eyes. It was a nostalgic moment. I couldn't believe my baby girl was standing in front of me looking like this incredibly beautiful young woman.

Where did all of the years go?

As I wiped my eyes, I chuckled. "I'm not sad. These are joyful tears." I wrapped my arms around Rosaline. "I'm so happy for you, sweet baby girl. I am happy for you."

"You're not mad at me anymore, Mom?" Rosie clutched me in her arms.

"Oh, Honey," I replied. "I was never mad at you. Perhaps I had a different vision for your life, but I was never mad." I tightened my arms around her. "And I understand now."

"I know I belong with Tony." Rosaline spoke confidently. "I know in my heart we will have a wonderful life together. He already has a job, and I'll get a salaried position in an office – it won't be difficult. I took shorthand and typing in high school, and I'm good at it. We're going to save for a house; then, we'll have a family. It's a great plan for us, Mom." She paused before continuing, "I don't want – no – I don't *need* to have a career to make me feel whole. That has never been important to me." Rosaline grinned slightly. "I don't want to change the world like you do, Mom." She pulled away so we could look directly into each other's eyes. "I'm proud of you for what you have done with *your* life, Mom. It's amazing. *You're* amazing!" She paused long enough to reward me with a gentle smile. "But it's not what I want for *me*. Those are *your* dreams." Rosaline's voice was firm but gentle. "*Your* dreams are not *my* dreams. I know I can and will be happy being Tony's wife – being a mother – staying home – taking care of my family. *That* is my dream."

Rosaline and I stood next to each other – wrapped in each other's arms – staring into the mirror. I had never been more proud of my little girl.

3

What a dilemma! Both our future daughter-in-law and our future son-in-law had their college graduations scheduled on the same day in May; as a result, Richard traveled to Elon with Rick to see Valerie get her diploma, while Brad, Rosaline and I drove to Lewistown to watch Tony walk across the stage in his cap and gown. It was difficult to be divided during such momentous occasions, but we all took dozens of pictures so we could share the memories with each other.

After Tony's ceremony, Rosaline road home with him while Brad rode with me. During the trip, Brad did most of the talking. He divulged the fact that he was disappointed with his ability to break into the photography field, and he was feeling less and less optimistic about making a career out of his passion. When he'd first arrived in New York two years ago, he'd gotten a position taking baby pictures for a diaper service. It required cold calling, and he was paid on commission. Unfortunately, the diaper company was on the verge of bankruptcy. It was struggling because disposable diapers were flooding the market. After all, what mother wanted a pail of soiled cotton cloths in her house when she could use a diaper once and throw it in the trash?

In a frustrated voice, Brad admitted he couldn't even get a contract to take pictures for store catalogs, much less get a job on a magazine or newspaper. His options were drying up and there was no money coming in. Brad's depression was evident as he spoke of his struggles to pay his bills. When I offered to give him money, Brad said, "A few extra bucks won't solve the problem, Mom." In a defeated voice he added, "I don't think I'm going to make it in New York."

"If there is anything I can do, Brad," I glanced in his direction. "All you have to do is ask."

"Thanks, Mom. Thanks for listening." He grinned half-heartedly. "Don't worry. I'll be okay."

4

A week later, the family came together for the first wedding of the year. The ceremony was simple but tastefully sophisticated. There were seventy-five guests in the pews of St. George's Church. Several of them were friends of the bride and groom from their respective colleges. Two dozen relatives from Tony's side of the family packed the groom's side; however, no extended family member filled our side of the chapel. A few of the couples in our neighborhood were invited and two of Tony and Rosaline's high school teachers were also included. All of the rest of the guests were business associates of Richard's and co-workers of mine.

The wedding party was small. Tony's sister Joanie and Rick's fiancée Valerie were Rosaline's attendants. They were dressed in sea-mist green floor-length gowns made of a light jersey material. Both wore big brimmed hats of the same color and matching satin shoes. The girls carried an assortment of daisies in a compact bouquet with trails of green ribbon cascading from it. Rick and Brad were Tony's ushers. The three young men wore black pants and white tuxedo jackets with wide black lapels. Their white shirts had four sets of ruffles edged with a black trim on each side of the buttons. They looked incredibly handsome standing next to the pastor at the altar waiting for Rosaline.

When the music cued *Here Comes the Bride*, we all stood up and faced the back of the church. I was next to the aisle and had a clear view. John was beside me. My husband filed for divorce five short days ago, but I didn't think my daughter's wedding was the proper time to make the announcement; as a result, we agreed to put on a charade for the family. As far as I was concerned, it wasn't difficult. We'd been doing it for years.

The moment I saw Rosaline standing next to her father, I momentarily stopped breathing. The oxygen seemed to be trapped in my throat. I wasn't sure how long I held my breath as I watched them walk slowly down the aisle – both smiling radiantly – Richard glowing with elation and Rosaline spreading her own personal bliss like intangible confetti floating all around her. The nostalgic scene created a fountain of emotions inside of my heart. Rosaline was a stunning bride. Her empire style dress with lace trim and pearl accent beads was subtle yet elegant. The Juliet cap and veil framed her face and highlighted her beautiful features. Rosaline carried a bouquet of white roses in a bed of rich green foliage that enhanced the buds. It was tilted slightly in her hands, which allowed me to see my mother's broach pinned to the ribbons laced underneath. I had given Rosaline the cameo two days ago in honor of her wedding. She couldn't find a place to put it on her dress, but apparently, she wanted it with her on this special day. As they passed my pew, Rosaline stared directly at Tony, but Richard was looking at me. He smiled – a smile I recognized from a long time ago. It was warm, inviting, and jubilant.

As I smiled back at Richard, the gesture mysteriously freed the air in my throat and I began to breathe again.

After they reached their destination, and the preacher stated, "Who giveth this woman?"

Richard replied, "Her mother and I do." When I heard him say those words, my heart skipped three – maybe four beats. I was unaware he planned to include me in his response. Tears burned my eyes. I watched as Richard leaned over and kissed Rosaline lightly on her cheek. He turned and came toward me. I moved to make room for him in the pew. As if it were the most natural of gestures, Richard brushed his lips across my forehead and reached for my hand. Again, my heart felt as if it leaped out of my chest.

The service was a blur of soft spoken words that barely registered in my mine. Instead of focusing on the altar, I was engrossed in the feel and the warmth of Richard's fingers intertwined in mine. It felt so natural. Once I glanced in his direction, but he was completely absorbed by the ceremony. The drumbeats of my heart filled my head and were incredibly distracting; as a result, I could not decipher any of the sentences spoken by the pastor.

Even though I couldn't hear the words, I did manage to savor the visual: my beautiful Rosaline and her loving Tony. The rocky roads Rosaline had traveled led her directly to him. Ever since Tony had come into her life, Rosaline had become more confident, more trusting and more certain of her future. She continuously called Tony her "earth angel." Watching them together – knowing their love was true – I believed God – with a little additional guidance from Sister Teresa – helped them find each other. I was convinced this union was a wonderful match.

The moment Tony placed the ring on Rosie's finger and began to repeat the vows, I focused on their voices. It was sweet music. The love that was transported between their eyes blended with the words they were speaking. Yes . . . sweet music indeed.

When we arrived at Carley's Place for the reception, I was awed by the transformation. Richard's staff had rearranged the room so there was an area for dancing. It was exactly the way I'd sketched it on a napkin and described to the headwaiter. Dining tables – set to perfection with white linens, china and crystal – completely surrounded the center stage.

Tiny white lights were laced on the banisters and in strategic places on the walls giving the room the illusion of candles everywhere. They flickered slightly like a flame. The flowers and decorations were festive and spotlighted the bride and groom's favorite spring colors. In addition, Brad had taken several dozen pictures of Tony and Rosaline over the years – some separately but most of them together. He enlarged them to various sizes, laminated them and hung them with invisible wire from the ceiling. The photographs looked like mobiles floating in the air. When the guests arrived, they admired the creation as they waited in the receiving line to greet the bride and groom.

Richard stood in the line with me until the last of the guests were greeted, and then he dashed off to the kitchen to make sure all was working smoothly. He wanted to make sure the steamship round was not over cooked and the mashed potatoes were going to be warm when served.

I proceeded to my table. John was already there, as were Tony's parents and Richard's girlfriend Sandy. All of them were nursing their first cocktail of the evening. The bride and groom were at the head table with the wedding party. Valerie sat next to Rick. Brad brought his current girlfriend Jill. And Tony's sister also had a date. Randy sat on the other side of the room with several young teens who had come with their parents. My twelve-year-old son looked like he was having a fabulous time flirting with a thirteen-year-old girl who was easily two inches taller than he was. I had a feeling he was going to enjoy this new experience.

The music from the DJ's table played softly in the background. It was a perfect setting. I was proud of the job Richard and I had done.

I heard the food was delicious, but I barely tasted it. I was too busy watching the bride and groom floating from table to table talking with their guests. I marveled at Brad, who carried his camera all around the room snapping pictures and capturing memories. Glancing at Rick and Valerie, I noticed they were absorbed in each other – probably discussing their upcoming wedding and envisioning their celebration. At our table, there was plenty of chatter. Tony's parents were easy conversationalists. I frequently glanced at Sandy and noticed she had a death grip on Richard's arm. She was clearly marking her territory.

When all of the guests were done eating, Richard tapped his champagne glass with his spoon. Everyone stopped talking and turned their attention in his direction. Richard held his glass up and motioned it toward Rosaline and Tony. The room was quiet; even the servers remained stationary out of respect for their boss.

"Rosaline," Richard spoke directly to his daughter, "You have filled my life with sunshine. On the day you were born – you were so small and vulnerable – I could hold you in the palm of my hand," he glanced in my direction, smiled and returned his attention to the bride. "Look at you now – all grown up – and incredibly beautiful."

Richard voice cracked ever so slightly. Most people wouldn't notice, but I did.

He continued his toast, "You have brought us great joy. No matter what roads you travel or how old you are, you will always be my little girl. I love you, Sweetheart." Richard smiled directly at his daughter. She beamed in response. Richard continued. This time, he directed his attention to the bride and the groom. "Today, you leave my home and begin your new life with your husband." Richard paused. "Over the last few years, I have seen both of you grow into such fine young adults. You have blossomed into strong, independent individuals – and you are amazing as a couple too. Your love – your commitment – your friendship – have created a solid bond." Richard paused to make sure the bride and groom were paying close attention before continuing, "Love each other. Be kind to each other." He spoke slowly and paused between each sentence. "Make patience a priority. Communicate your feelings. Give from your heart, and treat each other with the respect you both deserve. If you do this, you will find a lifetime of happiness together." Richard spanned the room with his eyes. "Let us all raise our glasses to this wonderful couple and toast their future together."

The guests cheered loudly and sipped their champagne. I was slow to lift my glass to my lips because I was too stunned by Richard's words. Never had he spoken so eloquently and with so much emotion. I was flabbergasted – even awed – by the sensitive and loving words coming from his mouth. In front of everyone, he verbally declared his love for his daughter.

If Richard could express his feelings so well for Rosaline – and also for Rick many times in the past – why then, could he never speak to Brad in that way? I watched Brad as he snapped pictures with his camera.

When he focused on his father, his face was etched with pain. It was as if I could see the pangs of jealousy set deeply in his expression. It was almost as if Richard used his love as a weapon against Brad, and Brad could feel the wounds.

The moment the toast was over, Sandy wedged herself between Richard and me. She stood on her tiptoes and kissed his cheek. "That was wonderful, Darling." I knew Richard's girlfriend was close to my age, but her voice sounded more like a lovesick teenager. I strained to see Richard's response, but I was denied access; Sandy's body blocked my view.

The DJ called the newlyweds onto the dance floor. The crowd applauded. Tony and Rosaline's first dance was to Elton John's *Your Song*. I'd heard it often during the last few years; Rosaline always referred to it as "our song." The lyrics suited them perfectly. As we watched the bride and groom swaying to the music, they seemed to be enveloped by the magical aura of the lyrics and the warmth of their love. Our guests could not help but smile as they watched the gorgeous couple. Multiple times, I tried to see Richard's face, but was at the wrong vantage point to see him clearly.

The moment the song ended, Rosaline walked to the DJ and requested a song for the parents' dance. Neither Tony's mother and father nor Richard and I had previous knowledge of this event.

The DJ spoke into the microphone, "This is a special request from the bride and groom. They would like their parents to join them on the dance floor."

Richard offered me his hand. I nodded, smiled bashfully and followed him. The moment the first notes from the piano keys came over the DJ's sound system, I recognized the tune. Instantly, I froze because I knew the beloved song was going to play havoc with my emotions. Richard, also, looked slightly taken aback for a moment; however, he quickly recovered his composure, took a formal bow in my direction before lifting his right hand to twirl me in slow motion under his arm. When the instrumental portion of the song was completed, Frank Sinatra's silky voice began singing *Someone to Watch Over Me*, and Richard gently pulled me into his arms. To my surprise, dancing with Richard felt like the most natural thing in the world.

"I wonder whose idea it was to play *this* song?" I whispered in Richard's ear.

"Does it matter?" Richard replied mischievously. He pulled away long enough to make eye contact. "I remember when this song was constantly playing on the radio," he whispered the words. "You were pregnant with Rosaline." He drew me back into his embrace, and we glided effortlessly to the romantic tempo.

I surrendered to the music and blocked out all of the other people in the room. Resting my head lightly upon Richard's shoulder, I absorbed the rhythm. It felt wonderful to be in his arms.

Through my veiled eyes, the images I saw were those from our past. A flood of memories washed over me. Richard . . . laying on the bed next to me . . . his ear glued to my protruding belly . . . commenting on the sounds and carrying on a conversation with the baby inside of me. Richard . . . wrapping his arms around me while I worked in the kitchen . . . telling me I was the most beautiful woman in the world . . . convincing me to leave the dishes in the sink and dance with him to this *exact same song*. Richard . . . holding our daughter . . . marveling at how pretty she was with her tiny, bow-shaped lips and sparkling eyes. Rosaline . . . barely old enough to walk . . . standing on her father's toes . . . dancing with her dad. The memories kept coming like waves in an ocean. They engulfed me with flashbacks that made me both happy and melancholy at the same time.

When the song came to a close, Richard successfully twirled me in an encore circle and then dipped me backwards as he had done countless times during the years of our marriage. As he cradled me in his arms, my back bowed and my head nearly touched the floor. Richard smiled. "I may be a few pounds heavier and a couple of decades older, but I'm still strong enough to do this." As the melody faded, the guests – who surrounded the dance floor – broke out in a huge round of applause. The abrupt sound brought me back to the present and reality.

"Thanks for not dropping me." My voice was more sarcastic than I'd intended.

"I wouldn't do that," he muttered defensively as the smile on his face vanished.

"I know that, Richard." I tried to smooth my words. "I

meant – everyone is looking at us. It would have been awful if we had fallen in front of all of the guests."

"You never did trust me," he paused. "Things might have worked out differently if you had." His sardonic comment was spoken with a lighthearted voice, but it was a definite stab at our failed marriage.

"What does that mean?" I inquired.

Richard didn't have time to answer. The DJ announced the next song and invited all of the guests to participate. *"You Are So Beautiful"* by Joe Cocker inspired every couple onto the dance floor. Sandy materialized at our side and asked Richard to dance with her. I surrendered and returned to the table where John was nursing his third drink. We were the only ones sitting; even Randy was dancing with a cute girl who towered over him.

By the time Tony and Rosie cut their wedding cake, John had consumed six cocktails. Once the rice was thrown and the bride and groom departed for their short honeymoon in the city, John announced his desire to go home. I stalled long enough to say good-bye to the last guest before we left the reception. After taking the keys from John, I got behind the steering wheel and drove us safely to the apartment. The only person talking in the car was Randy. He had thoroughly enjoyed the day.

14

Richard

It wasn't long after the wedding that I began to feel lonely and lost in my own home. The place felt overwhelmingly big, and I was the only one who lived in it. When I wasn't at the restaurant, I wandered the house aimlessly. The vacant rooms added to my growing depression.

Finally, I decided I needed a hobby for my spare time. Remembering how much I enjoyed the water, I decided to return to the river and my sailboat: *Caroline Sue*. Over the years, my sons had used the boat periodically, but it had been well over a decade since I'd set foot on the vessel. On occasion, I'd thought about selling it – even had a buyer at one point – but I'd never followed through on the transaction.

The teak needed some tender loving care. I bought new sails because the old ones were disintegrating; there was no way they'd catch the wind anymore. I filled my empty hours with a new goal – to get back on the water again. At least two times a week, I vowed to go to the river and work on her. Every time I stepped foot on the boat I felt my depression lifting. The labor was therapeutic.

I was in the kitchen packing a light lunch and looking forward to another day on the boat. After putting a few beers in a cooler and placing the food on top of it, I heard a bold knock at the front door. Apparently, I had left it unlocked because I heard the door open and close, but there was no greeting. I wasn't anticipating any visitors: Rosaline and Tony were living in Pennsylvania; Rick and Sandy were at work. There was no one else who would enter without an invitation. I walked into the foyer and was surprised to find Brad standing on the tile with a suitcase in his hand.

Startled and speechless, I managed to say one word, "Hi." Not once during the wedding weekend had Brad voluntarily spoken to me. I had approached him a few times, but he had never given me more than a single-word response to any conversation I attempted. Before the festive weekend was over, I had stopped trying to communicate with him. Now – here he was – standing in my foyer – motionless.

I broke the silence first, "Everything okay, Son?"

Brad's anxious expression was frozen on his face but his eyes darted around the room. He finally responded, "I was wondering if we could talk, Dad?"

"Sure," I answered. "Why don't we go into the family room?" Brad followed me through the kitchen and to the couch.

"Am I interrupting something?" Brad inquired as he pointed toward the cooler.

"Nothing that can't wait," I replied. "Would you like a beer?" I pulled two out of the refrigerator and chuckled slightly to myself. I'd never offered my son a beer before; in fact, Brad was twenty-four years old and I'd never even *had* a friendly beer with him. I popped the cap off of two Black Labels and handed one to Brad.

"Thanks." Brad did not utter another comment until after he had consumed half of the bottle. He simply sat quietly on the couch and looked anywhere but at me.

I knew Brad well enough to realize that nothing I said would make him move or speak any faster than when he was ready to do so. I waited.

Finally my son spoke. "Things haven't been too good in New York," he paused. "I'm broke, Dad. I need a job. Do you think there might be a position for me at Carley's Place?"

I'd never seen Brad look so defeated. I reached for him, but he pulled away, and he still wouldn't look at me.

"Of course, you can, Brad. The job's been waiting for your return." I tried not to be too enthusiastic, but I was thrilled to think of Brad joining my business. "I can train you for manager. You already have a solid foundation – my guess – it won't take long."

"Can I stay here for a little while until I can build a nest egg and get my own place?" He still wouldn't look in my direction.

"Of course you can, Brad. Stay as long as you need."

The signs of my depression were gone. I felt wonderful.

2

By the end of July, Brad was well established in a routine. He took to the business like I knew he would, but he was restless under my roof. My son might work for me, but he still wasn't comfortable in my home. Once he had a few paychecks in the bank, he opted to move out. His current girlfriend, Jill, lived ten minutes away and was thrilled to share the living expenses with him. Brad, of course, was glad to get away from me. I wondered if there would ever be a day when the two of us could enjoy shared time, but I didn't belabor the point; instead, I took comfort in having both of my sons working with me.

Once again, my house was empty. I considered asking Sandy to move in with me. After all, many in this younger generation preferred shacking up to marriage, why couldn't I? The trend was socially acceptable. It wasn't like I needed to be a role model for small children anymore. They were all grown and gone. Consequently, at least once – often twice – a week, I invited Sandy to spend the night at my house, but – for some reason – even though she was a wonderful substitute to ward off loneliness and she had a fabulous way of lifting my spirits with her infectious laughter – I wasn't ready to make a live-in commitment.

Sandy and I sporadically ventured in to the city. Shortly after the wedding, we saw an off-Broadway performance of *A Chorus Line* at The Public Theater. Sandy loved it and predicted it would be a winner *on* Broadway before much longer. She was right; as a result, I promised to take her to an encore performance at the Shubert Theatre in September for her birthday. Several times during the summer, we played tourist. We picnicked in Central Park, strolled through Time Square and visited the Statue of Liberty. I'd never been to Liberty Island; to my surprise, it was an entertaining and memorable day.

In addition, a couple of times a month, we went to the movies. Sandy loved the big screen. I liked *The Great Waldo Pepper* and *French Connection II* but her favorite to-date was *Once is Not Enough* mostly because she loved the Jacqueline Susann novel.

However, sailing was always my first choice when I had spare time. After finishing the repairs on my sailboat, I easily taught Sandy how to be my first mate. We enjoyed many lazy summer days on the river.

One Friday evening in early August, I left Brad and Rick in charge of the dinner crowd and took Sandy to see *Jaws* at our local theater. I'd been trying for weeks to clear my calendar to go to the much talked about film. As we stood in line to get tickets, I noticed Caroline at the booth. After she made her purchase, I called out to her. She spun around; a startled expression popped onto her face.

"Hi," I said. To my surprise, my voice was filled with an excitement I hadn't felt five minutes ago. It was the first time I'd seen Caroline since the wedding. "Where's John?" I inquired as I looked around in the crowd; he was nowhere to be seen.

"John's going to meet me here." Caroline seemed to be stumbling on her words.

Sandy curled her arm around mine and leaned against me. Smiling pleasantly at Caroline, she commented, "This is supposed to be a fabulous movie. I hear the music is sensational."

Caroline didn't respond; instead, she looked aimlessly around at the crowd and fiddled with her hands. I noticed there was one ticket – not two – wedged between her fingers.

I didn't know what possessed me to say it, but the words poured out of my mouth. "Would you like us to save you and John a couple of seats? There is quite a crowd, and it might be difficult to get good seats if you wait much longer."

"Sure," she replied.

Sandy tugged at my sleeve and encouraged me to move toward the door. As we walked away, I glanced back at Caroline. "See you inside," I smiled. She smiled, too, but she didn't respond. Sandy and I positioned ourselves directly in the center of the audience – about twelve rows back. I looked for John and Caroline until the lights dimmed and the movie began, but I never saw either of them. Eventually, two strangers sat in the seats we had been saving. The moment the movie started and the girl was devoured by the shark in the first scene, Sandy and I stayed on the edge of our seats. I didn't think about Caroline or John again until the movie was over; when the lights came on, I glanced around the theater. They were nowhere in sight. As Sandy and I filed out of the building, I jokingly said, "Want to go to the shore this weekend?"

"I am never going in the ocean again," Sandy said adamantly. The movie had terrified her.

I kept insisting the story was simply Hollywood at its best, but she was not convinced. Sandy confirmed, "It will be a cold day in Hell before I put even one toe in the ocean."

I laughed.

3

One night in mid-August, while Brad and I were working overlapping shifts at Carley's Place, my son approached me with an idea. It was a slow night and the dinner crowd was sparse, so he took advantage of the down time.

We sat at the bar sipping on a beer and looking out into the restaurant. "Have you ever thought about renovating – I mean – *really* remodeling Carley's Place?" Brad asked hesitantly.

I was slightly apprehensive about the topic. "What do you have in mind, Brad?"

"Discos are the latest fad in New York, Dad. They are packing in the crowds. Music is shifting and the songs are double in length giving dancers ample time to feel the rhythm. I know it won't be long before the trend migrates to smaller cities and suburbia." Brad's eyes sparkled with excitement as he talked, and his voice gained conviction with each word. "I'm certain it is a money-making proposition. It would be great to be a front-runner, not a follower, when the local population discovers it."

I watched my son. There was a passion in his voice and a certainty in his attitude. I had never seen him more confident. He pulled a napkin off of the table, opened it up and drew the layout of the building on it.

"If you took that wall down," Brad spoke as he pointed across the room and then drew several lines across the napkin. "It would open up the space. All of the booths would have to come out, and the bar would have to be moved over there." Brad continued to draw his plan. "If you did that, there would be plenty of room for a dance floor and a DJ." He continued to draw small boxes and lines on the napkin. "With smaller tables and compact seating, you could fit nearly two hundred in here comfortably. It wouldn't be about dinner anymore; it would be about selling drinks and entertainment. You would cater to an entirely different crowd."

"So, Brad, you think if we knock out that wall into the banquet room, close off that wall over there, and lay out a dance floor, we'd bring in a new type of crowd that would spend money on drinks instead of food."

"Well . . . you know, Dad, you've always said the big money is in the booze, and there isn't as much profit in food." He could barely contain his excitement.

I, too, was thrilled. This was the first time I could remember that Brad talked to me as an equal, instead of our usual strained conversations. I didn't feel like he hated me. I slapped him gently on the back. "I don't believe it, Brad." There was a teasing quality to my voice. "You actually were listening to me around the dinner table."

Brad continued filling me in on his thoughts of converting to a discotheque. "We could buy a huge glimmering ball – hang it from the ceiling – when it twirls slowly it reflects sparkling prisms over the entire room. It's the latest craze. Keep in mind, the DJ is the personality of the entire place. You can't scrimp there. It's the DJ who spins the web – mixing music and personality." Brad paused to finish his beer. "Right now, Dad, the music is basically black soul. The market hasn't been tapped yet, but I read in the paper that Hollywood is making this movie with John Travolta. The whole plot is centered on dancing. I know it's going to bust this concept wide open. If we hurry, we can be the first place in town; therefore, we'd have a monopoly on it. We could make a fortune."

"It's a lot of money, Brad. We're doing fairly well the way it is now." To be honest, profits were down in the last two years. Things had gotten stale. I wasn't losing money, but I wasn't making the profits I use to make either. "Why do you want to shake things up?" Brad's ideas appealed to me; however, my son didn't hear the potential interest in my voice – instead – he heard skepticism.

"That's what I thought you'd say," Brad shrugged. He seemed annoyed.

I didn't want to lose the chemistry we had created or the improvement we had made in communicating with each other. I paused long enough to relax my voice. "You remind me of the way I was at your age. Your eyes even light up when you talk about it." I grinned slightly. "Your mother always said that my eyes lit up like an electrical storm every time I got excited about a new idea. I was a little younger than you are now when I put this place together. I was so energized; I could barely contain myself. I was possessed by it." I took a long, slow look at every corner of the restaurant. A nostalgic wave passed over me. I smiled as much to myself as to Brad. "It's not much different than it was in the beginning." I paused. "Maybe it's time for a change." I hugged Brad. "I like your ideas, son. I think perhaps it's time to take a gamble on you. Get an architect in here. Call your friend, Bill. Doesn't he have his own construction company? Ask him for a bid. Compare it to a couple of others. Let's see if we can swing this brainstorm of yours."

Brad was floating on a cloud. I barely recognized him. He seemed genuinely shocked that I was considering his ideas.

"Brad, about your brother Rick – he's good in this business. He works his heart out, and I appreciate it. I can see what an effort he is making, but he doesn't have your innate ability or your insight. None of it comes as naturally to him as it does to you. You're a lot like me, Brad. Even if you've never wanted to admit it – you are. And the business is in your blood." I patted him gently on the shoulder. "I'm glad you're back. While you and Rick were growing up, I always dreamed that someday we'd be here together." I paused. "Your mother says you are a chip off of the old block. I've never been sure whether or not she's complimenting either one of us."

My son seemed to cringe slightly at the mention of his mother, but I broached the subject anyway. "Have you seen her recently?"

"Yeah. I had dinner with Mom last weekend."

"How is she?" I asked. By this time in our conversation, I was nursing my third beer. I hadn't eaten any dinner, and I was feeling a little of the effects. The alcohol relaxed me and made me willing to tread on unfamiliar ground.

"She looks good," Brad replied. He was clearly trying to avoid the subject.

"Your mother's a mighty fine-looking woman. You know something, Brad, she's even prettier now than she was in high school. Caroline was in my English class; she could really light up a room – positively radiant, even as a teenager. I couldn't take my eyes off of her."

"Let's cut the crap, Dad." Brad stood up – truly annoyed with the direction our conversation was heading.

I felt as if we were back to square one. *Why was it I could never do anything right with that boy!*

4

The sunrise on the morning of Rick and Valerie's wedding was a glorious blend of purple, orange and a soft yellow. The weatherman promised an afternoon in the low 70s, blue skies and no humidity: a picture-perfect fall day in Winston-Salem, North Carolina. Needless to say, everyone was breathing sighs of relief because rain had been predicted during the previous forecasts. The sunshine boosted our spirits.

The bride's parents hosted a brunch for the family and the wedding party. The food was delicious and the champagne was free flowing. Valerie and her mother, of course, were not there. The bride did not want to risk running into the groom; but the rest of the wedding party was present. Caroline and I sat at a table in the corner observing the young crowd as they interacted with each other.

"Rick sure looks happy, doesn't he?" I smiled.

"He's been waiting a long time for this day." Caroline replied, "But if he and Brad don't stop inhaling that champagne, they might pass out before the wedding starts."

"They're having fun… blowing off a little steam before the ceremony. It's nice to see them hanging out together." I remarked as I watched Rick and Brad laughing boisterously. "They had a couple of rough years while they were at Elon – they weren't close – a lot of visible tension. I never knew what it was about – but there was definitely a wedge between them."

"I agree," Caroline added. "Neither one of them would ever talk about it. Almost like – even in their anger – they still wanted to protect each other." She sipped on the last of her champagne. "Looks like they've ironed out the issues, and they're thick as thieves now – like when they were little. Remember how cute the boys were with their coonskin caps and their six-shooters." The corners of Caroline's lips turned upward and her eyes sparkled joyfully. "They were adorable."

We both laughed. The champagne and the flashbacks were merging together creating a blissful string of memories parading through our minds. We both were lost in thought as we individually recollected our favorites.

I finally broke the silence. "I think I'm going to sell the house." My voice was monotone when I spoke.

"What?" Caroline inquired. She truly looked stunned. "Why?"

"It's so big. Too big," I answered – still with a bland voice showing no emotion. It was not a snap decision on my part; I'd been thinking about it for a while. "It's kind of lonely rambling around those rooms all by myself." I leaned back in my chair. "Sometimes I think it's haunted."

"Haunted?"

"Yes."

"With ghosts?" Caroline snickered trying to make light of her question.

"No – not ghosts." I whispered pensively. "Haunted with . . ." I struggled for the right words. "Haunted with . . . the images of what could have been." The moment my personal thoughts were verbalized, I wanted to reclaim them. I couldn't believe I was expressing my feelings to Caroline in such a bold manner. My voice might have been steady, but my mind was racing with emotions I'd been suppressing for years. It must be the champagne. I felt vulnerable and didn't dare look at her.

"But you've always loved that house." Caroline seemed stunned. "That was your dream house."

I almost said it . . . I *almost* said . . . *That was **our** dream house – but once you left – it was nothing but an empty shell.* However, I caught myself. Looking down at my glass and twirling the stem with my fingers, I finally muttered, "It's just a house." After a short pause, I looked directly into Caroline's eyes. "Kids have grown – time to move on." Again, my voice was flat and impassive.

Caroline was quiet for a long time. She poured a little more champagne in her glass before asking, "How's Brad doing at Carley's Place?"

"Surprisingly well," I responded enthusiastically. This was a subject I felt comfortable discussing. "The construction is going great – renovations are right on schedule. The place is completely gutted. They are rebuilding now. Brad has definitely taken the bull by the horn – he's managing the entire project. Most of the ideas are *his*, but I insisted on a few of my own. Brad wanted *no* booths –just tables and chairs;

I wanted horseshoe-style booths in all of the corners that could hold as many as ten customers each. Brad wanted to spend an exorbitant amount of money on a brand new sound system; I convinced him to elaborate on the one we already have. He picked out new speakers and a few sub-woofers strategically placed." I chuckled as much to myself as to Caroline. "It amazes me. Brad and I have discussions – not arguments. Brad bends a little. I bend a little. We end up compromising. Feels like a miracle!" As I spoke, I noticed Caroline had tenderly placed her hand on top of mine. It felt warm and comfortable. Her gesture encouraged me to continue the conversation. "I go to Carley's Place several times a day to see how the construction is going, but I've given most of the authority to Brad. They are *Brad's* plans – *his* ideas – and I think it's all going to work out. The place should be open for business in a few more weeks."

"Brad is so excited." Caroline's brown eyes glittered with a gleeful expression that mirrored the way Brad's looked when he discussed the restaurant's transformation. "I'm so happy," Caroline said, "you and Brad have forged a bond. I always knew you'd make a great team."

"Brad has quite a vision for the future. He is determined, and he can't seem to focus on anything else." The elation I felt for my son was apparent in my voice. "It was a challenge to get him to come to Winston-Salem for the wedding. If he weren't Rick's Best Man, I think Brad might have opted out and stayed in Jersey to manage the construction workers. He didn't want to leave – not even for a couple of days."

"He's exactly like you, Richard," Caroline muttered with a hint of defiance in her tone, "always totally absorbed in his goals."

"Is that a compliment or an insult?" I asked – a little taken aback by the terse tone in her words.

"Only an observation." Caroline stiffened slightly and pulled her hand away.

The moment her hand left mine, I felt cold. Rarely did we touch, and having Caroline's fingers stroking my hand had been pleasant. It was a simple gesture, but heartwarming. I wanted to feel her touch again.

We sat in silence for a few moments, sipping the champagne. It seemed every subject we broached ended up being too sensitive to discuss – like poking a needle into our hearts and probing latent emotions.

Caroline pushed the food around on her plate, but didn't eat any of it. I was certain the remaining eggs were cold.

"What are you giving them for their wedding gift?" I inquired in hopes that changing the subject would lighten the mood.

"I had a set of eight coffee mugs and eight water tumblers personalized for them." Caroline voice became animated, and her expression reminded me of the one she wore on the day she'd given me the homemade tackle box – a lifetime ago. She was glowing with elation as she spoke, "I used the negatives from a few of the pictures Brad took of Rick and Valerie last summer when the wedding announcements went out. I found this company that puts pictures on ceramic and glass. Each one is different. They are gorgeous. I hope the kids think of them as keepsakes." Caroline smiled proudly. "What are you giving them?"

"I gave them a chunk of change so they can put a down payment on a house. Rick found a nice three-bedroom place on Western Avenue in Morristown. It's not far from my other restaurant. If he had to, he could walk to work. Last I heard, they are going to settlement a week from Monday – when they get back from their honeymoon. With my money and their savings, they might even have enough left over to buy some furniture."

"You always did overshadow any gift I ever gave the kids." Caroline voice dripped with cynicism. "I guess – after your present – mine won't make much of an impact." Caroline stiffened. Her lower lip curved inward; she bit it with her teeth.

"Why would you say something like that?" I was truly annoyed. Caroline could rip my heart to shreds with a solitary word or a single glance. This was no exception. For as long as I could remember, it was Caroline who gave the kids their favorite Christmas presents or the gifts they treasured for years. If I were honest with myself, part of me was jealous of her ability to relate to our children in such a poignant way. My voice was irritable when I added, "I gave Rick and Valerie money as a wedding gift – big damn deal! You gave them a present they will still be using when their grandchildren come to visit. Let's face it; by then, they will have long forgotten the money I gave them."

Again we sat in silent . . . and again Caroline pushed her food around on her plate.

When Caroline clammed up, I forged ahead even though I knew the subject was sensitive. "You always said, Caroline, that I spoiled the kids." I held my breath for several moments before I continued. "You were right."

Caroline stopped playing with her fork and looked at me. There was an expression of astonishment on her face. I could tell she was searching for a rhetorical statement, but I spoke before she could comment. "You accused me of buying their love." I paused. "I admit it . . . I didn't know how else to make them happy. In the beginning, I wanted to shower them with the things I never had as a child. I didn't want them to feel like less of a person because they didn't have the things other children took for granted." I was afraid to look at Caroline's face, so I gazed across the room at Brad and three of Valerie's bridesmaids who seemed spellbound by every word my son spoke. I paused a few moments before continuing, "Then – after you left me – I wanted them to be happy living with me. I was afraid if they weren't happy – they would leave me too."

I braved a glance in Caroline's direction. There was an expression of awe on her face, and tears misted her eyes. Neither of us spoke for several seconds.

"Richard, you didn't need to give them gifts to win their love – our kids adore you. Even Brad – who acts like he doesn't care – all he's ever wanted is your love and respect." Caroline reached for my hand – enveloping it again – this time with a firmer grasp. "They didn't want *things*, Richard. They wanted *you*."

I didn't trust my voice; as a result, I remained silent for a full minute. Finally, I changed the subject. "When is John coming?" I asked. Last night, during the rehearsal dinner Caroline and I hosted at Staley's Charcoal Steak House, she told me her husband was running late but would arrive in time for the ceremony. When Caroline avoided my question *yet again*, I looked at my watch and commented, "Don't you think John is cutting it a little close?"

Caroline sipped several times on her second glass of champagne. Finally she put the crystal down and stared directly into my eyes. "John's not coming."

"What?"

"He's not coming. John was never coming." Caroline squared her shoulders before continuing, "The kids don't know yet – not even Randy, but John and I are separated."

"Really?" I couldn't have been more surprised. "Did John move out?"

"Yes . . . about a year ago. He lives across town with his girlfriend."

"Girlfriend?" I asked – not even trying to conceal the shock in my voice. "John's having an affair?"

"I guess that is what you would call it," Caroline mumbled. "He claims to be in love with her."

"How have you kept Randy in the dark about this?"

"Randy is so wrapped up in the life of a thirteen-year-old boy – it's not hard to create an illusion of family for him. John and I don't fight. Hell – we don't even talk, but we do go to Randy's ball games, his parent-teacher conferences, and a field trip occasionally. When Randy asks where his dad is at night, I tell him he's working late or on the grave-yard shift. The explanation seems to satisfy him. I suppose our benign routine is better than volatile fighting or constant tension." Caroline paused as she contemplated her next comment. "I thought John and I could go on like that until Randy graduated from high school, but John wants a divorce. He's going to marry his girlfriend . . ." Caroline smirked, ". . . and live happily ever after."

"You sound bitter."

"I'm not." Caroline responded. "Really, I'm not. John and I have been living separate lives for several years. Roommates see each other more than we do. I suppose I should have seen a divorce coming – but I was so busy. I wasn't paying attention." She looked directly at me. "This is the first time I've talked about it." A forlorn expression covered her face. "I'm not bitter, but I do feel like a failure."

"You sure know how to put on a charade, Caroline. I had no idea."

"Please don't tell the kids. I don't want them to know – especially not this weekend." She sighed. "Rick thought it was odd that John and Randy didn't come, but I explained that Randy had a tournament for his select baseball team, and John had to stay home with him."

"Don't you think they are going to find out eventually?"

"John and I will tell them when the time is right." She paused.

"What happened?" I couldn't resist asking.

"Nothing . . . everything." Caroline looked down at the table and rubbed her forehead with all ten of her fingers. "John and I got married for all of the wrong reasons, and it finally caught up with us." She took a deep breath and made an effort to change the subject, "Enough about me," Caroline attempted a smile; however, her eyes were anything but happy. "How come Sandy didn't come with you?"

As if I was talking about the weather, I spontaneously replied, "We broke up a couple of weeks ago."

"Really?" It was Caroline's turn to be surprised. "Why?"

"Short version – Sandy wanted to get married." I paused. "If I married Sandy," I made direct eye contact with Caroline. "If I married Sandy," I repeated myself, "it would have been . . . for all of the wrong reasons."

My sentences hung in the air almost as if the words were an echo bouncing off of the walls. Caroline seemed to be processing my response, and neither of us added to the conversation. I knew the entire room was buzzing with festive activity; however, I could not hear or see anything but Caroline. There was an expression on her face I hadn't seen in such a long time. Her cheeks flushed a bright shade of crimson and her eyes danced with excitement – similar to the way they did – years ago when we were kids. I was instantly drawn to her – like a magnet – but I held back. I didn't want to risk being rebuked.

"Remember when we were young – like they are now?" Caroline's eyes darted into the room where our sons were standing with their peers. "Were you ever happy?" Her question rolled through the air like thick morning mist.

I did not respond right away. Instead, I allowed a flood of memories to fill my mind. Closing my eyes, I took a moment to enjoy the visions inside my head as if they were my own personal home movies playing from my projector.

I spoke without opening my eyes. "When we were together," I paused before adding, "those were the happiest years of my life." The words slipped out of my mouth like a silk scarf falling from a freshly waxed banister; I meant every single word.

Caroline embraced my hand with both of hers. When I opened my eyes, I watched her lift my hand to her lips. She gently kissed each knuckle. I could feel the heat from her breath; the warmth created an electric shock through my body. I felt weak and roused at the same time. After all five knuckles had been coated with a dew-like moisture from her lips, she turned my hand over and tenderly peeled my fingers open. In slow motion, she placed the palm of my hand on her face and closed her eyes as if she were absorbing the feel of my skin on hers. My fingers moved involuntarily across her cheek, over the bridge of her nose and slowly to the corner of her mouth. I could hear her catch her breath as my index finger tenderly tapped twice on her lips. Her eyes fluttered open.

Caroline traveled ever so slightly in my direction and tilted her head. I thought of her actions as an invitation. Every fiber of my being wanted desperately to kiss Caroline. I remembered exactly how her lips felt – soft like velvet – and how electrifying it had been to have her tongue entwine with mine. I waited for her to stop me; but she did not. Our eyes were locked and our breath mingled. Slowly, I moved toward her.

"Excuse me," an unfamiliar voice broke the spell.

"What?" Caroline managed to respond first.

"Would you like some coffee?" A petite waitress asked as she held a pot in one hand and a couple mugs in the other.

"Coffee?" Caroline mumbled. She seemed to be having trouble breathing as she leaned back in the booth, closed her eyes and took controlled oxygen through her nose. Without opening her eyes, she said, "No thank you. No. Wait. Yes. I'll have a cup."

"Caroline," I whispered as I noticed beads of perspiration dotting her forehead. "Are you okay?"

The waitress poured two cups and pointed to the creamer and sugar before she moved on to the next table. She seemed to take all of our sensual energy with her.

I repeated my question, "Really, Caroline. Are you okay?"

Caroline used her napkin to wipe her face. "I'm fine," she answered. A smile materialized on her lips. "I could say that you have swept me off of my feet," she responded in a teasing tone, "but I think I've simply had a little too much champagne. Nothing a cup of coffee won't cure." The magic of the moment was gone.

Damn that waitress and her bad timing.

6

Rick and Valerie's wedding ceremony was elegant – or as Caroline described – truly magical. Valerie's parents spared no expense. Trinity Church on Country Club Road was decorated to perfection with flowers hanging on the end of every pew and enormous bouquets in strategic locations on the altar. The chandeliers were dimmed, allowing the afternoon light filtering through the beautiful stained glass windows to fill the chapel with exactly the right amount of warmth and color to enhance the room.

Unlike Tony and Rosie's modest wedding ceremony in the spring, Valerie had eight bridesmaids and Rick had an equal number of groomsmen; many of them were friends from Elon. It was a huge wedding party. The girls all looked like charming southern belles wearing hooped dresses with a radius of nearly three feet of rustling petticoats that could be heard throughout the church. The groomsmen donned traditional black tuxedos with tails. In addition, Trinity Church was packed with guests. At the beginning of the ceremony – when I walked down the aisle with Caroline on my arm to our reserved pew at the front – I noticed there was not one empty spot in the entire chapel. Our son had a few dozen on his invitation list – all of whom were of the groom's generation; however, the Hunt family's guest list filled the church to capacity. The energy and love in the room was infectious.

Occasionally during the ceremony, I reached for Caroline's hand. To my surprise, she allowed me to hold it. In fact, several times she glanced in my direction and smiled. I saw sweet tears in her eyes.

The reception was held at Forsyth Country Club; to say it was beautiful would be a huge understatement. The grounds alone were incredibly impressive. The majestic oaks implied decades of regal Southern history. The glimmering white building looked like a castle, and the golf course provided visitors with a breathtaking view. After entering the Grand Ballroom, I leaned over to Caroline and muttered, "Bet this is costing the Hunts a pretty penny." To my surprise, for a fraction of a moment, old insecurities flooded over me. I felt like that little boy who lived in South Side – the one who was never invited to the North Side's social events. In a sarcastic tone, I leaned over and whispered into Caroline's ear. "This is probably what your wedding would have looked like if you had married Jerry Adams." I think I was more shocked than Caroline when I realized I'd said the words.

Caroline dropped my arm as if she didn't care if anyone noticed her antagonist gesture and abruptly walked past the guests in front of her – pushing her way into the room and leaving me in her wake. She walked through the ballroom and directly out onto the balcony. I could have gone to our assigned table; instead, I picked up two gin and tonics at the bar and followed Caroline. When I walked out onto the balcony, my skin was greeted with a gentle fall breeze that cooled the flames of embarrassment on my cheeks. I stood in the corner watching Caroline as she observed the wedding party. On the grounds below, the professional photographer lined up the bride and groom with the attendants. The rich green rolling hills of the golf course were in the background. No matter what the photographer said, the flower girl and the ring bearer were not cooperating. I wondered how long it would take before their parents removed them from the equation.

I handed Caroline a cocktail and sipped on mine. "Looks like pictures might take a while." Leaning my elbow on the railing, I scanned the horizon. Fall colors dotted the foliage with brilliant shades of oranges, yellows and reds. The trees were not yet peak; however, there were enough luminous shades to savor the season. The photographer seemed to be adjusting the frame of his camera to incorporate as much color as possible. I couldn't hear Brad's voice, but I could tell by his actions that he was making suggestions.

Finally, I broke the silence. "I'm sorry, Caroline." I knew I'd crossed the line. There was no other way but to apologize.

"Can we please get through this weekend without pounding each other with our past mistakes?" She didn't look at me when she spoke.

"Weddings and funerals," I muttered. "They seem to bring out the best and the worst in people." I tapped my glass against Caroline's. "Truce?"

Caroline didn't reply. Instead she stared at me – her eyes were pools of dark chocolate – an expression I could not read shrouding her face. Why did my tongue virtually tie itself in knots whenever I was close to Caroline? I could think of a dozen snappy comments and a hundred ways of saying them when she wasn't in the room with me – but the moment

Caroline was within my reach – I was rendered mute. No clever lines. No sophisticated remarks.

"Let's get through the weekend." With that comment, Caroline dismissed me. She sipped her beverage several times, but didn't say another word.

I downed my drink. When the waiter walked by, I picked two more cocktails off of his tray without even asking what they were.

It took forty-five minutes for the professional photographer to wrap up the pictures. By that time, the wedding party was parched and ready to celebrate with the rest of the guests. The moment they entered the ballroom, the energy was heightened. Once everyone had a glass of champagne, Valerie's father proposed a toast.

Cheers and applause filled the room as the bride and groom had their first dance to *Maybe I'm Amazed*. The band was not nearly as good as Paul McCartney's Wings, but they managed to perform a nice tribute to the couple's favorite melody. The musicians deliberately played the tune longer than expected because the DJ was instructed to invite the parents of the bride and groom onto the dance floor halfway through the song.

It was awkward for both Caroline and me because we had not exchanged a single word since we'd been on the balcony. However, I followed Valerie's parents' lead. Gently clasping Caroline's hand, I escorted her onto the floor. She flowed easily into my arms. As I always remembered – the perfect fit. I laid my cheek on hers and closed my eyes, listening to the lyrics; the words cut like a knife because there was nothing but truth in them.

Why is it that music can express volumes of emotions but I can't speak a single word?

Even though I knew everyone – including our children – was looking at us, I felt as if I was completely alone with Caroline. With my eyes closed, I could feel her entire body pressed against me as if there was no material separating us. When it came to Caroline, my memory was flawless. Her breasts heaved underneath her dress. I knew her nipples were taut – I could not only feel them – I could envision them: erect, full, inviting. The soft curve of her back, the inside of her thigh, the dimple directly above her right hip, the soft, tiny hairs on her abdomen – all treasured, secret spots on her body I had once known so well. Laying my nose on her hair, I savored a long, slow breath: roses. Was that her shampoo, her perfume or her corsage?

I wanted to say so much to Caroline – I wanted to pour my heart out to her. Why was it so difficult? She'd told me she was getting a divorce – John was no longer an obstacle.

Why did I always feel so insecure when I was around Caroline?

There was a portion on the timeline of my life when Caroline and I had been together – it was the *only* time that mattered to me. Without her – I was empty. I wanted to feel *whole* again. I wanted Caroline in my life!

How could I convey that to her? And would she even care if I did?

15

Caroline

Toward the end of the Paul McCartney song, every member of the wedding party was on the dance floor, but the only person I saw was Richard. The entire weekend, I felt breathless – like a school girl. Richard kept looking at me – as he once had – much like that day when we lived in the small room at Raffaele's. As if it were yesterday, I remembered walking out of the bathroom in the chiffon nightgown Rosa had purchased for me. When Richard saw me, his face had melted – the tension wiped from his expression – and only lust remained. I sensed the same chemistry from him today as I did all of those years ago.

Since our divorce, Richard barely acknowledged my presence; however, today I could feel his sexual tension mounting – and it seemed to be solely focused on me. Why was he playing with my heart in such a cruel manner? Women walked in and out of Richard's life; he was a revolving door – never at a loss for female companionship.

Why was he trying to hurt me when I was the most vulnerable?

The band hit the final note of the McCartney song and the room erupted in applause. I waited for Richard to let go of me – he didn't. I leaned against him hoping – praying – there would be another slow song so I could continue to stay in his arms. I was denied my silent request. Strobe lights flashed from the band's equipment as they broke out in the current hit by KC and the Sunshine Band: *Get Down Tonight*. It was not familiar to me. Richard didn't recognize it either. However, all of the young people flocked to the dance floor and moved to the beat.

Richard pulled away from me. "Maybe we should sit this one out." He had that cocky, confident expression on his face again. "Would you like another gin and tonic?"

"I think I'd like a glass of water – maybe a Coke." There was a tightening in my chest, and I felt light headed. My nerves were frazzled; I didn't want to pour any more alcohol onto my confusing emotions. I needed to catch my breath and get my composure before I embarrassed myself by saying *something stupid* – like that Nancy Sinatra song. The last thing I wanted to say was . . . "I love you" to Richard. Oh my God! Over the years, things were tense enough between us without me getting all gushy and sentimental.

Last spring – at Tony and Rosie's wedding – I had felt a similar connection with Richard – but I presumed it was the excitement of the wedding – the flood of memories and emotions as we'd witnessed our little girl getting married. I'd tried not to read too much into the twinges of fervent chemistry I'd felt because – once the weekend was over – our lives reverted to our normal rapport. As time progressed, we finally developed a pleasant relationship where we could be in the same room together without erupting into contentious disputes. I didn't want to lose the ground we'd gained.

Richard gently led me by my elbow to the bar. We stood in silence as we waited our turn with the bartender. I tried to think of something witty or profound to say, but nothing came to mind. I glanced at the wedding cake positioned strategically in the corner. It was a magnificent creation – no columns – one layer on top of the next – seven tiers high – each a little smaller in diameter. The white icing was sculpted to perfection. Flowers – roses, lilies and orchids – some live – some made with icing – circled the cake. On the top, there was a blown glass heart with an artificial bride and groom inside of it. The couple looked remarkably like Rick and Valerie. I finally broke the silence between us and said, "It's a beautiful wedding cake."

"Yes, it is," he replied – barely looking at it.

"Valerie's mother told me the cake was made by Dewey's Bakery." When Richard didn't respond to my comment, I continued. "Apparently, it is a famous bakery in Winston-Salem." I knew I was rambling, but I continued, "Valerie's mother said Dewey's doesn't make ordinary cakes – they make *masterpieces*. This one sure is gorgeous. I've been told it will taste every bit as good as it looks." Richard still did not participate in the conversation. "That coffee cake we had this morning at the brunch," I smiled as I talked, trying to get him to look at me. "It came from Dewey's too. You must have liked it – you had three helpings."

He did not respond.

"Richard. Oh my God!" I felt as if I was falling apart. Why wouldn't he at least *look* at me? "Please talk to me." There was a begging quality to my voice.

Not a word came out of Richard's mouth. Instead, he put both cocktails the bartender had given him back onto the counter and turned to face me. His eyes were wide and a deeper shade of blue than was the norm. His cheeks flushed with excitement. Without a word spoken, he grabbed my hand and pulled me out of the crowd. Richard had a tight hold on my wrist as he steered me through the string of guests congregating around the bar. At first, I thought he intended to take me to the balcony, but instead, he turned in the other direction. It was difficult to keep up with him in my three-inch heels, but I managed to follow without slowing his fevered pace. Richard proceeded to drag me down the stairs and out of the building. Silently, we rounded the clubhouse and raced passed the Crepe Myrtles that lined the 18th hole on the golf course. I had long since lost my heels in the grass by the patio, but I didn't care. I was with Richard – nothing else mattered.

We were running. I was breathless. Anxious. Excited. Aroused. I felt as if I were falling down the rabbit hole – spinning out of control – but I was not afraid.

Suddenly, we stopped. Our chests were heaving for much needed oxygen. I looked around – we were standing under a massive oak tree – sheltered from the sun – its crisp green leaves – not yet displaying the colors of fall.

"Richard . . ."

"Don't say anything . . ." His voice was deep – guttural, and he challenged me with his eyes.

Richard took both of my hands, lifted them above my head and pressed me passionately against the trunk of the tree. As our bodies melded into one, I could feel his heart fervidly pounding in sync with mine. Our faces – a few short inches apart. Our eyes – locked.

For a moment, I thought he was going to speak – his lips moved – but no audible sound emerged. His warm breath enveloped me – without question – the scent of gin and lime with a hint of mint – was my new favorite aroma. My breasts continued to heave against his chest. I could feel his desire through the material of our clothes, but we remained motionless.

I blinked. The simple action ignited Richard. There was nothing slow or methodical about the way he came at me – his lips were slightly parted – his tongue wild with sensations as it dove into my mouth. He continued to hold my hands over my head, but I did not feel like a prisoner. Our heated passion blended with a rhapsody only a poet can describe. In the back of my mind, I was certain the silk of my dress was being destroyed by the bark of the tree, but I did not care. Joy and passion – and liberation flowed wildly through my veins.

Richard was kissing me – Richard desired me – Richard *wanted* me.

One of my hands was freed – then the other. I threw my arms around him with an intensity that matched his. He placed his palm on my breast, diligently trying to by-pass the material and capture the warmth of my skin. He was not successful, but the disappointment did not stop him from roving over my body and clasping me from behind. He scooped me with both hands and forcefully pulled my pelvis toward him. It was such a powerful act – I felt our hips collide. The movement of our bodies was a ferocious action but it did not cause pain – only pleasure. I was lost in the euphoria.

Richard tried to reign in his desire and gain some composure. He steadied his breathing. "Let's get out of here." Richard muttered softly into my ear – still rhythmically moving his hip against me.

"What?"

"Let's get out of here," he repeated himself.

"They haven't even cut the cake, Richard."

"Shhhh," Richard gently kissed the words off of my lips. "No one will miss us." His eyes were still closed.

"What will the kids say?" There was a teasing quality to my question. As I spoke the words, I traced the outline of his ear with my tongue. The action increased the pace of Richard's breathing.

"Do you want me to take you right here – in broad daylight – where anyone can see?" Even though he chuckled slightly, there was a determined quality to his voice.

Richard nestled his nose in the curve of my neck. The tiny hairs above his lips brushed across my skin causing waves of tantalizing sensations that rippled through my body. He pulled at the material of my full-length gown – suggestively raising the hemline; I could feel a cool breeze above my knees and his warm hand on my thigh. Deep within my throat, a raspy groan emerged. Any common sense I might have fostered immediately evaporated. I was completely captivated by him.

"Come with me, Caroline," he whispered as he laid his cheek upon mine. "Come with me." It was not a demand . . . not even a request . . . he spoke the words as if they were an invitation.

"Okay." The moment I spoke the two syllables, sounds began to reenter my world. I could hear the birds chirping – the rustling of the leaves in the trees – I could even hear the band playing in the distant.

Richard, with his eyes still closed, chuckled. "How appropriate."

"What?"

"They're playing that Van Morrison song." Richard gently brushed the hair away from my face and kissed each of my eyes.

I tried to concentrate on the band in order to understand the meaning of his statement. Finally the song was audible. *Brown Eyed Girl.* Even though I could not see the ballroom, I intuitively knew the dance floor was packed. It was a hugely popular song. I loved it too. Everything about the tune made me feel like I was a kid again. Whenever I heard it, I instantly thought of childhood memories on the river – fishing, swimming, laughing– all of those fabulous memories I had shared with Richard.

"You've always been *my* brown-eyed girl." Again Richard placed tender kisses across my face. There was a seductive yet teasing element to his voice. My hair was piled in a French twist; however, a strand had escaped. Richard curled it around his finger as he stared into my eyes. I felt defenseless – like a teenager again – totally unsure of who I was and where I was going.

Why was Richard taking me on this journey?

As he kept me captive with his steel-blue eyes, Richard whispered the words along with the band's version of the song. His tone was suggestive – it purred with sensuality.

"We never did *that* in a football stadium . . ." I tried to sound coy and confident, but my voice was anything but strong.

"No we didn't . . ." he grinned. "We chose the backseat of my Chrysler." Richard continued to wrap my hair around his finger – in slow motion. "Perhaps . . . that was . . . the best day of my life."

As the memories enveloped me, a fiery hot explosion raced through my body. I felt an immediate weakness in my knees, and I leaned against the tree for support. Trying to appear sophisticated, I responded, "And I thought . . ." my lips curled upward in a coquettish smile. ". . . all of the magic was in that rickety old bed at Raffaele's." I tried to look innocent and inexperienced, but I could tell by the reflection in Richard's eyes – he did not view me in that manner. I glanced up at the branches and smiled again. "I remember an occasion under an oak tree – similar to this one – by a river – in the moonlight."

"You're teasing me again." Richard lowered his voice, "but don't stop. I'm enjoying the visuals." Richard nibbled at my ear; then, buried his face in my hair. "I swear to God, Caroline . . ." Richard's voice was steadfast. "If you don't leave with me now, I'm going to take you right here . . . in *this* green grass."

He waited for my reply. Perhaps I should have hesitated, but I didn't. Maybe tomorrow I could be rational – today – I wanted to be with Richard. "Yes. Let's get out of here."

We took a few seconds to compose ourselves. I readjusted my dress, and Richard straightened his tie. He looked down and noticed I wasn't wearing any shoes. "Where are your heels?" he grinned.

I couldn't help but laugh. "Somewhere between here and the ballroom."

"Let's go get them."

"No . . . I don't need them."

"How about your purse?"

"It's a clutch – there's a tube of lipstick and a compact inside. I don't need it." The frenzy to escape was monopolizing all of my senses. I wanted Richard's hands on me again. I didn't want to wait one moment longer than necessary. "Let's go."

"My car's in the parking lot." Richard reached for my hand. "My room or yours?"

"Yours," I replied. "Mine's a mess."

"Mine is too – but I don't care. We can push it all aside." He winked at me and an impish grin appeared on his face.

Hand-in-hand, we walked quickly around the building. The band's beautiful melody welcomed us, and David Gates' haunting lyrics floated nostalgically in the air.

I glanced at Richard, "I love this song."

"Me too . . ." Richard replied as he tenderly kissed me on the cheek. "Only now . . . it doesn't make me sad anymore." He gently pulled me toward him and wrapped his arms protectively around my shoulders as we continued to walk in the direction of the parking lot.

When we reached his Mustang, Richard opened the passenger door. He'd owned the sports car for a decade; however, this was the first time I'd been in it.

"Would you like me to put the top up?" he inquired as he rounded the hood and got in the driver's side.

"No . . ." I replied. "I think I'll take my hair down and feel the wind."

Richard leaned over and tenderly placed a hand on the back of my neck. He pulled me toward him and kissed me – it was a sweet, gentle kiss that left a promise of passion to come.

When our lips parted I spoke "Richard," I paused. "You and I . . . do you think there is a chance for us?"

With all of the confidence in the world, Richard replied, "Liz and Dick got back together. If they can do it – there's hope for us." Richard laughed.

I smiled at the comparison. Elizabeth Taylor and Richard Burton had gotten remarried last weekend; ever since *Cleopatra* in the early 1960s, their passionate and tumultuous affair was often in the headlines. The idea Richard compared our lives to their famous love story gave me confidence.

"I'm betting on us." Richard tenderly touched my cheek. "You and I . . . we belong together. We have always belonged together." He beamed. "We're going to make it. I promise."

Part of me felt like that scared little girl who packed all of her possessions in Ricky Malone's Chrysler – terrified of the unknown future and blindly moving forward. However, there was another part of me that was on fire with excitement – throwing caution to the wind and thrilled about all of my tomorrows. What a ride!

"Trust me." Richard winked in his confident way and turned the key. The ignition and the radio started simultaneously. Music filled the air. My favorite Beatles song blared from the speakers: *Here Comes to Sun*. Richard turned the knob to full volume. Putting the stick shift in first gear, he drove out of the parking lot.

The wind was on my face, and the song was in my heart.

The Malone Family Saga
continues
with the second novel
in the series:

Cobwebs of Time
by
Tesa Jones

CPSIA information can be obtained
at www.ICGtesting.com
Printed in the USA
LVOW12s0853081017
551660LV00002B/346/P